For Sam, with all my love

## Acknowledgements

Heart-felt thanks to my editor, Gaynor Eldon, and to Olivia Odiwe for all your wonderful support, help, and love!

A special thank you to dear friends and readers: Jenny, Caroline, Sara, Jade, Jan, John, Meg, Libby, Lisa, and Karen, for providing much-needed laughs, and inspiration for several chapters in this book.

Thanks also go to the fabulous Austen Authors for all their support - Abigail Reynolds, Sharon Lathan, Regina Jeffers Mary Simonsen, Diana Birchall, Marilyn Brant, C. Allyn Pierson, Susan Adriani, Jack Caldwell, Nina Benneton, Karen Doornebos, Alyssa Goodnight, Susan Mason-Milks, Shannon Winslow, Maria Grace, Colette Saucier, Syrie James, Cassandra Grafton, Sally Smith O'Rourke, and Monica Fairview.

Last, but not least, to my amazing husband Romanus - for all that you are and do - I thank you with all the love in my heart!

# PROJECT Darcy

WHO INSPIRED JANE AUSTEN'S PRIDE & PREJUDICE?

JANE ODIWE

TIME TRAVELS WITH JANE AUSTEN

PROJECT DARCY

Copyright © 2013 Jane Odiwe

First published 2013 by Paintbox Publishing

The right of Jane Odiwe to be identified as the Author of this Work has been asserted by her in accordance with the Copyright, Designs and Patents Act 1988

All characters and events in this publication, other than those clearly in the public domain, are fictitious and any resemblance to actual persons, living or dead, is purely coincidental

All rights reserved. No part of this publication may be reproduced, stored in a retrieval system, or transmitted in any form by any means, electronic, mechanical, photocopying, recording or otherwise, without the prior permission of the publisher or a licence permitting restricted copying. In the UK, such licences are issued by the Copyright Licensing Agency, 90 Tottenham Court Road, London, W1P 9HE

ISBN 978-0-9545722-3-5

## Chapter I

Ellie asked herself again, for the hundredth time, how it was that she'd been persuaded to join in. Archaeology was hardly her thing and for that matter, neither was Jane Austen. But, in the end, it was impossible to refuse Jess this small request. Jess, her best friend, who she loved like the sister she didn't have, had pleaded with them all. And it was Ellie who had made sure the others had agreed to come on the dig, reminding them when she'd managed to take them to one side that they were lucky to still have Jess around after her horrendous health scare of the previous year.

'It'll be fun,' said Ellie, packing her sketch book into her bag as she walked along in the sunshine, 'especially as it's our last summer together before most of us have to join the real world and work for our living.'

'So long as I can bring my straighteners,' said Liberty, admiring her reflection and flicking back her chestnut mane as they walked past the refectory window on their university campus. 'They do have electricity where we're going, don't they?'

'Of course they do,' Martha snapped, unable to disguise the irritation in her voice. With her nose buried in a book, she completely missed Liberty's rolling eyes and the grin that passed between her and Cara. Although the five girls had struck up a friendship since sharing a student house, the mix of characters and personalities could hardly have been more different. Martha always remained just a little outside the group. It was Ellie and Jess, Liberty and Cara, and Martha drifted between the two, happy, for the most part, to be on her own.

Ellie purposely left out any suggestion that the trip might involve hard work or dirt, and made light of the fact that the archaeological dig was in a tiny Hampshire village in the middle of nowhere. Jess was obsessed with Jane Austen's books and when she'd found out that volunteers were needed to find the remains of Jane's childhood home in Steventon, she'd not talked about much else. Jess would never have done anything like that by herself; she'd always been timid with strangers. Ellie knew Jess wanted them all to go with her, but also realised that if Liberty and Cara had any idea of what was really expected of them, they might refuse the invitation. Instead, she focused on the parts she knew would keep them interested.

'There's a film crew going, and they're making a documentary.'

Liberty, the drama student, could hardly contain herself. 'OMG, do you think we'll get to be in it?'

'Oh, Liberty, our fifteen minutes of fame,' said Cara, grabbing her friend's hand and twirling her round. 'I'll have to tell my mum. When do you think it will be on the telly?'

'I don't know exactly, sometime next year, I should think, but I can tell you who will be presenting it.'

'Who is it, somebody famous?' Liberty looked as if she might explode.

'Greg Whitely.' Ellie knew she did not have to say any more.

Liberty threw her arms around Ellie. 'But, I've been in love with him forever, and I've just always had this feeling that we were meant to be together. I think I might die at the thought of meeting him.' Her hands flew to her mouth. 'Do you think he'll be there, Ellie?'

'I don't know, maybe not for the whole dig, but perhaps for some of it.'

'Well, I shan't be in any hurry to meet him.' Martha closed her book and tucked her lank, mousy hair behind her ears. 'My mother's worked with him and she says he's an insatiable womaniser.'

'Even better! Perhaps I could be the one to tame him. I can just picture it – me in 'Hello' magazine on Greg's arm swathed in satin and crystals,' said Liberty, striking a pose, 'as the Duke and Duchess of Cambridge shower me with confetti.'

'Dream on, Liberty,' said Cara with a grin. 'Martha, you're so lucky. It must be wonderful to have an actress for a mother.'

'No, it's not,' said Martha, instantly turning scarlet to the roots of her hair, a frown wrinkling her forehead. 'I don't think you can have any idea. My childhood was spent largely alone with a succession of nannies in school holidays, none of whom ever showed me the slightest affection, whilst my mother travelled the world pursuing her career.'

'But, you must have seen some incredible actors and met some of them, too,' said Liberty, who really excelled at saying exactly the wrong thing at the worst possible moment.

Ellie knew she should step in before Martha started to say she wouldn't be able to come after all. 'There is someone going on the dig who I think you'll be interested to meet, Martha. He's been on that documentary series where they only have a week to dig up some bones and then reconstruct the faces. Will MacGourtey – you know him – he's an archaeologist – fair hair, young and quite good-looking.'

'At least there will be someone worth talking to, then,' Martha said as she opened her book again. 'Intelligent conversation coupled with the informed knowledge of a first-rate academic is my idea of heaven – something quite sadly lacking from my life right now.'

The other three exchanged smiles, and Ellie, who was glad that she now had all three girls on her side, sent up a silent prayer that they would all continue to be so happy.

Jess was beside herself with joy when Ellie told her the news. And Liberty looked even more excited when Jess told them that they'd been invited to stay at her godmother's house for the duration of the dig.

They were all gathered in the cramped sitting room of the student house they shared, which didn't seem big enough for the five personalities whose belongings lay strewn on every surface. Books and folders, half-finished essays and sketchbooks jostled for position with pens and pencils, bottles of nail varnish and tubes of paint.

'Isn't she the rich one with the big house?' Liberty never took long to get to the point. She put down the book of plays she was supposed to be reading to bounce onto the sofa next to Jess, hugging her knees and staring up at Jess's beautiful face with undisguised anticipation.

Jess laughed. 'I suppose she is quite wealthy and her house is a sizeable one. I must admit; I haven't been there for a while. I was just a young girl when I last visited. Aunt Mary has lived abroad for most of the last ten years.'

'Will she leave you all her money?' Cara chipped in, joining her on the other side so Jess was completely wedged in.

'That's not very likely, though goodness knows my family could do with it. My mum and Mary were at teacher training college together. My mum fell in love with a fellow teacher, but Mary was swept off her feet by a young man, who swiftly became a millionaire. We're comfortably off, but my parents have worked so hard all their lives and Aunt Mary doesn't really have a clue. But, she's always been incredibly generous to my family, and sadly was unable to have any children of her own.'

'It's really kind of her to invite us,' said Ellie, 'but does she know what she's letting herself in for having five girls come to stay?'

'Oh, Aunt Mary isn't going to be there,' Jess said, smiling as she recognised the fear in Ellie's eyes behind the question, 'she's in

Tuscany for the summer – we've got the place to ourselves!'

The coach picked them up from the university. It was already half full with an interesting mix of people who, like themselves, had volunteered for the dig. There was a group of male students from another university occupying the row at the back of the coach, and Ellie had to stop Liberty from marching up to them before they'd even found where they were sitting.

'We've got allocated seats, Liberty and Cara,' Jess called, pointing at the two in front of her. Martha sat next to Jess, which Ellie had agreed beforehand, so she wouldn't feel left out. As the coach headed out of Winchester, Ellie watched the urban sprawl gradually left behind: lanes of verdant green replaced shops, houses and flats. Fields and meadows, with tiny farmhouses in the distance looked like toy farm sets with cows and sheep grazing under oak trees dotted amongst the hedgerows. She was looking forward to the trip in many ways, and hoped there'd be some opportunities for her to paint. Google Earth had thrown up some beautiful images of the countryside around Steventon and Ellie loved nothing more than trying to capture a landscape in watercolours. It had been her ambition to study illustration for as long as she could remember and becoming a freelance illustrator was her goal. She was nervous about the future, but she'd already had a few commissions. Perhaps being in Jane Austen country would be an inspiration for her painting.

Ellie could hear the guys at the back, some of them talking far too loudly, showing off whilst evidently trying to get the attention of Liberty who was constantly looking round. Dressed like any other student, nevertheless, everything about them suggested out of the ordinary affluence and confidence exuded from every pore. Rather too much self-assurance, Ellie thought, and decided they were arrogance personified – snobs of the worst sort. It crossed her mind that perhaps she was being a little unfair but it seemed to her they expected everyone to be impressed by them. Ellie made up her mind, right then, to give them a wide berth.

'Isn't it exciting?' Jess's face materialised in the gap between the seats in front, a halo of short blonde curls giving her an elfin appearance. 'I can't believe we are going to be walking on hallowed ground tomorrow.'

Ellie nodded back as enthusiastically as she could for Jess's sake. It was fantastic to see Jess animated and looking well again. This last twelve months she'd been to hell and back. No one else could have suffered so much with such strength and courage. Ellie had watched her best friend grow pale and thin before her diagnosis, and then witnessed her growing sicker with every session of chemotherapy. When Jess's long, golden tresses had fallen out in clumps, it was Ellie who'd cried. Jess had borne it all bravely, saying what a relief it was not to have to fuss about with hairdryers and hairstyles. But, that was the type of person Jess was – never thinking of herself, only trying to make things better for everyone else. Her fellow lecturers and students were full of admiration for the girl who had managed through it all to hang on to her dream of becoming a teacher like her mum and dad. She'd had time off from university, but nothing was going to stop her from going back and completing her course.

'I hope we find something exciting. Can you imagine going to all the effort of digging and nothing of any interest turning up,' said Ellie.

'It will be enough for me just to walk in Jane's footsteps,' said Jess, a dreamy expression spreading over her face. 'I think they are supposed to be determining exactly where the house stood, initially. There's some debate about what the house looked like and its position on the land. Hopefully, the geophysics will be done by now and they'll have an idea where we can start digging!'

Liberty's head popped over the seat. 'I'm so glad I came,' she said, with one eye on the boys at the back, 'though, there are more old people than I expected.'

Martha made a shushing sound. 'You never know when to be quiet, do you, Liberty? I like the fact there are lots of different ages here. It's wonderful to think that not all people in their seventies are gaga and are still reasonably mentally alert.'

Ellie wanted to disappear into the fabric of her seat. The silver-haired woman sitting opposite them looked across disapprovingly and muttered something about 'the youth of today' under her breath.

There was a sudden crackling noise from loud speakers and a lady brandishing a microphone at the front of the coach stood up to make a welcome speech, introducing herself as Melanie Button, and thanking the volunteers for their participation. 'I hope you'll all be happy with the accommodation that's been arranged. Most of you will be staying in the village where you'll meet some of the local volunteers this evening at the reception party. According to my list, I believe Jess Leigh and her friends have made their own plans and also Henry Dorsey and Charlie Harden. Am I right?'

Jess waved and gesticulated in their direction. 'Yes, we're all sorted out, Mrs Button, thank you. We'll have use of a car and be walking in too, I hope. We're at Ashe, just a mile away.'

One of the students sitting with the Oxford group raised his hand. 'Charlie Harden here, Mrs Button. Henry and I are staying together – we're in Deane so we're not far, either.'

Ellie saw Jess looking at Charlie with interest. He was good-looking in a fresh-faced way with a mop of sun-bleached curls that looked even lighter against his tanned skin. He had the sort of piercing forget-me-not blue eyes that don't look quite real and it was easy to see why Jess looked at him, albeit in her own covert way. At least he seemed to have some manners, which was more than could be said for his friends. The one called Henry, by contrast, seemed to scowl at her when she caught his eye.

'Do call me Mel,' said Mrs Button, smiling broadly at Charlie and Henry, 'let's not stand on ceremony. We're going to be working very closely together.'

Liberty barely stifled a giggle and whispered to Cara, 'She's old enough to be their mother. Look at that gorgeous Charlie, he looks frightened to death at the thought of being personally intimate with Ms Button.'

'Now, we're all meeting in the village hall at seven thirty,' continued Melanie. 'We are enormously excited to have Greg Whitely and Will MacGourtey of *Dig your Ancestor* fame arriving to kick off the party, and tell us what's been accomplished so far. Are you *digging* that, ladies?'

There was a ripple of laughter from some of the older female volunteers and a few groans from some of the young men. And then the coach stopped. 'Ashe Rectory,' called the driver.

Ellie stared at the life-sized doll's house in front of them. A doorway surmounted by a beautiful fanlight was set in the centre of the elegant Georgian façade, its panelled doors opening as they stepped down from the coach. Wisteria and roses climbed over the rose brick walls and the windows on either side. On the upper floor, the window under the pediment caught the glow of the sun in its rectangular panes. The light was blinding, but Ellie sensed they were being watched and when she shielded her eyes to squint at the glass, she saw she was right. It was momentary, but the sight of a young man with pale hair and skin standing at the window made every hair on her body stand on end. He was looking down at them and, for a moment, Ellie thought that she knew him. There was something so familiar about the turn of his head and his stance that caused a flicker of pleasure to quicken inside her, and when, at last, their eyes met, the sense of recognition and consciousness felt almost like coming home.

## Chapter 2

The light bounced from the panes, the sun blinking in her eyes so strongly she was forced to close them and when she looked again, he was gone. As all five girls stood before the house with the noise of the coach rumbling away down the lane, the doors opened and a white-haired lady in a twin-set and tweed skirt stepped out, dogs barking at her heels.

'Now Mr Darcy and Mr Bingley, don't carry on so. You remember Jessica, there's no need to bark like that.'

The dogs were all over Jess, leaping up excitedly as they recognised their old friend. 'Mr Darcy and Mr Bingley,' cried Jess, laughing as they almost bowled her over. 'It's so long since I had the pleasure of seeing those wagging tails - you were always the most handsome and loving men of my acquaintance!'

'We should have known they'd have names from *Pride and Prejudice*,' said Cara, 'Is your godmother as obsessed as you, Jess?'

'No, not one bit,' said the apple-cheeked lady who greeted them after she'd bestowed affectionate kisses on Jess. 'Mrs Burke always says she prefers the Brontë sisters and has no time for

Elizabeth Bennet and Mr Darcy. It was Jessica who was allowed to christen the dogs, you might know. I'm Betty Hill, by the way, the housekeeper. Come inside – leave your suitcases in the hall, my dears, and my husband will see to those. The kettle is on, we'll have a nice cup of tea and then I'll show you to your rooms.'

The girls walked into a large hallway with a staircase in front leading to the upper floors, and rooms leading off left, right, and beyond. A polished circular table in the centre held a Chinese bowl of pot-pourri and a country arrangement of roses and lavender from the garden scented the air with its fragrance. Off to the right they were taken into a morning room, a pretty old-fashioned space with chairs and sofas sprigged in chintz. The walls were panelled and on each side of the marble fireplace the alcoves held shelves in the recesses topped with richly carved seashells, on which were displayed pretty, floral china.

'Oh, I thought we were to be on our own,' Ellie heard Liberty whispering to Cara, the disappointment in her voice plain to hear. 'I had high hopes of entertaining Greg Whitely here a bit later.'

'Liberty, you are too naughty for words,' Cara answered, giggling, as she plumped down onto an armchair covered in dove grey linen, sending the flowered cushions tumbling to the floor.

Mrs Hill appeared not to notice and when the tea came in they were introduced to the young girl, Nancy, who bore pots of Earl Grey tea, piles of chicken sandwiches and slabs of chocolate cake on delicate tea plates.

'Nancy comes in from the village to help me,' said Mrs Hill. 'If you need to know anything at all about Ashe, Steventon or Deane and the people that live here, she's the one to ask. Her people have lived here since before Jane Austen's day. In fact, they were a very special part of the family.'

Nancy wore an expression of pride as she set down the tray. 'Yes, my ancestors worked for the Austen family, they helped bring up the children. Mrs Austen used to send them off, once they were weaned, to live with my family until they were old enough to walk and talk and mind their manners. I suppose that seems an odd practice today, but that's what they did in the olden days. The children were visited every day, and, no doubt, were in and out of the respective houses as they were growing up.'

'So your family actually knew Jane Austen?' Ellie asked.

Nancy nodded. 'My granny told me that one of the Littleworths once dressed Jane Austen's hair for a ball. They were servants, really, but the Austens treated them as if they were their nearest and dearest. There's not much the Littleworths didn't know then, and there's not much we don't know about Steventon and all its neighbours now. And if there's any gossip to be had, we'll be the first to hear the news. It's not a place for keeping secrets, I can tell you,' Nancy said, lowering her voice to a whisper as if the walls themselves might hear something they shouldn't. 'It's just village life, but if you're not used to it, it can seem as if people are being very nosy and interfering, if you know what I mean.'

'I'd better be on my best behaviour then,' said Liberty, who pressed her lips together as if butter wouldn't melt in her mouth.

Everyone laughed. It was hard to get cross with Liberty who knew more than anyone else that trouble seemed to hunt her out like a heat-seeking missile.

'It's a beautiful house,' said Ellie, keen to change the conversation. 'It looks as if Jane Austen might walk out of a door at any moment.'

'Yes, indeed, my dears, this house is not without its associations to that great lady. It was a former rectory and belonged to a very great friend of Miss Austen,' Mrs Hill replied, as if the author was still alive. 'Her name was Madame Lefroy, that was how she was known. She was married to the Reverend Lefroy who was the rector at Ashe. Jane always ran to her dear friend for advice – they shared a great many interests, I believe, books and poetry, in particular.'

'I didn't know that,' said Jess, sitting up in her seat, instantly alert to the name of her favourite author. 'I've never heard Aunt Mary talk about Jane Austen being here in this house.'

'Well, Jane Austen and her books have never been of any

interest to her, and it's a few years since we've had the pleasure of seeing you in this house, Jessica. I suppose she thought you too young before, to be interested in the history of the rectory itself and the people who lived here.'

'Just think, Jane Austen might have sat in this very room,' said Jess.

'Without a doubt, she did,' answered Mrs Hill. 'Not only did she sit in this room, but Jane also attended a few dances here. Madame was quite a figure in the neighbourhood and loved to throw parties. You see the folding doors that separate the rooms? They were always thrown back to make room for the dancing couples.

Jess opened her mouth to speak again. Ellie could see how curious she was and longing to know more, but Mrs Hill stood up, gathering cups and saucers together on the tea-tray. 'I'll just pop these in the kitchen – Nancy will show you to your rooms whilst I tidy up. I understand you're all going out in an hour or so. I'll leave the side door open and there'll be a spot of supper, something cold left out for you when you get back. Have a lovely time, my dears.'

They followed Nancy upstairs and on reaching the first floor, Ellie remembered the haunting face that she'd seen earlier. 'Does anyone else live here, Nancy? I thought I saw someone at the window when we arrived ... could it have been Mrs Hill's son?'

'No, Mrs Hill's nephew stays here with her sometimes, but she and Mr Hill were never blessed with any children. It's such a pity because she would have made a lovely mum. Perhaps it was Mr Hill you saw – he's always seeing to odd jobs around the house.'

'I doubt it, unless Mr Hill is a very *young* man,' said Ellie, wondering if she had, in fact, imagined the face that had seemed to smile when he saw her.

'Oh, in that case it was probably the ghost you saw,' Nancy pronounced, in such a matter of fact way that Ellie wondered if she'd misheard her.

'Don't tell me there's a ghost,' cried Liberty, 'I shan't sleep tonight. I love nothing more than a horror film but I don't want to be in one!'

'I don't know anything about a ghost,' Jess joined in. 'Aunt Mary's never mentioned him to me. Where did you see him, Ellie?'

'Well, he must have been here standing at this window but, to be honest, I didn't see very much and it could just have been a trick of the light. The sun was really bright ... I got the impression of someone about our age, quite pale and fair. He was only there for a second – I probably imagined it.'

'That's not likely with your history, is it?' Jess had lowered her voice to a whisper and was looking at her friend earnestly. Ellie had only ever confided in Jess about the people she saw – not people exactly, they were more like shadows of real people, in three dimensions but dimmer in intensity, other worldly.

'There is a young man haunts the place from time to time,' said Nancy, opening the door of the first bedroom on the left. 'He's harmless enough, but I expect your aunt didn't want to say anything to you about him when you were a little girl, Jess, for fear of frightening you.'

Martha who'd been quiet for some time spoke up. 'I don't believe in ghosts. I've seen too many so-called séances with hysterical people, mostly ridiculously stupid actresses, who whipped themselves into a frenzy of believing all sorts of nonsense – contact with the dead, and even one who swore she'd lived in another time.'

Ellie didn't want to say too much. 'I think some people are more in tune or have a sensitivity to such things. I'd hate to dismiss it completely.'

'I agree with Ellie,' Jess chipped in, 'there is so much that we don't understand. I was reading about the Akashic records the other day, the belief that everything that happens in the world is imprinted on the unseen ether around us, present in every atom of the world and universe – like a multi-sensory photograph or holograph being constantly captured and kept on file.'

'Now you've lost me with all this talk of hollow graphs and

science. It sounds like a lot of gobbledygook to me,' said Liberty, hitching up her shoulder bag. 'I am dying to put this down, it is so heavy.'

'This is your room, Liberty.' Nancy waved her through and the others got a glimpse of a charming room in shades of eau de nil with flamboyant peonies and exotic birds perched on Chinese branches climbing over the walls.

The others heard her shouting with excitement and the sound of running taps as Liberty discovered her own bathroom before Nancy whisked them away and dropped them off one by one along the corridor. Cara's room was next in line to Liberty's with Martha on the opposite side. Ellie and Jess were given rooms at the back of the house overlooking the garden which rolled before them in varying sizes of green lawns, high yew hedges, and hidden spaces interspersed with traditional flower beds. Jess's bedroom with chalk pink walls boasted a French bed with buttoned silk upholstery and a chaise longue in one corner. On the walls was a collection of silhouettes of people from past times. The profiles of soldiers and debutantes looked across at one another from ebony frames ranged around the marble mantelpiece. It looked as if it had been designed with Jess in mind with its Regency furniture and vast portraits of ladies dressed in white muslin.

Ellie's room was perfection to her way of thinking; she loved anything vintage. In muted tones of Naples yellow in the patterned wallpaper and silvery grey satin falling to the floor in a cascade at the windows, the room was flooded in light. Sunbeams danced through the ancient embroidered lace like a bridal veil at a summer wedding, parted to give a stunning view over the beautiful garden. Touches of duck egg blue in the embroideries on the walls and in the milk glass vases on the mantelshelf were echoed in a shot of deeper blue silk in the dressing gown dangling from a padded hanger of cream silk. It looked like a film set left over from the 1930s and in contrast to Jess's room, which was a Regency haven, Ellie couldn't have wished for anything more glamorous. A deco dressing table complete with a mirrored surface and a triptych looking glass was topped with a selection of exquisite objects – a porcelain tray and boxes for jewels, a Japanese fan, a silver hairbrush enamelled with blue as vivid as a butterfly's wing, and a cloisonné vase filled with old-fashioned roses. The bed draped with grey satin and ivory lace was flanked either side with paintings typical of the era, watercolours of primroses or lilac in turquoise bowls, and a still life, of paper lanterns suspended from branches of white blossom, hung above the fireplace. She almost couldn't wait to go to bed when she'd be able to sink into the pile of satin covered cushions on her bed, pull the quilted eiderdown up to her throat and admire all the treats before her.

'I am so happy,' said Jess, sitting down at Ellie's dressing table and opening the lid of a jewel box. 'I don't know how you've persuaded the others to come but I'm so glad you did. You're the most wonderful friend a girl could wish for – thank you.'

'I only hope that you don't regret those words when Liberty and Cara realise they've got to get their hands dirty,' Ellie said, laughing as she sat down on a slipper chair in the corner.

Jess took out a diamonté necklace from the box and held it up against her collarbone. 'If Greg Whitely turns up tonight, I think Liberty will be pretty keen to impress, not to mention those other boys from Oxford.'

'Yes, I don't think we'll have much trouble keeping her engaged, though whether it will be on the task in hand, I'm not sure. I have to say, I thought you looked a little distracted at the sight of one Charlie Harden. He's not my type, but he is rather gorgeous. I saw him looking at you in a very studious way.'

'No, you did not. Ellie Bentley, you're always making things up.'

'I'm not – you'll see. I bet he makes a move tonight. I'm sure he's dying to meet you.'

Jess put the necklace back, closed the lid slowly and turned to face Ellie. 'Charlie seems very friendly and just the kind of person who is naturally sociable. Don't you go imagining things if he starts chatting to us.'

'Oh, I don't imagine he'll be chatting to *us* at all. To *you*, maybe.'

'Ellie, you're incorrigible! But, I will forgive you and who knows, perhaps you'll be the one who gets chatted up later.'

'I hardly think so, Jess. I know you'd love to see me in a romantic entanglement but you know as well as I, that there isn't a man alive who has yet taken my fancy to that extent. And your Charlie hasn't got a friend I like the look of – they all seem a bit immature ... or moody.'

'He isn't *my* Charlie, Ellie. But, I thought his friend Henry was *your* type, all dark hair and scowling looks.'

'No way! He's far too ... superior. I don't know, he just looks a bit arrogant, that's all.'

'Well, perhaps tonight he'll charm you. You never know, he could turn out to be 'The One'!'

Ellie grabbed a cushion and aimed. Jess leapt up, laughing as she ran from the room. 'Come on, we've got to get ready, Miss Bentley, or we'll be late.'

Half an hour later, Ellie was feeling refreshed for having had a scented soak in the bath. She'd washed her hair and was now standing in front of the wardrobe hanging her clothes, and trying to decide what she was going to wear for the party. It was still warm and light so she selected some cropped jeans and a short-sleeved cotton top, with a scoop neck and embroidered pin tucked front. The detail made it a little bit more special than the every day and to set it off, she picked a chunky necklace from her jewellery roll with turquoise stones and silver beads threaded on a long leather cord. Choosing a warm scarf in coral, scattered over with hummingbirds and edged in silk fringe in case it got cooler later on, Ellie then added a pair of canvas trainers to complete her outfit.

Jess knocked on the door. 'I'll just round up everyone else so I'll see you downstairs in a minute!'

Ellie shouted back that she'd join them in a second and looked around for her bag. It was her favourite, an antique bag that had belonged to her great-grandmother. Made of black silk moiré, it was embellished with a bluebird and had a long silk strap. She'd left it on the chest of drawers in front of the window next to a blue and white jug and bowl. Dashing to fetch it, she was stopped in her tracks by the sense of something or someone moving outside in the garden below. Ellie glimpsed what she thought might be a person moving between the trees but it was too difficult to see clearly. It was most likely Mr Hill or a gardener, she thought. The gardens were so immense, there had to be several people working on them to be kept as beautiful as they looked. Yet, she had a feeling that the person, whose shadow moved across the grass in shades of deep emerald, was someone other than a working man. And then she saw him again. Too far away to be able to see distinctly, nevertheless, she knew he was the same young man she'd seen before. Dressed like a character from a Jane Austen novel in a long coat with breeches and boots, he made an arresting figure. Striding towards the house, his white coat billowed out like the great wings of a swan before it takes flight into the sky. Ellie could see him unwinding the stock at his neck with impatient fingers, and as he did so his lawn shirt exposed pale skin, a muscular frame beneath the fine linen. Suddenly, she knew he was watching her. He raised his hand and waved.

## Chapter 3

It was pure instinct to look behind her to see if he was waving at someone else, but, of course, there was no one there. And when she turned back to see if he was still standing there, he had disappeared and Ellie began to wonder if she had imagined seeing him at all. There wasn't time to investigate further and so picking up her bag, she decided to try and forget about the mysterious gentleman for the time being and ran downstairs to meet the others.

Mrs Hill had kindly arranged a taxi to take them into Steventon and told them that it would pick them up again at 10.30. 'I don't suppose you'll be needing it any later than that,' she said, 'I know the caretaker insists on closing up at that time, whatever the event. I think if the queen herself arrived, he'd not allow it to stay open any longer.'

'Ten thirty!' Liberty's sigh was audible. 'That doesn't give me much time then.'

'Time for what?' asked Jess, as the taxi driver set off, speeding down the lanes with the confidence of one who knew them well.

'Time to charm Greg Whitely,' Liberty answered, 'By the time we've had the talks and everyone spouting off like in lectures, I'm guessing there'll only be about half an hour for chatting and that just isn't long enough!'

'Well, if I know Liberty Lovell, half an hour will be ample time,' said Ellie. 'I believe if you only had ten minutes you'd make the best of it. Don't be down-hearted – just think, you are actually going to see and possibly meet your hero.'

'There's no possibly about it,' said Liberty, applying her lipstick and checking her reflection in a hand mirror, 'If I don't get to talk to Greg tonight, then I will have definitely lost my touch!'

The village hall had been decked out for the occasion with strings of colourful bunting and a number of cloth-covered trestle tables lined one side of the long room. There was a veritable feast laid on with the usual sorts of buffet fare: sandwiches, sausage rolls, quiches, and salads at one end, and trifle, jellies and cakes at the other. Cara and Liberty nudged one another when they saw the bottles of sparkling wine lined up, though Liberty was quick to point out that there didn't seem to be enough of them for a proper party.

At the front near the stage were a series of displays and large graphic posters pinned up to illustrate maps of the area and the results of the geophysics that had already been done. Ellie spied several of the people she'd seen on the bus earlier though all looked as if they'd been spruced up for the occasion. She couldn't see Charlie and Henry from the university yet, though several of their friends were being just as loud as they had been on the coach. But, it was all quite exciting. There was a buzz in the air, lots of animated chatter as people met up again to compare notes on their new living arrangements and talk of what was to come.

Ellie saw Jess blush pink a moment later and when she followed her gaze, she soon saw the reason. Charlie and his friend Henry had arrived in a fragrant cloud of after-shave, looking rather smarter than they had earlier in freshly pressed shirts and chinos.

'Ooh, he's scrubbed up nicely, don't you think, Jess?' asked Liberty, who had seen Jess's blushing cheeks.

'I don't know what you're talking about, Liberty,' said Jess, taking a seat and rummaging in her bag in an effort to compose herself.

'Come on, Jess, he's gorgeous! You can't kid me, I know you like Charlie Harden.'

'I don't know him, so I couldn't possibly say, though, I must admit, he does look quite nice.'

Liberty rolled her eyes at Cara who grinned back. 'Jess has got a cru-ush,' she whispered back in the singsong way of a playground chant.

'That's enough, you two,' said Ellie.

'Shush, look, something's happening,' said Martha, fetching out her notebook and pen.

The door leading to the kitchen opened with a flourish and Melanie Button swept through with all the air of a celebrated opera singer. She had been transformed. Her waxed jacket, men's trousers and baggy jumper had been replaced with a long bohemian-style black dress. A lime green cardigan in jersey was draped around her shoulders and an amber necklace with a stone as large as a hen's egg nestled in her ample cleavage. Her hair had been tamed and twisted into a French pleat, which she patted every now and then as if to make sure it was still there. Just as some of the audience were wondering whom she could possibly be, her voice sounded loud and clear over the speaker system.

'Testing, testing, 1, 2, 3,' she bellowed, before blowing into the microphone to produce such a whistle that the audience immediately clapped their hands over their ears.

With the volume adjusted, she started again. 'Good evening, ladies and gentleman – welcome to *Project Darcy*, which, as you are all aware, is the codename for this special event, the first ever archaeological survey of Jane Austen's childhood home, Steventon. Aren't we a very privileged group? I must say you are all to be congratulated for keeping the secret thus far. There has not been one word leaked to the press and a good job, too, or we should be inundated with the likes of the paparazzi and I know Professor Whitely and Mr MacGourtey have quite enough to contend with on that score, without the rest of us having to be snapped at with long lenses the whole day long.'

Jess and Ellie exchanged a smirk. However pleased they were to be involved, they were quite sure the paparazzi would not be interested in either of them or Melanie Button.

'I hope you have all settled in well at your various lodgings and that you are ready to *get digging!*' Melanie shimmied like a disco diva and winked at her audience, which had Liberty snorting with undisguised laughter. 'And without further ado,' Melanie announced, with a flourish of her arm in the direction of the kitchen door, the gentlemen we've all been waiting for – Professor Greg Whitely and Mr Will MacGourtey!'

The audience burst into resounding applause as the two men walked in, beaming at their hostess.

'Why does she keep calling him a professor?' whispered Ellie in Jess's ear. 'If he's a professor, then I'm a Dame of the British Empire.'

Jess giggled. 'I expect some university has given him an honorary award.'

'Typical! I doubt he could 'dig up' two qualifications in anything much except curling pubescent girls around his little finger along with the art of leather trouser adjustment. Have you ever seen such tight trousers?'

Greg Whitely had clearly styled himself on a well-known film star. He'd gone for what Ellie could only describe as the 'pirate look' with a scarlet bandanna tied around his black curls, a waistcoat over a seersucker shirt with voluminous sleeves and those tight leather trousers tucked into boots.

'All he needs is a patch over one eye and his look will be complete,' she whispered.

'Well, he's very good at his job,' said Jess generously.

'You are always so kind and soft-hearted about people, Jess. But, even you must admit, he does look as if he really fancies himself. Will MacGourtey looks like a nice man, and he dresses really well. I love blue jeans with a white shirt.'

'Yes, I can see why Martha approves of him. He looks kind

and intelligent, too.'

Will MacGourtey spoke first. 'I expect you're all waiting to hear about the results of our findings so far, but I thought it might be useful to fill you in with a little of the history that we know about. Jane Austen was born in the rectory in 1775 at Steventon and it was to be her home for the next 25 years. Her father was the rector at St. Nicholas church at the top of the hill and it was in this small village where she drafted her first three novels, *Sense and Sensibility, Pride and Prejudice* and *Northanger Abbey*. Today, the site of the rectory is the corner of a field marked only by an iron pump, which stood in the Austen's courtyard. Further up the slope, behind the pump, are traces of terracing where a short walk across the top of the Austen's garden was formed. From the eastern end of this terrace a path called the Church Walk led through wood and meadow to the church. In the surrounding fields George Austen farmed the land. As you will see on the plan of the Glebe land at Steventon in 1821, the rectory lies nearest the road junction and was bordered by property belonging to his son Edward. This plan shows the layout of the rectory and the yard where it's thought the iron pump was positioned. A sweeping gravel drive bears out the descriptions left to us by descendants and we are told that the house had two projecting wings at the back, improvements possibly made by Mr Austen himself. Our initial findings indicate that we have a very good idea where to start with regard to the foundations, and if you would all like to follow me and gather around the exhibition boards, I can further explain.'

There was a scraping of chairs and a burst of chatter as the audience got up as one. The display was thoughtfully presented so even the least knowledgeable could grasp the implications of the job they had to do. Firstly, they would be trying to establish exactly where the house had stood, and though the geophysics were going to be helpful, it would really be a matter of testing the ground in the hope of finding the rectory. After Will MacGourtey's talk, Greg Whitely spoke next on how the television programme was going to be made. Liberty was the first to put up her hand to ask a question.

'Will there be any opportunities for presenting alongside you? It's just that I'm studying drama and I'd love to be of any help that I can.'

Greg smiled. 'Your name, young lady?'

'Liberty ... Liberty Lovell, Mr Whitely.'

'Lovelly by name and lovelly by nature, too, I don't doubt,' he said, grinning at the audience and pausing for the anticipated chuckle. 'Well, Liberty, there are always opportunities for promising students, and you will all be filmed, of course, as we go along. It may be that we want to interview people selectively, and a training in drama will, no doubt, be an advantage. However, what we're after is realism. The country will be transfixed at the idea of a group of non-experts coming together in secret, looking for the rectory that inspired the creation of the character of Mr Darcy and we are looking for personalities who will fuel the public's imagination. Liberty, I've a feeling you may well be a star in the making. And by the way, everyone, do call me Greg – I'm hoping we'll all get to know one another really well!'

There was an enthusiastic ripple of applause from the ladies in the audience. Liberty blushed red, her eyes shining with delight at the impression she'd made, which was exactly what she'd hoped.

Melanie Button bustled her way to the front once more to announce it was time for the party to start, declaring that she hoped they would meet promptly at nine o'clock sharp the next morning at the site. Corks popped, beer bottles were opened and a general sense of jubilation ensued as paper plates were filled, drinks were swigged, and people found someone to talk to.

Ellie was fascinated. She always loved people watching and she noticed how most stuck to the groups they had come with, though venturing nods and smiles at others they recognised from the coach.

'Well, that didn't take long, Liberty,' said Martha.

'Time and tide wait for no man,' answered Liberty, tucking into a ham sandwich and taking a large slug of wine. 'I am determined to make use of every opportunity. If I can get a presenting job out of this, I shall be made. And having a friend in Greg Whitely has got to be an advantage.'

'Just make sure he doesn't take advantage of you, that's all,' Martha swiftly returned, abstaining from the glass of sparkling wine that was being offered on a tray.

'I know how to handle him,' Liberty muttered.

'You've had enough practice, that's for sure,' Martha retorted, a little spitefully.

'Jess, have you tried the spinach and ricotta quiche? I know it's your favourite,' said Ellie, steering her friend over to the trestles groaning with food. She knew Jess hated it when her friends squabbled and Liberty and Martha were experts at it.

They reached the table just at the same time as Charlie Harden and his friend Henry. Ellie saw Jess hang back, but Charlie had caught Ellie's eye and was smiling.

'Hi, I'm Charlie,' he said.

Ellie shook the hand he held out to her, slightly bemused by his formal manners. 'Hi, I'm Ellie and this is my good friend Jess.'

'I'm really pleased to meet you,' said Charlie, taking Jess's hand and shaking it for what seemed, to Ellie, an unnecessary amount of time. 'This is my friend, Henry.'

He turned to introduce him, but Henry had disappeared. Charlie looked a little embarrassed and began talking rather quickly as if to cover up for the fact that he knew his friend must appear really rude.

'Where are you from? I remember seeing you on the coach. Did you have to travel far?'

'No, we're from Winchester Uni, so we're not far away,' said Jess. 'How did you get involved in the project? I heard you say you were from Oxford.'

'Yes, we're studying there, but I'm actually from around here. My family live not far away at Deane and my mother told me about it. I'd invited Henry to stay with me for the summer, and he's the one really interested in archaeology. It seemed like it might be fun. How about you?'

'I love Jane Austen's books, and my friend Ellie, here, persuaded my other friends to join in. It will be our last summer together and I'm so excited about what we might find.'

'Do you really think there will be an exciting discovery?' asked Charlie. 'To be honest, I don't know much about Jane Austen ... I haven't actually read any of her books, though I'd like to.'

'Jess will be only too pleased to tell you everything you need to know about Jane Austen's novels,' said Ellie. 'She would never say so, but she's a real expert.'

Jess's face was pink as she shot a warning glance at her friend. 'I've read them a few times. I'm just a bit obsessed, that's all.'

'And modest with it, by the sounds of things. I was sincere about wanting to know more. Which book would you start reading, if you were me?' said Charlie.

'Oh, *Pride and Prejudice*, without a doubt. It's by far her funniest and most sparkling of all her novels. I must admit it's my favourite and the one I turn to if I ever need cheering up,' Jess answered.

'*Pride and Prejudice*, it is, then. I shall rely on you for explaining to me what is going on. Literature was never my strong point.'

Jess grinned. She couldn't help herself. 'It would be my pleasure.'

Just as the conversation was really getting going between them, Ellie saw Henry out of the corner of her eye. He was on the other side of the room waving wildly at Charlie, trying to get his attention. Charlie excused himself as soon as it was polite to do so, and the girls were left alone.

'Don't you say anything, Ellie Bentley ... not one word.'

'But, he is rather lovely, and he clearly thinks you are, too. I can just picture you both, reading together.'

Jess tapped her friend, playfully, on the arm. 'You are determined to tease me, aren't you? He was just being polite. I don't expect he's really interested in *Pride and Prejudice* or me, for one minute. Come on, let's find the others.'

As they made their way back through the throng, Ellie nudged Jess when she spotted Liberty and Cara standing right next to Greg Whitely with most of the other females present. He was holding court, making them all laugh with jokes that made Ellie wince, and telling stories about his adventures in television. Liberty was talking now. Ellie recognised the unmistakable stature, Liberty's head bowed, but her eyes meeting Greg's, looking up at him from under her lashes.

'If anyone could write a thesis on the art of flirtation, it's our Liberty,' she said, directing Jess to where Liberty had now caught hold of Greg's hand and was peering at it intently.

'What's she doing now?' asked Jess.

'Telling his fortune, it's one of her favourite techniques. She gets to hold their hands and look into their eyes, whilst hopefully appearing to be perfectly innocent of any ulterior motive. Most guys fall for it, and by the looks of him, Greg Whitely is completely taken in.'

'What do you think we should do?' whispered Jess. She knew Liberty was a handful and needed looking after.

'I don't think there's much we can do right now, other than marching in and taking her off, which would surely cause embarrassment. I'll have a word with her later … at least Cara is there, and she's a little more sensible.'

'Oh dear,' Jess sighed, 'I've left my bag over at the food table. I put it down when I was wrestling with my conscience over whether to have both the ham sandwiches and the prawn tartlets.'

'I'll get it,' Ellie offered. 'You have a word with Martha – she looks miserable, as if she's lost a pound and found a penny. I notice she's all alone as usual.'

'Martha never finds it easy making new friends,' said Jess, 'I'll go and see if we can get her chatting to someone who's interested in archaeology. That should help things along.'

Ellie made her way back to the trestle tables and noticed Charlie and Henry standing right next to the one where Jess had left her bag. Fortunately, they were deep in conversation. If she was careful, she could nudge round, pick up Jess's bag, which lay just to the right of Charlie's elbow, and they might not notice her.

'I don't understand you, Henry,' she heard Charlie say, 'there are some really fabulous girls here. All it takes is for you to smile a little and start a conversation.'

'Why would I want to do that?' answered Henry. 'I haven't seen anyone out of the ordinary, you've been chatting up the only good-looking girl here.'

'Oh, come on, Henry, that's just not true. Her friend Ellie is gorgeous! Though, I have to say, Jess has to be the most beautiful looking girl I've ever seen.'

'I don't remember her friend, she can't be that amazing.'

'They were here just a moment ago. She has long dark hair.'

'Oh, I know who you mean, the plain hippyish one with dull brown hair. Charlie, I'm not that desperate, for goodness sake.'

Ellie had heard every word, and when they turned round in the next second to see if they could spot the girls, there was nowhere she could go. Charlie looked the most embarrassed when he saw her, and Henry glared at her as if she were a bad smell under his nose. His lip curled with distaste and he moved away at speed.

'I've just come for Jess's bag,' Ellie said, pointing to where it lay.

Charlie was there before she could pick it up. He put it into her hands and seemed reluctant to let it go. She met his eyes.

'It's really good to meet you both,' he said, colour flaring in his cheeks. 'It's always fun to make new friends.'

Ellie recognised the sincerity behind those blue eyes, which she felt studying her face. 'And, it's a pleasure to meet *you*, Charlie.'

He looked as if he might say something more, but Ellie turned before he could speak, clutching Jess's bag as if her life depended on it.

It was dark by the time the taxi turned in at Ashe Rectory. The chatter all the way home had been about the day's events and the day to come. Liberty was delighted with the way that Greg had responded, and Jess was already privately thinking that Charlie seemed like a young man she'd like to know better. Cara had been in awe of the whole proceedings and had watched Liberty in action with admiration. Martha was disappointed that she hadn't got to speak to Will MacGourtey but knew that the chances to do so would be increased on the following day. Ellie, quite simply, felt exhausted. She was pleased that Jess had found someone who seemed as sweet as she, but she'd been a bit disturbed by the fact that the person who seemed to be his closest friend was clearly idiotic, and that was putting it politely.

She looked out of the window watching the car headlamps lighting up the narrow lanes. Cow parsley, frothing white in the hedgerows, loomed and tapped on the car windows, and the branches of summer trees arched over them like fan vaulting in a cathedral. Summer in all her lush greenery flashed past in a blink of the eye. Ellie felt her eyes closing, the rhythm of the car lulling her to sleep, and it was only when she felt the car stop that Ellie looked out once more. She shivered in her thin top. And it wasn't only her tiredness and the lack of sunshine that made her feel quite so cold. The scene she saw outside could not be explained. There was a picture from a Christmas card in front of her – snow covered the ground, lit up from the moon above and from the candlelight in the windows, which threw bars of gold against the blue snow shadowed by tall trees. Powdering every surface, snow crystals were piled in pillows up to the steps and weighed down lacy boughs on trees, bending them to the smooth white blankets on the ground. The house was alight, the gardens and surrounding fields, dark, icy and mysterious. Feathery showers whirled to the earth, and as Ellie peered through the swirling snow she glimpsed moving figures at the windows. Like enchanted shadows at first, the spectres became alive, vital with life, real. It looked like a party, the rooms were full, and the strains of music, a piano and a harp, could be heard.

## Chapter 4

'I am so hot!' Liberty announced, 'I'll never be able to sleep, though it shan't only be this sweltering weather that will keep me awake. My dreams will be all about handsome Greg tonight.'

'Did you really like him?' asked Martha, who clearly could not see the attraction. 'He was a bit oily, if you want my opinion.'

'Well, I don't want it,' Liberty snapped, fanning herself with the paper they'd been given on the programme for the next day.

Ellie, whilst privately agreeing with Martha, was distracted from the view outside for a moment, but turned back to witness the wintry scene melting before her eyes. Like a dream on waking; the figures vanished into thin air, the trees and gardens were lush with greenery and blooms under a pale moon. The house sat in darkness, in midnight blue, with only the sprinkling of stars studding the black dome of a clear night sky.

'Are you okay?' asked Jess. She, of all people, was most attuned to Ellie's sensitivity to such experiences.

Ellie nodded. 'Yes, I'm fine, a little overwrought, I think. It feels as if it's been a long day.'

The girls scrambled from the taxi and up the steps into the house. Mrs Hill had been as good as her word, leaving them some supper on a tray. Only Liberty and Cara were hungry, the others contented themselves with filling the chocolate pot that had been left for them with hot milk. Taking their mugs up to bed with them, Ellie and Jess left Cara and Liberty still chatting downstairs. Martha had already gone up ahead, saying she must go, as she would, no doubt, have to be the alarm clock for them all in the morning.

Ellie undressed and put on her pyjamas, deciding that one last chat with Jess before they went to sleep would be a lovely idea. It all sounded quiet beyond her friend's bedroom door so she knocked gently before cautiously opening it, but was completely unprepared for the sight she saw. The shock made her close the door again and glance behind her, in case by some mistake she'd opened the wrong door, even though she knew that was impossible. Warily, she slowly pulled the door back again. In an enormous four-poster bed in the middle of the room, hung with festoons of embroidered linen and lit by candlelight, a young man lay. He was in a deep sleep, his fair hair falling over one eye in a plume of gold, tousled and dampened into curls at his temples. Ellie recognised him at once as the mysterious figure she'd seen in the house before. He wore a crumpled shirt with a frilled collar, which was open at his neck where a pulse throbbed. His breathing was even and slow; his lips slightly parting with each exhalation, and like the chiselled cheekbones above were rosy pink from the heat of sleep and the linen and blankets partially covering him. It was a handsome face, Ellie thought. One long muscular leg poked out from under the patchwork quilt, smooth and firm like white marble, and diametrically opposite, an arm cradled his head. There was strength in the tapered fingers; and in his hands, one nestled next to his hair on the pillow, the other on the outstretched leg. He looked like a sculpture of Eros she'd once seen, and she stared, hardly able to tear her eyes away. On the bedside table she could see a pile of books, a candlestick whose candle had burned almost to nothing, and what looked to be a half-written letter. Curiosity got the better of her and creeping forward she tried to take a closer look. But before she could take another step, the body twitched. He was coming to, and rubbing his eyes. Ellie panicked, and running out of the room she shut the door with a bang, not daring to look back.

A knock at her own door a second later had Ellie trembling but when Jess bounced in and tumbled onto the large bed, Ellie was able to laugh even if she felt all her hair was standing on end.

'Gosh, Ellie, you look as if you've seen a ghost. I've never seen you so pale!'

The last thing Ellie wanted was to frighten Jess by saying she'd seen the young man in her room, so she stuck to partial truths. 'I did see something earlier. When we drew up in the taxi, I saw the rectory deep in snow, as if it was winter. There was candlelight at the windows, and I saw people dancing. It looked like a party – I could hear music.'

'Wow, that's amazing. I wish I had your talent.'

'I'm not sure you would if you were me. It can be very unnerving. Things seem to happen when you least expect it. I don't have any control over what and when I see it.'

'Do you have any idea how far back you are seeing? Could you see anything of the clothes people were wearing, or get an idea of the time period they're living in?'

'Not really ... though I did see that young man again before we left for the meeting. I'm not an expert, but his clothes looked like the ones in the portraits in your room.'

'Ellie! How exciting – now, I really am very envious. Where did you see him? Was he any clearer this time?'

'I saw him in the garden when I was looking out of the window. He was a little sharper, but it was such a fleeting moment, he'd gone before I got a really good look, and as we were just about to go out, I didn't think any more about him.'

'How I wish I could see him, too.'

Ellie looked at her friend whose expression was wistful. She'd never believe he'd just been occupying her room at the same time if she told her. 'I wish you could, Jess. There seems such a thin veil between this world and the one I saw today. It's just a heartbeat away. I can't really describe what happens ... it's almost like being in a trance, I suppose.'

'Well, next time it happens, you'll be sure to tell me. Perhaps if I knew he was there, I could see him. I'd like to see your handsome ghost.'

'He is good-looking, but whether he is as beautiful as young Charlie Harden, I would not like to say.'

'Oh, Ellie! I wondered how long it would be before you brought him into the conversation again. But, I will say, he is very charming, and I like him. There, will that do?'

'The word 'like' is rather insipid, I feel, but at least you've admitted a stirring of the heart. No, do not protest, Jess.'

'No, I won't. I will admit to a stirring of the heart ... just a slight one.'

'And you'll be seeing much more of him, which can only be something to look forward to.'

'Perhaps his friend might turn out to be more promising when we get to know him better, Ellie.'

'That's a nice idea, Jess, but I don't think you should be matchmaking with the idea of him in mind for me. I happen to know he doesn't find me very attractive. I heard him telling Charlie when I went to retrieve your bag. They didn't see me. Henry called me a hippy, which I suppose is true, and I'm proud of it.'

'Maybe he meant it as a compliment, Ellie.'

'No, Jess, he indicated that he wasn't so desperate as to find me in the remotest bit attractive. It's fine; I don't like him, either. Guess I'll just have to stick to Mr Darcy's ghost.'

Jess found this very funny. 'I can't imagine anything less likely, you're such a modern kind of girl.'

'You're right! Though, let's face it; most blokes we know are still living in the dark ages. I'm a hopeless case. Still, I shall be a very good godmother to your 2.3 children, and as long as I can see you being happy in love, that will be quite enough. And now all this reminds me that if we don't get you to bed very soon, you'll have such black circles under your eyes that even Charlie may change his mind.'

'Change his mind about what?'

'About the fact that perhaps you are the most beautiful girl he has ever set eyes on.'

'Did he really say that?'

Ellie nodded. 'Jess Harden, it has quite a nice ring to it, don't you think?'

Jess picked up the pillow from behind her golden head and threw it before running off into the next room, only reappearing seconds later to shout goodnight. She was resigned. Ellie had always teased her, and nothing was going to change that!

The next morning dawned bright and sunny without a cloud in the sky, and felt even warmer than usual for the middle of May. Mrs Hill prepared a hearty breakfast of bacon and eggs for them all before they set off in the car. According to the instructions they'd been given the night before, the kind vicar at St. Nicholas church had said anyone who needed to could use the church car park. It was quite a walk back down the hill but they took a short cut through the fields along what they imagined must have been the same route that the Austen family had used themselves, two hundred years ago. They could see people gathering at the bottom, and halfway up the field, a marquee had been erected where they could see Melanie Button, Greg Whitely and Will MacGourtey deep in conversation. There were a couple of cameramen training their huge cameras on the landscape every now and again. Several other people who were clearly technicians of one sort or other milled about, running up and down to the vans parked in the lane with miles of cable and sound equipment.

Liberty wasted no time in alerting Greg to the fact that she'd arrived, waving enthusiastically and calling out his name, and Martha wasted no time in telling her off. However, Greg appeared quite pleased to have been distracted from the attentions of Melanie Button, who was standing so close to him that she was completely invading his personal space, and excusing himself, he strolled over to join the girls.

'Good morning, ladies! How are we today?'

'We're fantastic, Greg, and ready for anything,' said Liberty, turning on her big beam smile and displaying a set of perfect, white teeth.

'I'm glad to hear that, Miss Lovelly,' said Greg, staring into her eyes, 'because I've got a special job for you.'

Liberty couldn't help showing her excitement and a whoop of sheer joy escaped before she could stop herself.

'I was wondering if you'd like to shadow me, be my assistant for the day?' said Greg.

Martha groaned audibly, but Greg appeared not to notice. Liberty jumped up and down with pure excitement.

'Would I? You bet!'

'Then, come with me to the operations centre, and we'll discuss what's required of your new role.'

Liberty turned to make a face at the others, her eyes wide and knowing, a huge grin spreading over her face. Cara looked disappointed. She'd clearly hoped she would be part of Greg's team.

As they watched Liberty waltz away, Ellie spoke up. 'Do you think she'll be all right? Why do I feel I've just fed her to the lions?'

'I'm sure she'll be fine,' answered Jess. 'And you know Liberty, she won't be happy until she's got a starring role. I'm pleased for her if this turns out to be the opportunity she wants.'

'She may get more than she bargains for,' said Martha, 'and I'll certainly be there to say, I told you so. But, Liberty never listens, least of all to me.'

'Let's try to keep an eye on her,' said Ellie. 'In any case, it's a bit unfair of us to assume Greg Whitely hasn't her best interests at heart.'

'Precisely,' Jess agreed, 'I think it's really kind of him to give her a break. For Liberty, this is a dream come true.'

'Are we ready now?' Martha asked. 'It looks as if everyone is waiting for us.'

Melanie Button, Greg Whitely, Will MacGourtey and the film crew were soon in full flow. The cameramen and the director took up their places at the corner of the field by the gate whilst Melanie and Greg explained that they wanted the volunteer team to walk in, as if they had just arrived, so that the film crew could capture the moment.

'We want this to look as natural as possible so don't be put off by all the equipment. Just walk through the gate, as you would normally do, chatting to your friends. And whatever you do, don't look at the camera.'

Liberty, who had been standing at Greg's side with a clipboard to hand, passed it back to him and rushed to join Jess and Ellie, Martha and Cara. 'I'm not missing out on this,' she said. 'Anyway, Greg said it would be quite all right if I wanted to be in the filming.'

'It's all so exciting, I do envy you, Liberty,' said Cara, 'but at least we all get a chance at being on television ... my mum will be so proud!'

'My mother won't believe it,' said Martha, 'it will be a dream come true for her. She's spent her entire life trying to get me in front of a camera, but I'd rather be anywhere else! I may not tell her; she will just not stop going on about this being the start of my acting career if she gets wind of it.'

A couple of rehearsals had the entire team in fits of laughter. The director encouraged them, saying he wanted them all to look happy to be there.

'Please remember not to look into the lens of the camera,' he said, looking at Liberty, and finishing with, 'and most particularly, please do not make any gestures like winking.'

Cara nudged Liberty and they both laughed. 'I'm sorry,' shouted Liberty, 'I just couldn't help myself, the whole experience brings out the actress in me.'

'Right, from the top, ladies and gentleman,' said the director, 'and please, Miss Lovell, look at your friend instead.'

'It's actually more difficult than it looks,' whispered Jess to

Ellie. 'I suppose it's because those cameras are huge and you're so aware of those massive lenses trained on you.'

'Exactly, I've never thought about it before but I'm pretty sure I couldn't cope with being a celebrity,' answered Ellie.

Once the initial filming was over, the activities of the day were able to start. Melanie Button introduced the archaeological experts who'd be in charge of the dig and they took over, explaining how they had a good idea where some of the main features of walls and foundations might be, and had been able to mark out excavation units where they'd be working. The team of volunteers were split into groups, those who would be digging, those who would be involved with note-taking and recording of artefacts, as well as people who would be helping with washing, labelling and recording into a computer database. Martha wanted to be right in the dig itself, Cara thought she'd be best washing or dry brushing found objects, and Ellie and Jess opted for helping to label and record everything. When Will MacGourtey spotted Ellie's painting equipment, he suggested she might like to make some paintings, a record of the progress made.

'I'd like you to come and look at the drawings we have of Steventon Rectory that were made by descendants of the family. Sadly, they don't quite correlate, but perhaps when we've started digging and can make out the basic layout, we might have more of an idea. If you think you could work from what we've got, that would be so helpful. We could do with one or two sketches and paintings of the landscape as it is now, before we've done too much.'

'I'd love to be useful,' said Ellie, setting up the little stool she always kept with her for painting *en plein air*, 'I'll start straight away.'

'Thank you, Ellie, your input will be invaluable for making the whole project come alive,' said Will. He smiled warmly and Ellie was filled with confidence.

She made a start, but the sun's heat felt very fierce on the back of her neck, and without the floppy hat she usually wore when outside working, she felt sure she'd get burnt very easily. It was typical of her to have left something behind, but at least she'd remembered her bag with paints and paper. There was nothing for it but to go and fetch the forgotten hat. Ellie ran back up the hill, her heart thumping in her chest as she reached the top. She'd left it in the boot of the car, which she soon retrieved, and found her way to the gap in the hedgerow where they'd walked earlier. The weather was really warm, and as soon as she put on the straw hat she felt instantly cooler. Everywhere looked so beautiful, light dappled the floor with golden coins, and the smell of earth, green leaves and nature, running riot, flooded her being with happiness.

The moment she stepped through the hedges and trees that screened the fields, Ellie knew something was different – her world was changed in more ways than she could ever have imagined. Like the little girl in *Alice in Wonderland*, she'd grown smaller and everything around her had doubled in size. Trees were so tall she could not see the top of them and the grass that tickled her bare legs nearly came up to her knees. Ellie looked back towards the way she had come but she knew it was fruitless. There was only one way to go, and that was to follow the sound that beckoned her. It was as if she saw everything through mist, layers of white vapour that rose to reveal a reality that became sharper with every passing minute. She was no longer Ellie Bentley; that she knew. She was a child, perhaps no more than five years old, and her thoughts intruded until Ellie had none left of her own. Her world was larger, more defined, sounds and smells were fresher, brighter and vivid. More than that, she felt different. Ellie saw life through the eyes of someone else, and when she heard the boy's voice calling her name she knew him to be her brother.

## Chapter 5

'Come on, Jane, let us go again!'

Henry pulled me up the slope to the top of the field where the elm trees stood like sentinels and whispered over our heads in their hushing, leaf language. The day was hot like the one I'd left behind, and my legs struggled to keep up with him in the heat. He sensed that my small legs were tiring and he turned to wait, looking at me with a grin. Light flickered in his hazel eyes, those that I knew grown-ups said were so like mine, but his were almost golden on this day, like Baltic amber. The grass up at the top of the terrace was so long; it prickled the back of my legs. Beads of dew, like fairy necklaces strung along green blades, felt cold under my feet. When we reached the top, he showed me how to lie down in line with the trees, my toes pointing one way and my arms stretched over my head.

'Jane, wait until I count to three,' I heard him say.

Lying in the sweetly fragrant meadow, I felt so excited I started to giggle, and my body fidgeted in response. And before he'd managed to shout out the number three, I'd started going, rolling down the hill, and gathering momentum until the world was spinning. There was a blur of blue sky; then green fields, and then over I went again like a flyer on Nanny Littleworth's spinning wheel. I could see Henry overtake me, going faster than ever. He got to the bottom before me but I came to a standstill at last, my heart beating with pure pleasure as I lay in the grass chuckling and laughing. There were grass stains on my dress and daisies in my hair, which Henry picked out, one by one.

Sitting up, I could see a house that I knew was my home and I had a sudden longing to see my father.

'Are you not coming up again, little Jenny?' Henry asked, using the pet name my family used when they wanted to appeal to my better nature. He had his hands in the pockets of his breeches. His shirt was crumpled and stained like my gown. Brown curls flopped over his eyes, which looked into mine so tenderly that I almost changed my mind. I ran to hug him, stood on my tiptoes and planted a kiss on his cheek. Henry was my protector, and my beloved playmate. I longed to be just like him but my mother scolded me when I behaved too much like a tomboy. I knew I should not run or jump or shout, as my brothers did, but nothing she said would deter me, so when Henry begged me to play with him I did not usually need to be asked twice. But, as much as I wanted to be with him, home was calling.

I shook my head and muttered, 'I'm going to see Papa.'

I ran through the glittering garden, past the sundial and the rose beds, where rosy blooms were crumpled like crushed paper in the heat. Along the pink bricks of the walled garden scented with apricots, I ran my fingers along the roughened surface, not stopping to pick the sweet strawberries lying below in their straw bed nests, and at last I saw him. I could see his white head as he sat at his desk by the window. There were piles of dusty books and yellowed papers on every side of him, and I knew his fingers would be stained black with ink as he corrected his accounts or marked his scholars' work. I knew before I reached the house that the room he occupied would be wreathed in sweet-scented pipe smoke, just one ingredient in the magical elixir that conjured up his special smell. Gilt-edged books, paper and ink all had their own aroma as dear to me as any exotic perfume from India, and were as much a part of him as the glass of Madeira that he took in the evening, and his own cologne of bergamot, neroli and lavender. I could not reach him quickly enough, and at that moment he seemed to sense my presence and looked up to wave and smile. I waved back, and my heart was filled with love.

I ran into the house, dark and cool after the sunny day outside to find him still busy with his books. I brought the smell of the outdoors with me and knew I looked like a wild child with leaves in my hair.

'Little Jenny, you have had a very busy afternoon, I think. Those grass stains tell a certain tale.'

I hung my head waiting for him to scold me, but I should have known better. He simply laughed and held out his arms to me.

'Tell me a story, Papa.'

I loved to hear his voice and the tales of fairyland, wizards and magicians that he conjured up in a moment. Every word fashioned another golden link in an elfin chain; each phrase wrought an ivory tower or an enchanted castle. All my favourite objects on the window-sill found their part in the tale – the tiny bleached skeleton of a cat's skull was a witch's talisman, a peacock feather was a fallen treasure from a princess's satin cap, and a blue glass bottle held a powerful potion.

'And what happened next?' my father asked after the wicked queen had imprisoned the princess in the castle tower.

It was my turn. I loved to watch his eyes grow wider as I spun my tale though I could not think of all the words I wanted even if I could see it all in my head. Mermen and mermaids steered the prince's boat to the shore, which looked exactly like my father's model ship made by my brother Frank. And, of course, there was always a happy ending.

'That's my Jane, my little storyteller. You will write great tales one day, I am certain.'

There was a face at the window watching us. Henry had his nose pressed up against the casement. 'Come on, Jenny, come and play. Leave Papa alone now.'

Hopping down, I gave my father one last hug, burying my face in his chest, savouring his smell, his smile and the twinkle in his hazel eyes, before running back to the garden and my darling Henry. But as I took up my tiny watering can, made specially by my friend the blacksmith, the sun that was shining so brightly seemed blotted out by more than just clouds that were turning pink in the sky above on that golden afternoon. As I stood trying to make sense of it all, everything started to fade, the rich colours of a moment ago washed into pale tones like the silk embroideries mama had stitched as a child. The stark, bright reality of the scene just played out to me disappeared on the summer breeze that blew my hair back in the wind, and was gone forever.

Ellie blinked. She was back, as if she had never been away. The sun still felt as warm as the one she'd just experienced, but it took her a moment to recover. Her head felt light, and a feeling of fatigue was strong. But, as much as she would have liked to lie down in the field and sleep, she knew she would have to get a move on. She wasn't sure how long she'd 'been away' and hoped that her absence had not been any cause for alarm. Running down the hill, she was reminded of the little girl whose pleasure she'd felt in rolling down, a far more enjoyable exercise.

'I'm sorry it took me so long,' she said to Jess as she caught up with the others.

'I don't think you could have been any quicker, you must have run there and back,' answered her friend.

'Really?' Ellie queried. 'I feel as if I've been gone a while.'

Jess looked at Ellie, a puzzled expression on her face. 'Are you okay? You do look a bit washed out.'

Ellie nodded. 'I'm fine, just feeling a bit tired that's all.'

'I expect it's the sun, we're not used to this kind of heat in England, are we? At least you've got your hat now. Don't worry, you haven't been missed.'

Ellie settled down on her stool and picked up her pencil but nothing could have prepared her for the ease with which she drew. It was almost as if she were possessed, and just half an hour later, though she hardly had any memory of executing it, there on the paper before her was an exquisite watercolour painting of the house she'd just been visiting, captured in sunshine exactly as she'd seen it. It was even possible to see the white head of Jane Austen's father as he marked his books, and Ellie knew, without a shadow of a doubt, that she'd been 'helped' to see it.

The rest of the day passed swiftly and by the time the girls were back home they were feeling very pleased with what they'd already accomplished. Even Liberty was happy she'd decided to come along on the dig, and Ellie felt relieved that it had been a good decision for them all. They couldn't have asked for better weather and it was good to be making new friends and discoveries. She could only hope that such an excellent beginning was a good omen, and feeling optimistic she looked forward to the coming weeks. As for her strange experiences, she had learned in the past to shelve them somewhere entirely different in her mind. They belonged to another world and time, one that she felt privileged to experience. If she was able to have another glimpse, that would be well and good, but she never took such things for granted, and knew time in all its guises would only make itself known to her as it wished.

## Chapter 6

Over the next week or so, the girls threw themselves into their new jobs and the dig got truly underway. Removing the topsoil was a slow process and the team covered every square inch of the excavation units methodically with shovels, picks and trowels. Martha was happy in her work. She didn't feel the need to chat away like the other students around her, and no one bothered her as she dug enthusiastically into the earth with her shovel.

Jess was in the operations tent, and already unidentified objects were appearing, carried in with all due reverence, to be washed, labelled, recorded and identified. Charlie, by luck or design, Jess wasn't quite sure, worked there also, though he was working on the computer at the other end of the space. Whenever he had a moment, he was at Jess's side, taking note of whatever she was doing.

'Are you coming to the pub tonight?' he asked, as he watched Jess working. 'There are a few of us meeting at the Deane Gate Inn.'

'I'd like that, thank you,' said Jess. 'I'm sure Ellie and the other girls would like to come, too.'

'Now, you've made my day,' said Charlie, smiling into her

eyes. 'I've persuaded Henry to come ... he's a nice guy when you get to know him.'

'I'm sure he is,' Jess agreed, 'what is he doing this morning?'

'He's at the sharp end with the diggers, you might know. This is a bit of a dream for Henry; he loves nothing more than scrabbling about in the dirt looking for history. He's reading archaeology at university, he's very clever and very thorough.'

'What are you studying, Charlie?' asked Jess.

'Music.'

'How wonderful; what's your instrument?'

'I play double bass ... but to be honest, it's my electric bass I love playing best.'

'Oh, wow, and I bet you're really brilliant, too. Do you ever perform?'

'I'm in a band at college.'

'I'd love to see you play!'

'Well, I've a few gigs at the weekends – there are some local festivals coming up. It would be great if you could come along. Bring your friends.'

'Oh, that sounds really exciting.'

'It is the passion of my life, I must admit. How about you? Do you like music?'

'I love music but I was never good enough to pursue music to your level ... I play a little piano. I suppose I can play a recognisable tune, but that's about it.'

'And what are you studying?'

'I want to be a teacher. I come from a teaching family ... my mum, dad, and most of my aunts and uncles are teachers. It must be in my blood, I suppose. It sounds a bit boring, but I've been on teaching practice a few times now, and I simply love it.'

'It doesn't sound boring at all. I remember the teachers I had who were passionate about teaching. They gave me a love of my own in music. If it hadn't been for my music teacher at school, I doubt very much that I'd be doing music, right now. And besides, I'm sure you'd be an inspiration for anyone.'

Jess blushed. 'Well, I don't know about that. It can be quite daunting facing a class of teenagers and trying to get them enthusiastic about Jane Austen.'

'That reminds me; I've found a copy of *Pride and Prejudice* at home. I shall start reading it later, and then we can discuss it, chapter by chapter.'

'I shall look forward to that,' said Jess, putting down the dirt-encrusted object to meet his eyes that seemed to see all the way into her soul.

'Anyway, it was lovely talking to you,' said Charlie. 'I'd best go, I can see someone waving at me by the desk.'

Back at the dig, there was great excitement. Will MacGourtey let out a whoop of elation, as the first line of bricks was located. Photographers, cameramen, presenters, experts and volunteers crowded round as if a treasure trove of precious jewels had been unearthed. The whole team turned up to see the line of exposed brickwork, still recognisable as such. Henry Dorsey stood at Will's side as the archaeologist praised the volunteers working with him.

Ellie couldn't help herself. She was standing next to Martha as the news broke. 'You might know Henry would be credited with discovering the first significant find. And, just look at his face … he looks as if he found them single-handed.'

'Well, it's a huge deal, Ellie. I think I'd be feeling pretty pleased with myself if I was heading up the team.'

'I don't know, there's just something so smug about him that I don't like. Any one of you might have had the same good fortune if you'd been working right next to Will MacGourtey.'

'I've enjoyed it, bricks or not,' answered Martha, her eyes shining. 'I must have found fifty nails this morning. It's fascinating to think they might have been in the very floorboards Jane walked upon.'

Ellie wasn't sure she could have got so excited about a few dirty nails. 'I'm just saying, you've been toiling away just as hard, Martha, but no one has thanked you. Look at him, puffed up like a … peacock.'

'He's only doing his job. I don't know why you find him so irritating,' said Martha. 'You're being rather a snob, you know. He can't help being so rich or privileged.'

'What do you mean?' asked Ellie.

'I heard one of the girls from the university saying that Henry Dorsey comes from a hugely wealthy family. He's from Surrey, apparently, and his family live in some enormous pile in Weybridge when they're not in their Chelsea townhouse or their villa on the Italian lakes.'

'Oh, that explains it,' said Ellie, inwardly groaning, 'no wonder he looks so pleased with himself all the time.'

'He's going into the family business, apparently, though one of the others said all he'd really like to do is become an archaeologist.'

'I wouldn't expect anything less from him,' answered Ellie. 'Clearly, he'd rather be making more millions than following his heart.'

'Still, it might turn out well for Jess if Charlie falls in love with her,' said Cara, who'd been hanging back, eavesdropping.

'I don't understand, unless you mean Henry is going to give Charlie a job, perhaps.'

'No, Charlie's got money of his own, and a family pile. It's a massive mansion not far from here, I've been told.'

Before Ellie could comment, Jess arrived, bouncing over to join the girls, a huge smile spreading over her face. ' Isn't it wonderful? I can almost see it, can't you? Just imagine, the rectory must have been right there.'

Ellie was taken back for a moment, almost pulled to the other dimension where she'd stood as a child. She could picture the house perfectly and she heard a voice in her head.

'My home, my home ... my beloved Steventon,' the voice whispered so closely in her ear that she turned to see if there was someone who could have possibly spoken to her, but there were only the crowds of people all chatting away, glad to have an unexpected break from the work in progress.

'Have you had a good morning?' asked Jess. 'I've been so busy; I really didn't expect to be. I thought it would be ages before anything would be found.'

'I've done some sketches,' said Ellie, 'some of them a bit fanciful, I'm afraid, but I've also painted a watercolour showing the landscape today. I've really enjoyed it. I've missed you, though you know what I'm like once I'm in the zone.'

'Exactly. You go all quiet on me. I missed you, too, but I have had some company.'

Ellie looked at her friend who was looking back at her rather sheepishly. 'It wouldn't be a certain Charlie Harden, would it?'

'It might be.'

'And did he tell you all about his big house and all the money he's inherited?'

'I don't know what you're talking about, Ellie. I don't think that can be right, he seems so grounded and normal.'

Cara turned once more. 'His family own a great big house at Deane, apparently. I heard some of the Oxford girls talking. And they said his sister is here, but I'm not sure what she looks like or what she's been doing. They said she's at Oxford too, and that she's supposed to be brilliant. His family are all really clever and talented.'

'Charlie's a musician,' said Jess, nodding her head. 'He sounds very passionate about his music.'

'Well, it does seem you've been busy this morning,' said Ellie, raising her eyebrows at the others who all laughed.

'Ellie Bentley, you stop right there. I shan't tell you any more if you're going to be this teasing. However, what I will tell you, is that we've all been invited to meet Charlie and his friends at the pub tonight!'

When they finally reached home again they found Mrs Hill preparing an evening meal for them all. Delicious smells of grilled lamb chops and potatoes cooked with garlic and rosemary made them realise how hungry they were, and a fantastic spread laid out on the scrubbed table in the kitchen was a sight to see.

'Well, you can't go out to an evening like that without a good lining,' said Mrs Hill, 'and I know how hungry you can get out in the fresh air all day. Mr Hill is always ravenous when he's been out in the gardens working. You're growing girls and you need to keep up your strength!'

Apart from Liberty who raised her eyes, the other girls said how cherished they felt under Mrs Hill's loving care. She was a very generous lady with her time, and wanted to hear all about the work they'd been doing. The girls were happy to talk all about the lovely day they'd had and the anticipation of the evening in store, and Mrs Hill listened as if she was enraptured by every word. The moment they'd finished the first course, she fetched a dish of stewed apples and a jug of cream for their pudding from the larder and sat down to listen to the rest of their tales.

As soon as the meal was over Jess and Ellie started clearing the table, but Mrs Hill insisted they could have a night off from helping.

'I'll see to the clearing up. You go and get ready for you've to make yourselves lovely for all those young men I've been hearing about!'

'Don't you wish you were coming too, Mrs Hill?' said Liberty. 'I'm sure we could find you a nice young man.'

Mrs Hill laughed. 'Get away with you. I'm not tempted in the least ... no, Mr Hill is the only young man I've ever wanted!'

That had Liberty and Cara in stitches of laughter and even Ellie admitted to Jess she could not quite picture the dour and silent Mr Hill as a romantic hero.

As soon as supper was over, the girls disappeared off to their various rooms agreeing to meet downstairs in the drawing room before they went out to meet Charlie and the others. Ellie got changed in about five minutes and with plenty of time before they were due to go out she fetched her sketchbook from her bedroom and ran downstairs. She had an idea to try a drawing of the front elevation of Steventon Rectory based on what she'd learned that day, and was really looking forward to talking to the other girls about all the ideas she had. The door to the drawing room was closed, but as soon as Ellie touched the handle, she could sense that the very air was different. Sounds, smells and furniture were all changing before her eyes beyond anything she recognised. Gone was the circular table in the hall, and instead a pier table and ornate looking glass graced one side of the corridor. There was an umbrella stand and a bookcase full of heavy tomes, two mahogany chairs either side of the doorway, and a familiar object in the recess where it had probably stood for over two hundred years telling of the moments, seconds, minutes and hours that passed. She heard the Grandfather clock in the hall whirr into action and chime again and again, with each sonorous strike of the bell seeming to take her further and further back in time.

## Chapter 7

I brushed my hands over the blue and white checked poplin of my morning gown, and despaired. The hem was spattered with mud from the walk but more than that I knew my faded dress had seen better days, and would have been improved for having another three inches added to its length. My hair, always unruly and curly to the point of being wild, was threatening to fall entirely down my back from the knot on top of my head, and tucking stray strands behind my ears was not doing a very sufficient tidy-up. Though why I was so keen to impress the stranger come to Ashe, I could not think. I'd lived in the world for very nearly twenty years and had not yet worried about my appearance when meeting any single young man. But, I'd heard enough from my dear friend, Madame Lefroy, to be exceedingly curious about her nephew Tom – his coming to visit his aunt and uncle had often been talked about, but never accomplished. When at last he'd been expected, every morning visit in Steventon had included a mention of the well-composed letter his aunt had received. Every lady in the village had been full of the news.

'I suppose you have heard of the handsome letter Mr Tom Lefroy has written to Madame?' said Mrs Bramston. 'I understand it was a very handsome letter, indeed. Mrs Harwood told me of it. Mrs Harwood saw the letter, and she says she never saw such a splendid letter in her life.'

We knew that he hailed from Ireland, which lent him an air of romanticism. I loved some of the country airs and songs that were composed by his countrymen, and I suppose I had imagined him to be something of a romantic figure. We were told he was clever, and I remembered someone saying that overwork was the reason for his visit. After a suitable rest, he was going to study law in London and until then he was to spend Christmas with his relations. When the invitation came, I couldn't quite believe I was to meet him. He'd achieved almost mythical status, and he surely couldn't live up to the nonpareil of my imagination.

'Jane, your hair!' my mother exclaimed. 'Why did you not let Rebecca see to it this morning?'

'I do not like to be always asking her to be looking after me with tasks I can do for myself. She has quite enough to do with running errands for Nanny Littleworth and Nanny Hilliard.'

'You will have to do, I suppose. Just remember not to talk too much and run on like you do at home.'

We entered by the parlour door, and saw a young gentleman sitting with Madame. The Tom Lefroy so long talked of, so high in interest, was actually before me. He was introduced, and at first, I did not think too much had been said in his praise. He was very tall and fair, his hair the colour of buttercups in sunshine. But, it wasn't his shock of yellow hair that drew my attention. It was his eyes I noticed straight away. They were the colour of the sea on a winter's day and as restless as the waves crashing to the shore. The grey coat he wore intensified the shade – one minute they were as lavender as sea thrift, the next as pale as pebbles in sand. He was a very good-looking young man; and his countenance had a great deal of spirit and liveliness. I felt immediately that I would like him; but as the afternoon wore on I found I was completely deceived in my first impressions. There was no well-bred ease of manner, or a readiness to talk, which convinced me that he had no intention to be really acquainted with me. Taciturn and proud were the words that sprang to mind. He looked as if he were there on sufferance, that the invitation from his aunt was most unwelcome.

My mother and Madame did most of the talking, but on feeling that perhaps we were a little overwhelming for someone who was not entirely well, I moved from my chair on the opposite side of the room to sit next to him.

'You have come from Ireland, I understand, Mr Lefroy.'

'Yes, from Dublin, Miss Austen.'

'Ah, and is Dublin the town where you were born?'

'No, that is Limerick.'

'Thomas has been studying at Trinity College,' Madame offered, as she caught our rather one-sided conversation.

Thomas nodded in assent, got up and walked over to the window where he stood looking out. It was then that I gave up trying to engage him further. Every now and then, I felt his eyes on me, and when once I dared to look back at him, he stared at me in such a way as to make me feel decidedly uncomfortable. I did not know what to make of him.

'Well,' said my mother on the walk home, 'what a very proud and conceited young man. And never to open his mouth the whole time ... Irish airs are all very well, but he'll not make many friends if he looks down his nose at his aunt's Hampshire neighbours. I suppose his father is a Colonel and fancies himself very high and mighty, and there I was thinking that I'd heard his mother was a very sensible woman.'

'I understood from Madame that Thomas has been ill, that he is suffering the effects of too much work and that his eyesight has been affected.'

'A poor excuse to behave badly, in my opinion,' answered my mother. 'He is most disagreeable, and rude. Why, I should have given him a dressing down if I were his aunt. To stand up and walk away when you were trying your very best to converse with him, I never heard of such a thing!'

He was dressed in a dark coat and satin breeches for the Basingstoke Assembly just a day later, a distinguished figure who seemed to have no wish to join in either the conversation or the dancing, merely standing at the edge of the dance floor with the Lefroy party almost as if he looked down on anyone who chose to take part. He walked here and there, occasionally whispering something in his cousin Lucy's ear, which despite his serious expression seemed to make her laugh heartily. Nevertheless, there was something about him I could not dismiss, and I was intrigued by his haughty manner. It seemed improbable that he'd look my way, and yet I wished he would. I wanted him to notice me. He intrigued me in a way no other person ever had, and yet, he made me cross. I was angry with him for being so superior in his manners, but I loved a puzzle, and there was no doubt, Tom Lefroy was an enigma. I could not help staring at him, enjoying the way his yellow hair curled into the collar of the coat that closely fitted broad shoulders and skimmed over neat hips. He didn't smile; he only observed the other dancers. I wondered if he knew that I watched him, but all I could see was his static expression, and an eyebrow twitching in response to his observations.

My admirers were plentiful, and I sat down not once, getting up with Mr Heartley, Reverend Powlett and Mr John Warren, to name but a few. As I danced, I felt him watching me, those grey eyes of his followed me about the room as I whirled and skipped. Once, I glanced towards him and our eyes met. He made the smallest bow before looking away so I could not be sure if it was intended for me at all.

Sitting at the edge of the ballroom my mother observed everything, gossiping with the other Hampshire mamas, punctuated by complaints of being too hot. I was tempted to say that was bound to be the case if one sat almost on top of the fire, but I bit my tongue and offered to fetch her fan. That meant I had to run back through the cold, narrow passageway that separated the ballroom from the inn, and I shivered in my thin, muslin gown. It was there that I bumped into him. We were alone in the dimly lit space with hardly room to pass the other, and I was so shocked to see him, so conscious of every unspoken thought of mine, that I jumped.

Tom nodded, and clearing his throat, muttered, 'Miss Austen', the smallest smile curving upon his lips. He could see my discomfort and for a moment I felt he held all the power. It was just that the space was so small; we were so close, almost intimate. I knew I would have to be the one to speak, but then he surprised me.

'I have been to fetch my Aunt Lefroy's fan,' he said, waving the forgotten accessory, by way of explanation.

'And I am on my way to collect my mother's,' I rejoined, unable to suppress a laugh at the absurdity of discussing nothing in particular and in such polite terms in the freezing, draughty corridor. The balance of power was shifting.

Tom bowed and moved to walk past me as I stepped the same way, more by design than accident. He instantly coloured, and made another attempt to escape after a cursory, 'Forgive me'. But I was in a teasing mood and moved again, springing with a light foot to block his path once more. I was determined to get a reaction from him, one that was real and human. When he saw me laughing with such open friendliness, he could not help but smile also. It lit up his eyes, the flint-grey warmed by tones of sapphire.

'Why, we are almost dancing, Mr Lefroy,' I said, adding with a serious expression, 'but, I am quite wrong, I think, because you do not dance ... or perhaps, cannot dance.'

This time his glowering eyes met mine. 'Indeed, you are quite mistaken, Miss Austen. I enjoy dancing quite as much as you do amongst my own friends and neighbours who would be only too happy to assure you of my pleasure in the activity.'

'So, you do not consider yourself to be amongst friends, Mr Lefroy? I am sorry to hear it, for the generous hospitality of Hampshire folk has often been remarked upon. Indeed, I hoped that my own efforts to welcome you into our small circle yesterday would satisfy.'

'I was very happy to be introduced to you by my aunt, Miss Austen.'

'Yet, I daresay you are used to finer company in Ireland. In Basingstoke we are a little rougher round the edges, I think. Perhaps we are too countrified for your taste. No doubt, Limerick and Dublin have far finer assemblies to boast of than a country dance in an upstairs room above an inn, and far more rarefied company.'

Tom Lefroy looked completely shocked at my speech. I felt I had done all I could to startle him into conversation and made my way to leave.

'Please forgive me, Miss Austen, if I have given the impression that I am above my company or that I have no desire to dance. Nothing could be further from the truth.'

He hesitated. I felt a little shame-faced. Now that he'd spoken and hinted at his wish to dance in a most gentleman-like manner, I felt I should not have been so frank. I detected something more from the grey eyes that peered at me under fair lashes. Was there a reason for his rudeness?

'I confess, I am apt to be ill at ease with strangers. I certainly have not the talent which some people possess of conversing easily with those I have never seen before.'

He looked sincere and suddenly, I had a change of heart. Could he be shy, after all? My judgement that he considered himself too good for the company could be false. Perhaps Tom's behaviour was understandable if he was attempting to protect his shyness from being exposed, shielding a vulnerability within. Yet, his whole manner had led me to believe that the idea of dancing was the furthest thing from his mind.

Well, even if he'd contemplated asking me before, I felt certain he would not ask me to dance now. On the other hand, I decided, how was I to have known that his haughty demeanour, which I had first decided was the result of misplaced pride was a mask he wore to hide his diffident nature?

I turned to go. Tom held out his hand, touched my arm slightly to arrest me. 'Miss Austen,' he faltered, 'Will you dance with me?'

My first inclination was to say no, to spite him. I reminded myself that he was the son of a gentleman, Colonel Anthony Lefroy, and as such, had received a fine education and was now taking a step on the ladder of his chosen profession. He could not be ignorant about the ways of the world. Being shy was a poor excuse. Why would a man of sense and education, who has lived in the world, be ill qualified to recommend himself to strangers? Was it simply the case that Mr Thomas Lefroy had forgotten his manners until I reminded him of them? I hesitated, and willed myself to refuse him.

'I have promised to dance with Mr Powlett next,' I said promptly, unable to completely dismiss his request yet avoiding those steel grey eyes I felt regarding me steadily.

I met his gaze with an expression of defiance.

'But, Miss Austen, do you think it would be wise to dance with Mr Powlett for a second time this evening?'

I looked up to regard the eyes that looked so intensely into mine. Mr Lefroy's countenance bore such a serious expression that I couldn't think what his thoughts must be. Surely he did not disapprove of dancing twice with the same gentleman, though I admitted to myself that dancing again with Charles Powlett was not an event to which I looked forward. That young clergyman was the clumsiest partner I knew.

'I ... do not think it imprudent to step up with a gentleman for two dances, Mr Lefroy. Perhaps in Ireland it is not the custom, but I assure you, that here in England it is quite good form.'

'And does good form and fashion allow for the abuse of one's toes whilst dancing? I could not help but notice that yours were thoroughly and most cruelly mistreated the first time round.'

I could not help laughing especially when Tom's eyes crinkled at the corners and he grinned, unable to keep his serious expression.

'Mr Lefroy, you are provoking me, I think, for your own amusement, and I cannot agree with your wicked observations though I will allow that dancing has its hazards as well as its joys.'

'Then, on the grounds of safety, and the preservation of your good health, I implore you, Miss Austen, to forget your promise and to dance with me instead.'

I could not help but be amused by Tom, and was almost prepared to forgive him anything, even his pride.

'I cannot break my promise to my dancing partner, Mr Lefroy, but I will dance with you directly afterwards, if you wish.'

To my complete surprise Tom took my hand and raised it to his lips planting a kiss as he observed my expression with an intensity I found most disconcerting. I felt scorched, almost branded: my heart was hammering so loudly I feared he would hear it. These were not the manners of a shy boy; I could not make him out. And whilst in the midst of such thoughts, he seemed to vanish as quickly as he had appeared. I hurried away to retrieve my mother's fan and though the temperature in the corridor was somewhere approaching freezing, I felt the heat upon my cheeks as if I had been standing before an open log fire.

Entering the ballroom once more, I was struck by the fact that there appeared to be a heightened expectation in the very air of the place, a sense of excitement in the vibrations of the fiddles tuning up again, and in the incessant chatter of the observers and dancers, as they frantically rushed for places on the dance floor. Everywhere looked fresh and bright, a picture of Christmas celebration in the evergreens strung along the mantelpieces at either end of the room, and in the looking glasses above them reflecting green wreaths and scarlet berries winking like ruby jewels in amongst the towering plumes of the dancers and the twinkling lustres of the chandeliers.

Mr Powlett claimed his dance and my hand. I felt a sea of faces turned in our direction as the country dance began. I noticed Mrs Terry who had travelled from Dummer turn to her neighbour and pass comment as she fixed her eyes upon us. Whilst I loved dancing, being scrutinised by all the ladies eager to marry off every single young woman or gossip about her particular prospects with a partner was most disagreeable. And, I knew every dance was remarked upon and my partners numbered. All this could be endured, however, if I could just make sure that the one person I most minded watching me dance with Mr Powlett could keep his countenance. I would not seek him out, I would maintain eye contact with my partner and take little notice of those who sat or stood at the edges of the ballroom.

But, I might have known it would be impossible. Far from behaving as he had before, silently regarding the scene with an expression of hauteur, Mr Thomas Lefroy did not once remove his eyes from my face and every time I passed once more along the dance, he merely inclined his head towards me with such a saucy expression I was sure the whole room observed it! Far from keeping my head, I became flustered even to the point of moving the wrong way down the set to my utter mortification.

At last, the tortuous dance was over, Charles led me back to my place and I waited for Tom to claim me. Looking about, he was nowhere to be seen, and as the seconds ticked by, I perched up out of my seat looking eagerly round for him. He simply wasn't there. Oh, I was so vexed! To think I had been looking forward to dancing with that proud puppy, and now, he was going back on his word. Well, I was not going to be fooled like that again, I decided. Miss Jane Austen was not to be toyed with by some upstart with a honeyed Irish lilt to his voice that was such pleasure to my ears that I wondered if he'd bewitched me by fairy means. I swore there and then I'd never be taken in by such fairness of face or feature again. How dare he!

'Are you by chance looking for someone?' whispered a voice very close to my ear that had me jumping out of my seat.

Tom Lefroy was standing behind me, bending his handsome head down toward mine to tease me yet again. On seeing my expression he merely bowed, and holding out his hand said, 'Miss Austen, I do hope you will do me the honour of dancing with me.'

I could not refuse him, however much I wished. And when he took my hand and led me out onto the floor, I knew he would be the perfect partner. Tom and I danced three times together during the course of the evening, and though I knew I should not, I could not help myself.

'Miss Jane Austen of Steventon has found a new beau,' I heard the gossiping neighbours whisper. 'My, she is a lively one tonight. How many times has she stood up with that young man? She is certainly setting her cap at young Mr Lefroy, and well, she might!'

The gossips might remark all they liked and my mother could scold me all night. I did not care: I was only intent on enjoying myself.

## Chapter 8

On the following morning, I awoke with thoughts of Tom still in my head. I was dying to tell my sister Cassy all about him, but she was away visiting her beloved fiancé Tom, and spending Christmas with his family once he went away to sea. I wished to tell her everything, but then I was not sure she would be very pleased with the way I'd behaved. To dance three times with him had raised some eyebrows, and I knew those who liked to talk would be watching me even more carefully the next time we were together. I would write and tell her something about him, but perhaps not just yet.

In my bedchamber, hidden under the bed was my box of delights, all my writing to date. I fetched it out hauling the mahogany box onto the coverlet, disturbing the dust lurking below to sparkle in sunlit shafts like powdered diamonds. Opening the heavy lid with impatient fingers I couldn't wait to fetch my scribblings out, to glance through the familiar pages. I stroked the papers one by one as if greeting old friends, and stopped to look through my latest manuscript. It was more or less finished, but at the editing stage, which took rather more ink and paper than I liked. Written in letters, *Elinor and Marianne* was my first full-length attempt at writing a novel. I liked writing about women's lives, and this book about two sisters – Elinor and Marianne Dashwood, was to explore the differences between acting with the head or the heart. It was something I struggled with myself on a daily basis, and I was finding it harder to write about as the novel concluded. Behaving sensibly wasn't always easy, but I tried to be a model of goodness and duty like my sister. My heart overruled my head on too many occasions, and finding a balance was always difficult.

I wanted to write great novels like those of Samuel Richardson or Fanny Burney – books that inspired others with heroines that were strong, bold and capable. But, they also had to include a hero, and I spent much time imagining how such a gentleman might look and behave. Leafing through the pages, I read aloud my description of Willoughby again. He was a hero at the start of the novel and I wanted my readers to fall in love with him as much as Marianne and I had done. Marianne was writing to tell her friend all about her new acquaintance.

*A gentleman carrying a gun, with two pointers playing round him, was passing up the hill and within a few yards of me, when my accident happened. He put down his gun and ran to my assistance. I raised myself from the ground, but my foot had been twisted in the fall, and I was scarcely able to stand. The gentleman offered his services, and perceiving that my modesty declined what my situation rendered necessary, took me up in his arms without farther delay, and carried me down the hill. Then passing through the garden, the gate of which had been left open by Margaret, he bore me directly into the house, whither Margaret was just arrived, and quitted not his hold till he had seated me in a chair in the parlour.*

Closing my eyes, I lay back against the pillows to imagine the scene. Willoughby was very handsome, but his dark hair that fell on his cheekbones in loose black curls, in my imagination, looked rather blonde now, and the eyes that stared into mine had turned from brown to light grey. Tom Lefroy now held me in his arms, his heart was next to mine and his lips were so close I could feel his breath, warm upon my face, stirring the curls under my bonnet. His eyes lingered on my cheeks tinged with dusky pink, dropping to the slope of my breasts where a fine lace tucker was fastened with a silk rose.

How I wanted to see Tom – I had to know if last night had been as momentous for him as for me, and I would know when I saw him, in the very second our eyes spoke to one another as they had last night. Perhaps he would call with his aunt later on, or maybe even sooner, and I leapt out of bed to get washed and dressed. It would never do to be still in bed if Madame were to call with her nephew. Tom occupied all my thoughts. Was he washing too? I imagined the pale skin beneath the white shirt, his hair sleek with liquid, and drops of water falling from those limpid eyes.

I dressed as quickly as I could, before the cold air could freeze my fingers and toes to numbness. Morning sounds, of creaking wooden boards, of fires being laid, maids' footsteps running up and down, buckets slopping, curtains rattling, clocks ticking, mice scampering, doors closing, jugs pouring, water splashing, scent pots clinking, snatched voices, and stolen whispers, greeted the day. I put on layers of my warmest clothes but I didn't want to look bundled up if Tom were to come. If only ladies could wear breeches, I thought, which would be so much more practical. Running down to the kitchen, I knew Nanny Littleworth would be there, raking out the range, fetching out the breakfast set and giving Rebecca instructions about the first meal of the day. It was one of my favourite rooms in the house filled with homely smells, of hot meat and turnips, spruce beer and cinnamon, and now scented with tea and nutmeg, ginger, and coffee from the dresser. Despite the tallow candles burning, the light was dim that shone on a favourite print of Nanny's, the sole picture in the room, showing a dish of sugared fruit. A slice of daylight glimmered on a velvet peach, a green gooseberry, and a silver knife. Texts from the bible featured on either side with stern words for the lazy and encouragement for the hardworking. Strung up high upon the walls, sides of bacon and great hams dangled from hooks, and on the shelves were displayed jugs and bowls, bottles and pots, some filled with jam, made with blackberries gleaned from the hedgerows and plums from the fruit trees. Glass pots filled with the sweet smells of strawberry, apple jelly or golden honey from Cassy's bees sat side by side with the pungent tang of onions and spices, red cabbage and cucumbers pickled in dark vinegar. In the larder I knew there were mince pies and plum puddings waiting to be sent as gifts for our neighbours or to be eaten on Christmas Day. There were bottles of elderflower, ginger and cowslip wine and bowls of butter and cream waiting on the cold marble shelf to add a little bit of magic to the festive food. There was a pie stuffed with ham and eggs, its pastry crust crisp and brown, a pound cake rich with dried fruit, strings of sausages in a china dish, and a large turkey waiting to be plucked.

In the dining parlour, I set the kettle on a trivet to boil water for the tea and heaped too many spoons of black leaves into the teapot whilst watching the lane outside for any sign of life. I knew it was too early but every sound, and any figure of a man that loomed towards the window set my heart thumping. I drifted from one window to the other until my mother called out in exasperation, to bring the pot to the table. She regarded me with stealthy looks as I jumped in my seat at the sound of the bell clanging at the front door. It was only my father returning home after helping the men dig some sheep out of the snow, and it was so hard not to show my disappointment. Knowing I was being scrutinised I ate a piece of toast, which I didn't want, and drank my tea.

'You're as fidgety as an old maid today,' said my mother. 'What are you about, Jane?'

'I'm perfectly fine, Mama, I thank you.'

'Expecting visitors, perhaps?' said Henry, winking at me. He always had the ability to see into my mind and my heart.

My blushes were about to betray me when my father interjected, 'Could you run me an errand, Jenny?'

He still called me by the name of my childhood, but he was the only one I didn't mind using it.

'I've got a pile of books for Madame Lefroy. I promised I'd

send them over this morning.'

'I'll take them, Father,' I said. I couldn't believe my luck, and yet, when presented with the perfect excuse, I felt nervous at the thought of seeing him. Before Henry could make any more mischievous comments, I grabbed my cloak and left.

The morning was cold but sunny, and as I walked down the snow-covered lanes I could see icicles melting and snow falling from branches. By the time I got to Ashe the sun was so warm the muddy earth was showing through slushy ice, but I had a feeling I might be running out of time in the past. As I approached the house, I had the sense I was being watched, and when I looked up to the window above the door, I saw him. Tom smiled, before disappearing from view.

'Madame Lefroy is not at home,' said the housemaid, and I dithered, not sure what to do.

I looked up at the window but there was no sign of my Irish friend. I could not stand waiting all morning, and it began to be rather obvious that my hesitation had no purpose. Tom was not going to make an appearance I realised, and so I ran up the steps and into the hallway, handing the books into the maid's hands. I couldn't help wondering if Madame was really somewhere there in the house, that my behaviour of the night before had prompted this turn of events. But, I knew Madame had smiled when she saw us dancing together: she'd positively encouraged us to be friendly. But why did *he* not come downstairs? Was he now ashamed of his partiality, and regretted dancing with me so much?

As I turned to leave, I experienced the strangest sensations of time slowing which prevented me from moving quickly. It was like wading through treacle and my feet felt glued to the floor. The clock ticked loudly, but every second seemed to last an age, and then I saw that the hand on the painted dial was spinning, gathering momentum as the seconds passed by. The clock started striking with the sound of bells clanging as loudly as in a cathedral tower and I covered my ears and closed my eyes to shut it out. When at last I opened them I could see that everything of the world that had felt so real a few minutes ago had melted away. Steadying myself, I gripped the round table and staring past the open door I heard the last chimes of the Grandfather clock softly die away.

It took Ellie a few minutes to adjust being back at Ashe in the present. She felt stunned by the intensity of the emotions she'd felt and the scenes she'd witnessed. Never before had she experienced such a sense of belonging to the body that claimed her own. The attraction that Jane felt towards Tom was powerful. Ellie felt really shockedby that idea, because the impression she'd got from anything she'd ever read about Jane Austen was that the famous author was often described as a bit of a cantankerous old spinster. And that was certainly not how she'd perceived Jane herself. Ellie couldn't begin to imagine how or why it was that she was being given such a privileged glimpse into her youth. A similar age to herself, she guessed that would make the year 1795 or thereabouts. So, Tom Lefroy had arrived at Ashe Rectory that December to stay with his aunt who was Jane's friend and neighbour, and it was definitely he that Ellie had seen haunting the house. No doubt they would meet again. Ellie felt quite torn, and even though she knew what she was feeling were not really her sensations and passionate feelings, her body had responded to those exquisite emotions. But, as much as she would have liked to linger in the past, time and fate had other ideas, and she was well aware that she would have to wait until she was summoned by whatever forces controlled her travels through time.

## Chapter 9

When the girls got to the Deane Gate Inn that evening, (an old tavern Mrs Hill told them Jane would have known well as a coaching stop) they could see quite a number of the volunteers gathered in the main room, a large space with a low-beamed ceiling. Liberty said that she knew Greg and Will were going, and suspected Melanie and some of her friends would be there. The film crew were all staying at the inn so the chances were that they'd make an appearance too.

Ellie got some drinks and found her way to the others who'd managed to find a table opposite the door so they could see who was arriving. They soon spotted Charlie and Henry who walked in with a young girl none of them had noticed before. The three of them came over to say hello though Ellie saw that Henry hung back and seemed more interested in looking round the room than he did at them, and as usual his response to their greeting was hardly a grunt.

'This is my sister, Zara,' Charlie said introducing them to a tall, slim girl with long blonde hair. She was pretty and expensively dressed, but Ellie thought she looked a little out of place in a country pub. Zara nodded her head by way of acknowledgement before turning back to Henry to continue their conversation.

Charlie sat down next to Jess on the banquette. There wasn't any more room for Henry and Zara but it seemed as if they weren't too interested in joining their group anyway. Ellie decided that she wasn't too impressed with Zara. It was hard to believe that Charlie would have a sister who seemed so unpleasant. She hadn't even been bothered to say hello properly, and she clearly thought she was better than everyone else there by the sneering expression on her face. Dressed in white trousers and an oyster silk blouse, Ellie watched Zara flick at her seat with a tissue before she sat down. Henry was fussing round her now, she noticed, and then their heads were together, whispering. Zara laughed affectedly, a device used to draw attention, and clearly one she'd used many times before, Ellie thought. She flicked back her hair, which was the colour of spun gold, and crossed her long legs, smiling at Henry before she gave the room the benefit of a sultry pout.

Greg Whitely and Will MacGourtey came in next and soon joined them. There wasn't a seat left by Liberty so Greg made his way to the other side, sitting down next to Ellie. Liberty didn't look too happy but Will, it seemed, was happy to stand whilst talking to her and as long as she had some male attention, she was in high spirits.

'You're Ellie, aren't you, a friend of my good assistant Liberty? Will's been telling me what a talented artist you are,' said Greg. 'I'd love to see your work.'

Ellie considered he was probably just being polite, but felt flattered that he'd remembered what must have been a passing conversation. She blushed pink and to hide her discomfort gulped rather too much wine. 'Well, I love to paint and a project like this is a fascinating mix of fact and fiction. I didn't think I'd be asked to do anything special so it's a real bonus for me.'

'Will speaks very highly of you ... you're clearly very talented. I like to paint when I get the chance. I take any opportunity I can to escape from London and spend time in the countryside with my sketchbook and pencils. I must admit, I take a lot of photographs, which is cheating, I suppose, but I prefer working in a studio where it's warm.'

Ellie was so surprised by what he was saying that she found herself almost tongue-tied. 'I like to do both, but working outside is definitely favourite with me when the weather is good.'

'Do you come from an artistic family?' Greg asked taking a slug of beer and peering at her over the top of his glass.

'Not really,' Ellie answered, 'at least, there are no artists in my family. I'm a vicar's daughter, and my mum has always been at home being the vicar's wife. She's a very creative lady in her own right and can put her hand to anything from dressmaking to flower arranging, and seeing to all sorts of events at the vicarage.'

'So, I have this picture in my mind,' said Greg, looking far off into the distance, screwing up his eyes as if in deep contemplation. 'A large Georgian rectory, summer fetes and harvest festivals in a quintessentially English village, with you, the vicar's daughter, taking on commissions of portraits for the local ladies in the Townswomen's Guild and the Women's Institute.'

Ellie laughed. 'You couldn't be further from the truth. I come from a London suburb, where the vicarage is appointed on the wrong side of town. It's a 1970s modern box, and though there are summer fetes and harvest festivals, I doubt you'd recognise them as being particularly English. It's what I love about the area I live in, there's such an interesting mix of people and cultures. I find it quite strange to come here, and find that places like this still exist. It's lovely, but a bit on the quiet side for me. As for commissions, I haven't really started yet. I've got some of my work on Instagram and there's been a bit of interest, but it's early days and I'm more concerned with having a relaxing holiday right now than selling my work.'

'There speaks a lady I can identify with – I intend to take a holiday as soon as this little project is finished. I hate to take them on my own, however, and it's some time since I had the luxury of sharing a vacation. I love travelling, don't you, Ellie?'

'I do, though I haven't done much outside Europe. I would

love to explore India and Thailand if I ever got the chance.'

'You'd enjoy it, undoubtedly. There is so much inspiration for a painter. India is magical, a land of colour, scents and experiences unlike any other. I know you'd love the breathtaking scenery of the Himalayas … you can take a train from the town of New Jalpaiguri to the lovely hill station of Darjeeling, which has to be one of the most incredible journeys I've ever made. Or, if you're feeling rich, you can take a luxury train from Mumbai and travel as they used to in the past. I can just see you in your element, stopping off en route, paintbrush in hand, conjuring up a Goan temple with a few strokes of translucent colour, as the sun sets to an apricot glow.'

'You make it sound so wonderful,' Ellie enthused. Now that she'd spoken to Greg her initial impressions were changing. He was clearly more intelligent than she'd reasoned and he genuinely seemed interested in her. With some guys, all they wanted to do was talk about their own interests, but despite what she'd initially thought, he didn't seem like that. And though he enjoyed a certain 'celebrity' status, he was just being one of them, keen to join in the conversation. Martha's mother must have her reasons for disliking him, but she wasn't going to listen to idle gossip. Ellie decided she would give Greg a chance.

They were in deep conversation when she noticed Zara staring at the pair of them in a really unfriendly way. When their eyes met, Ellie saw her look away with a disdainful expression and watched Zara pointedly whisper in Henry's ear.

'Do you know Zara Harden or Henry Dorsey?' Ellie asked Greg.

'A little, why do you ask?'

'I don't know either of them, but they were just looking over here, and to be honest, they didn't look as if they might be about to join us. In fact, I'd go as far as to say, they looked rather hostile.'

Greg nodded and sighed deeply, picking up his beer and taking another long draught. 'I went to the same boarding school as Henry, though I'm a bit older than him. Not that he'd have had anything to do with me if we'd been in the same year. I was surprised to see him here; actually, I wouldn't have had him down as one ready to get his hands dirty.'

'I didn't think people like him still existed,' said Ellie. 'I've met lots of people who have money but none ever behaved as if they were still 'lord of the manor'. If there's one thing I really don't like, it's a snob.'

'His family are very wealthy, and were old friends of my family, once upon a time. They were in business together some years ago, but the Dorsey's ideas of expansion meant that they cut out my father, and, consequently, any chances I had of taking over my family business when we were dissolved.'

'Oh, that's awful. I knew I didn't like the look of him from the very first. He's a typical arrogant rich kid who has probably been spoiled rotten by his mother.'

'Well, it all happened a while ago, and I've moved on.'

'You're a success, and you've done it all by yourself, despite being trampled all over. You should be proud of your achievements.'

'I am, but being in television isn't all that glamorous, you know. Everyone thinks we're rolling in it, that all presenters have million pound contracts, but, sadly, that isn't the case for us all.'

'You're really popular,' said Ellie, 'and even if you haven't got that contract now, I'm sure it's only a matter of time.'

She wasn't quite sure why she was giving so much support and reassurance to someone who probably didn't need it, but Ellie really felt sorry for him. She hated injustice and knew how much her parents struggled to get by, and she could imagine the effect it must have had when Greg's family had found themselves in reduced circumstances through no fault of their own.

Greg was smiling at her and she was struck for the first time by his good looks. He had dark hair, which was very much her preference, and in contrast, a pair of striking blue eyes shone out from a handsome face. She'd seen his picture in magazines and always thought he seemed a bit slick, but now she saw his personality coming through she could forgive him his piratical style, which thankfully, he'd toned down a lot tonight.

'Ah, I see Melanie has just arrived ... I'd better go; I promised I'd get her the first drink. I've really enjoyed our chat,' he said, draining his glass and standing up. 'That's why it's so good to work on a project like this; you get to meet the most interesting people.'

'Yes, it's lovely to meet you; it's been so kind of you to take Liberty under your wing. It's a dream for her.'

Greg smiled again. 'I hope we'll be able to catch up again very soon. I'd love to hear some more tales of the vicarage.'

When he'd gone, Ellie was happy to sit and watch the goings on for a minute or two. In a place like this where groups intermingled, it was fascinating to see who was mixing and who preferred to stay talking to the same person. Jess and Charlie seemed very clear in their preference. Ellie doubted they knew anyone else existed. Their eyes met and looked away again as in a dance, each step taking longer to accomplish and each tender expression lingering until forced to look elsewhere. They were talking, but it was their body language that communicated far more. Ellie was so pleased for Jess. She deserved happiness like no one else she knew.

As she scanned the room, Ellie suddenly realised she was being scrutinised herself. Henry Dorsey was staring at her, and she wondered for a moment if her hair was sticking up or if her buttons had come undone. She smoothed back her long mahogany hair, and made a quick check on her appearance as best as she could. His eyes were still on her face, she sensed it, and when she looked, he was really studying every feature. She smiled, reasoning that friendly attack might be the best defence and something seemed to quiver about his lips. Not quite a smile perhaps, but there was definitely some progress. Ellie couldn't wait to tell Jess – the haughty Henry had cracked his face!

Getting up, she saw Cara and Liberty had moved to the bar to talk to some of the film crew and decided to join them. Henry's eyes burned into the back of her as she walked away, and a quick glance behind confirmed the truth. It was all a little unnerving.

'I see you've made a conquest,' said Cara, opening a bag of crisps and offering the packet to Ellie.

'Whatever do you mean?' Ellie thought she was probably making some reference to Greg.

'Henry Dorsey can't take his eyes off you.'

'Oh, yes I noticed that. It's a bit creepy, to be honest, this trying to stare me out. He just doesn't like me, though goodness knows what I've done to warrant such contempt.'

'It doesn't look like contempt from where I'm standing,' said Cara. 'It looks like lust.'

'Cara!'

'I'm only describing what I'm seeing; the bloke is positively drooling into his beer.'

Ellie purposely turned so she could no longer see him, even out of the corner of her eye.

Cara laughed. 'That's done it … he's taking in all your best features now, starting at your toes and he's going up. Now, where do you think he's looking?'

Ellie couldn't help laughing at Cara. 'You're making it all up now, you wicked girl.'

'I'm not, I swear, and even though he knows that I've seen him staring at your legs it's not deterred him. Up and down he goes like a rat in a drainpipe.'

'That description most aptly suits him, I fear,' said Ellie thinking back to her conversation with Greg.

Liberty was looking slightly worse for wear. Several empty glasses lined up on the bar told why she was slurring her words and giggling every ten seconds. She was draped over one of the film crew, a man in his thirties who was wearing a wedding ring. 'I'd love to be on the end of *your* lens, Jake,' she was saying, loud enough for the entire pub to hear, and when the rest of the crew heard what she'd said, there were guffaws of laughter. Liberty didn't seem to care even when she realised how her words had been misconstrued and she just laughed all the more.

'Come on, Liberty, I think it's time we headed home,' said

Ellie moving over to her and quietly whispering in her ear.

'I don't wanna go home,' she shouted, 'I'm having such fun with ... what did you say your name was again?'

Ellie sighed. When Liberty was in this kind of mood, it was hard to reason with her or extract her without making a fuss. She looked over at Jess and their eyes met, but they weren't the only eyes that had registered what was going on. Charlie, Zara and Henry were looking on aghast. Ellie felt she wanted to curl up and die rather than have Henry witness her friend's behaviour. Jess came over in seconds. If anyone could reason with Liberty it was Jess, but not before Liberty knocked back her glass and started demanding more. In the next breath she declared she wanted to be sick, and by that time Jess was able to march her off to the Ladies' room.

Ellie fetched Martha and together with Cara they all went to see how Liberty was doing. Thankfully, she seemed much better and as she was in no fit state to argue, she did as she was told. Jess bathed Liberty's face, and once they'd established whether she was fit to walk home, they decided that would be the best course. Supporting Liberty between them as they'd done on many occasions before, Ellie and Jess realised it was going to seem a long walk home. What they hadn't reckoned on was that Charlie would be waiting outside for them.

He seemed genuinely concerned. 'Is she all right?'

'Nothing that a few cups of black coffee won't sort out,' said Ellie, biting her lip.

Liberty's head rolled from side to side, but she managed to look up when she heard she was being talked about. 'I'm fine, Charlie. You are gorgeous; do you know that? You need to get with our Jess, you'd make a lovely couple!'

Jess was turning a deep shade of beetroot and couldn't meet Charlie's eyes. He was looking at her and grinning. 'Listen, my car is not five minutes away. I'll get it and take you home.'

'We wouldn't want to put you to so much trouble.' Jess managed to look up to meet his unerring gaze.

'No, it's no trouble. In fact, I insist. Wait here, I'll just pop home. I won't be long.'

Cara and Martha decided there probably wouldn't be enough room for them in the car too, what with Liberty hardly being able to stand or sit up, and so after saying their goodbyes they began the walk back home along the lane together.

It seemed no time at all before Charlie was back pulling up outside in a sleek, black Mercedes. Ellie offered to sit with Liberty in the back of the car, which meant Jess could sit with Charlie in the front. No one seemed to know what to say as they sped off noiselessly down the road.

'It's just a bit of high spirits,' Charlie said, breaking the silence. 'We all do something daft from time to time.'

Ellie saw Jess look across at him and smile. 'Thank you, Charlie, for being so kind and taking us home.'

'It's a pleasure,' he said, leaning over and squeezing her hand.

In the back of the car Ellie couldn't help smiling to herself.

## Chapter 10

When they arrived back at the rectory, Ellie whipped Liberty out of the car as quickly as she could so that Jess might have a chance to say goodnight to Charlie on her own. She heard her coming upstairs half an hour later but pretended to be asleep as Ellie was sure Jess wouldn't really appreciate being cross-examined there and then. That could wait for another day.

Liberty was not very well in the night, and predictably, in the morning said she couldn't possibly get up and go to the dig. Everyone agreed that it would probably be best if she stayed in bed to sleep it off and when Mrs Hill was told a little white lie that Liberty had eaten something that hadn't agreed with her, she seemed unperturbed, saying she would keep an eye on her though she was due to go out later to visit one of her sisters at Dummer, a nearby village. Ellie volunteered to come back in the afternoon to check on her and so they all left for Steventon, choosing to walk as it was yet another beautiful day.

Jess was in two states of mind. 'I don't know what Charlie must have thought of us all last night,' she confided to Ellie as they walked along. Even though it was still early, the sun was beating through the canopy of trees that arched over their heads. It was going to be another hot day.

'I don't think he was shocked at all,' Ellie answered. 'I'm sure he's seen a few people worse for wear in his time, though she was spectacularly loud. And who was that guy? Didn't she see his wedding ring?'

'You know Liberty, it's not that she would purposely do such a thing, she just doesn't think. I wonder why she craves such attention; though I know her home life is a bit chaotic. Her father's never been one for being at home. He's always away on business and, even when he is there, he doesn't seem very interested in spending time with her. Perhaps if he took a little more notice, she wouldn't be so desperate for any man's attention. I must admit, I feel sorry for her.'

'I do. Her mother doesn't seem much better. Liberty told me she has an allowance on top of her student loan and her mother encourages her to spend it. It seems a bit irresponsible to support such reckless spending, especially as Liberty told me she has an overdraft as well.'

'Oh, I didn't realise it was as bad as that; it's a cry for help, I think. I'm not sure what we *can* do to help, but I'll try to keep an eye on her.'

'We'll just have to make sure she doesn't get into any more trouble that could easily be avoided. Anyway, the upside of last night is that you got a drive home in Charlie's very smart car,' said Ellie, grinning at her friend. 'And, I couldn't help noticing that it seemed to take you a little while to say goodnight to him.'

'Ellie, he is gorgeous. I think he's one of the nicest guys I've ever met. His sister seems very friendly too.'

'Does she?' Ellie didn't know quite what to say. That wasn't the impression she'd got, but then Jess always saw something good to say about everybody.

'I was talking to her just before you alerted me to Liberty's escapade. She's younger than Charlie, but at Oxford like him. I got the impression she hangs around with her brother and Henry quite a lot. It's really nice that they're so close. They must have a good family background.'

'I'm sure they have,' answered Ellie, 'and it's very clear she likes Henry. Perhaps that's why she was glaring at anyone who looked at them together. Not that I'd ever be interested in *him*, but I suppose *some* people might be attracted to a hateful, rich boy.'

Jess laughed. 'I think you'll like Zara when you get to know her, and really, Henry can't be that bad if he's a friend of Charlie's. He is such a lovely person; I don't believe he'd make friends with anyone awful.'

'You are a truly wonderful person. I hope Charlie is good enough to deserve you. Are you excited at the thought of seeing him again?'

'I must admit I am.'

Ellie took her friend's arm. 'I have such a good feeling about you two. And I'm so excited to witness the pair of you falling in love!'

'And, how about you, Ellie? Have you met your handsome Mr Darcy again?'

'I have, Jess, though I am sure you'll not believe it when I tell you. I cannot believe it myself!'

'It's Tom, isn't it – Tom Lefroy?'

'How could you possibly know that?'

'Oh, Ellie, I've suspected it from your very first encounter. You are witnessing Jane and Tom falling in love, I think.'

'I cannot understand how or why this is happening to me. I'm visiting the past, travelling through time, if you like, and it's so real when I'm there that nothing else exists. But, I sincerely wish it were all happening to you, and not me ... none of it makes any sense.'

'I'm sure there is a reason, Ellie, and despite what you think, I do not envy you. I know a little about Jane Austen's life, and I do not think I am strong enough, emotionally or physically, to experience anyone else's time on earth. I'm having enough trouble with my own.'

'That's true; Jess, and I know from experience that these

'happenings' rarely last long. Even so, they are exhausting. I just hope it will all resolve itself in the end.'

'Don't worry, Ellie, I have a feeling that everything will become clear before long, and in the meantime, I shall be here to hold your hand all the way.'

When Jess and Charlie caught sight of one another they instantly made a beeline for the other. Charlie had contrived to get his computer placed a desk nearer to Jess in the operations tent, and whenever they had a spare moment, one or other of them would sidle over for a chat, often on the pretext of having found some nugget of treasure that had just been brought in.

Martha settled to her careful digging. Using a trowel, the painstaking work was in progress. To her great excitement several shards of china were showing up, encrusted with dark soil. When she carefully removed the dirt, she could make out a very distinctive design. Still in use today, the blue and white willow pattern was easily recognisable. Several pieces looked as if they might fit together to form part of a large platter. Everyone was thrilled for her, and the hunt for more treasures continued in earnest. Martha carefully bagged up her find to take it over to Cara and the others who were waiting to inspect anything that might be carefully washed and sorted. Passing Ellie, who was sketching the landscape, she stopped to show her what she'd found.

Ellie smiled in recognition at the blue and white willow pattern shards of porcelain, and when she reached out to inspect the pieces, taking one or two carefully from the bag, she almost felt herself being pulled back again into the past. It was like looking down a long telescope at images that flickered like those on a silent cinema screen. She could see the dining parlour of the old rectory with every shelf, and every windowsill decorated with holly, ivy and paper streamers cut from gold paper. Sprays of holly hung from every picture, and even the clock had its own crown. Festoons of fir were strung across the mantle and twisted in garlands and a kissing bunch dangled from the ceiling with mistletoe and ribbon.

The maidservants were lighting candles, fires roared in the grates and the table groaned with such delights as a roasted turkey resting on a willow platter in the middle of the table, rabbits with sorrel sauce, mince pies, a side of ham, gooseberry tart and fruit jellies. Nanny Littleworth and Rebecca were bringing in hot food from the oven, tureens of soup, platters of roast beef, dishes of snowy potatoes and sauceboats of rich gravy. The figures were shadowy, but there were Mr and Mrs Austen at either end of the gleaming table, which was set out for a banquet, on blue and white china. Jane in white muslin with a pale blue sash had her hair piled high, showing small pale ears like pink shells and a ribbon of the same cornflower hue as her sash, wreathed through her chestnut curls. Brothers Henry, Frank and Charles, were laughing at some shared joke, all looking very handsome. Ellie wished she could see more, but the pictures were already fading. As she placed the precious bag of shards back into Martha's hands she felt grateful for this extra glimpse of life at Steventon.

'Are you okay?' asked Martha, looking at her with a puzzled expression. 'You have a really faraway look on your face.'

'Yes, I'm just lost in time, I suppose,' she answered truthfully, and with a secret smile on her face she picked up her paintbrush. 'Don't mind me, Martha; it's just that sometimes I get totally absorbed. I'm having a lovely time imagining the past and thinking about how it might have looked then.'

'It's a dangerous thing, the imagination,' said Martha in her typically dry fashion before she walked off clutching her bag of treasure.

The morning passed off well though nothing more remarkable than some extra pieces of pottery were found in the excavation areas. By mid-afternoon, Ellie had finished her painting and both Will MacGourtey and Greg Whitely had been over to inspect and praise it. There was no sign of Liberty so she was obviously still feeling poorly. After checking with Jess who looked happy enough labelling a box full of pottery pieces with Charlie by her side, she set off for the rectory. The sun had continued to blaze down all morning and it was quite delicious to walk in the cool shade under trees. By the time she got to Ashe, the heat was almost unbearable. Entering the house, it was very quiet and there was such a sense of stillness about the place; Ellie didn't think there could be anyone at home. Mrs Hill had clearly been there earlier; the fragrances of beeswax on polished wood and lavender in the bowls of pot-pourri smelt fresh and new. Perhaps Liberty was still asleep, she thought, and made her way up the staircase to Liberty's room. She knocked on her door but there was no answer, and it was only when she heard a noise downstairs that she went to investigate.

Liberty appeared then, dressed in a bikini with a towel slung over her shoulder, and a drink in her hand. 'OMG!' she shouted, completely taken by surprise. 'Ellie, you've totally freaked me out! Why didn't you call me to say you were coming back?'

'I didn't want to disturb you in case you were still asleep,' said Ellie. 'Are you feeling better now?'

Liberty raised her glass, full of pink liquid and tinkling with ice. 'I'm fine, nothing that a French Martini won't sort out, hair of the dog and all that!'

'I'm not sure that's a very good idea, Liberty. Well, I just came to check on you, make sure you weren't dying.'

Liberty smiled before draining her glass. 'Thanks, Ellie, you are lovely. I'm just taking it easy by the swimming pool. It's so hot and I couldn't bear the thought of spending all day at the dig.'

Ellie knew Liberty could be thoughtless but this behaviour exceeded everything that had ever gone before. She could easily have phoned one of them to let them know she was up and fine. They would be bound to be worried about her, but she supposed such a thought would never enter Liberty's head.

'I won't keep you from your swimming,' Ellie said, thinking it was not worth saying anything else. 'I'm just going to change into something cooler and I'll head back. See you later.'

Liberty turned, tossing her hair over her shoulders and waving one hand in the air as she made her way back to the kitchen, no doubt with the idea of replenishing her glass.

Back at the dig, Ellie found Jess. She knew she would be worrying about Liberty, even if it were clear that Liberty suffered no qualms on that score.

'How was Liberty?' Jess smiled when she saw Ellie and put down her pen, glad to have an excuse to stop labelling for a minute.

'Right as rain, and knocking back vodka cocktails by the swimming pool,' said Ellie, unable to disguise her feelings. 'I almost wished I hadn't bothered, but at least you can stop worrying about her. She is still alive.'

'Thank you for checking up on her for me,' said Jess. 'I couldn't rest after the state she was in last night.'

'Well, I don't suppose for one minute that Liberty has been worrying about how her behaviour might have impacted on us. You must stop taking the responsibility of her upon your shoulders, Jess. She's old enough to look after herself.'

'I know, but I do feel responsible. It was me who suggested she come on the trip, after all.'

'Just don't go losing any sleep and worrying too much. I'll keep an eye on her, she'll be fine.'

Charlie joined them just then, sauntering over with that easy style he had. Ellie almost felt a twinge of envy. She wished someone would look at her like Charlie was looking at Jess. He was very boyish, and his blue eyes twinkled with obvious pleasure at the sight of her.

'I've come to ask a special favour. My mother runs this annual charity ball at home, and she's asked me to pass on an invitation. I'm sorry it's such short notice, but I'd love it if you'd like to come ... all of you, of course. Henry and my sister will be there, and I'm asking the other volunteers too.'

Jess looked at her friend with pleading eyes.

'When is it?' Ellie asked.

'A week today ... please say yes, it would make my day if you could come.'

'Yes, we'd love to,' Jess said, before Ellie had a chance to speak. And she didn't need to, because it seemed that Jess and

Charlie were oblivious to everything around them.

It was Ellie's idea that they should look into the church before they went home. St. Nicholas church, a simple building built of grey stone and flint, guarded by giant yew trees, felt homely and cared for inside. There were hassocks lovingly stitched in needlepoint, embroidered pennants, brass candelabra and vases of flowers on every surface, some cultivated and some wild, which filled the interior with the scent of summer roses and lilies. Upon a display table, they found leaflets and postcards about the church and some information on Jane Austen. The church was early English, built sometime at the beginning of the 13th century.

'We have to imagine the church without the spire, said Jess, reading from a leaflet, 'if we are to 'see' it as Jane did ... that wasn't added until the middle of the 19th century, apparently. There's a bronze memorial in the nave, which commemorates her life.'

The simple plaque was soon found. Erected by Jane's great grandniece, Emma Austen-Leigh, in 1936, the simple tablet confirmed the dates of birth and death of the famous author and the fact that she'd worshipped in the church. Below it, someone had thoughtfully arranged a brass vase of tea roses with peach-pink hearts and fading petals of an old-fashioned variety, their yellow stamens shedding on the linen sampler.

'It's too cold in here for me,' said Cara. 'It's all very lovely, but churches give me the creeps, I'm afraid, all those dead people under our feet. You can almost feel them, somehow, and I'm not sure I want to stick around. I'll see you all back at the car. Are you coming, Martha?'

They wandered off outside, and Martha soon followed saying she wanted to investigate the gravestones to see if she could find any of the Steventon dignitaries mentioned in one of the pamphlets she'd picked up.

Ellie and Jess sat on one of the oak pews near the front.

'Just think, Jane Austen might have sat right here in this very seat,' said Jess. 'In any case, we know she worshipped here and that her father stood right there to deliver his sermons.'

Ellie shivered. She suddenly felt terribly cold. The stone walls of the church seemed to prevent any of the sun's warmth from penetrating and her thin cardigan felt completely inadequate. Looking up to the window set high above her head, she noticed that grey clouds were passing overhead, the sky a sheet of dark steel. The interior was plunged into darkness for a moment and she knew time was shifting again. She tried calling out to Jess, but her friend seemed oblivious, trapped in another dimension. Reality was blurring, everything around her shimmered and quivered so that she glimpsed images from both the present and the past. Ellie felt she was slipping once more into another world and there was nothing she could do to prevent it. She was drifting outside towards the churchyard, and the real world seemed a million miles away. The leaves on the trees above were turning, she noticed, from summer greens to autumn yellows, and heaps of them lay in drifts of amber and lemon, cinnamon and tangerine. Long skirts replaced her jeans, which slowed her progress over the snow-covered grass. An icy feather flicked her nose as it fell to the ground, and was swiftly followed by another. As if a great goose were being plucked in the skies above, the feathers grew thicker and faster, as big as two pound pieces. Ellie felt grateful for the warm layers she wore as the snow whirled from the heavens, and pulling up the scarlet hood on her long cape, she tucked her hands inside to keep them warm. And then she was aware of a voice calling to her. It was difficult to hear at first, and she couldn't tell from which direction it came so she had to close her eyes to focus all her attention. When she opened them again, she was standing in a real-life snowglobe, and the voice was more insistent. She turned her head to see Anne Lefroy's Irish hunter, but it wasn't Madame who was exercising him that morning. Tom sat astride the beautiful horse, reins in hand and then he called her name again.

## Chapter 11

'Miss Austen, how do you do?'

I wanted him to say my name again. If he said it a thousand times it would not be enough. No one ever before had spoken it so softly. I dropped a mock curtsey, but I did not smile. I could not forgive him for not receiving me when I'd called at Ashe, and I was far too proud to allow him to see the effect his voice had on me.

'How do you do, Mr Lefroy?' I answered looking up to meet his eyes which stared steadily back at mine. 'And where are you going on this cold morning?'

'I'm visiting a local family, as it happens – a clergyman, his wife and his children. There is a daughter who lives in the parsonage – I believe she considers herself to be quite the dancer. Do you happen to know of such a young lady in the district?' His grey eyes were twinkling with merriment and I knew he was teasing me.

I felt my mouth twitching, but I was determined not to laugh. 'I think I might happen to know the family,' I said, 'though I have heard reports that the daughter of whom you speak is not merely a boastful creature. Her dancing prowess is talked of as far as Basingstoke, sir.'

Tom threw back his head and laughed. ''Tis a fearful distance you speak of, my lady – as far as Basingstoke, you say? This lady must, indeed, be a celebrated performer!'

He dismounted, leaping down with a jump to the ground, the white tails of his coat flapping with a snap. I'd forgotten how tall he was and his coat gave him a greater stature. Broad shoulders narrowed to a fitted waist and great skirts of voluminous fabric fell to the snowy earth. He smoothed down the wide lapels and adjusted his coat. Watching him tweak the tilt of his hat, I thought him a perfect coxcomb; even if his hair reminded me of spring cowslips, and it crossed my mind that he must be one of the most handsome young men I ever saw. Yet, his white coat symbolised everything I'd thought of him on first meeting: that he had rather too high an opinion of himself, and that he was a mere dandy, even if my first impressions were changing ... just a little. I liked his teasing ways, and I knew that on occasion he'd shown that he didn't take himself too seriously.

'I'm sorry I was unable to speak to you yesterday,' said Tom. 'My aunt and uncle were out on parish business.'

He didn't offer another excuse or say why he hadn't invited me in to the rectory himself, and I wondered why he'd felt unable to speak to me. It was rather strange behaviour. I felt I'd established that although he might be a little shy with strangers, I was sure he'd overcome that with me. Talking to people I didn't know well was an irksome activity, but I tried to make the effort where I could. With Tom, I'd glimpsed such a warm personality at the Basingstoke ball, but here in this snowbound lane, I was unsure of anything and I felt I could no longer see into the soul that had seemed so akin to mine.

'Do you miss your home, Mr Lefroy?' I asked, wondering if he was homesick. After all, he was living in a different country whose customs and ways were surely different.

'No,' he said, but he had such a faraway expression at that moment as if perhaps it was not his home that he was thinking about, but a person – someone dear to him. And then he smiled. 'I have a great friend, Tom Paul, who would love it here – he'd think the scenery to his taste, I'm sure.'

He was studying my face all the time. His eyes travelled from the top of my bonnet to the curls on my forehead and followed the line of my cheek. I watched him take a step towards me and saw him stare at my mouth. I held my breath as his face came nearer, his eyes holding mine, before he put up his hand to hook an unruly curl around his finger. He tucked the offending hair under my bonnet. I felt my face flood with heat, but I didn't flinch, nor could I move away.

'You remind me of someone,' he said.

I couldn't speak, every sense in my body was alive to sensation, a quickening, heart-beating desire to possess and be possessed, which both thrilled and frightened me.

'*Her cheeks were of the oval kind; and in her right she had a dimple, which the least smile discovered.*' Tom placed a finger on my dimpled cheek and softly stroked my skin. '*Her chin had certainly its share in forming the beauty of her face; but it was difficult to say if it was either large or small, though perhaps it was rather of the former kind.*' He held my chin and tilted it towards him. '*Her complexion had rather more of the lily than of the rose; but when exercise or modesty increased her natural colour, no vermilion could equal it.*'

I gasped and whispered, 'Sophia Western.'

'So, Miss Austen, you are a reader of great literature also, I surmise,' he said, laughing as he released me, and I blushed even more if that was possible when he finished his quote from one of my favourite books, *Tom Jones*. And then I realised he fancied himself as the hero who also wore a white coat.

'I must admit, I am a great admirer of Mr Fielding's work.'

'*Her pure and eloquent blood spoke in her cheeks,*' Tom continued, '*and so distinctly wrought that one might almost say her body thought.*'

My hands flew to my face. It was true, every emotion showed in my countenance: I'd always been teased about my scarlet complexion, but this was worse than anything I'd ever endured before.

I was anxious to change the subject. 'Will you come to the house? I am sure my mother and father would be very pleased to see you.'

Tom looked thoughtful. 'Whilst I am diverted by the idea of such convivial entertainment, my preference would be for some increase of fresh air. Besides, my horse needs some exercise. Would you care to join me?'

'I'm afraid I do not ride, Mr Lefroy. The horses on our land have always been needed for work, and I have not the leisure …'

I did not know what else to say. I certainly didn't want him to know that we were too poor to have such an activity as a given right.

'But I know how much you would enjoy the pursuit, Miss Austen. You have such a vigorous look about you.'

I considered the fact that my face must be the colour of beetroot by now. 'It is of no disadvantage to me, but I must admit, I like the idea of riding a horse.'

'You were born for it, Miss Austen. And, if you will permit me, I shall help you to ride mine, though you may not like to ride astride the animal.'

My first instinct was to protest, but I didn't want to appear as if I was frightened by it or bothered by the fact that there was no lady's saddle. I could never resist a challenge.

'I'd prefer to ride like a man, I must admit. When I was a little girl Mr Hilliard used to put me on top of the horses and lead me round for my pleasure.'

Tom showed me how to hold the reins, and I watched him put his foot in the stirrup and bounce up onto the horse. He dismounted and then it was my turn. I clung to the reins as he'd done, put my hand on the pommel and placed my foot in the iron. I started to bounce, and then strong hands were about my waist, the touch of his fingers staying with me long after I was lifted to my seat.

'You will not be frightened, Miss Austen, if my horse should dance about a little at first setting off. He will, most likely, give a plunge or two, and he is full of spirits, playful as can be, but there is no vice in him.'

I was fearless, and I felt supremely confident as if I was formed for a horsewoman; and to the true joy of the exercise something was added in Tom's attendance and instructions, which made me unwilling to dismount. At first my companion and I made a circuit of the neighbouring field at a foot's pace; then, at my suggestion, we rose into a canter, Tom running alongside. After a few minutes we stopped entirely. Tom was near to me; he spoke with that faint trace of an Irish burr, so softly, I had to lean in close to hear him. He was directing my management of the bridle; he took hold of my hand and his fingers entwined with mine. It was exhilarating, every moment flooded my being with pure pleasure, and I could not think when I had ever felt so happy.

'If only we were both mounted,' said Tom, 'we could take a ride together. I could show you how fast this horse can ride.'

'But, that must be impossible, Mr Lefroy!'

'It can be done, I assure you, Miss Austen.'

'If someone should see us ...'

'There is no one about on such a cold morning, but if you care only for your reputation, and have no wish to experience the thrill of a gallop, Miss Austen, there is little I can do to persuade you.'

'I do wish to gallop through the lanes, Mr Lefroy.'

'No, Miss Austen. Indeed, you are right, it would not be seemly. Please forgive me for suggesting such an outrageous proposal.'

'Why not climb up beside me,' I heard myself say, and then realised how shocking that sounded. But, in the next moment, he gently released the reins from my grasp and pulled himself into the saddle shifting his body behind me. It was a snug fit, his thighs gripped mine, and he drew me closely to him, one arm encircling my waist. Tom urged the horse on, our breath misting on the frosty air as we galloped through the lanes powdered in white. We moved in rhythm together, flying faster and faster, as if chased by the devil himself. Blood pounded in my ears, and my heart was beating so fast I felt Tom must be aware of it through the gloved hand that gripped my ribcage so tightly. I didn't want it to end, but when I saw the church looming in the distance, I felt some shame for what I had done. I did not want to imagine what Madame Lefroy might think if she saw me, and begged Tom to stop. He jumped down with a grin before turning to face me, encircling his hands round my waist. They stayed there, his thumbs resting above my hipbones and when he clasped me tighter to release me to the ground, my body clenched with longing.

'Miss Austen, you are a bold rider, indeed, and as fearless as any Irish friend I have.'

I could not help but smile, but when he pulled me down and I fell into his arms, I was all confusion. He held me for a moment, and I lost myself in those eyes, which enchanted me. I wanted to feel his lips on mine, and I willed him to kiss me. His eyes strayed to my lips and his mouth moved towards mine. Then he seemed to think better of it and let me go.

'Perhaps this was not a very good idea after all, Miss Austen.' He started to walk away leading the horse with him. 'Are you trying to bewitch me?'

I didn't know how to answer. 'I am not certain what you are about, Mr Lefroy.'

'What would your parents say if they knew we'd been spending time alone together? Forgive me, I should never have suggested that we ride.'

'I enjoyed it. I thank you, Mr Lefroy. No one has ever taken the time to show me how to be a horsewoman. It is a lesson I shall not forget.'

'But, it is one we can never repeat.'

Tom wore an odd expression. Something between a scowl and a look of regret, I could not fathom what he was thinking. He had withdrawn from me and the Tom who had laughed and been so warm was gone. I began to regret what I'd done. How could I have let my guard down so much? I couldn't begin to wonder what he must think of me. Stepping back, I started to speak of mundane subjects but Tom was already fading. In shades of sepia, I saw the past fold and collapse as if it were a piece of ancient origami, the paper disintegrating before my eyes. I watched it bend and crumble, diminish and fragment until the snow-splintered pictures vanished into the summer sun, and the fields and meadows, where just a moment ago I had been with Tom. Keeping in the shade, I saw the sweeping hillsides in the distance, the villages separated by hedgerows running through them like green ribbon, tall spires of pink foxgloves growing on the bank, and the woods, dark and mysterious with beeches, oaks and silver birch trees. Dappled cows sat in the shade of a giant oak tree in the middle of a golden field, whisking their tails as a blackbird sang above my head. As I walked along I tried to recall where I'd been that morning. Yet, somehow, it all looked a lot different, the road seemed dustier and narrower, and it wasn't long before I began to question whether I'd taken a wrong turning. I looked behind to get a better sense of the way I had come and didn't recognise where I was at all. In front, the lane became little more than a dirt track where patches of fresh green grass grew down the middle. If I left the road I was sure to get lost, but then as the road inclined again, I saw the church, and I knew I was home.

Ellie felt stunned by everything she'd just seen and felt. Every sense in her body echoed that of the girl whose life she'd been playing out, and for a moment all she could think about was Tom. It was so real when she was there in the past, and every time it happened the experience seemed to take on a greater significance. It was more than just seeing through Jane's eyes, she decided. Ellie became Jane in those moments and she knew that the feelings that stirred inside did not only belong to her. Ellie admitted to herself that she felt attracted to Tom in a way she would never have thought possible.

## Chapter 12

'Ellie, are you there? Ellie, speak to me!'

Someone was rubbing her hand and saying her name. Ellie heard a voice from another world, calling her back. It was a voice she loved, though she couldn't think to whom it belonged.

It was like coming out of a deep sleep where the dream is very real, and when she opened her eyes Jess was there, a huge smile on her face. 'Oh, thank goodness you came back to me; I was beginning to think you might not make it. It was only for a few seconds but you looked as if you'd stopped breathing.'

'I'm fine, Jess, though I feel completely wiped out,' Ellie replied, rubbing her eyes and sitting up.

'Were you back with Tom?'

Ellie nodded. 'Oh, Jess, it's as if it's happening to *me*, and I cannot separate my feelings from the reality. I've had some experiences before, but nothing like this has ever felt so real or affected the way I'm feeling.'

'I wish I could do something to help.'

'Oh, but just being able to talk to you is all the help I need. Thank you for being such an incredible friend.'

Just as Ellie was telling Jess everything she could remember they were interrupted by Cara, popping her head round the church door. 'Come on, let's go home now,' she cried. 'I'm absolutely starving!'

The girls were soon returned to Ashe. They were all very tired for as they were discovering, working outside in the fresh air was apt to make them sleepy, and even Liberty was ready for an early night. Not that she had been hard at work, but she yawned her way through supper.

Mrs Hill had prepared a lovely meal of roast chicken and new potatoes with green beans from the vegetable plot. 'You'll all be hungry, I'm sure,' she said, putting out pretty Spode plates before them, ready plated up, 'to save on the washing up'.

'Mrs Hill, you are so kind,' said Jess, echoing the thoughts of all the others. 'It would be awful to have to come home and start cooking, and this smells simply heavenly.'

'I'm only doing my job,' Mrs Hill said very matter-of-factly, smoothing down her floral apron, 'it's what I'm paid for.'

However, the girls could see that she was pleased, especially when they all joined in and said what a good cook she was and how delicious it tasted.

'We're all going to the ball at Charlie Harden's, next Friday,' said Cara. 'Do you know the family, Mrs Hill?'

'I should say so. One of my sisters is the housekeeper there. They are a very nice employer from what she says, and young Charles has a heart of gold, though I don't think she has quite the same high opinion of his sister who is rather spoiled by all accounts. Mrs Harden is a good sort, a lady who thrives on charity events. She keeps herself busy, especially since Mr Harden passed away last year. It's been very hard on them all.'

'Oh, I didn't know that,' said Jess, her eyes welling with tears. 'Poor Charlie, he didn't mention it to me.'

'Well, I expect what with him being a sensitive lad; he might find it difficult to talk about. He was very close to his father. They were alike as two peas in a pod.'

'And what about the house, Mrs Hill, is it very grand?' Ellie couldn't resist asking.

'It is a big house, but what I call a comfortable size, not too grand like the Vyne, for instance. I worked there myself, many years ago. There are a good nine bedrooms, and four receptions downstairs, at least, with a lovely couple of wood panelled rooms with doors that can be flung back to make room for dancing. Oh, it's a party house, I'd say, and I hope the one they hold tomorrow will bring a little bit of joy back into the place.'

'I don't know what I'm going to wear,' wailed Liberty, 'I've hardly anything decent, and there's no time to go shopping. Stuck out here in the middle of nowhere, how is a girl to get her retail therapy fix?'

'I thought you liked being in the country,' said Cara, 'or at least you keep saying the scenery is very inspiring, though somehow I'm not convinced you were talking about trees.'

Liberty and Cara fell into giggles, and couldn't stop. 'I always think a man on the horizon is the best thing, especially when he's coming into view,' said Liberty, with another smirk that had her and Cara falling about with uncontrolled giggling.

Jess, Martha and Ellie rolled their eyes in despair. 'She has a point though,' said Jess, 'I want to wear the right thing, and make a good impression.'

Everyone stopped and looked at Jess. 'Absolutely,' said Ellie, 'for we are all relying on you to make our fortune!'

Jess shook her head in disbelief. 'And to think I genuinely thought you were my real friends.'

'Oh, but we are,' Liberty announced, ' and if you're nice to me, I shall let you borrow my snakeskin jumpsuit.'

It was Jess's turn to laugh, and Ellie laughed alongside.

Liberty didn't take offence. 'If you don't want it, I shall wear the jumpsuit. I couldn't care less, I haven't got any long dresses, anyway, and I'm sure that's what you're supposed to wear at formal dances. That sweet guy, Matt, the friend of the cameraman I was chatting to the other night, said I'd look delicious in anything. Said my skin made him think of ice cream, and when I asked him why, he said he liked nothing better than licking a vanilla ice.'

Martha groaned. 'That's really disgusting, Liberty.'

'I thought it was rather complimentary, myself.' Liberty yawned loudly, and fiddled with the expensive, over-sized watchstrap round her wrist, twisting it round, running her thumb over the smooth dial. 'I really need to go to bed, I am so worn out.'

'But, you've done nothing all day!' Martha held up her hands like an actress in a third-rate comedy. 'I heard you were lying by the pool most of the time, getting a suntan.'

'I *was* lying down for the greater part of the day, as a matter of fact,' Liberty retorted, as she swaggered out of the kitchen, 'but I wasn't necessarily by the pool or by myself!'

The others watched her departing figure, their mouths falling open.

'I'm sure she's just saying that for a reaction,' said Jess. 'You know what she's like; she loves to shock.'

Ellie wasn't so sure. She'd seen the distinctive, man-size watch that Liberty was wearing on someone else, but for the life of her, she could not remember on whose wrist.

Time was passing quickly by at Steventon. Almost another week had gone in the blink of an eye and the month of June burst into being in a blaze of glory and sultry weather. Ellie was glad there had been no more weird experiences or sightings of Tom though it was impossible not to think of him from time to time. She was doing her best to concentrate on being in the present and resolved on putting the past, well and truly behind her. Working her way round the site, drawing sketches and annotating the old maps she was studying, was exactly the kind of job she loved to do and was helping, she was sure, to keep her firmly in the present. On this particular morning, she set herself up at some distance from the dig and was busy making more records looking north to the sloping landscape. Using a pencil to sketch out the lie of the land, she was completely absorbed when a shadow fell across the white paper.

'How's it going, Ellie?'

It was Greg Whitely, and when Ellie looked up to meet his eyes, she was caught unawares by the unexpected lurch in her stomach. It was almost as if she hadn't really noticed before, but she couldn't help thinking how his looks were growing on her. His eyes were the deepest blue she had ever seen, and fringed with long dark lashes that any girl would have been proud to possess. His long legs were encased in blue denim, and he wore a white shirt, which contrasted with his tanned skin, and his dark hair, which curled past his collar.

'I've not done very much today, but I'm really enjoying the work,' Ellie said feeling shy under his scrutiny.

Greg bounced down to her level, resting on one knee, but still managing to tower above her. She caught his scent, a lemon fragrance that made her heart flutter.

'That landscape's looking great, Ellie. I love your work, by the way. I was hoping to do an interview. I'd like to hear some more about you as the artist, and what makes you tick.'

'Oh, Greg, that's so kind of you. I'd love to do an interview.'

'Good! I thought perhaps if we have a little chat first, off camera, how would that suit you?'

Ellie nodded. 'Yes, that sounds fantastic, then I won't be so nervous when it's on.' She laughed, relieved to find Greg so very different to how she'd assumed he would be. He obviously was a really caring, sensitive person.

'Tomorrow night suit you? I know a little restaurant not too far away where we could chat in private.' He put his hand over hers. 'I'd really like to get to know you better.'

It was a brief touch, but enough to set Ellie's heart pumping. She could feel the adrenalin coursing through her veins. But, it was impossible to answer. As much as she liked him, she was getting the feeling he wanted more than just a chat, and though the idea of being in Greg's arms seemed quite a lovely idea, right then, going out on a date seemed a step too far. And then she remembered. Charlie's ball would be the perfect excuse to refuse his invitation.

'I'm sorry, Greg, but I've already said I'd go to Charlie's ball tomorrow night. I know Jess really wants me to go with her ... and, in any case, Charlie's inviting everyone. I'm sure he'll ask you to go, too. It'll be fun, and you can ask me all the questions you like at the party.'

Greg didn't answer straight away, and Ellie noticed his hesitation. But, then he smiled, nodding his head so enthusiastically that his curls shook. 'Yes, that's a brilliant idea. Come to think of it, I had heard something about a ball. It slipped my mind. I suppose I just liked the idea of getting you all to myself.'

Ellie felt herself blush and when she managed to look up, saw that Greg was smiling into her eyes. It was quite nice, really, she admitted to herself. He made her feel special. She was warming to him, and it felt good. But, she had no intention of getting too close. Besides, she was sure Liberty had her heart set on Greg and she wouldn't be the one to shatter her dreams.

The next morning the girls were all awake early, keen to think about the preparations for the evening. There was much to discuss, as everyone tried to find something to wear so they'd all feel special. Even Martha, who was not generally so fussy about how she was dressed, came to ask Ellie's advice about what she had chosen. The atmosphere in the house was exciting: girls ran from one end of the corridor to the other, dashing in and out of one another's rooms, as dresses were swapped and armfuls of clothes traded. Mrs Hill said it did her heart glad to see them so happy, and how it reminded her of being young herself when she was courting Mr Hill.

Jess and Ellie decided they were quite happy with the long dresses they'd brought with them, after all. Jess's was cornflower blue to match her eyes, and Ellie's was a soft shade of coral, which suited her dark hair and brown skin tone beautifully. Jewellery and accessories could be sorted out later after the day's work at the dig. Both girls were really looking forward to the evening and Jess confided that she couldn't wait to have a dance with Charlie.

They were sitting eating breakfast at the large table in the kitchen when the doorbell rang. Everyone assumed it must be the postman and each one got a little excited in case they'd received a letter or a parcel from home. Mr Hill came through the door empty-handed, but just behind him they could see a young man. He was tall and thin with pale skin and rather red-rimmed eyes. His sandy hair, parted on one side was carefully combed into place. Liberty was transfixed by both his Adam's apple, that moved rapidly above his dog-collar when he spoke, and the dewdrop on the end of his nose which was growing longer and longer. Although it was still very warm, he wore the clothes of a country vicar, a black suit with a black jumper underneath, and he dabbed at his face with a large and dirty, crumpled handkerchief.

'Donald! What a surprise.' Ellie clearly knew the young man, but also did not look exactly pleased to see him, however hard she was trying to appear otherwise.

'Hello Ellie, your mother didn't telephone you, then?'

Ellie shook her head, looking rather bemused. 'No, did she say she would?' She suddenly remembered her manners and instead of looking as if he was the last person on earth that she wanted to see, introduced him instead. 'Girls, this is Donald Smith, my father's curate. Donald, these are my friends from university. I must admit; I'm shocked to see you. Is everything all right at home?'

'Yes, your mother and father are both very well. I'm visiting the area, actually attending a conference in Dummer that your mother signed me up for. Isn't that a coincidence?'

Privately, Ellie thought it was probably a very calculated move on her mother's part. How to get rid of him would be no mean feat. 'I see. Are you staying far?'

Donald reddened, colour flooding his white cheeks. 'Well, I'm rather throwing myself on your mercy, as it happens. I do apologise, I thought it was all arranged. Your mother said she was sure it would be absolutely fine, what with this being such a large house and all.'

Ellie's eyes swivelled to Jess's, and back to Donald's, who had put down the large holdall he was carrying. 'I'm sorry, Donald, I don't understand.'

Donald ignored her and proceeded to snap his fingers. 'Excuse me ... Mrs Hill, isn't it? Do be so good as to take my bag upstairs. I've got to be in Dummer for nine o'clock and I do hate being late. Ellie, it's so good to see you, and if I may say so, you are looking as lovely as ever ... and so are your friends. My goodness, Ellie, you've kept very quiet about these adorable creatures.'

'I don't know if it will be possible to put you up, Donald,' said Ellie, clearly exasperated. 'Mrs Hill is very busy and she has enough to do without adding to her burdens.'

Ellie stood defensively in front of the bag to prevent Mrs Hill from picking it up. The latter was looking none too impressed with the young man who'd blundered into her kitchen, but they could all see she was relenting.

'I can put you in the Red Room, if that will do. It's rather small, having only a single bed, and is high in the attics. It can get rather warm up there in summer.'

Donald was unperturbed. 'That sounds splendid, Mrs Hill, and without further ado, I must be off. Right-ho, I'll see you all later. What time is supper?'

Mrs Hill didn't quite know what to say. She could hardly object, especially with him being a 'man of the cloth'. Being left in charge whilst Mrs Burke was away gave her the necessary power to sanction such a thing, but she felt uneasy. Betty Hill could see that Ellie wasn't happy, and she didn't want anything upsetting her jolly household.

'We'll be eating earlier this evening on account of ...' Mrs Hill stopped, as she caught Ellie's wide-eyed expression, and the almost imperceptible shake of her head, and knew she must not divulge any of the evening plans. 'Supper's at six tonight.'

Donald beamed at them, shouted 'cheerio' like a character from a 1940s black and white movie, and waved before departing without another word.

'I will kill my mother!' Ellie was fuming, and paced round the table like a lion caught in a cage.

'Don't worry, there wasn't very much you could have done,' said Jess, coming over to her friend and stopping her to stroke her arm. 'He would only have turned up later even if we'd said there was no room, and it'll only be for a few days, I expect.'

'You don't know him; he thinks nothing of inviting himself to places for weeks on end. We'll never get rid of him, Jess, and I just can't bear the thought.'

'I'm sorry, Ellie, I feel I'm partly to blame,' said Mrs Hill, collecting up the plates from the table. 'I could never say no to a clergyman.'

'Please don't fret, Mrs Hill, you did very well under the circumstances. At least, he knows nothing about tonight's ball.'

'This might be a daft question, but why do you dislike him so much?' asked Cara, echoing the thoughts of everyone else in the room. Though most of them thought he was a little rude and forthright, Ellie's reaction was so over the top.

'Because my mother wants to fix me up with him, and she won't be happy until I'm walking down the aisle by his side. She's been trying to get us together since he started working for my father last year. She knows his mother and thinks he's very eligible. What she doesn't know is that he's a creep.'

'Well, that was very apparent to me,' said Liberty. 'I nearly asked him to put his eyes back in when he was so obviously looking at my cleavage.'

'It's very difficult, I don't want the guy to lose his job, but I can't tell you how many times he's tried to back me up a corner. He's never done anything, but he just stares ... a lot, and is always trying to hold my hand or peck my cheek. I can't explain, but he just irritates me.'

'Perhaps he's just shy, and doesn't know how to talk to girls,' Jess offered.

Ellie raised an eyebrow. 'Okay, Jess, when he's chased you round the kitchen table later, I'll ask you again how shy he is. I can't stress enough how much I dislike him. I am phoning my mother right now! You go on ahead without me. I won't be long.'

After further reassurance that she would be quite all right and calm again once she had spoken to her mother, the other girls left for the dig. Jess was worried about Ellie but knew that it would blow over in time.

Picking up her phone, Ellie walked outside to the garden that stretched endlessly before her. She passed lawns and stables, the tennis courts and the swimming pool until she found a seat in a secluded garden 'room' at the end of a velvet, clipped lawn, and under a rose-covered arbour where the sight and smells of the beautiful garden in perfect sunshine eased her mind and senses. The phone call was brief and, as usual, Ellie was made to feel she was being unreasonable when she explained that it had put her in a difficult position. She didn't feel any better after the conversation, just angry, because she really did wonder if her mother was right. Putting away her phone in the back pocket of her jeans she made her way back to the house with a heavy heart.

## Chapter 13

Ellie was still unable to concentrate properly when she reached Steventon. She was standing at the top of the slope looking down at the views trying to decide where to paint next. All her painting equipment was out at her feet, but she felt very distracted. Thinking about Tom was proving to be the best way of putting Donald out of her mind, but she didn't like to dwell on thoughts of him for too long. Being unable to fully understand what was happening was hard work, and longing to see Tom again relied on time playing its part.

'Penny for them?'

Aware that she was staring into space, she hadn't even realised Greg was there. 'Oh, I was just contemplating the mystery of time,' she said. 'You know, if time really exists, and if we all perceive time in the same way.'

'That all sounds very philosophical for so early in the morning,' said Greg. 'Are you always so thoughtful?'

'Ellie nodded. 'Generally, I'd say so, I probably think too much for my own good! How are you, this morning, Greg? Is filming going well?'

'Excellent, in fact, I've just been doing a piece with Liberty, as it happens.'

'I expect she enjoyed that very much,' Ellie answered, 'it's good of you to mentor her like this. It's all she ever talks about, being on television.'

'Well, I aim to please.' Greg smiled, and Ellie watched him rake his fingers through his dark curls. She noticed his hands; his fingers were long, and tanned. 'Are you still going to the ball tonight, Cinders?'

'Yes, I am, though I don't think I'll be arriving in a pumpkin carriage. Are you and the team going?'

'We've all been invited. I don't think any one of them will want to miss out on a free party and free booze ... And I wouldn't want to miss a dance with you.'

Ellie could imagine Greg holding her in a slow dance, and though she tried to push the picture away, it stayed with her. She saw herself from a distance moving slowly, her head on his shoulder, his arm tucked around her waist, and she knew that Greg was looking at her and thinking the same thing. His eyes travelled from hers to her lips, which made her bite them, and then he was looking into her eyes again, which made her heart beat all the faster. 'You are leading me astray, Miss Bentley, with your wicked beauty.'

Ellie didn't know what to say. She felt herself crimson and looked away.

'And with those delicious thoughts running round my head, I'd best be getting back to work,' he said.

She watched him stride away and was left feeling bewildered. Although Ellie didn't want to feel attracted to Greg, she was experiencing a sense of longing that she'd never known before. Perhaps it was seeing the way Jane and Tom reacted to one another that was stirring all these emotions. Not as intense as the feelings Jane had experienced for Tom, she knew, but they were there, nevertheless. It disturbed her, and she didn't quite know what to make of it. When she closed her eyes to banish his image, all she saw was his head bending to hers, as she tilted her lips to meet his.

Ellie blinked, snapped out of her reverie, and was suddenly aware of a figure standing somewhere just in the line of her vision. Henry Dorsey was staring at her. She wondered if he'd been watching them, and judging by the scowl on his face she would bet money on it. Turning on her heel, she ignored his reproachful expression and marched up the slope. It was suddenly very important that she should see Jess, and find out what she was doing.

Activity on the dig was slow. Everyone was full of the ball at Deane House, even those who normally would be far more interested in poring over a shard of clay brought up from the ground. Cara and Liberty had their outfits planned down to the last hair-clip, and Martha had allowed herself to wonder if Will MacGourtey might ask her to dance. Jess and Charlie had hardly left one another's side all day, and Melanie, unable to resist making a comment about the tardiness of young lovers had shooed Charles back to his computer more than once.

Ellie found her friend, and was just admiring the cracked tea-bowls and the clay pipes they'd found that morning when she noticed Jess looking beyond her shoulder with a round-eyed expression.

'Oh, Ellie, don't look now, but it's Donald Smith. I'm sure he's looking for you – I saw him a few minutes ago asking people about your whereabouts.'

'Please say you're wrong,' cried Ellie. 'And what is he doing here so early? I thought he was at a conference.'

Before she could say another word, Donald appeared at the door of the tent looking rather hot and bothered. Beads of sweat along his top lip were mopped away by the same grubby handkerchief they'd seen earlier. He was looking decidedly flustered, the heat making his hair stick to his forehead in a greasy quiff, and large dark circles were staining his cheap suit under the armpits. Despite Ellie diving behind a supporting tent pole, much to the amusement of Jess who declared it would never make a good hiding place, Donald soon found them.

'Good afternoon, my lovely ladies! Isn't this splendid? – I'm so glad that I found you. I'm very happy to say my meeting was over even sooner than I hoped and so I just couldn't resist coming to see where you toil away your happy hours. Your mother told me all about this dig, and I couldn't wait to see it for myself. Do introduce me to your sweet friend, Ells.'

'Donald, this is my best friend, Jess,' said Ellie, speaking as shortly and succinctly as she could.

Donald took Jess's hand, raised it to his lips and kissed it, much to her mortification. Jess tried to ease her hand away, politely, but was unsuccessful. He held onto it, and gazed into her eyes. 'Where has Ells been hiding *you*, then? You've got the face of an angel, or the Madonna herself.'

Jess was looking really uncomfortable, and tried once more to release her hand from his grip.

'Let her go, Donald, you're crushing her hand', said Ellie.

Reluctantly, he let her hand drop but his eyes didn't leave hers and the wide smile that showed the large gap between his two front teeth was reserved especially for her. He didn't stop talking for ten minutes, asking Jess about herself, and in turn, telling her all about his prospects and his ambitions. After this had been accomplished, he excused himself and whisking Ellie away, he marched her off to a quiet corner under the shade of some trees by the nearest hedgerow.

'I simply must go out with that girl, Ells. What's her name, again?'

'It's Jess, Donald, and you've as much chance of going out with her as you have with Princess Beatrice.'

'Oh, come on, Ellie. You can put a good word in for me.'

'You are unbelievable, Donald. Why would I do that?'

'Because you are secretly in love with me, and desire me, to boot. I've seen the way you look at me, you minx. I've seen you admiring the ripped muscles beneath my cassock, admit it.'

Ellie knew it was pointless to go on, to say or deny anything would only prompt further ridiculous speeches from him. She gave him one last look of contempt before marching back to the tent and her friend. Donald followed on behind, running to keep up with Ellie's vigorous strides. 'Don't follow me,' were the only words that passed her lips. He stopped, knowing it was useless to pursue her when she was in this kind of mood.

Ellie was glad she'd shaken him off for the moment, and at least, she told Jess, they would enjoy one evening without him leering in their direction. Or so they thought. Just as they were leaving, Charlie bounded over to say how much he was looking forward to seeing them later at the ball.

'I've invited Donald too, Ellie,' he said, with a large grin on his face. 'I didn't realise he was your boyfriend. Well, he's very welcome.'

'He's not my boyfriend,' said Ellie. 'Who on earth gave you that idea?'

'Donald did ... he said you and he had an understanding. I think that's the way he put it.'

Ellie was far too polite to reveal her true anger to Charlie. 'Let's just say he is a little deluded. He is not my boyfriend, I can assure you.'

'But, he is a family friend?'

'I suppose so, he is a friend of my mother's, at least.'

'And we are all looking forward to seeing you and your family at the ball tonight, Charlie,' Jess interjected. She knew Ellie was trying her hardest, but could completely understand how frustrated she was by Donald's behaviour.

Charlie was spellbound by Jess. He looked as if the world had all but disappeared as he looked at Jess with love in his eyes.

'I'm just going to walk up to the church to make a few sketches of the outside,' said Ellie. 'I'll meet you in an hour, Jess, and then we can go back together.'

Ellie could only smile at Jess who looked back at her with such happiness on her face. At least there would be two people who would truly enjoy each other's company at the ball tonight, she thought.

Making her way up the lane, her thoughts drifted back to her last timeslip experience. She couldn't help wondering what, if anything, had happened next between Jane and Tom. Had they ever seen one another again? She wished she had more control over her coming and going back into the past, and she thought about how last time there had been such a heightened concentration of awareness on her senses, and how closing her eyes had helped to calm and transport her safely back to the present. What if she could will herself back to the past in the same way? Closing her eyes she stood, feeling the sun burning down on her head and thinking herself back to that other time. It was no good. Half opening one eye, she knew she had accomplished nothing. The others were coming up the lane behind her and hearing their voices brought her solidly into the present. She remembered that Charlie's party was about to take place and as she thought about how much she was looking forward to it and to seeing Greg, the past and Tom seemed to settle back into its proper place. Ellie knew she had no control over her experiences and told herself it would be unwise to get too embroiled in a history that had already taken place.

## Chapter 14

The same excitement that had started the day at Ashe Rectory was now heightened to almost fever pitch, with Liberty and Cara hardly able to contain themselves. They were upstairs giggling at the most ridiculous things, and discussing every little rumour they'd heard discussed amongst the volunteers that afternoon.

Along the corridor Martha stood in front of the mirror in her room. She would never be glamorous, no matter how hard she tried, but she was quite pleased with her appearance. Mrs Hill had helped her to curl her usually straight locks, and Nancy Littleworth from the village had found her a long dress to wear. It was too much to hope that any man might notice her enough to ask her to dance, but she really did think she'd never looked better. The dress was plain, at least, not like Liberty's, which she was thankful for. The latter had complained so much about being forced to wear a jumpsuit because she had nothing else that Nancy had begged and borrowed another from a sister who lived in the next village.

'I know you'll love it!' said Nancy, unzipping the black and white Zebra printed silk from its plastic protective bag.

And Liberty did. Black and white stripes, sequins, and a fushia pink ribbon sash were the stuff of her dreams. 'I heard

Charlie say there was a European prince going to the ball,' said Liberty who was standing in front of a tall cheval mirror admiring herself. 'I don't think he's still got a kingdom, but I reckon he's probably still worth a few million pounds. How do you think that will sound?'

'How do I think what will sound?' asked Cara, firstly tying up her hair, but then letting it fall down her back in loose waves like Kate Middleton wore hers.

'Princess Liberty, of course,' answered Liberty, waving her hand regally before falling back into a chair and throwing her head back in gales of laughter.

'You never fail to amaze me, my friend,' said Cara stepping into a pale pink dress. 'I truly believe you could be Princess Liberty – especially if you become a television presenter. You never know who'll you'll end up meeting in the media world.'

'Well, a girl has to have her dreams,' Liberty agreed, liberally applying fuschia lipstick to match the sash on her dress.

Ellie and Jess were putting the final touches to their appearance.

'Jess, Charlie will be even more in love with you than he is already,' said Ellie, tying the strap on her dainty heels. 'You look so beautiful, he'd better watch out because there will be a queue waiting behind him.'

'Oh, Ellie, you're so good for my confidence, but I'm not sure if Charlie is in love with me. I think he likes me, but any more than that I could not say. Anyway, it's you that the guys will be lining up for tonight. You are simply stunning, and that dress looks wonderful!'

Ellie was quite pleased with the girl she saw in the mirror. It was amazing what a little scrubbing up and a bit of blusher could do for a girl, she thought. She wondered if Greg would like the way she looked. It would be nice to have a dance with him.

As if Jess could read her mind, she said, 'I'm sure Greg Whitely will love you in that dress – I've noticed you two chatting quite a lot recently. He looks fairly moonstruck when he looks at you, and he's just your type, though it wouldn't surprise me if Henry Dorsey doesn't step in tonight.'

'What do you mean?' asked Ellie unable to keep the note of incredulity from her voice. 'Henry Dorsey hates me. He spends all his time staring at me as if I'm some common peasant that's got in his way.'

'That's not what I've heard from Cara, or been a witness to myself. I've seen him positively relishing the sight of you – he can hardly stop looking at you.'

'Well, he can look all he likes ... he's not going to ask me to dance, and even if he did, I'd run in the opposite direction. Anyway, he's the least of my worries. Donald has already hinted that he's going to be at my side all night. I don't know what I'll do because if I don't dance with him at least once, I know he'll never leave me alone.'

'Oh, one little dance won't be so bad, will it?' asked Jess. 'You can always hide or make sure you're dancing with other people for the rest of the night.'

Ellie sighed. 'You have absolutely no idea, do you, my darling? You have never seen him in action. Now, don't accuse me of being cruel until you've seen the exhibition that is Donald Smith on the dance floor. I don't require every man that I meet to be able to dance, but if he can't then I don't expect him to fling himself about like a madman. I shall be laughed at and yet, I hope there will be pity.'

Jess laughed. 'I have quite a picture in my mind!'

'Trust me,' said Ellie with a grim smile, 'you haven't seen anything yet!'

Mrs Hill and Nancy were in the hall to see them off with Donald who sat patiently waiting for them on a chair by the Grandfather clock. For once, his appearance didn't make Ellie wince. Dressed in evening wear he looked almost smart, but for his jacket lapels which were ironed to a silky shininess. His mouth literally fell open when he saw the girls descending in their dresses. Naked shoulders and creamy flesh were almost too much for him, and Liberty shuddered when she caught him ogling her once again.

'I'll see you there later,' said Nancy. 'I'm taking some of my canapés for Mrs Harden, and once they've been served, I shall be joining in with the party!'

Everyone was really pleased that Nancy who had been so kind would be able to join in the fun. And she was getting paid really well, she said, for what would only amount to an hour's work at most.

'Girls, you look a picture, every last one of you,' said Mrs Hill. 'And every time I look at you I'm reminded of something from my own past. I'm being silly, I know, bringing up all these memories, but I spent many a time at a ball there in my youth. It was not quite what you're going to tonight, but there were plenty of dances for the servants during the 1950s. Deane House is where I met Mr Hill. He was a gardener there then, and I was a lady's maid.'

'Oh, Mrs Hill, how romantic,' cried Jess. 'Do tell us all about it.'

'Well, we always used to joke that it was Jane Austen that brought us together. She used to go to dances at Deane in her youth, you know. The house belonged to the Harwood family back then, and it was there that they say she fell in love, and was inspired to write *Pride and Prejudice*.'

'Really? I didn't know that,' said Jess. 'I'm sure Charlie doesn't know, either.'

'I've forgotten his name,' said Mrs Hill, 'the boy they said she was in love with. Was it Tom? I can't remember, but, anyway, my Bill started talking about it, and I said how much I liked *Pride and Prejudice*. It turned out that he was a great reader of Miss Austen too, and the rest is history, as they say.'

'How wonderful,' said Ellie, 'to meet someone who loved the same books as you. That's very rare, I'm sure.'

'You wouldn't think it to look at him, but he's a shrewd observer, an avid reader, and he likes dry wit. We've been very happy for sixty years, and I don't think it would be going too far to say that Miss Austen had her hand in it. Well, off you go now. You have a wonderful time and tell me all about it in the morning.'

When the taxi entered the road leading up to the old manor house, Ellie thought how beautiful it looked. A red-bricked house built in the time of Queen Anne stood at the head of a great lawn with a pale, stuccoed church to one side. It was quite a grand house compared to the Austen's rectory of her recollection and she could imagine how Jane must have felt when coming to the house for a ball. Would she have been as nervous and excited as she felt now, she wondered, as the girls piled out of the car, smoothing down their dresses and crunching across the gravel in their high heels.

Once through the large double doors they were directed to the long drawing room by the butler, a friendly chap in traditional black. There were already many guests assembled, and a few familiar faces loomed. Liberty and Cara broke off from the group as soon as they saw anyone they knew, and Charlie came rushing up to greet Jess, Ellie and Martha.

'I'm so pleased you could come,' he said, taking Jess's arm. Ellie smiled – she could see the two of them only had eyes for the other. They were offered glasses of champagne from a tray, and as Ellie took a sip of the golden bubbles, she looked about eagerly to see Greg.

Jake, one of the cameramen that Liberty liked, was moving through the crush. He looked very handsome in black tie, and it passed through Ellie's mind that she ought to keep her friend well away from him tonight.

'Hi Ellie,' he said, 'Isn't this great? And wow, you look simply edible.'

Ellie couldn't stop herself from smiling, even if she knew he was a bit of a lady's man. She stopped to chat, partly because she knew he would have the information she wanted.

'Is Greg here?' she said, trying not to look as if her hopes would be disappointed if he didn't appear.

'I'm afraid not. Actually, he asked me to pass on a message to you. He's had to go to London ... something about a new presenting job that was just too good to pass up on. Greg is really sorry. I know how much he was looking forward to seeing you all.'

Ellie was disappointed even if she didn't like to admit it to herself. And before she'd got used to the fact, Donald was standing at her side. He grabbed her free hand. 'Are you ready to dance the night away, Ellie?' he said. 'Don't forget you promised you'd dance with me first, Ellie.'

She'd resigned herself to the fact that she would have to dance with him at some point and nodded. When she looked up, Henry was standing just a few feet away looking from her to Donald and back again. Zara stood at his side, her arm in his, dressed like an ice maiden in a blue silk deco-style gown. Ellie smiled, and was shocked when Henry smiled back. It was only a curve of the lips, not a full, pearly-white teeth-showing smile, but a smile nevertheless.

Charlie insisted on introducing them both to his mother who turned out to be a whole lot better than Ellie had imagined. She'd thought the haughty Zara might be a replica of her mother, but Mrs Harden turned out to be rather like Charlie himself in character, really friendly and welcoming. She was a classic beauty dressed in a stylish rather than fashionable evening gown with a velvet hairband being the only adornment on her silver hair. When Nancy came round with the canapés Arabella Harden told her how wonderful they were, and then insisted she go and get ready as the dancing was about to start. Ellie thought Jess could do a lot worse than have a mother-in-law like Mrs Harden, and was glad to see how well the two women seemed to get on.

Everyone made their way to a large marquee which had been set up outside. The girls thought they'd never seen anything so magical. Strung with paper lanterns and strings of white lights, there were tables dressed with snowy cloths, vases tumbling with fresh flowers and gilt chairs at one end, and a dance floor at the other. There was to be a surprise later on, Charlie said, but his lips were sealed for now.

As soon as the music started, Donald appeared at Ellie's side.

There were only one or two couples on the floor, and Ellie, though a natural dancer, felt reluctant about getting up and dancing just yet. Liberty and Cara were dancing with several of the film crew, and when Donald insisted that they join them, Ellie felt she had no choice. She didn't want to cause a scene, which was a real possibility if she refused the promised dance. To her relief, she saw Jess and Charlie start dancing, and nodding to Donald allowed him to usher her onto the floor. But, it wasn't long before she was regretting that she'd agreed to dance after all. Oh, the embarrassment and shame she felt. Not content with shuffling from foot to foot like most people who couldn't dance, Donald was literally throwing himself about, arms and legs flailing willy-nilly. The worst of it was that he thought he was really good, and kept grabbing Ellie, to spin her round or look longingly into her eyes.

'I always loved the film, *Saturday Night Fever*,' he said. 'I'd have worn a white suit tonight, like John Travolta in the movie, if I could have. The Eighties were so magical, don't you think?'

'I'm more of a contemporary dance girl, myself,' said Ellie, and when Donald suggested his dance style was an improvement on modern dance, she gave up trying to talk to him. The track was endless seeming to go on forever, and with every step he took, her toes were squashed and trodden on. Thank goodness, Greg wasn't there to witness the exhibition, and she was even more pleased when there was no sign of Henry either. She couldn't say why, but she would have hated him to see her dancing like some demented disco diva from a long-gone era. He must still be in the drawing room with Zara, she thought, being too cool to actually break a sweat and start dancing. And then, she saw him. He was actually walking onto the dance floor to stand next to her and Donald. Of course he was with Zara who looked like elegance personified. Far from being too cool, they danced as if they had always partnered the other. They were brilliant dancers and moved together so well. It was hard not to be aware of the contrast between the two couples, and she saw Henry glance across to meet her eyes. Zara could hardly stop from smirking, and now seemed to be performing even more to the rest of the audience who stood at the edges clapping them on. It was hard to endure the pointing fingers of Liberty and her friends, but at last it was over, and Ellie was released. Donald was begging for another and hanging onto her hand, but she had to get out of there. Feeling humiliated, her face was beetroot, and she knew her hair must look like some kind of bird's nest on top of her head after being thrown about so wildly.

Ellie snatched her hand away and headed for the nearest exit. As she stepped outside into fresh air, she felt a hand on her elbow, and spinning round was surprised to see it was Henry gripping her arm. He was taller than she'd realised, and she noticed how his dark hair fell over his eyes in one lustrous sweep. There was no denying he was really good-looking, even if she reminded herself that he was the most arrogant guy she'd ever met.

'Ellie, would you dance with me? That is, when you come back from wherever it is you're going.'

He looked sincere, as far as she could tell, but Ellie wasn't at all sure whether he was just enjoying watching her squirm with embarrassment after the last dance. Her first reaction was to say no, but then her mind and mouth disobeyed her.

'Yes, thank you, Henry. I'll be back in a minute.'

He didn't smile or say anything but dismissed her with a nod. All the way back to the house Ellie scolded herself for agreeing to partner him. How could she have said yes?

She made her way up the grand staircase to the room allocated for ladies to powder noses and to freshen up. There were one or two chatting in a corner, clearly enjoying a spot of gossip and too immersed to notice Ellie. She sat down in front of the dressing table and drew a comb through her hair, put on a little lipstick and gathered her thoughts. The idea of being pursued by Donald all night was almost too much, and her heart sank when she realised that she still had the ordeal of a dance with Henry to face. Taking a few deep breaths she stood up at last, and as if about to enter a battle scene walked towards the door with courage in her heart. Opening it, she knew at once she was about to step through a portal into the past.

## Chapter 15

I descended the staircase and made my way through the hall to the saloon. There were so many people it was difficult to make any progress without stopping to greet neighbours and friends. The Portals from Laverstoke, the Terrys from Dummer, the Bramstons from Oakley Hall, and the Biggs from Manydown were crammed into the panelled space and all chattering at once.

'Oh, Miss Austen, how very pleased I am to see you,' said Mrs Bramston. 'Is this not a pleasant party? We were so late I feared we'd miss the dancing, and Mr Bramston felt so poorly yesterday, I worried we'd not be here at all. It's nothing more than a little cough – just what's to be expected in this cold damp weather. Is your mother here? I should like so very much to see her – I didn't catch her at Basingstoke to talk to, but it's very difficult to see just everyone you would like to speak with. Everywhere looks so very festive, do you not think? And at this time of year it adds to the pleasures of the season, does it not? I am sure you are of the same opinion. I remember coming to one of the theatricals at Steventon once and the barn was fitted up like a fairyland with lanterns and candles and Christmas greenery. I never saw anything so pretty, not even in London when Mr Bramston took me to see Mr Kean in *As*

*You Like It.* Are you putting on a play this year? Your cousin Eliza was quite a wonderful actress – Mr Bramston talked about her for a month together afterwards. Now, what was the name of the play – I've quite forgotten, but she was so good in it.'

All the time Mrs Bramston was talking, it proved quite unnecessary for me to answer or even contribute to the conversation, as she was perfectly happy to supply the responses. I smiled and nodded in all the right places and soon enough she moved on to Mrs Mildmay who was just arriving.

My brother Henry's friend from Oxford, John 'Willing' Warren, stopped me to beg that I should dance with him and I agreed for the third because I'd promised James I'd start the ball with him. Poor James was still mourning Anne, his beloved wife of three short years and was finding life too difficult to be the light-hearted swain he once had been. But, this season had seen a great improvement in my brother's dancing and I had high hopes for him that he might be able to look for another wife in time. I was to dance with beloved Henry after that and had already teased him about the fact that he was not wearing his regimentals tonight. He wore his scarlet coat whenever he could and knew exactly the effect his militia uniform had on any ladies present. That he would not be happy until he had a commission in the regulars, I was certain, and I was also sure that although he'd deny it, my cousin Eliza had much to do with influencing his choice.

When I walked into the saloon I had not reckoned on the fact that the Lefroys would already be there. I could see Madame deep in conversation with my mother, and accompanied by her husband and one of her sons, Ben, and her daughter Lucy. Tom stood slightly to one side and I found I could hardly look at him. I was sure he'd seen me but he neither regarded me now nor sought me out. I felt I knew him no more than the very first time we'd ever met and he looked just as grim-faced and silent. I longed for my father at that moment. He'd not wanted to come to the ball, an ever-increasing habit, as he was getting older. He much preferred to stay at home with his books and how I wished I'd done the same. The memory of the last meeting I'd had with Tom pricked me with feelings of shame. Since that day when we'd ridden Madame's horse, our hearts beating together as we rode through the wintry lanes, I'd suffered such a torment of feeling, from elation on the one hand to the feeling that I'd disgraced myself. But, I couldn't think about that now or I would never have the courage to speak to him.

The musicians were tuning up their instruments, a certain preamble to their playing and the dancing that was to begin. Before I could reach the other side of the room, my brother James was there to take my hand and lead me onto the floor. There were at least twenty couples in the set and I saw Tom take his cousin's hand.

'It's good to see so many of our friends here,' said James. 'I daresay you've promised many dances to all your admirers.'

'Oh, Jemmy, I've one or two, but to be perfectly frank, I could well do without some of the attention.'

James laughed and I thought how good it was to see him smile again. 'Now, who might be a troublesome suitor? I'll see them off, if you should need help, but I daresay Mr Lyford is quite harmless.'

'How could you possibly know that he is a cause of my distress?'

'You might think you are a good actress, my dear sister, but your distaste shows a little too well on your countenance. Besides, it's well known that he is an ardent pursuer of ladies.'

'At least, I am not the only one he is chasing. I am glad of it because I do not think I have the speed or the energy for such pursuit.'

'Unless hunted by a particular Irishman, I would hazard a guess.'

'I do not know what you mean, Jemmy. The only gentleman here who hails from that far-off island is far too proud and above himself to be truly interested in anyone here.'

I instantly regretted being quite so forthright. James would think that I harboured a secret admiration for Mr Lefroy, and I was determined that my heart, though it had betrayed me before, was not to be toyed with.

'Methinks the lady doth protest too much.'

James stopped when he caught my expression. He knew he'd gone too far but he couldn't help adding, 'And so you shall refuse him if he should ask you to dance?'

'I can assure you, I never mean to dance with Mr Lefroy again.'

The rest of the dance passed by in silence but I congratulated Jemmy on his dancing as we came off the floor and he said he'd enjoyed himself. I knew it would be a while before he'd be dancing like a young bachelor again, but at least we'd made a start.

My dear friend Catherine Bigg was waiting for me. She looked very elegant in pink silk with a carmine sash; reminding me of a summer rose whose petals are unfurling towards the sun. 'Who is the lucky man to take your hand for the second?' I asked. Catherine had been rather unfortunate to have Charles Powlett first but her expression told me she was to be better pleased with her second.

'Mr Lefroy has asked me for the next. He is a very handsome man, is he not?'

'He certainly thinks he's good-looking,' I commented, rather ungenerously.

'Jane, do I detect some partiality of your own? I thought you danced rather well together at the Basingstoke assembly and I daresay he has marked you out for more than one dance tonight.'

I couldn't help feeling a little cross that I had to answer in the negative. There had not been enough time, I explained, and then I felt rather silly for it was beginning to look as if I minded very much that the opportunity to have him ask for a dance had not occurred. I changed the subject.

'So whom do you think your sister will choose?'

Two gentlemen were presently courting Elizabeth and gossip was rife about which gentleman would win the day. Not only was she handsome, but she also had some money, which meant fitting suitors were vying for her hand, buzzing round like Cassy's bees upon a honey pot.

'Well, she opened the ball with John Harwood tonight though that doesn't signify anything other than a wish to please him in his father's house at his own ball. Between ourselves, I think she'll take the baronet's son if she can get him. Not that William Heathcote will inherit as a second son, but he is already the rector of Worting and has a good deal of money. And besides all that; William is as good-looking as she is beautiful, and I know she expressed a preference for his father's beautiful grounds at Hursley Park.'

Catherine made me laugh so much that it seemed to catch the attention of a certain young man standing on the other side of the room.

'I think your partner is ready for you,' I said, nodding in his direction.

'Though it does not appear that he looks to me for his next dance. He has been regarding you in that steady way of his for the last ten minutes.'

'He can regard all he likes. In any case, I've promised to dance with Henry next and Warren for the two after that, at least. And even if he should beg for a dance, I think it probable that I may refuse him.'

'But Jane, you would be a simpleton to refuse him on the grounds of pride alone. Especially if you like him, and I believe you do.'

Catherine knew me too well, but when I saw Tom start to move, I wished her luck with her handsome Irishman, and left the scene before I would have to either acknowledge or speak to him.

Thankfully, Henry appeared at my side though after his own teasing remarks about him not expecting to have claimed one dance with me for he was certain I'd only be occupied with dancing Irish jigs, I was ready to ignore both my brothers for the rest of the night. They really could be very vexing.

How I wished Cassandra were here tonight. I always felt odd

when she was away, as if a little of myself was missing, and in a way that was true. She was as much a part of me as I was of her. I hoped she was having as good a time as it was possible to have with the Fowle family even if Tom could not be there. When he was offered the post of chaplain in Lord Craven's regiment it seemed too good an opportunity to pass up. Cassy's Tom was keen to make his fortune so that they could at last get married. But, neither of them had reckoned on how hard it would be to spend so much time apart.

John Warren was always fun, and always 'willing' to dance or do anything for the comfort of my sister and me. I hardly liked to encourage him because I had a feeling he was falling in love with me and though I liked him very much, I did not think of him in 'that way'. He came to claim my hand as did all the others, my so-called admirers. Mr Lefroy would be lucky to find a dance free if he should change his mind about being civil. Now and again, I was aware of him out of the corner of my eye, and one time I was sure his eyes were upon me but on glancing back at him, he looked stonily ahead. I knew he'd partnered almost every girl in the room, except me. Was he trying to ignore me or wound me? He was making it very obvious that he had nothing to say to me. Anyone else might be intimidated by his hauteur and his snubbing ways but as the evening wore on, my courage rose. What did I care if I never spoke or danced with him again? I had more partners than any other girl in the room!

The bell rang for supper and the crowd dispersed, heading for the dining parlour with its tables groaning with Christmas delights. Roast beef, venison, goose and pheasant, all ready for carving were arranged at one end, whilst tureens of white soup, and dishes of buttered prawns, chickens with tongues, and lobster pies were placed in the centre. Puddings and desserts made a pretty picture on the other side: syllabubs and trifles, pyramid creams, jellies and cake, would soon be washed down with punch cups of Negus and glasses of orange wine. I wasn't hungry and wished to avoid the teasing attentions of my brothers and the constant questioning from my mother. I found my cloak and made my way outside. The garden at night looked mysterious under its veil of snow. The lake was frozen, glowing like a tarnished mirror under the silver moon and the temple beyond hardly visible against the night sky studded with bright diamonds. I followed the path skirting the formal gardens, but as the temple came closer into view I felt a certain trepidation. The doors, which were usually closed, were now slightly ajar and the faintest light seemed to glow from within. Perhaps a lovers tryst was taking place, I thought, and for a moment I hesitated before curiosity got the better of me. I wandered up to the door and peeped in.

The scene was certainly set for a pair of lovers. There were rugs and cushions scattered over the stone seats, and a picnic of sorts, though everything was set out on a table covered in a white cloth and beautifully arranged on gleaming white china with a gold motif. Everything was lit by lantern light, and vast candles burned in lustrous candlesticks. It was still and silent except for the soft sound of dripping wax. There was no one there. Or so I thought.

No sooner had I stepped inside than he stepped out of the shadows. Tom Lefroy stood, his hands on his hips, with what I can only describe as a triumphant smile on his face. He looked so pleased with himself that I wanted to turn tail and leave, but I could not. I was stunned and shocked. Shocked that I knew he had designed this scenario with me in mind, and I couldn't fathom it out.

'You are wondering how, are you not, Miss Austen?'

I completely lost my tongue.

'Please come in and join me.'

I did not want to go in, but he held out his hand, and I happened at that moment to look into those grey eyes, which I knew was a mistake. They were no longer mocking or challenging, but they seemed to offer genuine affection. I took his hand, which closed over mine so tenderly I thought he'd hear my heart beat out loud, and I sat down on a velvet cushion. I had a thousand questions and did not know where to start.

'How did you know that I'd come out into the garden and how on earth did you manage to arrange it all?'

'If I dare to tell you, do you promise you will stay?'

'Why do I think I may not like the answer to my question, Mr Lefroy?'

'Promise me.'

'You have my word.'

'I think you are a lady who does not enjoy being ignored. I knew if I failed to acknowledge you or speak to you that you would not like it. Added to that, my refusal to request your company on the dance floor would be enough to make you vexed beyond wishing to stay in the company of others. You love to walk and your preference is for the outdoors. And your romantic nature made it impossible to walk by without looking in. There it is, Miss Austen, my simple plan to secure your company.'

I was almost beyond speech. I was the one who enjoyed dissecting the intricacies of the characters and personalities of my friends and neighbours. I was the expert on human behaviour and could anticipate the next move of most people I knew. But, I had not expected this. He'd seen through me and understood every secret thought of my soul. And, for all my bravado, I knew Tom was right, but I was not going to forgive him that easily.

'You're insufferable, Mr Lefroy!'

Tom bowed. 'I fear I am, Miss Austen, but please hear me out. I wanted so much to talk to you and we cannot do so without half the world aware of it. Forgive me?'

I watched him pour a glass of wine and I took it from his outstretched hand. He settled beside me on the seat and there was no need for any more words. The cool liquid soon worked its magic and though my head felt strange, I was more composed and certainly not so cross. Outside, beyond the open doors we looked to the night sky where the stars sparkled and the moon lit up the snow-covered trees and woods beyond.

'On such a night, Jane, we have all time and beauty before us,' said Tom. 'I am sorry to have been so underhand.'

'It is all forgiven. Look what you have presented me with – here's what may leave all painting and all music behind, and what poetry can only attempt to describe! Here's what may soothe every care, and lift the heart to ecstasy! When I look out on such a night as this, I feel as if there could be neither wickedness nor sorrow in the world; and there certainly would be less of both if the sublimity of Nature were more attended to, and people were carried more out of themselves by contemplating such a scene.'

'I like to hear your enthusiasm, Jane. It is a lovely night, and they are much to be pitied who have not been taught to feel, as we do. They lose a great deal.'

'There's Arcturus looking very bright.'

'Yes, and the Bear.'

' I wish I could see Cassiopeia.'

'We must go out on the lawn for that.'

'And yet, I find I am happy enough to star-gaze from here.'

'Do you think we will be missed, Miss Austen?'

'Not for a little while, but I suppose we must go back soon.'

'And will you dance with me?'

'If you wish it, Mr Lefroy.'

'Oh, I do, Miss Austen.'

## Chapter 16

Before Ellie reached the house she knew her time with Tom was about to end. She could hear music throbbing into the night air, and suddenly after the stillness of the temple, the world seemed very loud. Ellie turned to see that Tom was disappearing before her eyes, fading like a wisp of mist in a morning haze. The marquee was looming out of darkness glowing with light and shadows, silhouettes of dancing couples flared into life or diminished in size like the very shades she was leaving behind. Was it possible that Tom was still there, but it was just that she couldn't see him and no longer felt his touch? Did he still trail after Jane and continue to hold her hand? Ellie could feel the warmth of his fingers, though he was no longer there. The whole experience was so real, and yet, she had to remind herself that everything that she was seeing and feeling was not of this time. Standing in the darkness, she tried to picture them in her mind. Tom and Jane running across the snow, late to be getting back because they couldn't stop talking. She could see them in her mind's eye. They were dancing. And she knew Jane had never felt happier.

Such a time had passed by that Ellie had completely forgotten her promise to dance with Henry until she saw him standing with

Zara at the side of the dance floor. It was possible he'd forgotten his request for a dance so with a determination to avoid all eye contact she made her way over to Jess who was standing on her own.

'Oh, Ellie, isn't this lovely?'

'Yes, it's gorgeous, a simply heavenly evening,' answered Ellie truthfully, thinking back to the lovely time spent with Tom. 'Where's Charlie?'

'He's having a dance with his mum – don't they make a wonderful couple? She is such a kind lady, Ellie.'

'I'm very pleased to hear she is being pleasant to you, and so she should be. You'd make a wonderful daughter-in-law for anyone.'

'I shall ignore that last comment,' said Jess, unable to stop laughing. 'I am sure Charlie doesn't think of me like that, and his mother certainly won't. It's too early, anyway, I hardly know him even if he is the nicest guy I've met in a long time. I just wish he had a lovely friend for you.'

'Well, we can't have everything,' Ellie answered, and was instantly reminded of the dance she'd promised.

Just at that moment, Ellie spotted Donald making a beeline for them. 'Oh, watch out, Donald is on the rampage. I'm going to have to go. And if I were you, I'd go too, unless you want to be caught by him.'

'Although,' Jess added, 'it looks as if Henry Dorsey might cut him off before he gets to you. It's rather funny, don't you think?'

From opposing sides of the ballroom space, Donald and Henry moved at a pace. If Henry was aware of Donald bearing down in Ellie's direction, he gave no indication. He kept his eyes ahead, on the prize. Donald, however, was suddenly made aware of his rival and with eyes swivelling maniacally from Henry to Ellie as if judging the distance to the object of his desire and his chances of achieving his goal, he practically broke into a trot.

To Jess's utter amazement Henry was there first and whisked Ellie away before she had a chance to accept or refuse him. Donald was not giving up that easily, however, and whenever he could would dance up to and around the pair, until Henry turned and glared at him in such a way that the latter quickly danced his way to another unwilling partner.

Glaring at people seemed to be rather a speciality of Henry's, Ellie thought. He was a good dancer but he looked incredibly moody and so far, he hadn't spoken a word. What was the point of it all, she wondered? Why had he bothered asking her to dance if he so clearly was going to hate every minute? Ellie decided she would make him talk if it killed him to answer.

'I love dancing, don't you?' Ellie said, and then thought how pathetic she'd sounded, not to mention the fact that it was highly likely she'd only get a one-word answer in reply.

She was almost right. Henry nodded, and didn't offer any more.

After a minute, she tried again. 'You like dancing more than you like talking, I think.'

Ellie knew she'd provoked a reaction as his face twitched into action.

'I like talking just as much as I like dancing where there is something worth saying, and a conversation worth the trouble of joining in.'

Touché – that one almost hurt, but Ellie was inclined to laugh. 'And what would you consider a topic worthy of your discussion, Henry?'

'Well, the merits of scientific analysis in an archaeological dig, versus the conjectures of an artist who makes it all up as she goes along, might be a good starting point.'

'Ouch!' cried Ellie, who was even more amused. 'And I cannot begin to think where you'd stand on that particular debate.'

Henry smiled, and for the first time Ellie warmed to him.

'Are you enjoying the work you're doing?' asked Henry.

'I am, very much. As you no doubt realise, I'm much happier being creative than scientific, and I've had some really positive support. Will MacGourtey and Greg Whitely have been particularly helpful.'

Ellie watched Henry, keen to see how he would react when she mentioned Greg's name. He looked a little uncomfortable and she could not resist adding. 'Greg is an artist, too, apparently. He's so kind and friendly, not a bit like I'd thought he would be. I've really missed his friendship tonight.'

Henry coloured, blushing deeply. 'He was always good at making friends, though in my experience he rarely keeps them.'

'Well, he's certainly lost your friendship, that I do know, said Ellie, stopping to make her point. 'And in a way that he or his family is never going to recover from.'

Henry looked very thoughtful, as he glowered at Ellie, but he didn't say anymore. The music was stopping and without saying another word he walked right off the dance floor leaving Ellie standing alone and open-mouthed, as she watched him heading for the exit. She felt incredibly frustrated. He was so rude, it was impossible to understand him, and what was more, she really didn't want to take the trouble over trying to make head nor tail of anything about him. What seemed very clear was that everything Greg had said about the Dorseys must be true or surely he would have explained. Ellie took a deep breath and headed back to the main house. She hadn't seen either Liberty or Cara for a while and from her experience that wasn't a good thing.

Ellie made her way to the bar that had been set up in the dining room. She should have known that the loud chanting of male voices and the banging of fists on tables she could hear might have something to do with Liberty and Cara. There they were with a line of cocktails set up before them, and a crowd of hangers-on all eager to make the girls knock them back in one. Liberty was sitting on the bar itself and loving all the attention, clapping in time to the mantra of every admiring man. It was useless to say anything or attempt to intervene, but as Ellie rushed out of the room again she bumped straight into Henry who gave her such a look of disdain that she wished the ground would open to swallow her up. She knew he would see her friends behaving badly and though she'd decided he wasn't worth bothering about, Ellie hated the thought that he'd think anything dreadful about any of them. It was time to find Jess. Perhaps together they could reason with Liberty and Cara.

Luckily, Martha and Jess were just coming out of the drawing room when they saw Ellie. They'd already seen what was going on with Liberty and Cara, but even Jess had no ready answers.

'It's about time they started behaving responsibly,' said Martha. 'I don't see why we always have to pick up the pieces. It's not fair, I'm not a nursemaid!'

'No,' said Jess, 'you're not, but I can't just leave them, either.'

Before Jess could make up her mind about what was best to do, Charlie made an appearance with a younger cousin at his heels, rushing through the hallway and banging a small brass gong. 'Ladies and gentlemen,' he announced in a loud voice, 'please make your way to the marquee where we have a little entertainment laid on.'

'Thank heavens for that – a diversion is just what we need,' said Ellie, as they were swept along in the crowd heading for the door. 'With a bit of luck our friends might just be curious enough to find out what's going on.'

Ellie was proved right. Liberty and Cara joined in, bringing a 'conga' line of followers with them as everyone gathered in the marquee where on the stage at one end, there was much activity. There was all the evidence of a band being set up – drum kit, guitars, keyboards and microphones were having final arrangements and adjustments made. The guitars were being tuned, and the mikes tested for sound.

Jess caught Ellie's eye. 'Are you thinking what I'm thinking?'

Ellie smiled. 'Oh Jess, do you think you'll be able to cope? Charlie with a guitar might prove too much for you.'

'He didn't say anything about playing tonight, but, Ellie, I hope you're right. Oh, how exciting!'

The crowd was getting larger as they all rushed to get the best possible view and when Jess saw Charlie's mum walk onto the stage, she squeezed Ellie's hand.

'Ladies and gentlemen, thank you so much for making

tonight's ball such fun and for contributing to the charitable funds which depend so much on every donation they receive. I hope you are all enjoying yourselves immensely.'

There was a huge cheer from the crowd as Arabella Harden stood patiently until it had died down enough to announce the entertainment. 'I'm hugely proud of my son Charlie and his band, as most of you know. They are going to be playing for us tonight, a little taste of what will be on offer when they go on tour. So, please put your hands together for the Charlie Harden band!'

The crowd roared and stamped their feet when Charlie came onto the stage. The girls recognised a couple of the other boys from Oxford, but were totally aghast in the next moment when they saw who picked up the lead guitar.

For once, Ellie was lost for words, and both girls felt their mouths drop open in shock. For none other than Henry Dorsey was adjusting the strap on his guitar and testing the pedals at his feet. He'd changed, and looked far more casual than she'd ever seen him. He wore slim-fitting dark jeans and a short-sleeved T-shirt emblazoned with a picture of Jimi Hendrix, and despite herself, Ellie caught her breath. Henry looked so different and far from being stiff and looking uncomfortable, he appeared to be totally at home on stage. When he started playing, she found she couldn't take her eyes off him. Every muscle in his body seemed to be at one with the music and his guitar, and when he moved, she melted inside.

'Ellie, look at Henry,' said Jess. 'Wow, he is really good.'

Ellie was completely transfixed. He was an amazingly brilliant guitarist, she could see. So was Charlie, and Jess was looking up at him even more adoringly.

'OMG! Mr Dorsey has one hot body!' said a voice in her ear.

Ellie knew before she turned round that Liberty must be ogling Henry, and she was right.

'Who'd a thought he could actually be sexy! And he likes you, Ellie. You're in there, all right.'

If only Liberty could keep her ideas to herself, thought Ellie, but five minutes later she was still going on about Henry being sex on legs in a really loud voice.

'You could do a lot worse than go out with him, Ellie. He's good-looking and disgustingly rich ... I don't know what's holding you back.'

Ellie told her to lower her voice especially when she saw Zara looking across and glaring at them both.

'Lets go a little closer,' said Jess, 'we'll be able to see better.'

Glad of a reason to leave Liberty behind, the girls threaded their way through the throng to the front of the stage. When Charlie caught sight of Jess, he smiled and blew her a kiss.

'This next song is for Jess,' he said, looking down at her, which made her blush furiously. 'It's called, 'Loving you.'

Neither Ellie nor Jess could look at the other, but Ellie sensed every emotion Jess was feeling. She knew how much her friend adored Charlie and it was becoming very clear that his feelings totally mirrored her own. Throughout the song, he gazed into her eyes, and when Jess was brave enough to do the same she looked back into those blue eyes that held hers so lovingly.

Once or twice, as Ellie was dancing she caught Henry looking at her, and it was as if he was someone else entirely. Concentrating on his long fingers, she watched him pluck and strum the strings of his guitar and all she could think about was how she'd love him to cradle her as he was holding his guitar. Ellie tried so hard to blot out the image but she could feel those fingers on her skin, and what was more, she wanted to experience their touch. When she saw him looking, she smiled at him and, unbelievably, he smiled back. It was a smile that touched her soul. Her body disobeyed every thought and sheer instinct took over. Somewhere deep inside, her senses burned with a desire she hardly recognised. She tried to think with her head but Ellie was confused. She couldn't figure him out, but decided there really wasn't much point in trying to understand him and told herself to snap out of it. He couldn't be a very nice person after what he'd said about Greg, and if he and his family had behaved so badly they really weren't worth knowing.

She wondered what Greg was doing, and thought how much she was missing him.

Charlie announced that they were going to open up the stage to anyone who'd like to join in.

'If you've got what it takes, we'd love to hear you sing,' he said, looking particularly at Jess who shook her head. Liberty looked as if she might make a move, to Ellie's horror, but before she could get anywhere near, there was someone else bounding up the steps.

'Oh no, it's Donald!' Ellie muttered through gritted teeth. 'Please make him stop, someone. Believe me, I've heard him sing and he'd make a cat's choir sound good.'

Donald took the mike, and shielding his eyes from the lights as he looked out into the crowd he declared, 'This song is for someone very special to me. Ellie, are you there?'

'Oh please, no ... he's completely drunk,' Ellie couldn't help saying out loud.

Whilst Donald swayed from side to side, the searchlight beam of a spotlight roamed over the crowd. Ellie tried to hide behind Jess, but then she saw Henry pointing her out. It was impossible to think of anything for him but hatred, at that moment, and as she stood enduring the stares of everyone in the room, Donald began to sing. It was a love song. Donald opened his mouth wide and the noise that came out could only be likened to a caterwauling vixen looking for her mate. Ellie wanted to die right there and then, but instead she looked inanely ahead with a stupefied expression. How she would ever recover she did not know. Ellie had to get out of there. It was time to disappear.

As she headed back for the house she could see Zara making her way over. Thinking she couldn't possibly want to talk to her, Ellie carried on until Zara put out her arm to stop her.

'It's Ellie, isn't it? Can I have a word?'

Ellie couldn't help feeling a little troubled. 'Yes, of course, how can I help you?'

The queen of the withering glance wore her usual haughty

expression along with the sheer fitting dress in blue. She was smiling, but at the same time her eyes, which Ellie likened to ice chips, held no warmth. Zara's manner was hostile, not that she had ever come across as being friendly in the slightest.

'I hear you've been seeing a lot of Greg Whitely, but I just wanted to pass on a word of warning. He's got some history, if you know what I mean, and the Dorsey family will tell you that he's always been pretty awful. Anyway, I think you should be careful – his motives are not always in the best interests of his friends.'

'What do you mean?'

'I don't know any details, exactly, but I know Henry can't stand him and he has good reason. Well, he's hardly top drawer, you know. His family come from one of those sink estates.'

'I don't care what he's done, where he comes from or which class he belongs to – how dare you presume that such things would matter to me. My judgement of people, if indeed it can be called that, is based on my experience and personal knowledge, and so far, nothing you or Henry could say to me would alter the impression I have of Greg Whitely as being one of the nicest people I know.'

'I was only trying to help,' Zara insisted, as her eyebrows rose disdainfully. She stood with her hands on her hipbones, barring Ellie's way. 'I'm only telling you for your own good, and I shan't bother another time.'

Ellie watched Zara sashay away thinking what a nerve she had. Obviously, Henry must have had something to do with Zara's unexpected outburst and she thought what a dismal attempt it had been to salvage his own reputation. When she thought how she had almost changed her mind about Henry after watching him play, she was glad she'd been reminded of the situation with Greg and reprimanded herself for being so shallow as to be taken in by Henry's glamorous side.

Bearing a tray of drinks, she returned to the marquee a quarter of an hour later, by which time the band had finished their set to resounding applause. Another group of Charlie's friends had taken to the stage, all students from his course, and the dancing was resuming. And for a wonderful moment, Donald was nowhere to be seen.

Jess was talking to Charlie, and when she had the chance Ellie asked her to make some enquiries about Greg and Henry. Surely Charlie would know the truth. But, a little later she was only disappointed to hear that Charlie didn't know Greg, although he had backed up what Henry had said.

'Charlie has no reason to dispute what Henry says about Greg,' said Jess. 'He says he's never known a friend like Henry ... he's loyal and honest, and he has the highest opinion of him in the world.'

Ellie was determined that no one would persuade her to think differently about either Greg or Henry, whatever they might say. Suddenly, she felt very tired. When Donald appeared again at her side, all Ellie could hope was that she could soon go home to bed. Tomorrow couldn't come soon enough.

Ellie felt very subdued for the rest of the following week. She couldn't put her finger on why, exactly, but she supposed it had quite a lot to do with the fact that she was missing Greg more than she wanted to admit, and also because she hadn't recovered from being relentlessly pursued by Donald at Charlie's ball. A new week promised a fresh approach and a new start. Arriving at Steventon early on Monday morning, everyone soon settled into their routine and was busy working. Jess eagerly headed up to the operations tent to see Charlie, whilst Liberty and Cara searched for any sign of Greg. Ellie noticed there was still no sign of him and wondered if he'd decided to stay in London even longer. She decided to concentrate on the excavations for a new painting. It would be lovely to have some figures in a composition, and the area they were working on would make a great contrast to the undulating landscape behind them.

Will MacGourtey came over to watch her progress. 'I can't thank you enough, Ellie, for the work you're doing. It really is bringing everything to life, whether it's factual or imagined. Now we've got more of an idea of the layout of the rectory, we can see it was built on very traditional Georgian lines, and your painting of the rectory is spot on.'

'Thank you, Will, that really means a lot,' said Ellie, who wished she could tell him that she knew her painting was very accurate.

'I love the way you've managed to draw from all the sources we have, and there's something so real and authentic about your work.'

'I'm just letting my imagination run riot.'

'No, it's more than that. The architectural details are exquisite, not to mention the particulars like the tiny watering can by the sundial, and the flower beds in front of the windows. I see you've got Mr Austen reading in his study at the back of the house – it's looking incredible. You've such a light touch with colour and form – the sign of a true artist.'

Ellie was almost overwhelmed by Will's praise. He really was lovely to talk to, and he was clearly very knowledgeable about art. 'Thank you, Will, you're so kind.'

'Well, it's the truth. You carry on – you're doing a fantastic job. I've come to ask my excavators to join me up at the top for a little recapitulation. Will you be able to work without them for a while?'

'Oh yes, I've sketched in most of what I need for this painting. I'll just get on with it.'

Will called the others away and Ellie was left to the pleasure of sitting outdoors alone. It was incredibly quiet with everyone gone off to the tent for a talk. There was no camera crew today, no endless shifting of equipment and filming going on, and she thought how wonderful it was to soak up the atmosphere. She put down her paints for a moment and went to stand in the space, which she reckoned must have been the parlour of the rectory, once upon a time. Somewhere up above a bird was singing a most delightful song, and the soft Hampshire breeze stirred her long hair. It felt so good to be in Steventon. Ellie closed her eyes and felt the sun on her face.

## Chapter 17

'It's Mr Lefroy, ma'am,' said the maid, curtseying at the door.

I was more shocked than I could say. I was not expecting him to call, nor had I expected my heart to flutter quite so much at the sight of him. I'd been writing. I was making some notes about a new novel I was thinking about. For once, my mother and I had spent the morning companionably, but I supposed the success of that was due to the fact that we neither of us were talking. We worked best together in silence.

My mother put down her darning, but made no disguise of the fact that she was working. I doubt she would have tidied it away for the king himself. She lifted her noble head and looked down her long nose to scrutinise our guest from the point of his brown leather boots to the yellow hair on his head.

'Come in, dear boy,' she said. 'Come out of the cold and warm yourself by the fire. I'll just get Nanny Hilliard to fetch us a drink to warm us up. Now, what will you have? Our housekeeper makes a splendid posset.'

Tom walked in, twisting his hat in his hand, and he grinned at me when he was sure my mother was looking elsewhere. 'That sounds quite wonderful, Mrs Austen, I thank you.'

My mother left the room and we were alone at last. We looked at one another for what seemed an age, and I felt myself drowning in those eyes that were so like dark seas. I could hardly look at him for any length of time for fear of losing myself forever.

'I hope your journey home was pleasant last night, Miss Austen.'

'It was most agreeable, I thank you, Mr Lefroy.'

'It was late, I expect, by the time you arrived home.'

'It was, indeed.'

'But, not too late for you to make mention of me in your journal, I hope?'

I regarded him steadily. 'How can you be so sure that I keep a journal?'

'Perhaps the sun will not rise tomorrow, and maybe we are not standing here in this room where I may observe every emotion that flits across your mind and affects your figure. Every young woman from seventeen to twenty-five keeps a diary, Miss Austen. No matter, I think I can be certain that I will find my name in it.'

'Insufferable puppy! In any case, you shall never see it.'

'No matter, I shall tell you what's in it. Went to a ball at the Harwoods, where I was quite the belle of the ball. Was accosted by a young man who stole me away to a stone temple and afterwards made me dance the night away with him. Hope to see him again.'

I gasped audibly. 'Tom Lefroy, you are wickedness personified.'

Tom laughed. 'I will not disagree with you, my sweet Jane. Every word you speak is true.'

My heart took a moment to recover from the sound of his voice saying my name. I wished to hear him say it again.

'Did you sleep well after our dancing?'

I laughed. 'It would take many more hours of such activity to put me to sleep, Mr Lefroy. But, I did sleep well.'

'And did you dream or had you thought of me even before your head touched the pillow – perhaps whilst partaking of a little warm wine before bed?'

My blushes gave me away. I ought to have been cross with him, but all I could do was laugh. I offered to take his coat as a diversion from the conversation. I watched him remove his gloves and unbutton his coat, and I wished I'd stayed silent. The moment was so intimate, and when he pulled a sheaf of papers from his chest pocket, I was taken by surprise.

'I've written out some of the songs you requested. They are favourites of mine and I know how much you enjoy an Irish love song from what you told me last night. Perhaps we could sing them together.'

There's nothing I like more than new music, and I moved to the pianoforte and sat down before he could comment on my countenance, which I knew betrayed every feeling, every thought. There were several songs and I was touched that he'd taken the time to write them out. I rifled through them – some of the titles made me want to chuckle.

'*The Yellow-Haired Laddie*, I said, reading from the lyrics. 'And here's one called, *The Irishman*. Are all these songs about you, Mr Lefroy?'

Tom threw back his head and laughed. 'I daresay, but you have seen through me, Miss Austen. I confess; I did not want you to forget me. And I thought, perhaps when I am no longer here, you might be reminded of me in the songs we have shared.'

'Are you going away?'

'Not yet, but I will be leaving soon to continue my studies.'

I did not want to think about the fact that he'd be going to London where he was to study the law.

'We have been to London to spend time with my cousin Eliza,' I said. 'Everyone is rich there and lead the most exotic lives. I have been to the theatre, and the Royal Academy, and seen the wild beasts in the Tower of London.'

'There are wild animals to be had in all parts of London and I'm glad you have seen only the high side of life, Miss Austen. Have you ever been to Astley's Amphitheatre?'

'No, though I have heard it is a great entertainment, and I

should love to see it.'

'Well, should you come for a visit, I should love to take you. I've never seen such an exhibition of horsemanship – quite surpassing even that of the riding one sees in Steventon's own lanes.'

I was blushing when my mother returned just at that moment with Nanny Hilliard who bore a tray with steaming cups of hot milk posset.

'Here we are, just the thing to warm you through, Mr Lefroy.'

Tom took a seat by the fire. He looked very thoughtful for a moment as he stared into the flickering flames.

'How are your mother and the Colonel?' asked my mother.

'They are both very well. I had a letter from Mama only yesterday. Her sister Gardiner is staying with her for Christmas.'

'It will be good for her to have the company of a sister, I'm sure. And, are all your brothers and sisters at home?'

'Yes, my brother Anthony will be home from his regiment, and my sisters will be glad to see him. With five elder sisters there will be balls aplenty, you can imagine, and they are always hankering after a partner.'

'Sisters always miss their brothers when they are gone,' I said. 'Men are so lucky to have employment to take them away. As much as I love my beloved home, I must admit I would like an adventure.'

'You always were a restless soul,' said my mother, 'and I am sure if anyone can find a way, it will be you who will find that adventure you seek. Jane loves to travel, Mr Lefroy.'

'Except I have not travelled very far! But, the idea of seeing fresh places is so exciting to me.'

'I wish you could see Ireland, Miss Austen. I think you would love the country where I grew up. Limerick has become a prosperous town but when one gets beyond the city walls there is beautiful Irish landscape as far as the eye can see.'

'Ireland is celebrated in much folklore and famed for its beauty. I am certain I would not be disappointed.'

'You should come when the first cuckoo calls and the bluebells flourish in the woods and drift into the fields. Or when the swallows return to bring summer with them. You'll never see the like of wildflowers as there are in Ireland, planted by the pixies they say. Buttercups as large as a saucer, poppies enamelled in scarlet and wild geranium in swathes of purple over the meadows ... to walk barefoot across the dew-drenched fields of emerald green is a favourite delight of mine.'

I could see it in my head. 'You paint a beautiful picture.'

There was silence for a moment as we became thoughtful. I could not help watching Tom and the way the firelight flickered across his face, highlighting his fair eyelashes and his cheekbones. He wore a light grey coat which I thought became him far more than his favourite white one, perhaps because it brought out the colour of his rain-washed eyes.

'Are you attending the Manydown Ball with your aunt and uncle?' my mother said, at last.

'Yes, I believe we are going. I have had the pleasure of meeting the Bigg-Wither family, and danced with Catherine and Alethea at Deane.'

My mother pursed her lips, a sure sign that she was about to be indiscreet. 'Poor Harris will never be as clever as his sisters though he has Manydown Park in his favour. He is rich, to be sure, but nothing will ever cure of him of that terrible stammer. I've seen it before, and I'm certain it can only get worse. However, he is a gentleman and that might stand him in good stead even if his manners may not always belong to that class. And, I've a mind to say; someone could do a lot worse than marry him. They'll have a comfortable life, and be able to look after their relatives with ease.'

I knew Harris was on a list of suitors my mother preferred. That he was somewhere near the bottom of the list did not make the fact any easier. Constantly reminded that Cassandra and I should look to money for happiness, I shuddered to think of the sacrifice I might have to make one day.

Tom didn't speak when I looked up and caught his eye, but he knew what I was thinking and I was shamed to think how easily he had seen through my mother's outburst. He rolled his eyes in sympathy and I almost burst out laughing.

'Mr Lefroy has been so good as to bring us some new music, Mama.'

'How very kind. Do you play yourself?

'I enjoy rattling out a tune, Mrs Austen, though with so many sisters at home it's not often that I get the chance. I am required as a dancing partner for many a practice performance. I was dancing a reel at the age of two to oblige the ladies in my house.'

My mother laughed. 'Brothers are very useful in the dancing class especially those that are happy to comply. Henry has always been the great dancer in this family, though I think Charles may well prove to be his equal.'

Nanny Hilliard appeared at the door. 'I'm sorry, Mrs Austen, but John Bond sent me to fetch you about one of the dairy herd. He says he didn't want to worry you earlier but he's concerned about one of them.'

My mother removed her spectacles. 'Forgive me, Mr Lefroy, but there's always farm business to attend. Perhaps Jane will play for you whilst I'm about the cows.'

We burst out laughing when she'd gone. 'What a picture she conjures up – my mother always did have a way with words.'

Tom stood up. 'There's room for two on that seat if you move up a little.'

I shuffled along the seat and took a moment to look through the sheaf of music again – anything to attempt to hide my discomposure. Tom sat down next to me. It was impossible not to touch him and I felt the length of his thigh through my gown. His arm went around the back of me. I started and jumped, but he was only reaching for a piece of music. I did not know how I should play for my fingers trembled. I laid them in my lap but they would not be still.

'This one is my favourite.'

I turned to look at him. He was looking at my mouth and his

eyes told me of his desire, so much that I was sure he was going to kiss my lips. I longed to feel them on mine and when his mouth moved towards mine, I closed my eyes.

'It's called *Robin Adair*.'

My eyes flickered open. Tom was staring ahead studying the music with intent.

'My family are not rich, Miss Austen.'

Why he had chosen to divulge that particular piece of information at that second in time I could not imagine. 'Then we have something in common.'

'Precisely.'

I looked at him, and the warmth had gone out of his face. He looked the same sulky boy I had first seen in Madame's parlour. 'You have no idea, do you?'

'I'm afraid I do not know what you are talking about, Mr Lefroy.'

His face softened into a smile. 'It is not good for me to spend time with you, Miss Austen. You arouse such feelings …'

'I share them,' I dared to say.

'Then, I must go.'

Without another word or glance, he grabbed his coat and rushed out of the room.

## Chapter 18

    Ellie was so used to falling in and out of time that she didn't question what had just happened. But, every encounter with Tom Lefroy left her feeling more immersed in that world and more confused by her feelings. All she knew was that even though Jane was the one left sitting alone at the pianoforte, it was Ellie who had longed for him to kiss her. She knew that she was falling in love with Tom. However stupid or impossible, she couldn't help the way she felt. Each meeting made her feel more vulnerable and she knew that if Tom had chosen to kiss her then she would have kissed him right back. Ellie refused to listen to the voice that told her not to be ridiculous, that Tom wasn't falling for *her* but for a girl who had lived two hundred years ago. Every look, every touch, she felt was for her alone. If she closed her eyes she could see him as clearly as if he were here now, but no amount of willing herself to return would do any good. It wasn't happening. Wondering how long she'd been sitting there, she glanced at her watch though she knew, as on any other occasion, time would not have changed. It seemed time in the present did not alter. Whilst she could live for hours and perhaps days in the past, if a second passed in the present she would have been surprised. She could only liken the experience to dreaming where whole days away could pass so fleetingly.

Looking up the field at the tent in the distance, she imagined they'd still be talking and so she had time to collect her thoughts and feelings. As she watched, a figure came out, someone in a hurry. She watched them as they started to run and Ellie knew it was Jess and that she was also looking really upset. By the time she reached her, Ellie could see her tears coursing down her cheeks.

'Whatever is the matter? Jess, what's wrong?'

Jess threw herself into Ellie's arms. 'Charlie's gone!'

In between sobs, Ellie heard the tale. 'Apparently, something's come up in London. Will MacGourtey told me. It's something to do with the tour; they're starting it earlier. He said it sounded like a big break for the band. They've all gone, even Henry and Zara.'

Privately, whilst Ellie felt sorry about Charlie she didn't think losing the other two would be any great loss, but she was surprised. She thought Henry loved the work on the dig. It was supposed to be his passion in life. 'Perhaps it's just for a couple of days. They'll be back soon. Charlie won't stay away from you for long, I'm sure.'

'Oh, Ellie, I don't know what to think. I've tried phoning his mobile but it just goes to voicemail. He didn't even tell me he was going.'

'Look, he probably just hasn't had time. Give it a few hours. I'm sure he'll be in touch and you'll see, your worries are for nothing. It's probably something really exciting, and who knows, maybe he wants to surprise you. You never know, perhaps it's a record deal or something.'

Jess stopped crying and Ellie dried her eyes with a tissue. 'That's better. It's obvious to the whole world that Charlie is as in love with you as you are with him. Try not to worry, he'll come through in the end.'

Whilst they were standing there, Ellie noticed someone else make an appearance. She had no chance to get away, what with Jess being really upset, and so she gritted her teeth in readiness for the usual assault.

'Whatever you do, don't leave me,' Ellie mouthed.

Jess looked up and managed a smile. 'He doesn't give up easily, does he?'

'Hi girls,' said Donald, striding over the grass towards them. He was sucking on a piece of grass, bits of which were left sticking between his teeth.

'Why aren't you at the conference?' Ellie asked.

'Oh, that's finished now. It was just a matter of tying up loose ends this morning, and saying goodbye.'

'So, you'll be going back home now then?'

'Not exactly. Listen, Ells, I need to talk to you about something.'

Ellie gripped Jess's hand. 'I haven't got time now. Jess has just received some distressing news and I'm really busy. Sorry, Donald, some other time, perhaps.'

Donald looked very disappointed. 'Right, I'll talk to you later if you're sure we can't have a word now.'

'I'm quite sure, Donald.'

'Okey dokey! I'll see you at supper then.'

Ellie didn't answer. They watched him walk away, both breathing a sigh of relief when he disappeared out of view.

'I told you he was persistent,' said Ellie, raking her fingers through her hair in frustration. 'I know exactly what he's going to ask me. How many times do I have to tell him that I don't want to go out with him.'

Jess was looking despondent again. 'Oh, Ellie, I miss him so much already. I really had no idea just how much I'd fallen in love with Charlie until this happened.'

Ellie would have shaken Charlie if she'd seen him. How could he do this to her best friend without giving her any word of it? Jess was still in a very vulnerable state and something like this could really knock her back. Men were so thoughtless at times.

'I'm sure you'll hear from him before the end of the day. I know I'm right about his feelings for you and that there must be a good reason that he hasn't been in touch.'

'When you put it like that, I must admit I feel reassured. He's probably got a lot on his mind and if something interesting for him has come up, he probably hasn't even had the opportunity to think about letting me know.'

'That's the spirit, Jess. He's probably locked in some dungeon of a rehearsal room. And, you know what creative types are like ... once they're composing, everything else just doesn't figure on their radar.'

Jess looked much happier. 'I'm being very selfish, I know, just thinking about myself and how much I'm going to miss him. I hope it is going to be a big break for him. His mother would love him to be in an orchestra, but I know Charlie's writing music and playing for his band means so much to him. I'm not sure about Henry, though Charlie kept saying that he was really committed. It was a shock, wasn't it? I hadn't taken him for a musician at all.'

Ellie instantly conjured up a picture of Henry playing his guitar and though she would never admit it to Jess, she was surprised by the strength of her emotions. When he was playing she'd seen him in a totally different light. He'd moved her and had made her face some pretty basic feelings. Henry had stirred something deep inside her soul, but whilst Ellie recognised that she'd been aroused by the very sight of him, she quickly pushed those thoughts to the back of her mind. He was every bit as arrogant and one-dimensional as she'd always believed him to be and she was going to hang on to those memories.

'Yes, it was a surprise, and for a single moment, I thought he might be human after all.'

'Oh, Ellie, I'm sure he's not as bad as all that.'

'Well, I for one am glad I'm not going to have to find out for the time being. I expect he feels far more at home in London with the Shoreditch in-crowd. I can just picture him with a bunch of his egotistical friends all trying so hard to be cool and trendy in their too-skinny jeans.'

Jess was laughing now and looking far more relaxed. 'Ellie,

you are wickedly funny and observant, but I don't think I really know Henry that well to dismiss him completely.'

'I wouldn't expect anything less from you, Jess. You are so kind I think you'd find something good to say about a serial killer. I'm glad to see you smiling and you'll see, Charlie will be back before you can dance the Hoxton Hoedown.'

'Is that a real dance, Ellie?'

'I've no idea, but I'm sure if there is such a thing, they'll be doing it in the fashionable East End.'

Ellie watched Jess walk away looking a little happier than she had ten minutes before, but she knew her friend would soon feel despondent again if Charlie failed to get in touch. At least she didn't have to see Henry or Charlie's irritating sister, and for that she felt happy.

She'd just picked up her paintbrush and was busy putting in the details of the trees on the horizon when a shadow fell across the white page of her sketchpad. Her heart leapt before she'd even looked up because in that split second she'd already decided it must be Greg returned from London.

'Hi, Baby.'

Ellie looked up as she recognised the voice. Donald was standing there and she couldn't have felt less happy.

'What are you doing here, Donald? I'm busy, I haven't got time to chat, I'm afraid.'

'Ellie, I have to speak to you.'

The volunteers were returning, picking up their implements and carrying on their careful work though Ellie could see one or two people were clearly fascinated by the exchange that was taking place between her and Donald.

'Please, Donald, not now,' Ellie whispered as quietly as it was possible to do. 'Can't it wait until later?'

'No, it can't.' Donald had a look of determination about him. He took a deep breath before he raised his voice. 'I've something to say that I'd like everyone to hear.'

Suddenly, Ellie felt really frightened. Her powers of intuition and her sixth sense were communicating very strongly that Donald was about to reveal the inner workings of his heart to the whole world and there was nothing she could do to stop him.

In one swift moment, Donald fell to his knees and almost simultaneously pulled an object from his pocket, except his hand got stuck and a loud ripping noise announced the fact that the fabric of his suit was now torn. Ellie knew before she looked that the object he held before her was a box. It was a ring box and in its velvet interior a large diamond ring sparkled.

'Ellie Bentley, will you marry me?'

Ellie was so shocked, she couldn't think what to do or say straight away. The fact that a large crowd was gathering around them and most of the ladies in the audience were making oohing and aahing noises only made it worse.

'I see you are at a loss for words, and dearest, Ellie, I understand only too well that this must come as a huge surprise, though I think you know how long I have loved and adored you. Last night put the final seal on my affections and with your encouragement; I couldn't wait to share my feelings with the world. Your very silence on the matter is testament to your sensitive and insightful personality, those traits in your character that I have long since admired and praised, and only make you more perfect in my eyes.'

Ellie found her tongue at last. 'Please get up off your knees at once, Donald. I am very sorry if I have encouraged you in any way to think that the feelings you have for me are in any way reciprocated. This is truly difficult for me to express, as I have no wish to hurt your feelings, but I cannot marry you.'

Donald appealed to the crowd who were still looking on and showed no inclination to stop. 'She doesn't mean it, does she? I know all of you ladies like a little drama and a little pretence. It's not the thing to look too eager, now is it? I'll ask you one more time. Ellie …'

The crowd were now clapping and cheering Donald on, the

noise rising to a crescendo as some of the Oxford crowd were beginning to see the humour in the situation.

'Please don't say it again, Donald. This is hard enough. Why would I say no when I mean yes, for goodness' sake?'

The crowd were very quiet all of a sudden. It was beginning to look as if they didn't want to be witness to any more now it was all going so horribly wrong. Ellie was trying so hard to keep her temper but was losing it rapidly especially when she heard some of the whispering from a few of the volunteers who seemed to be blaming her for leading on 'that nice vicar'.

'Did my mother put you up to this?' Ellie asked, 'because I honestly can't see how anyone could possibly have got the wrong idea about my feelings. From the very first time you tried to get my attention, I think I made it perfectly clear that I was not interested in you. We haven't even dated. How could you possibly think that I would say yes to a proposal of marriage?'

'Well, I suppose your mother did encourage me a little.'

'I knew it. Just wait until I see her.'

'You might not have to wait too long.'

Out of the corner of her eye she saw a battered mini pull up and in the next second the door was open and her mother was running across the field towards them. 'Ellie! Just a minute ... think what you are doing!'

'What are you doing here, Mum?'

'Ellie, you'll never get another chance like this. Don't do what I did and settle for anything less than a man with good prospects. Donald, tell her about your inheritance.'

'You have to be kidding, Mum! Why are you doing this?'

'It's about time you got your head out of the clouds. You're never going to make any money being an artist and Donald is offering you a life where you'll be able to indulge every creative whim you have, plus, you'll never want for another thing. When I think of all the years I've scrimped and saved and made the best of that poky little house that we don't even own ourselves. You have an opportunity and you'd be a very silly girl not to take it.'

As if matters could not get any worse, Ellie observed one or two of the film crew turning up and reaching for their cameras, and then she saw her father get out of the car, striding across the grass. When he reached her she threw herself into his arms.

'Reginald, tell your daughter that she's making a huge mistake.'

Ellie's father looked completely perplexed. 'I'm not sure I understand. Sorry, Ellie, your mother hasn't exactly told me what's going on.'

'Ellie is determined to refuse Donald's proposal.'

'And what has that to do with me?'

'For heavens sake, Reggie, tell her she must marry him.'

'Is this correct? Donald has asked you to marry him?'

'Yes.'

'But, you have refused him?'

'I have.'

'Right. Well, your mother insists that you accept him. Isn't that right, Margaret?'

'Yes ... or I will never speak to her again.'

'So, now you have a difficult decision to make. From this moment, you will have to make the sad choice of cutting off one of your parents. Your mother will not see you again if you refuse to marry Donald, and I will never see you if you do!'

The crowd, who far from dispersing, were now laughing wholeheartedly and Ellie couldn't help but join in. She saw her mother stomp off and her father saunter back to the car. Ellie knew her mother would probably not speak to him for a couple of days, but as silly as she was, she didn't bear a grudge for long, and her darling dad would not take any notice. He'd bury himself in his study with his sermons and that would be the end of it.

Donald didn't look any worse for being humiliated. Ellie couldn't believe someone could be so thick-skinned and her only fear was that this little episode would not alter anything. Whatever the exchange, Donald did not give up easily.

'Well, I just hope you don't live to regret your choice, Ellie, because if you truly don't want me, I shall look for someone else. Did you really mean no? You will not consider marrying me?'

'No, Donald, I will not consider marrying you. I'm sorry, but it would never work.'

There was a groan from the crowd. Some were returning to their work, as it seemed they were satisfied there was not much more to be seen. Ellie and Donald were left quite alone.

'You'll be very lucky if you find someone else willing to put up with your bohemian ways, Ellie. Not to mention the fact that I already have a house of my own and will inherit my father's on his death, plus a cash sum of at least a million pounds.'

'And, I hope you and your money will be very happy, Donald. I'm sure there is a young lady out there just waiting for you, but it's not me.'

Donald gave her one last lingering glance before he loped back down over the field and out into the lane. Ellie knew it was probably too much to hope that he'd now leave, but she was ever optimistic. She turned to see Martha standing with a concerned expression.

'Oh, Ellie, how desperately awful.'

'It's all right, no harm done.'

'But, he looks absolutely heartbroken.'

Ellie realised she'd completely misinterpreted Martha's sympathy. 'Don't worry; he'll get over it. In fact, I am completely convinced that he'll be thoroughly recovered by teatime.'

Martha looked thoughtful. 'Does he really have all that money and a house of his own?'

'I think he does, but as far as I'm concerned, all the money in the world would not induce me to marry Donald.'

'He's not an unpleasant person,' Martha continued. 'Anyone who married him would have a very good life, I think.'

'And I wish them the greatest luck,' said Ellie, picking up her paintbrush and thinking how relieved she felt that it was all over.

## Chapter 19

To Ellie's great surprise, Donald was still in residence at Ashe when they returned that evening. Supper was very subdued, and the atmosphere in the house was understandably strained. Donald refused to speak to Ellie, but Jess managed to find out that despite what had happened, he was going to stay until a fortnight on Saturday exactly as he had always planned. Martha seemed happy to chat to Donald and for that Ellie was immensely grateful. Even if all she received were resentful silences when she attempted to speak to him, Martha was able to draw him out and engage him in some conversation.

The next day brought some news from London but Jess was still as puzzled and upset as ever.

'I've had a text from Zara, but it's very brief and doesn't really tell me very much that I didn't already know. She says that Charlie is busy with some unexpected business to do with the band, and that it's very hush-hush. That's about it, and still nothing from Charlie himself.'

'Does she say how long they'll be in London?' asked Ellie.

'No, there's nothing more. I texted her back, but I've had no reply. I would have phoned but she's being so evasive I'm getting definite signals that I shouldn't. And I really couldn't bear it if it went to voicemail again. Above everything else, I don't want to look desperate and I'm beginning to think I've been reading far too much into what happened between Charlie and me.'

'Jess, believe me, if you've read too much into Charlie's obvious attraction to you then I think the whole world will be under the same impression. There couldn't have been a single person at the Deane ball who didn't think the same as I do. Charlie is in love with you, that I know. For goodness' sake, he even sang how much he loved you in a song dedicated to you.'

'I don't know, Ellie, it was just a song.'

Ellie was about to argue when the sound of Jess's phone sending another text caught them both by surprise. 'Who is it?'

'It's Zara.'

Jess's face looked crestfallen. Tears were welling in her eyes.

'Whatever is the matter?' cried Ellie, rushing over to Jess and putting a comforting arm round her shoulders.

Jess read the text out loud. 'V. exciting! Henry's sis Pippa's joined the band – on vocals with Charlie. They had a fling last year – never seen 2 peeps so much in love as they were. Looks like it's back on!!! More soon. Love Z x.'

Jess handed over the phone and Ellie saw it in black and white.

'This doesn't mean anything, Jess.'

'I think Zara is telling me in no uncertain terms that Charlie has another girl in his life, and that he's never had any feelings for me other than that of friendship. It's perfectly clear that's what she thinks or surely she could never have written to me like that.'

'Well, I take the opposite view, Jess. Zara knows that Charlie is in love with you, but she wants him to be with Pippa. No doubt, because she wants Henry for herself and thinks she might have more of a shot with him if Pippa is putting in a good word for her. I wouldn't believe a word she says ... it's just wishful thinking on her part ... on both counts.'

Jess shook her head. 'Ellie, you are so sweet, but you cannot be right.'

'I would bet money on the fact that Zara is keeping Charlie away from you on purpose. Who knows what she's said to him. She clearly sees an opportunity. And talking of money – the Dorseys are rich, and whatever people say about us living in a classless society in the modern age, it's a load of rubbish. Zara wants Henry and she wants Pippa for her brother in a 'money begets more money' scenario. But, this doesn't mean that Charlie will be capable of changing his mind or feeling any less for you.'

'But, the facts are there. Charlie was in love before, and I'm sure Zara isn't making it up.'

'Charlie may well have had some sort of fling with this Pippa girl, but it isn't necessarily the case that he was in love with her. It's more likely it wasn't very serious or it would have been extremely difficult for them to work together again.'

'I still think Zara is telling the truth, or at least, that's what she truly believes. I'm sure she wouldn't purposely want to hurt me.'

'If you want to believe that, go ahead.'

'But, if you're right, how could I possibly think about being with Charlie if his sister dislikes me so much.'

'You'll have to make a decision about that,' said Ellie, 'and if you think that the distress of offending his sister is more than equal to the happiness of being with him, then perhaps you'd better not be with him.'

'How can you say such a thing? You must know nothing Zara could say or do would ever separate me from Charlie if I thought he was truly in love with me.'

'Precisely!'

'But, I may never get the opportunity to see him again. I don't even know where he's staying.'

'That is immaterial, Jess. You'll see, in time. I know Charlie just won't be able to stay away for long. Whatever's he's doing and however pre-occupied with work, he will not be able to resist seeing you again. Stay just where you are. He'll soon be back!'

The next fortnight passed in a quiet way. Work at the dig carried on in the same methodical fashion and the mapping out of the old rectory was almost completed. Ellie was worried about Jess, and hoped her disappointment with Charlie's disappearance would not impact on her health. She was still vulnerable, and to see such sadness in Jess's eyes made her heart ache.

The evenings were spent at Ashe. Long days meant that the girls could swim or play tennis in the courts at the back of the garden, or sit and read a book in the walled garden where pink bricks glowed in the warmth of the setting sunshine and lances of light speared the trees to illuminate hollyhocks and larkspur, delphiniums and sweet stocks in the beds below. Mrs Hill spoiled them with treats from the garden. Finding out how much Jess loved meringue, she made a Pavlova and topped it with thick cream and fresh strawberries. Jess smiled with pleasure, but Ellie knew she was not happy, however hard she was trying to hide it. Charlie made no effort to contact her, and Ellie knew her hope was fading further. Jess stopped talking about him altogether. After sending Zara another text and having received no answer, Jess seemed resigned to the fact that she'd been completely forgotten and that Charlie was gone forever.

At least there were two people in the house who seemed happy. Ellie had never seen Martha so animated. She and Donald spent much time together chatting, and Ellie couldn't have been more grateful. He'd stopped giving her long, silent stares, and simply ignored her. Several times, Ellie came across them in a quiet spot in the garden. Donald would be reading to Martha from a book, and she didn't even appear to be bored or find him irritating. On Friday, Ellie took Martha to one side.

'I can't thank you enough for looking after Donald,' she said.

'It's a pleasure, Ellie. I don't mind, really.'

'Well, it's very kind, but I must admit, I'm feeling a little guilty. Honestly, you really don't need to give him all your attention. He's quite capable of looking after himself, and it's not as if he has a broken heart or anything.'

'Oh, I know,' said Martha. 'He told me he's quite recovered, and can't think now what he ever saw in you. I don't mind being with him. Anyway, it's our duty to think of others before ourselves.'

Ellie had to stop herself from laughing out loud. She wasn't quite sure how to reply, and could only be thankful that he had seen sense at last.

Saturday came but by mid-afternoon Ellie feared that Donald may have changed his mind about leaving to go back to his job. He and Martha were closeted together for much of the day, and even Ellie began to think she was taking her sense of social responsibility too far. After supper, Donald made an appearance in the kitchen with his suitcase in hand. Liberty and Cara were outside sunbathing by the swimming pool, whilst Ellie, Jess and Mrs Hill were clearing the last of the supper dishes.

'I'm off now,' he said, pulling at the collar round his neck. The heat was making his face rather red, and the old hanky was dabbed ineffectually over his forehead, moist with sweat. 'I'm getting the last train, but I wanted to thank you, Mrs Hill, for your wonderful hospitality, and, to say goodbye … until next time.'

Ellie noticed Martha coming through the kitchen door. Her normally lank and greasy hair was shining brightly like a chestnut, and she wore a summer dress and matching sandals with a rope of old-fashioned pearls around her neck. She looked almost pretty, and as she stood looking slightly pink and self-conscious, Ellie noticed something else. Martha wore a ring on the third finger of her left hand. It was a jewel she recognised, and when she saw the diamond winking in the light, Ellie had to clamp her mouth together for fear of it dropping to the floor.

'Before I go, we have an announcement to make,' said Donald, frantically mopping his head. Martha came to stand at his side, and before she could say another word, Donald had taken her in his arms and was slobbering over her, sucking her lips until the others didn't know where to look.

Jess and Mrs Hill were equally shocked; both by the exhibition of lip-locking and the unexpected turn in events.

Donald finally let go of Martha who seemed to be struggling for air. 'Martha has agreed to become my wife. We are engaged!'

It seemed it had all been arranged in the time it took Liberty to down a vodka and tonic. There was a moment of shocked silence before the others remembered to offer their congratulations. Donald and Martha beamed before clamping lips together once more, leaving the others to exchange glances with wry smiles and raised eyebrows.

'I think I speak for my fiancée when I say that we have never experienced such happiness, and can only look forward to a very happy life together. And, it goes without saying, that I shall look forward to us all being together again very soon.'

When Ellie waved him off from the door and watched Martha's tears as he stepped into the taxi, she could hardly believe her eyes. She noticed Martha dabbed at her eyes with the same grubby handkerchief that Donald had been using ever since he arrived.

'I know what you're thinking, Ellie, but your mother made a lot of sense.'

'Martha, you hardly know him! And, I cannot understand why you'd get engaged before you've even been out with him. You know what he is ... how could you?'

Martha blew her nose into the grimy cloth. 'It's all very well for you to say, Ellie. I've never had anyone look at me, let alone have a boyfriend. When Donald asked me to marry him, I had to say yes, and I might as well spend the rest of my life with someone, as not. I can't bear the thought of living under my mother's influence for even the foreseeable future. If I could afford to buy my own home or even rent somewhere it might be different, but in London that's impossible for a single girl, and the thought of sharing again with a lot of people is perfectly horrid to me. With Donald I'll have a good chance to be happy.'

'I fail to see how you could possibly be happy – you cannot be in love with him.'

'All I want is a nice house. Every good-looking girl on the

planet gets a handsome husband and a lovely home. Having both would be an impossible feat. Would you really deny me at least one of them?'

'I suppose not.' Ellie did not know what else to say. She knew she could not ever behave in the same way and would never understand Martha's decision. To live without love or to sacrifice oneself for a compromise, especially when that involved someone as hideous as Donald, was unthinkable.

Ellie went in search of Jess. The announcement of the engagement between Martha and Donald would not only have been a shock but would most likely have reminded Jess of Charlie and their estrangement. She headed back to the kitchen to find her, but before she got to the green baize door, which separated the domestic part of the house from the rest, she heard the grandfather clock striking. Each silver strike sounded longer than the last and as the mechanism whirred into action, Ellie felt her surroundings subtly shifting and changing. The binding hold of the present was slipping and an all-pervading stillness reigned. Grasping the moment out of eternity Ellie held on, absorbing every second. She turned, not knowing which way to go, and then she saw him. There was Tom in evening dress looking more handsome than ever.

## Chapter 20

Madame Lefroy rushed into the hallway looking more beautiful and younger than her years.

'Ah, Jane, here you are. Thank you for your kindness in taking Thomas to Manydown. Do thank James very much for taking pity on us. Now, where is my cloak and where is the rest of my family? Come along! We should make haste!'

Reverend Lefroy, Ben and Lucy appeared in a flurry of movement as coats and pelisses, cloaks and capes were thrown on. All was noise, bustle and motion before we were left alone in the echoing hallway at last. I was determined not to be intimidated by him and the grave looks he was giving me. I tried to look past his dark coat, which contrasted so beautifully with the golden curls touching his collar, and I steeled myself to look anywhere but into those cold eyes of slate grey.

'Good evening, Mr Lefroy. I've been sent to fetch you, and our carriage awaits. Do not look alarmed, sir, my brothers share the vehicle and will ensure you come to no harm.'

'Miss Austen ...'

'It is no matter to me, Mr Lefroy, whether you should stay or run away from me, though it seems 'tis happening with alarming regularity. But, I would only add that if your idea is to lessen the wagging tongues that start simply because we are having a conversation, then your hope is a false one. It is too late.'

'You do not understand, Miss Austen.'

'On the contrary, I understand you very well. But, hear this. Whatever gossip may have been repeated, I am not 'setting my cap at you' or trying to 'catch you', both common-place phrases by which wit is intended, and which are quite odious and abhorrent to me. If I choose to speak to you or dance with you, it is because I like talking and I enjoy dancing. I have no other motive. Is that perfectly clear?'

'I did not mean to give you the wrong impression. Yesterday, when you called, I had just received ...'

Tom faltered. I could see he was at a loss for words.

'You had a letter from Ireland, I suppose, and wanted time to read it. Was it from your sweetheart?'

His pale skin was tinged with pink to the very tips of his ears. 'It was a letter ... requiring some attention.'

I knew it was from a girl, and I would have staked my life upon the fact that this particular girl was someone special to him. But, I would not find out anything like this.

'Come, let us not quarrel,' I said. 'If you smile at me I shall allow you to open the ball with me.'

Manydown, the beautiful home of my friends, Elizabeth, Catherine and Alethea Bigg, sparkled in snow and moonlight, the illuminations from the glasshouse throwing coloured light across the deep blue drifts. There were a great many carriages arriving, and many of our neighbours were handed down to carefully pick their way across icy paths to the welcoming glow of the house. James, Henry and Tom chatted companionably all the way, and I would not be telling the truth if I did not admit how much that gladdened my heart. He fitted in so easily. They shared the same sense of humour, and the same easy attitude to life in general, as they talked of the sport they'd enjoyed in the week after Christmas.

The room was full of the usual company. Everyone who had

danced at Deane was set to do it again, though perhaps with less zeal of the festive period just passed. Added to them were the Grants, St. Johns, Lady Rivers, her three daughters and a son, Mr and Miss Heathcote, Mrs Lefevre, two Mr Watkins, Mr J. Portal, the Miss Deanes, two Miss Ledgers, and a tall clergyman who came with them.

My mother and Madame had taken up their habitual places by one of the fires in the ballroom, and as we approached I heard her telling mama that it was Tom's birthday.

'Thomas has received so many letters from home this week, have you not?'

I was surprised for he'd given me no inkling of it. He was looking at me with a smirk on his face and I knew what he was thinking. He wanted me to feel shame-faced about teasing him for the letter from a supposed sweetheart. I would not be so obliging. As far as I was concerned, I was sure it was a lover's missive.

'I did, indeed,' said Tom, looking to his aunt. 'Birthday greetings are always welcome, and my sisters are great letter writers.'

'I have often thought that ladies write so much better letters than gentlemen!' I said. 'Indeed, I think the superiority was always on our side.'

'Jane, do not run on so,' scolded my mother. 'Your father is an excellent example of a gentleman who writes a most diverting letter.'

'I am sure there are exceptions to the rule, Mrs Austen,' said Tom, bowing in her direction, 'though in general I would agree with Miss Jane. As far as I have had the opportunity of judging, it appears to me that the usual style of letter-writing among women is faultless ... except in three particulars.'

'And what are they?'

'A general deficiency of subject, a total inattention to stops, and a very frequent ignorance of grammar.'

My mother and Madame seemed to find this amusing, but I could not laugh. He had the upper hand, and that I did not find diverting in the least.

'Well, fancy that, a birthday just a day before our very own Cassandra's. Many Happy Returns, Mr Lefroy,' said my mother. 'I hope you're enjoying your visit.'

Tom was much easier in my mother's company these days. She'd stopped saying what a foolish and proud puppy he was, and I was glad that she seemed to like him. It would be difficult not to like him, I thought, however much he vexed me when he was enjoying a 'superior' moment.

'I am enjoying my aunt's hospitality exceedingly, Mrs Austen,' said Tom. 'And, it has been such a pleasure to meet all your family, though I am very sorry not to have met the beautiful Miss Austen of whom I have heard so much. I believe she is away at present.'

'Yes, and I'm afraid that you may well be gone before she comes home. She is a very handsome girl, Mr Lefroy, with the sweetest temper you will ever find. All the young gentlemen here are anxious for her return. Why, Benjamin Portal called this morning especially to ask after her health. Now, he is a handsome fellow.'

I noticed she said nothing of Cassandra's engagement. It was not common knowledge, and I suspected that my mother still harboured hopes that Cassy would do better for herself. One of us would have to marry well, as we had nothing to attract anyone of high rank except our beauty. It was unlikely that Cassy's Tom would find riches as a clergyman so it looked as if I might be expected to find a wealthy husband. I disliked my mother's scheming however well she tried to conceal her efforts. She was always sending me to Kent in the hopes that one of Edward's friends might take a liking to me, whilst pretending that seeing new places was an education. Fortunately, I was not averse to travelling, if not always wishing to be in Kent. Cassandra and my sister-in-law, Elizabeth, were better housemates. It was difficult when I was away from home to be able to write freely. Whole days in Steventon would disappear sitting at my writing box. Darling papa had presented me with this delicious gift on my birthday, not quite a month ago. Made from mahogany, with a glass inkstand and brass lock and key, it was my delight, and it would mean that when travelling all my precious manuscripts could come with me hidden away inside.

Tom asked me for the first dance, and I couldn't have been happier. All stiffness and reserve melted away, and he was just as much fun as he'd been on previous occasions when he'd let me glimpse the real Tom. There wasn't anyone else in the world I'd rather dance with, but I did not want for partners. I danced twice with John Warren, and once with Mr Charles Watkins, and, to my inexpressible astonishment, I entirely escaped John Lyford. I was forced to fight hard for it, however, as I found myself quite alone with him in the corridor, and he was most insistent. I escaped as soon as I could, finding a chair away from my mother's watching eyes. Mindful that my sister had already cautioned me in a letter about singling out certain partners or dancing too many times with the same young man, I found that I had no wish to abide by her rules, and by the time I'd had a glass of punch or two, I'd entirely forgotten them.

James danced with Alethea, and Henry with everyone else. I heard him tell Catherine that he was still hankering after a commission in the Regulars, and as his project of purchasing the adjutancy of the Oxfordshire was now over, he'd got a scheme in his head about getting a lieutenancy and adjutancy in the 86th, a new-raised regiment, which he fancied would be ordered to the Cape of Good Hope. What a Henry! I could only wish all his schemes would come to naught.

I was enjoying watching him dance as I caught my breath and sipped my glass of Negus. Tom was dancing with Alethea, but when he could, I noticed he was looking over at me. Thankfully, Alethea didn't seem to mind or notice. I tried to look around the room at other things and concentrated hard on watching anyone else dance, but I felt Tom's eyes were always upon me, and when the dance finished, I knew he would find me.

'Sitting down, Miss Austen? That is not like you.'

'Believe me, if you'd just been chased down the hallway by Mr Lyford you might well be sitting down trying to compose yourself. A glass of punch is steadying my nerves!'

Tom laughed. 'I often thank the stars for being a gentleman, and am grateful that the fates did not decree otherwise.'

'Men have it all, and I am sure they have no idea how truly fortunate they are,' I answered, draining my glass and clasping it in my lap.

'Oh, Miss Austen, now your pretty face looks sad. How unlike you to be so melancholy.'

I could not look at him. He'd said I was pretty and I couldn't help smiling at that. I took a sidelong look and he grinned.

'You look very beautiful tonight, Miss Jane.'

His voice was so low only I could hear it. How my heart was singing at the sound of his voice. 'Thank you, Tom.'

'Ah, she speaks my name, albeit in a whisper. But, how lovely the sound.'

He leaned across, unlacing my fingers from the grasp of my punch cup, his own threading through mine for just a moment before he took the glass and set it on the floor. He held out his hand. 'Dance with me.'

I felt his hand grasp mine, his thumb finding the fleshy part of my palm as he stroked it again. The feeling was so momentous I almost pulled my hand away. Every time he touched me I felt I might singe and burn, that the passion I felt for him would ignite and set me in flames. I hardly remembered the dance or the steps we were making. I only felt his physical presence, his hand on my waist, and his very soul in my being.

We were rather quiet when we came from the dance floor. We were sitting on a window-seat, which forced our proximity to one another, wedged in the narrow space. Like the day when we'd sat together at the pianoforte, and on the day when we'd ridden together, I felt his body next to mine, the length of his leg beneath my thin gown. Long and muscular, his legs stretched out before him. I gazed at him in the candlelight, which flickered over his face making his eyes dark and his cheeks bright. If he turned his golden head, his breath was on my cheek, our lips just inches from the other.

John Warren sauntered over. He looked rather pleased with himself. I hoped against hope that he would not ask me to dance. He'd become ever more attentive at the last few balls and more than anything I did not want to give him a false impression of there being anything more than friendship. Besides, I did not want to leave Tom's side. I wasn't sure how many more occasions we'd be able to spend time together, and I wanted nothing to take me away.

'I have something for you, Miss Austen.'

He held out what looked like a folded letter, but on closer inspection it turned out to be something else entirely. I hesitated to open it, as I knew Tom would clearly see whatever was inside. It was a painting, executed in watercolour on an oval background, and a very good likeness. Thomas Langlois Lefroy, as his full name would have it, stared back at me. John Warren had captured Tom's grey eyes and fair hair to perfection, and even included the infamous white coat.

'And, what makes you think I would be willing to accept your gift, Mr Warren?' I said, folding it up again hastily, before it drew any attention from an unwanted direction.

Mr Warren was looking to Tom to take the lead.

'I hoped you'd like it, I sat especially for the portrait,' said Tom staring straight into my eyes.

The gentlemen were smiling at one another, as if they shared a huge secret, and suddenly, I knew what it meant. Tom had known as much about the picture as Mr Warren, and I'd clearly been wrong about *him*. Or was it just the case that my feelings for Tom were so clear to everyone else that Mr Warren had given up trying to get my attention. Whatever the case, he knew that I would love the painting, and the fact that Tom had sat especially made the picture the most precious one I'd ever owned. I could deny my feelings no longer, and if Tom wanted me to have his picture to remember him by, I knew he must have some regard for me, whatever he pretended.

'I think it an extraordinary likeness, and I will treasure it.'

Both gentlemen seemed satisfied with my answer. Tom leaned towards me and whispered in my ear. 'I should like one of *you* as a keepsake, if you'd let our friend make the commission.'

My spirits were dancing in silent rapture just as much as my feet when Tom escorted me to the dance floor. I think something of the joy we felt on the occasion pervaded the whole room like the fragrance lingering on the air as the atmosphere lightened. There was laughter and movement and flurries of white muslin as dashing young men spun their partners round, satin slippers kicking up the chalk. As the musicians played faster the handclaps and boot stomping grew louder. Everywhere looked a blaze of colour and sparkle under glittering chandeliers as the dancers skipped and hopped, galloping down the set to reach their place in time. It was wonderful to feel his hand in mine, to catch his eye, and to have his fingers linger in the small of my back like a caress.

By the time the supper bell rang, we were all starving hungry. Such a spread, like a king's feast, was laid out on the dining table. My brother James carved the turkey with great perseverance, whilst Henry made it his job to help all the young ladies. He was on fine form and had encouraged his brother to dance every dance. Catherine and Alethea exchanged smiles with me. I knew Catherine would tease me about Tom as soon as she had the chance. Catherine's brother Harris was helping James. He was growing up, and looked quite the young gentleman in his evening attire. I saw him look up and catch my eye. He was very shy, but I knew that he liked me. Knowing that I was one of the few people he preferred to talk to, I gave him my best smile back again.

'Come on, Jane,' whispered Tom, 'surely there's a corner where we can sit without the whole world attending to our every word.'

'Tom Lefroy, you will have people talking about me, if they are not already, but there is a little place in the greenhouse where we might find a seat.'

I led him from the room and along the corridor. Everyone was so busy eating, drinking and swapping gossip that I was certain we would not be missed, but I knew we should not be long. At the back of my mind, a voice told me I was behaving badly but it felt we were the only two people in the whole world who mattered. We abandoned our plates and glasses, and ran tiptoeing, hand in hand, as soon as we were out of sight. Amongst the Persian orange trees and exotic plants, I found my rustic bench, a favourite spot where I often took a book when staying with my friends. Screened by greenery, we could not be seen. The space was a cosy one, warm from the glow of candles set in coloured lamps that lent a magical glow to the darkness of the interior.

'Thank you for making this Christmas visit so enjoyable,' said Tom, turning to face me. 'I must admit that I was truly dreading being away from my family.'

'I, too, have enjoyed every minute of your company ... even when you were behaving like an arrogant coxcomb.'

'You wound me, Miss Austen, and in more ways than you will ever know.'

I fiddled with my reticule and thought of the picture hidden inside. 'You will have to go away soon, I think.'

Tom nodded. 'I have to study, and I have a long way ahead of me before I shall be started in my chosen career.'

'And I suppose you will not stop at being a mere lawyer. I can see you as a judge, Tom, with a long white wig on your head looking rather stern.'

Tom threw back his head and laughed. 'If my Uncle Benjamin has anything to do with it, you're right. He is my sponsor and I do so hope to make him proud. I wish to do the best for my family. With so many children, you know yourself, money is stretched to its limits.'

'I wish you weren't going away,' I said. The words were out, and the secrets of my heart were unleashed. It was too late to go back.

'But, I will go and you'll soon forget me. It's probably for the best, you know. Besides, you have so many ardent suitors I could not flatter myself that you would wish to confine yourself to me alone.'

He took up my hand between two of his own and turned it, as if studying my fingers before entwining his in mine and holding them up to the curve of his mouth, pressing his lips against the kid leather. I wanted to feel his mouth on mine, and I knew I might never have another moment so exquisitely right.

'Kiss me,' I dared to say.

'Jane ... we should not.'

I heard his words but I did not believe them. I tried again. 'Do you not wish to kiss me, Mr Lefroy?'

Tom stroked the flesh exposed above my wrist where he hooked a finger beneath the buttoned opening of my glove. 'Jane, it's not that ... but I do not think kissing you is a good idea.'

'It would just be a kiss between friends. I am always kissing Catherine and Alethea. It would signify nothing more than a seal to friendship.'

Tom shook his head. 'Oh, Jane, you have no idea how much I've dreamed of kissing you, and it would be a terrible thing if I did.'

'I don't understand. If we both wish it, why is it so wrong?'

Tom gazed into my eyes and I saw his anguish. 'Because I do not trust myself to behave like a gentleman.'

'Kiss me, Tom, or I will kiss you.'

His hand caressed my face and a finger traced my mouth before he placed his lips on mine so gently that tears filled my eyes. I touched his cheek, threaded my fingers through his hair, and felt our lips and our breath join as one. I fell into his arms and he drew me closer with kisses of love and tenderness.

## Chapter 21

I rose early after the Manydown Ball despite hardly being able to sleep. Opening my eyes, for a moment I couldn't begin to fathom the reason for the feelings of inexplicable happiness that seemed to start from my toes radiating throughout my whole being. Lying in bed with thoughts of Tom and his wonderful kisses was thrilling and all I wanted was to live over the sensation again and again. How I wished Cassandra were at home. At last I knew how she felt for her Tom. All the times I'd watched her with him, I had not really understood the wonder of those stolen glances, and the discreet lingering touches that brought such a smile to her countenance. Could it be that she felt the same way as me? When I was with Tom the world was brighter, sharper in focus and brilliant in colour. Happiness flowed through every pore of my being and when he'd kissed me I felt I'd been set free. Like a captive bird released into the wild I'd soared to the heavens on a flight of ecstasy, and I knew I was truly in love for the very first time.

Hopping about on the cold floor pulling on long, woollen stockings I reached for my dressing robe, and tip-toed to the window avoiding those places on the oak boards that I knew would creak with a loud retort and wake the rest of the house. Outside, beyond the snow-powdered casement, pine trees glittered with ice crystals in the pearly morning light, and the fields stretched away under billowing, white folds like sheets flapping in the wind on washday. It had been snowing again and all pathways and the road beyond had vanished save for the trails made by pheasants and foxes, rabbits and other small creatures that had been up and around in the night searching for food.

All of a sudden, my thoughts were interrupted by the thud of something white and icy being hurled against the glass. It was a snowball! Looking out through the window once more, I could see nothing at first until the sight of a figure stepping out to look up caught my attention. Running downstairs with my hair flying and giving not a care for anything except opening the front door, I felt the same kind of excitement that I'd been conscious of at the Manydown ball. I opened the door with caution but the figure had gone, and although I'd only glimpsed him I knew exactly who had thrown the snowball at my window. I looked all about, but Tom had truly disappeared. I was about to shut the door when I noticed a small package at my feet on the step.

I ran to my room with the precious parcel. With trembling fingers I untied the scarlet ribbon that bound the small box to discover a sprig of mistletoe inside, tied with the same ribbon, its milky pearls still glistening with snow. There was a note.

*To Miss Jane Austen - a poem, with apologies to Mr William Cowper from whom I have stolen said verse and rearranged for my own ends. Please think on me when you behold this token.*

*To a Friend*

*What Nature, alas! has deni'd*
*To the delicate growth of our isle,*
*Art has in a measure suppli'd,*
*And winter is deck'd with a smile.*
*See, Jane, what beauties I bring*

> *From the shelter of an obliging tree,*
> *Where the flowers have the charms of the spring,*
> *Though abroad they are frozen and dead.*
> *'Tis a bower of Arcadian sweets,*
> *Where Flora is still in her prime;*
> *A fortress to which she retreats,*
> *From the cruel assaults of the clime.*
> *While earth wears a mantle of snow,*
> *This mistletoe is as fresh and as gay,*
> *As the fairest and sweetest that blow*
> *On the beautiful bosom of May.*
>
> *Thank you for so many exquisite moments last night, dearest Jane,*
> *Your friend,*
> *T. L.*

Holding the be-ribboned mistletoe to my cheek I delighted in his simple gift as if it had been a token of gold. How clever and unexpected of Tom. I'd hoped I might see him, but this was the next best thing and could only remind me of last night. It hadn't been a dream and Tom was clearly thinking of those stolen kisses just as much.

With thoughts of my handsome Irishman dancing in my head, I washed and dressed in a dream. The house was stirring. I could hear the familiar murmur of my parents talking in the next room, and knew they would be wishing to break their fast very soon. I rushed downstairs to help Nanny Hilliard and Nanny Littleworth who insisted they needed no help at all so I dashed to the quiet parlour to sit at my writing box and fetch out a piece of pressed paper. Cassandra must be told my latest news about Tom if she were not able to meet him herself.

As if my very thoughts had been read the post was brought in, and there was a letter from my dear sister. Cassy told me how she was passing her time pleasantly with the Fowles, but that it meant she missed her Tom even more. Spending time with his brother who reminded her of him so much was very hard, but in her usual stoical style she wrote that she had time to spend on sewing shirts for him and thinking about her wedding clothes and much else. The letter went on:

*I am certain your Tom is as much the gentleman as you describe and I am very sorry not to meet him, but I cannot read your last letter without giving you a hint of caution. Please be sensible of those people who will take pleasure in gossiping about the pair of you if you do not disguise your partiality. You should not show your preference for any gentleman, and, in any case, I do not think you should neglect those you have been pleased to call your dancing partners in the past – there are always those who are 'willing'. Do not let Tom single you out for more than two dances or for too much conversation – it may not be safe – Tom will not be in Steventon forever, and it might be propitious to look closer to home for a husband.*

*Besides, if you have set your cap at Mr Lefroy, you will leave these other fellows broken-hearted. Can it really be true that you are to dance your last with the beaux of Steventon? The Hampshire lanes will be strewn with lovelorn gentleman, and on my return, I will, no doubt, have to counsel them all!*

*But, I cannot believe that you truly mean never to dance again, except with a charming Irishman – especially one who chooses to display his shocking want of taste by dashing around Steventon in a light coloured morning coat! Now I understand why the pink Persian silk was so important – no doubt, you shall wear it under muslin for the next ball.*

*Now, I have given you my sisterly advice, I shall say only this: I hope you have a wonderful time at the next evening party and have many partners with which to dance, although I fear that you and your Tom may expose yourselves too much for propriety. In any event, I will allow you to step out for the first two with the handsome Mr Lefroy, and I remain,*

    *Yours affectionately,*

*Cassandra*
*p. s. I long to hear all about the ball at Manydown!*

As much as I longed to write pages about Tom, one scolding was quite enough, though I couldn't help wondering if my mother had directed her writing. It would not surprise me if she hadn't given Cassandra her version of the events and would know that instead of trying to reason with me herself, a word from my sister might do a better trick. So, I should be cautious in my letter writing and I would try not to be too effusive. However, that proved to be far too difficult.

Firstly, I wished her a very happy birthday, but could not help telling her that yesterday had been Tom's birthday. I had to include details of who had been there and then I couldn't resist adding that Elizabeth and William Heathcote danced together. And who could fail to laugh out loud at this next part?

*Mr H. began with Elizabeth, and afterwards danced with her again; but they do not know how to be particular. I flatter myself, however, that they will profit by the three successive lessons, which I have given them.*

*You scold me so much in the nice long letter, which I have this moment received from you, that I am almost afraid to tell you how my Irish friend and I behaved. Imagine to yourself everything most profligate and shocking in the way of dancing and sitting down together. I can expose myself however, only once more, because he leaves the country soon after next Friday, on which day we are to have a dance at Ashe after all. He is a very gentlemanlike, good-looking, pleasant young man, I assure you. But as to our having ever met, except at the three last balls, I cannot say much; for he is so excessively laughed at about me at Ashe, that he is ashamed of coming to Steventon, and ran away when we called on Mrs Lefroy a few days ago.*

It would not be wise to tell her anything else until she came home, but I felt certain this letter would satisfy – she needed to know that everything between Tom and I was being conducted in a very light-hearted manner. She did not need to know the whole truth. In any case, I could not write of stolen moments and kisses in a letter. I added that we'd left Warren at Deane Gate to catch a carriage and that Henry had also gone to Harden in his way to his Master's degree. Both of them would be exceedingly missed for they were always such fun at an evening party and there was to be another – at Ashe.

I stopped and hid my letter when I heard voices. It would only draw curious glances and questions about its contents and my mother thought nothing of looking over my shoulder when composing. Breakfast was a quiet affair: I was far too pre-occupied to converse with anyone though I knew my mother would pass comment. The morning after a ball was usually a sombre one with everyone tired from the exertions of the night before and so I was glad that no one really expected me to say very much.

The grandfather clock ticked insistently, speaking of the past and the future, whilst the fire crackled in the grate sending up tongues of flame, antlered like a golden stag. The smell of wood burning into cinders, crusty bread toasted on a fork, the fragrant smells of tea, and coffee were the pleasant odours of the start to a new day and conjured up the best of home. The worn tapestry cushions on the settle by the fire, the oak bureau and the old books on its shelves all gave out their own delicious perfume. The best porcelain arranged on the dresser in the alcove was polished to brightness, and displayed with pride alongside the wicker basket overflowing with mending, the family Bible and my mother's writing desk containing precious letters, sealing wax and old seals secreted in the drawers. Great meat dishes and painted plates with Chinese willow pattern were set on shelves above. There were hooks in the ceiling for lanterns, baskets of dried lavender and the birdcage where we could talk to the canary. There were some ancient jugs and cups, that were too old and fragile for ordinary use, hanging up in the ceiling – their painted faces staring down to watch the family meals.

Through the window poured the clear light from the

Hampshire downs across the valley to the house nestled in white fields, freckled with sunshine and shadow. Stars of light spotted the top of the collection of elephant flowerpots in blue and white, as they waited for spring to come and for small hands to fill them with wildflowers again, a task for my little niece Anna.

My thoughts wandered over hill and dale until they rested upon another dwelling I knew very well – Ashe House and its inextricable associations with Tom Lefroy. I spoke his name in my head as I pictured him in my mind producing an image of the 'yellow-haired laddie' I would forever associate with that song, twinned with the recollection of his soft grey, Irish eyes, and his proud, Irish airs. I wished he'd not run away and I longed for him so much I pictured him in my mind walking through the snowy woods to reach me.

And then, as if I'd conjured him up by fairy magic, there was Nanny Hilliard at the dining parlour door proclaiming that we had two guests – Mr Lefroy and his cousin George!

## Chapter 22

Ellie found herself outsidein the middle of the dig site as the sun was lowering in the sky. Standing in the very place where the dining parlour of Steventon rectory once stood, she'd returned with a jolt, and so abruptly that she felt as if she'd been dropped through time with too sudden a bump. It was a shock, especially when she recollected everything that was happening in the past. Longing to see Tom again, she tried very hard to wish herself back into the past but it just wasn't possible, no matter how hard she tried. Ellie had no idea what time it was, though from her experience she assumed it could be no more than a few seconds since she went to find Jess. Time in the past had its own rules and she knew she would have to wait until she was enchanted again. The past seemed to find her when it wanted to show or share something and no amount of longing to be taken back could alter that fact. There was nothing else to be done but walk home along the darkening lanes and try to slip back into the house unnoticed.

Luckily, no one seemed to have missed her very much except Jess who was sitting alone in the kitchen. When Jess saw her she pulled out a chair for her then put on a pan of hot milk and made two steaming mugs of hot chocolate.

'You're frozen cold,' said Jess putting down the mug on the scrubbed pine table. 'Where have you been?'

'Oh, just back to 1796,' said Ellie, noting how anxious her friend appeared to be.

'I must admit, I'm worried about you,' said Jess. 'And, I'm feeling a little guilty.'

'*You're* feeling guilty? I don't see why. I've felt so bad, Jess, because it should be you who is experiencing all these magical trips back in time with your favourite author. I don't know why it's happening to me.'

'You're a very special person, Ellie, with a gift that few possess. To be honest, I'm grateful that I do not have the power myself. I really don't want to be able to go back and see Jane Austen's life played out, as tempting as it might be.'

Ellie picked up her mug and looked thoughtfully into the warming chocolate. 'I never know precisely when it's going to happen, but I'm fine, really. The past is the past, and when I'm here in the present it's almost as if nothing has happened.'

Jess took a long look at her friend. 'I'm sorry; Ellie, but I know you too well. I can see how you've changed. You're so distracted, and although it might not be obvious to everyone, I can see exactly how much you've been affected. I've never really seen you quite like this before, and I know just how you feel – it's obvious in every way.'

'What are you trying to say, Jess?'

'You're in love, aren't you?' You have fallen in love with Mr Darcy's ghost every bit as much as I've fallen in love with Charlie.'

'No ... that's a ridiculous thing to say.'

'So, if you couldn't go back again and you never saw Tom Lefroy again ... that would be fine, would it?'

Ellie did not want to consider why that thought upset her so much. If she never saw Tom again, she would be devastated. 'What can I do? I'm feeling her thoughts and feelings, Jess, and I don't know how to stop it.'

'Is it just *her* emotions you're experiencing, Ellie?'

'Oh, Jess, it feels so real and yet, my common sense tells me it's impossible. We've hardly had time to get to know one another.'

'As Jane had Marianne say in *Sense and Sensibility*, *'It is not time or opportunity that is to determine intimacy: - it is disposition alone.'* Perhaps there is a reason for all of this, and that you will find out why this is happening to you. But, I can't help thinking that being tied to Steventon is not helping. I know a little about Jane's relationship with Tom Lefroy, and perhaps when the dig is over it will be better for you to get away.'

'There's to be a ball at Ashe. If I can get back again it will be the last time I'll get to dance with Tom for a while. I don't know what will happen next; though I see from the way you're looking at me that you do. I have a feeling of foreboding, but I have to see him, Jess. I just need to dance with him, at least one more time. You do understand, don't you?'

Jess nodded and stretching over the table, she caught Ellie's hand in hers. 'Of course I do. But, do be careful. After all, you know what that great lady said?'

Ellie shook her head.

'To be fond of dancing is a certain step towards falling in love.'

When the girls arrived at the dig next morning, there was great excitement. Melanie Button told them all that Greg Whitely was returning from London, and the last stages of filming would be completed.

'Ellie, it's on the list that you're down to have an interview with him, and Liberty, I believe you're shadowing him for the rest of the day,' Melanie said, ticking items off on her clipboard.

Setting up her stool, and fetching out her watercolour box, Ellie didn't know quite how she felt at the prospect of seeing Greg. She was looking forward to seeing him, but she recognised that any romantic feelings she might have had for him had subsided somewhat. When he strolled over, half an hour later, to talk about meeting up in the afternoon at the church for the interview, she was able to look at him without suffering any fluttering or beating of her heart. Ellie couldn't help comparing him with Tom but however ridiculous that might be she simply couldn't stop it. In every way, Tom was exactly the type of guy who suited her. He was good-looking and talented with a temperament and outlook so like her own that she felt they'd been made for the other, that somehow it was always meant to be. Was it only true that she was just seeing life as Jane saw it or was it possible that she might be making those moments with Tom her own? Jess had hinted that there were difficulties to be faced in the future. All Ellie could hope was that her travels through time were all for a purpose, and that eventually it might all make sense.

Ellie had agreed to meet Greg at two o'clock inside the church. She'd arrived a little early and there was no one in sight when she entered and took a seat on an oak pew. It was such a peaceful building and the sight of bunches of wildflowers filling the vases on the altar and on every surface made her feel entirely calm and ready for anything Greg might have to question her about. It was lovely and cool after the heat outside and Ellie took time to rest and luxuriate in the quiet atmosphere within the ancient walls. Below, at her feet, were a row of beautifully embroidered hassocks, the padded cushions made for parishioners to kneel on for saying prayers. There were so many brightly coloured and intricately executed patterns worked in wool and silks, in large stitches and small, cross-stitch and satin stitch, every one a different design. The one at the end caught her eye. It looked a little different to the others, and was propped up on one side with a little note attached. *Do not use*, said the note. The cushion looked rather fragile and she wondered why anyone would have thought it was a good idea to use such flimsy fabrics on something that would be knelt upon. There were at least two panels of pale silk stitched into the centre of the design, which was overlaid with more layers of transparent organza to protect the delicate fabric underneath. Held in place with small pearls and miniature embroidery stitches in white silk twist, it looked as if the needlework had been executed by one of Beatrix

Potter's Gloucester mice. There was something so familiar about it that she leaned over to pick it up for a closer look. And that's when her heart skipped a beat. Yellowed through age, the little bag she'd held at Manydown Park now formed part of an exquisite design on the cushion. The organza that shielded the reticule was coming away slightly and was also frayed on one side, which was inevitable when it was so obviously delicate. Ellie ran her fingers over the fabric, hoping that somehow the vibrations of the past would be picked up. She could feel something like stiffened paper underneath and heard the accompanying crackle. With mounting feelings of excitement, she stroked the organza again. It was too much to hope that what was concealed could be anything but a piece of card put beneath to stabilise the material, but she couldn't help remembering how she'd hidden Tom Lefroy's portrait inside. Was it possible that it might still be there? It was frustrating that there was nothing she could do about examining it further, even if she thought her hopes were false ones. Just to see the bag confirmed that she had been at the ball with Tom and that was nearly enough.

It was then that she heard sounds from the vestry. Putting down the hassock she went to investigate. As she reached the door it was obvious that there was more than one person inside, and she stiffened when she recognised the quietly spoken voice of one and the giggling laughter of the other.

'Kiss me again, Greg,' said Liberty, unable to stop laughing.

'Shush, you're making too much noise. Ellie will be here in a minute, and we don't want to be disturbed, do we?'

Liberty stopped laughing abruptly. Ellie didn't need to go any further to know exactly what was happening beyond the vestry door, and as she tiptoed away down the aisle and outside into the fresh air, she had a sudden memory of seeing Liberty on the day after she'd been ill at the Deane Inn. She remembered the man's watch she'd been wearing, and had worn ever since, and now she knew exactly whom it belonged to and where she had seen it before.

## Chapter 23

It was the last week of the dig. Ellie had enjoyed the experience for the most part, but she was glad she wouldn't be seeing any more of Greg Whitely. Although she'd returned to the church some time later and the interview had gone reasonably well, she'd found it hard to concentrate and her answers had been short and succinct. When Greg had taken her to one side afterwards and asked her out for dinner she'd declined, saying she had too much work to do. The truth was she was beginning to realise that Greg was a bit of a player, though she wasn't prepared to paint him quite as Henry had done. He was no different from most of the guys she had ever known, not that that excused his behaviour, but she decided perhaps it was a twenty-first century problem. All the men she'd met in the past were so gallant, charming and gentlemanly. The fact that Tom made her see them all through rose-tinted specs would not shake her from the belief, but as much as she longed to be transported back into the past again to see them, nothing happened.

Jess carried on valiantly even though Ellie knew her heart was breaking. She wasn't used to seeing her friend looking so sad and defeated and she couldn't think what to do to improve things. If she could have got hold of Charlie she would have given him a piece of her mind. By the middle of the week, Ellie decided it might be better for them all to leave Steventon, however much the idea tore her heart in two. As time was marching on, she was beginning to think that any charm she had over the place was gone. The enchantment was over, and she would never again return to the past.

After a long day working outdoors Jess and Ellie were finally back at Ashe, sitting in the drawing room. Liberty and Cara were out, and though Ellie had a good idea where they might be, most likely entertaining Greg and the camera crew somewhere, she'd decided there wasn't really too much she could do about it. Liberty was an outrageous flirt, and as much as she'd been concerned when she caught Greg kissing her in the vestry, since then, she hadn't seen the pair of them together. If anything, Greg seemed to be spending his time increasingly with Melanie, and Liberty and Cara seemed happy with any attention from whoever was left.

The weather, like their mood, had changed for the worse. The temperature had plummeted and dark clouds were turning the sky to gunpowder grey. The air crackled with electricity and thunder rumbled overhead.

'It wouldn't be so bad if it wasn't for the fact that just everything here reminds me so much of Charlie,' said Jess, stretching her toes to warm them before the fire that Mrs Hill had kindly laid to take off the chill. 'Every time I look over and see his empty chair in the operations tent, the wound strikes an inch deeper. I shall be so glad when it's all finished.'

'Well, I have mixed feelings, as you know. I don't really want to cut off my only connection to Tom, and now, with this bombshell of Martha's that she and Donald are getting married in under a month, I don't know what to think.'

It had been a total shock to all the girls when Martha had presented them with engraved wedding invitations, embossed in silver, the day before. Liberty and Cara were most excited at the news, as the wedding would be taking place in a London church near Sloane Square at the beginning of August. They were already discussing hats, fascinators and dresses and Liberty mused on the fact that it might be a great opportunity to meet eligible men. Martha's mother had it all in hand and, for once, seemed to be completely behind her daughter's decision.

'I can't say it's been a total surprise. Martha is just taking the only chance she thinks she's got,' Jess said with a sigh. 'I expect it's got a lot to do with her home life. Martha didn't have a very happy childhood, from what she's told me, and I think she just wants to make up for it. Apparently, they've talked of having at least five children.'

'Ugh! Rather her than me. That's definitely a picture I do not want jumping into my mind, thank you, Jess! I just don't understand her – I could not even contemplate ...'

'No. But, I think we have to support her in her decision. He's not a bad person, Ellie, and they actually look quite sweet together. And surprisingly, they seem to have a lot in common.'

'I just hope she doesn't live to regret her decision, that's all.'

'Who knows? Maybe she'll be happier than any of us. I think she just wants someone to love and a brood of children may well be the making of her.'

'Perhaps we'll see Charlie in London,' said Ellie, hardly daring to look over at her friend who was gazing into the fire watching the flames lick up the chimney.

'I doubt it, and, in any case, I don't think I could handle it at the moment. I think it might just be a better idea to forget all about him, hard as that is proving to be.'

There was a timely knock on the door. Nancy Littleworth popped her head round to give them a huge smile.

'Hi, Nancy – come in!' cried Ellie. 'We haven't seen you for ages.'

'No, I've been busy with my other cleaning jobs and helping out with my enormous family where I can, but I just thought I'd pop in and say hello. And, to be honest, I've got a favour to ask. I hope you don't mind, Jess and Ellie, but it's a little project I thought might appeal to both of you.'

Nancy took the proffered seat sitting down in a flowered chintz armchair and setting the plastic carrier she was carrying on her lap. 'I'm one of the volunteers at St. Nicholas, and it's my job to look after some of the ancient possessions we have. There is a dear old soul who normally helps me with work like this, but she's not too well this week, and I don't like to ask her.'

Both girls were intrigued. 'I'm very happy to help if there's anything I can do,' said Jess, as Ellie agreed with her.

Ellie had an idea what it was going to be before Nancy removed the large, tissue-wrapped object from the bag. She lovingly unwrapped it, taking off each layer, until the hassock was revealed.

Jess reached out to take it from Nancy who passed it across. 'It's beautiful ... if a little in need of attention.'

'Yes,' Nancy replied, 'it's over two hundred years old. I don't know why anyone thought it was a good idea to put such a lovely thing in so prominent a place where much harm could come to it, but it's generally not used. People prefer to look at it. The white silk is very lovely even if it has faded with age.'

Ellie's heart was beating so fast and so loud she was sure the other two would hear it.

'Anyway, I wondered if you'd mind having a look at it. I've got a little more organza and it only wants stitching into place. I know you love history, and I've just got a feeling you're both good at crafts. Ellie, Mrs Hill has been showing me some of your paintings. You are so talented!'

'Thank you, you're very kind,' said Ellie, who was dying to get a closer look at the cushion.

'I remember my granny saying that her grandmother was given the little bag ... she called it a reticule. She said it had belonged to Jane Austen once upon a time, but I don't know how true that can be.'

'We'd be very happy to look, wouldn't we, Ellie?'

'Yes, though I'm not certain if my own embroidery skills are up to the mark,' said Ellie. 'Did your Granny say anything else about the bag, Nancy?'

'I often wished I'd written down more of what my Granny said, but to my great sorrow, I didn't. All I remember was that it was to be kept in the family until someone came to claim it. I get a little mixed up because she was always talking about Jane Austen. There is a letter somewhere explaining it all – I must look it out, but I've got an idea the reticule was meant for someone named Elizabeth. Well, she's not turned up yet, and I can't help thinking it's all too late.'

'It's getting more and more like *Pride and Prejudice*,' said Jess with a laugh. 'Jane and Elizabeth, my favourite names in the whole world. You are so lucky to have one of them, Ellie, even if you insist on it being shortened.'

'Elizabeth always sounds so formal,' said Ellie. 'I will have to read *P&P* – see if it changes my mind. Would I make a good Elizabeth, do you think?'

'You would, indeed!' said Jess, in a style not unlike Jane Austen herself. I will convert you to *Pride and Prejudice*, yet.'

'Oh, it's lovely,' said Nancy, 'not that I've ever actually read the book, but Colin Firth and Matthew MacFadyen make very yummy Mr Darcys.'

'It's the heroines for me, every time,' said Jess. 'I could leave both Mr Darcy and Mr Bingley for a chance to become Jane or Elizabeth, two of literature's most wonderful characters ... they're so modern even if they were created so long ago.'

'Okay, you've sold it to me,' said Ellie. 'I will try the book and the films sometime soon.'

'It makes me want to go home and put the telly on,' said Nancy standing up and folding the plastic bag before popping it in her handbag. 'All those swaggering men in flowing capes and ruffled shirts, not to mention the tight satin pantaloons – does a girl's heart good to see them.'

'I know just what you mean,' said Jess smiling at Nancy's

comment. 'I always feel better when I've read a little Jane Austen.'

'I'm afraid it's a bit more basic and less intellectual with me,' Nancy replied, laughing at the thought. 'Still, each to his own!'

Jess laughed. 'I think we all swoon at Mr Darcy in our own way, and in whatever form. Thank you again for coming to see us and thanks so much for bringing the hassock round – I'll get to work on it straight away.'

'That's very kind, Jess, I'm sure you'll do a wonderful job. Well, I'll be off and see you again on Friday evening. I'm so sad at the thought of you leaving, now the dig is almost over, but we're going to give you and all the other volunteers a great send-off. Your godmother was most insistent before she left for Italy. This house loves a party, and I'm sure it's seen a fair few.'

When she'd gone, Ellie was rather quiet. She was dying to have a closer look at the cushion but she was unsure about what, if anything, she should say to Jess or even if it was a good idea to touch the bag. It might just be the very object to send her back in time and as much as she wished that would happen, she felt frightened. The sense of foreboding apprehension had not left her. All of a sudden she wasn't sure what to do.

'You've seen it before, haven't you?' said Jess, gazing at Ellie's face silhouetted in the darkening room, yet lit by the flames, highlighting her dark hair with slithers of gold.

'I can never keep anything away from you, can I?'

Jess produced a tiny pair of scissors from her handbag and started snipping at the organza threads that were coming away to release the reticule trapped beneath. 'Ellie, we will never discover the truth if we don't explore everything. This bag holds a clue, I am certain. It's so beautiful and fragile that I hardly want to touch it.'

Carefully placing the reticule in Ellie's hands, Jess sat back to wait. Tears misted in Ellie's eyes at the remembrance of the last time she'd seen the bag, which had looked bright and new, shining and white with silver threads stitched into pansies, pinks and roses gathered in bunches on the front. The faded silk and the metal thread were dull with age, the grey fringes at the end of the drawstrings flattened with time. Undoing it as carefully as she could, the fabric did not tear or disintegrate as she loosened the strings and placed her fingers inside. She could feel strong card and stiff paper, not one sheet but two, and when, at last, she pulled them out, Ellie gasped in surprise.

## Chapter 24

With trembling fingers Ellie held out the papers to Jess. She was utterly speechless, quite unlike Jess who had no hesitation in making her thoughts known.

'Oh my goodness! It's you, Ellie!'

Ellie nodded and managed to find her tongue. 'It certainly looks a bit like me, don't you think?'

'I think it's an amazing likeness, and there's something about the hazel eyes that are completely your own. And I'm guessing, this other miniature is of Tom.'

'John Warren gave it to me the last time I was back in that other world. And Tom said he'd like me … that he wanted Jane to sit for her portrait. What I don't fully understand is why the picture looks like me.'

'Unless you look like Jane Austen, of course. Come to think of it, you do look like a younger, prettier, and less cross version of the portrait her sister painted. And that would make sense of what Nancy said about someone coming to claim it. You must be the Elizabeth that Jane Austen mentioned.'

'Now, I think you're going too far.'

'No, Ellie, it makes perfect sense to me. Perhaps Jane was

aware that she was 'taken over' in spirit from time to time. I believe you were her inspiration for Elizabeth Bennet, a heroine like Jane, but perhaps with more spirit and daring than she possessed or allowed herself to have.'

Ellie laughed at that and took another look at the painting. 'Oh, Jess, you really are inhabiting the realms of the imagination, well and truly!'

Jess was studying Tom's portrait. 'He is very handsome and fair, not quite your usual choice.'

'No, I suppose not.'

'Is it a good likeness?'

'Yes. I think Mr Warren has captured him perfectly, especially those moody grey eyes.'

'Ellie, I can see how much this all means to you. I think you've just got to go with it, don't try to fight it. Perhaps your recent reticence is acting like a block and that's why you haven't been able to get back again. I'm sure when you feel right and the time and opportunity arises, you'll return once more.'

Holding the painting in her hands and gazing into those eyes, Ellie felt such a yearning to see Tom that she felt a wave of overwhelming love rise inside, washing over her with such an intensity that tears spilled over her cheeks.

The last day of the dig was a very subdued affair with everything being finally returned to the same order, as much as that was possible. The last of the excavation finds were sorted, labelled and bagged before being sent back to their new home at Will MacGourtey's university. In time there would be an exhibition and there was talk of a local author writing a book. It felt like the last day of a holiday where people are reluctant to pack up and go home. The new friendships that had been made were being cemented with promises of meeting up and staying in touch. There was plenty of hugging and kissing, but the whole atmosphere was one of sadness, and despite the additional sorrow that both Jess and Ellie were feeling, they both recognised that they'd enjoyed a wonderful experience never to be forgotten.

Jess confided in Ellie that she was sorry that nothing out of the ordinary had been found on the dig. Her hopes that a box full of Jane Austen diaries would be found were now entirely gone, but as far as both girls were concerned they had found something even more spectacular. What to do with the miniatures presented a problem. On the one hand it seemed the easiest solution was to leave them in the reticule, and stitch the bag back into place, but they were of such historical significance that neither Jess nor Ellie knew what was best. There was nothing written on either painting so they had no provenance to speak of, and as Ellie pointed out, there wasn't anything else to prove that the miniatures were of Tom and Jane, even if she'd seen him with her own eyes. Jess said she'd seen a painting of Tom in a Jane Austen book, and the miniature looked very similar. She said that she'd started reading Jane Austen's letters and that she was sure in one of the first letters there'd been a reference to a painting of Tom, but she would have to check. The other problem was that as good as the paintings were, they'd obviously been executed by an amateur and clearly, Ellie could not tell anyone they were the real thing. They decided they'd consult Nancy first as the bag had belonged to her grandmother and see what she thought about the matter. She would be coming to Ashe for the party later and they'd ask her then.

Ellie wandered round trying to help pack up where she could. Her paintings were set out and being admired on a table in the operations tent and although she was sorry she wouldn't be doing any more, she was happy that she'd been able to produce such a body of work. Will MacGourtey said he wanted to talk to her about them, and said he had a little surprise for her.

'Have you thought about what you might do with your paintings eventually? I suppose I'm asking if you'd consider selling them.'

'I haven't really thought about it, but yes, selling some would be a definite possibility. I hate to admit it, but I really need the money.'

'I hope you don't mind, Ellie, but I contacted a friend of mine about your work,' he said. Obviously, they will feature in the exhibition we have later on in the year when everything has been collated, but I think they deserve being seen by a much wider audience. Would you consider letting them be shown in an exhibition of landscape painting in London?'

'Oh, Will, that sounds wonderful. Are you sure?'

'My friend owns a gallery in Mayfair. I didn't want to say anything before he'd seen them but I had him take a look first thing this morning, and he thinks they're amazing.'

Ellie couldn't believe it. Will was grinning from ear to ear making his grey eyes twinkle. She'd not really considered it before but he was turning out to be a really lovely and valued friend.

'In Mayfair?' Ellie repeated.

'Yes, in the most famous area for art galleries, actually, and in *the* most prestigious gallery in Cork Street.'

'I'm overwhelmed, Will. It's the stuff of dreams!'

'I'll let Oliver know. There's just one snag. You'd have to be prepared to let them go off to London as soon as next week. Oliver knows we will want them back again for the exhibition we have planned later on, but he sees no reason why buyers can't wait until after that before they take possession of them.'

'Does he think they'll sell then?'

'He thinks you're going to be huge. I don't want to get your hopes up too high, but he confided in me that he hasn't seen work like yours for a long time. It's an opportunity of a lifetime, Ellie. What do I tell him?'

'Oh, tell him yes!'

'Brilliant! You will need to go down there yourself, as soon as you can … Oliver always likes artists to be there for the hanging, and there's bound to be a launch of some sort, though this first one will be something of a rush.'

'Will, I don't know what to say.'

'You don't need to say anything – the pleasure for me is seeing your face. I'm so glad you're pleased.'

'Pleased is a bit of an understatement! Thank you so much, I won't let you down, Will, I promise. I've just got to think of a way to get down to London. We were going later for Martha's wedding but I wasn't really expecting to go quite so soon.'

'Good, I'm glad we have that sorted.' Will put out his hand and Ellie found her tiny hand completely engulfed by his large one as he shook her hand enthusiastically. Then, he was striding away with a wave goodbye, in his usual brisk manner. 'That's fantastic, Ellie, I'll let the news sink in – perhaps I'll see you to speak to at the party tonight.'

Jess was almost as excited as Ellie by the news. 'I always knew you were going to be famous,' she said, hugging her friend until Ellie was gasping for air.

'There's just one tiny problem,' said Ellie. 'They want me to go to London next week. I've no idea how long for, and I just got so caught up in everything that Will was saying that I didn't even think about stuff like where I was going to stay or what I was going to do for money.'

'Leave it with me,' said Jess. 'It's only Friday and I've got an idea. Trust me?'

'You know I do, but please don't do anything that won't have my approval like paying for things that I can never afford to pay you back. I know what you're like!'

'I promise I shan't do anything without consulting you first. Oh, Ellie, this is so exciting. London here we come!'

Mrs Hill and Jess were being very secretive after dinner that evening. They disappeared off together whilst the other girls went to their rooms to change into their party clothes. Liberty and Cara knew exactly what they were wearing; they'd been discussing it for days. Not so formal as the ball at Deane, they'd chosen shorter dresses, Liberty's was scarlet bandage with cut-outs; Cara's was pink, plunging and floaty. Ellie couldn't make up her mind what to wear. She really wasn't too interested in making any statement or impact, and in the end turned to an old favourite. Pulling on the white broderie anglaise summer dress she looked at her choice with approval, as she stood before the mirror. Teamed with some silver pumps which she felt added a dash of glamour, Ellie felt ready for the evening ahead. At least she didn't need to fend off Greg any more. He seemed totally disinterested in her, preferring to spend time with those who hung on his every word.

Just as she was about to head downstairs to meet the others, there was a knock at the door. Jess was summoned in, and by the look on her face Ellie knew she had good news.

'It's all arranged, Ellie. I've just been talking to Aunty Mary on the phone. We're going to her mews house in Mayfair. As soon as you mentioned the gallery I thought of it and with Mrs Hill's help we've been able to secure it. I don't think my aunt needed much convincing but Mrs Hill was wonderful, putting in a good word for us all. Hay's Mews is not far away from Cork Street and it will be perfect for us all. It's not far from the school where I'll be doing some work experience. I'll be able to visit and start making plans. There's room for Martha, Cara and Liberty, too, though we'll have to be prepared to share.'

'Jess, you are wonderful,' Ellie cried, 'how will I ever thank you?'

'There's no need for that,' said Jess who looked quite misty eyed. 'I'd never have got through this last year, never mind these last couple of weeks without you ... it's the least I could do.'

'How wonderful it is to have rich relations,' Ellie chimed in, 'how I wish I had an Aunty Mary of my own!'

Jess laughed. 'What's mine is yours, Ellie. I think Aunt Mary likes the idea of all these young people living it up in her houses. She didn't have any children so she loves the fact that she can 'borrow' some without having the bother of looking after them permanently or the all round expense. Come on, it's our last night in Hampshire. Charlie or no Charlie, I am determined to enjoy myself, and with your success we've much to celebrate!'

The temperature had steadily risen throughout the day. Every window and door was open to let the breezes circulate, but by the evening the hot July air was still and it was stiflingly hot. Out in the garden there were plenty of areas in cool shade although the sun was striking the back of the house with a fierce heat that seemed almost Mediterranean. The sun was a ball of crimson lighting up snow-white trumpet lilies, irises and dianthus in the herbaceous borders with brushstrokes of pink and lilac. The scent of jasmine and honeysuckle floated through the long French doors combining with the perfumes of cut flowers burgeoning from glass vases and ancient epergné to create a heady fragrance. Blooms wilted and drooped, their petals drifting onto polished mahogany tabletops and marble mantels.

Mrs Hill had arranged for welcoming drinks to be served on the terrace. Ice-cold buckets of champagne were placed in rows with Mr Hill guarding them like a sergeant major on duty, and Nancy was hovering about with trays of her delicious canapés ready to serve the guests as they came through into the garden.

Melanie Button was the first to arrive. She floated in on a cloud of peach chiffon, laden with mysterious packages. 'I thought we'd make a little presentation to the gentlemen,' she said. 'I know they won't be expecting anything, but I thought a couple of their favourite bottles of wine might be nice, and I've got a little speech prepared.'

'That's a lovely idea,' said Jess relieving her of her bags. 'I'll hide them in the kitchen and we can fetch them out later.'

Melanie was looking more than a little tearful. 'I know it's probably very silly of me,' she said, 'but I'm going to miss everyone so much. It's just been such fun, and I feel as if I shall be saying goodbye to real family.'

'It will be strange to think we shan't be spending any more time in a field,' said Ellie whose thoughts didn't quite echo those of Melanie's. 'I've become quite used to spending every day out in the fresh air, though we've been so incredibly lucky with the weather. Just imagine, if it had rained every day we'd have had a completely different experience.'

'Well, they say a change is coming,' Melanie answered. 'But, it's almost as if the weather was ordered for us – I think that's why I feel it's been so special. We've been under some sort of enchantment with everything being so perfect ... people, place and the weather all coming together in quite a magical way.'

Ellie could see Jess was lost in her thoughts and she knew exactly what or whom she was thinking of.

'It *was* perfect,' Jess murmured, and then turned to beam brightly at the other two. 'And we're not finished yet. Does Melanie know about your exhibition, Ellie?'

It was typical of Jess to turn the attention onto her friend and she proceeded to tell Melanie all about the gallery in Cork Street, and how at last Ellie's great talent would be recognised. Melanie appeared interested until a flux of people, mostly volunteers, arrived. Bringing up the rear were Greg Whitely and Will MacGourtey who Melanie latched onto as soon as she saw them. She lost no time in waving at them both, even though she was in mid-sentence replying to Jess and, shrieking like a schoolgirl, she took an arm each to lead them to the terrace. Neither Will nor Greg had a chance to even say hello to the girls, but Ellie was quite grateful. She hadn't realised quite how much the sight of Greg looking very handsome in a blue shirt to match his eyes would stir the feelings she'd thought were safely buried. He reminded her of Tom in some ways, she supposed, and knew that was where her true feelings lay.

'Oh, Jess, this is going to be more difficult than I thought.'

'Ellie, don't worry. I know it's hard for you to think you might never see Tom again, but there is London to look forward to, and I promise, this is a new beginning.'

Ellie took Jess's hands in her own. 'Yes, my darling friend ... it will be a new start for both of us. I don't know about you, but right now, I could do with a glass of champagne!'

Jess went in search of drinks for them both and Ellie wandered off to find a quieter spot. She left the laughing crowds behind her and disappeared into one of the smaller garden 'rooms' where she could observe but remain undiscovered. The sun had disappeared but the garden was twinkling with fairy lights, which Mr Hill had strung across the terrace and along the rose arbour. Ellie sat down on a bench to watch the couples drifting down the garden hand in hand. Donald was back again and there with Martha, both looking very pleased with themselves, even if Ellie was not entirely convinced by their relationship. Perhaps there was something in what Melanie had said. Like a midsummer night's dream, *Project Darcy* had been under a spell and she knew several romances were in full flow. In her heart she wished them all happy, though she felt a deep sadness that Jess could not be a part of all the excitement.

'I thought I saw you slip away. You look very deep in thought, as usual.'

Ellie looked up to see Greg standing in the archway; holding out a glass of champagne and gazing at her with an intensity she found disturbing. Moonlight highlighted his dark hair, which rippled from his forehead in black waves. His blue eyes seemed to sear a path into her consciousness and she could hardly look back at him. With every step he took towards her, Ellie felt increasingly nervous. She watched him take the seat next to her and felt her hand shake as she took the glass. Ellie heard her voice tremble as she spoke.

'I was just thinking what a pity it all has to end.'

'It doesn't really have to end, you know,' Greg replied, lowering his voice to almost a whisper. He put his hand over hers. 'Whatever shall I do without you, Ellie?'

Ellie took a long drink. She felt his fingers lightly stroking her wrist on the tender skin where her pulse throbbed. His touch brought forward an image of Tom that was so strong that she didn't want him to stop. She took another slug of champagne. The bubbles had an immediate effect, making her feel very fuzzy and light-headed. As a rule, she didn't drink very much, but Ellie was beginning to feel that the world was a very lonely place and her heart was aching for a time and a someone who seemed so far away.

Greg started nuzzling her ear in pretence of whispering to her. 'Ellie, you are so beautiful tonight.' His lips followed the length of her neck and she felt his mouth kiss her skin. The sensation of being kissed made her yearn for Tom. Closing her eyes for a second she almost groaned with desire. Greg's hand slid round her waist and Ellie gasped.

'Come and walk with me, Ellie. There's the sweetest boathouse down by the lake. I think it's time we got to know one another a little better.'

Suddenly, Ellie saw all too clearly what was happening, and then she remembered the last time she'd seen Greg with Liberty and was brought back to earth in a second. It was impossible not to think about what Henry had told her, yet she felt cross about being reminded of him. However, he was soon forgotten as events were happening rather too quickly. She pulled her hand away. 'I'm sorry, Greg, but I don't really feel like walking. Besides, I'm sure there are plenty of others happy to 'know' you as much as you'd like.'

'Oh, come on, Ellie, why don't you let yourself go, a little. I know you want me just as much as I do you. You can't fool me; I've seen it in your eyes every day we've been working together ... and you can't deny the fact that I just heard how much you want me ... you gasped with sheer pleasure. I promise, you won't be disappointed ... come, let's make beautiful love together down by the moonlit lake.'

Greg was pulling her closer and Ellie had to push him away. She felt revolted. What was more, she felt sick. The last slug of wine had been so quickly drunk that the whole world seemed to be revolving, and when she stood up her head was spinning. She was swaying on her feet and now it looked as if Greg were laughing at her. She stumbled through the yew archway, and ran back to the house, bumping into Liberty on the way.

'Ellie, have you seen Greg anywhere? He promised to get me a drink and I haven't seen him since.'

'No,' Ellie lied, 'I haven't seen him.' The last thing she wanted to do was encourage Liberty to go after him. Besides, she was sure

Greg would find someone else very soon.

'No worries,' Liberty shouted, dismissing Ellie with a wave. 'I can see Jake over there, and he'll do just as well!'

Some things never change, thought Ellie, as her friend disappeared, and she headed for the house. Liberty would never be happy until she'd allowed some guy to take complete advantage of her. Ellie tried to remember who Jake was and whether he was a nice person, but her brain felt completely befuddled.

'That's some champagne Greg gave me,' she muttered out loud, as she staggered inside, making for the stairs. Several times, she stopped in order to right the images that overlapped before her eyes. When she got to the first landing, she had to pause. She was seeing double and waves of nausea were overwhelming her. If she concentrated really hard, she might make it to her bedroom. Conscious that she ought to appear to be sober, she tried to walk in a straight line past a couple who were totally oblivious to her being there. Ellie watched them with a certain amount of envy, knowing they just didn't see her. They only had eyes for each other. At the end of the corridor she opened her bedroom door at last, and collapsing onto the bed with relief, she passed out as she hit the pillow.

## Chapter 25

When I opened my eyes, I couldn't think where I was for a moment. I was sitting on a bed that looked nothing like the one I'd collapsed onto earlier. This one was a four-poster, simply carved with reeded motifs and dressed with drapes and swags of sprigged cotton. The panelled walls were painted a dusky blue-grey which echoed the tones in the long curtains at the floor-length windows. A chest of drawers and a dressing table were the only other items of furniture, but the biggest clue to its owner lay in the elaborate powdered wigs set on stands, the silver-topped scent bottles, and the set of ivory-backed brushes, upon the dressing table. An open box of jewels glinted in the candlelight, and I recognised one or two of Madame's favourite Rivière necklaces, one of amethysts, and the other of topaz. The fireplace looked the same though a fire roared in the grate, and a glimmer of starlight pierced the blinds to kiss the enamelled shepherdess on top of the little gilt clock on the mantle. A jug and bowl of steaming water with a discarded piece of rumpled linen and a ball of soap in a dish looked as if it had been set there especially for me.

I knew when I examined myself that I was dressed for a ball. My white muslin with a glossy spot fell stiffly in starched folds, the glazed fabric showing my pink underskirt beneath. I felt rather grand in my new dress, which was a rare treat, and I was equally delighted with the grey velvet slippers, which nudged under my gown. Catching a glimpse of myself in the looking glass, I didn't recognise the girl whose pink cheeks were glowing with excitement. And then I remembered. That other time to which I belonged was fading into another landscape, one that was disappearing so rapidly I could only think about the here and now. I was at Ashe, a place that was a second home to me with all my friends so dear. I loved Madame for so many reasons, and I knew how delighted she was about my friendship with her nephew. This evening had been arranged with us in mind, I knew, and the invitation to come for the day had been given so that Tom and I could spend as much time together as was possible. I didn't want to think about the fact that we'd be parted from one another after tonight. All I could hope was that Tom would continue to visit his aunt, and Steventon, whenever he could.

The afternoon had been delicious. Tom and I stole away from the house, and walked down to the lake. Set in the woods, the old boathouse at the edge of the sandy shore was open. Rowing boats tethered underneath rocked like empty cradles with the rhythm of the lapping water, confined by the ice that lay in a thin sheet dusted with frost. We climbed the steps to the first floor and stood on the verandah overlooking the lake. It was beautiful in the pearly light. Mist hung in white veils above the glassy water, the willow and beech trees trailing their branches along the ice like the sweeping trains of dowager duchesses. The occasional trout could be glimpsed, golden underbelly glowing, and speckled with silver gleaming under the ice like mother of pearl on a lacquered tray.

'I've enjoyed our walks, Miss Austen,' said Tom, resting his arms on the balustrade, looking straight before him. 'Indeed, I shall miss them very much.'

I turned my head to look at him. He was more handsome than he'd ever been to me. I wanted to gaze upon his countenance forever, and I tried to commit every feature, each hair on his head to memory.

'I will miss your company,' I admitted, 'even if you attempt to vex me at every turn.'

Tom raised an eyebrow, but when his eyes met mine, he smiled. 'What will you do when I am gone away?'

'If you mean will I pine for you, re-tracing our footsteps and weeping into my handkerchief, then I hate to disappoint you, but I shall be far too busy.'

'Mending your brother's shirts, I suppose, and seeing to the hens.'

'Mr Lefroy, I shall be doing no such thing. I will be working on my new project. My brothers may take care of their own needlework if they so choose.'

'Ah, some book writing, no doubt.'

'Not just any writing, sir. But the creation of a novel of such great literary merit that it will be read in every house up and down the land.'

'And may I ask the title of this great work, Miss Jane?'

'*First Impressions*, Mr Lefroy. It is a tale of love and money, great pride and a little prejudice.'

Tom turned to study my face. 'You look entirely different to me now. When first I beheld you, I thought you were rather priggish ... that was *my* first impression.'

'And I thought *you* rather proud. You hardly strung a sentence together, and looked down your nose on everyone.'

'I was just a little shy in company ...'

'And I never heard such nonsense in my life before.'

Tom covered my hand and took it up, bringing the fingers of my York tan gloves to his lips. Melting snow showered from the decorated gable above, falling on my head, slipping into the gap between my bonnet and my cloak, making me shriek at the icy cold. Tom grabbed my arm and drew me to him as another, heavier slab shifted and slid off the roof narrowly missing us both.

'Stay close to me, Miss Austen, I'll see you come to no harm.'

I curtseyed in mock style. 'Why, kind sir, whatever should I do without you to guard and protect me and my reputation?'

Tom wasn't laughing any more. He looked thoughtful with a faraway expression I'd seen before. 'Would that I could, Jane ... life is not always so simple, and I will not always be here to look after you.'

'Do I need looking after, Mr Lefroy?'

'You are an innocent, unused to the ways of the world, Jane. I've seen the way gentlemen look at you.'

'And you think I am in some danger?'

'Promise me that you will not marry John Warren or Benjamin Portal.'

'And, why on earth would I do that?'

'What I mean to say is that I hope you will not think of marrying anyone, just yet. Promise me.'

'It has never been my intention to marry anyone if I can help it. I do not know that I am the marrying sort, Mr Lefroy. How would I pursue my writing if I were shackled to a husband and turned into a brood mare? Children are adorable, but they take up so much time. And besides all that, no one ever asked me to marry them, and I am certain my lack of fortune will prove prohibitive in that endeavour.'

'A lack of money on both sides is indeed an obstacle for the most earnest lovers. And yet, where there is talent and ambition, fortunes may be made. Would you wait for a lover who had no money, Miss Austen?'

'If I were to marry, it would be for love, and if I ever chanced to happen upon the young man who might suit me above the rest, then yes, I would wait for him, Mr Lefroy.'

'Would you wait for me if I asked you to, Jane?'

I could not tell if he were teasing me. His grey eyes reflected the black ice of the lake, and I glimpsed amusement twinkling in their depths.

'That is a question I cannot answer ... as you have not asked it.'

Tom laughed and raised my hand to his lips. He kept his eyes on mine, and I felt myself sinking into those limpid pools, reflecting the greyness of the lake and sky. I watched him kiss my fingers. When he let go my hand, he removed his glove. 'Give me the ribbon from your hair,' he said.

I reached up to untie the scarlet ribbon, and handed it to him thinking he wanted it for a keepsake. He slipped off a gold ring from his little finger, and I watched him thread it onto the piece of silk before he beckoned me to lower my head. 'This token will guard you from all harm, and from the attentions of those you do not seek.'

A smile played upon his lips. His fingers tied the ribbon round my neck, and I felt them brush my ears, as he held my head in his hands, lowering his lips upon mine to kiss them tenderly.

The ring was one I'd seen him always wear, and was clearly precious to him. 'But Tom, this is your family ring. I can see the crest of the wyvern,' I said.

'I wish you to have it … a talisman against marriage, if you like.'

It was my turn to laugh, and as I slipped my finger through the ring, I believed every word he said was true.

The precious ring was hidden next to my heart. Of course, it was impossible to wear it for show, and I would have to be very careful about wearing it round my neck. On my finger, it was a little too big, but I liked the feel of it. I felt close to Tom when I wore it, and together with the scarlet ribbon, the two of us were joined and represented. Although he had not said in so many words, I felt sure it was more than a talisman, a token of his high regard for me. Before we'd parted to prepare for the evening festivities, we'd promised to write to one another. His cousin George would act as go-between, he said, and the thought of exchanging letters on all the subjects we wished to discuss delighted me. I could not wait for the evening to come. To dance again with Tom and feel him close to me one more time were most delightful thoughts.

When I entered the drawing room, I noted with a frisson of

pleasure that the room was completely changed. Preparations had been taking place all day, but the last adjustments meant that the carpets were rolled up and the connecting doors flung back to make some room for dancing. There would be little space compared to the other balls we'd danced at lately, but I was not one to complain. In such a small area, we'd be dancing even closer together, and the thought of Tom's arms linked with mine was immensely exciting.

'Good evening, Miss Austen.'

At the sound of his voice, I wanted to prolong the moment of turning – as soon as I did I knew the evening would start and it would all be over in the time a breeze ruffled the lake beyond the formal gardens, stippling the surface into beaten silver. Every second felt like an eternity as I revolved. At last, it was time to stare and take a memory picture in my mind. Fair hair shining in candlelight, a golden curl falling on an eyebrow, brooding grey eyes contemplating me with a steady scrutiny, broad shoulders, black coat, white cravat, silk waistcoat, satin breeches, gleaming shoes – a promising list, but the whole married into an epicurean feast for the senses – my senses. He bowed, and I curtseyed.

The room was full of people in the next second and our moment was over. From now on our every move and action would be observed. I was past caring. If I never saw Tom after tonight, it would not deter me from flirting, dancing or sitting down with him as many times as I liked. I could not care how profligate my behaviour might seem – why should gentlemen be the only ones to have fun? I'd teased Cassandra in my last letter that I fully expected an offer of marriage from my Irish friend – tonight I believed anything was possible!

Tom and I sat together on our favourite window seat. Winter still held its grip over the countryside though the snow had abated. Beyond the sash window, moonlight illuminated the white fields as smooth as a dish of cream on top of a Christmas trifle. Narrow carriages plunged down the frosted lanes, full with revellers in high anticipation of the party, a snowy barn owl swooping along in their path.

I felt Tom's eyes upon my face.

'You should not stare so, Mr Lefroy. Did your mother never teach you any manners?'

'I am not staring, Miss Austen. I am merely gazing and thinking.'

I felt my mouth twitch with amusement, but I was determined he should not see my lip curl.

'And may I ask, on what subject you are gazing and thinking?'

'I have been meditating on the very great pleasure which a pair of fine eyes in the face of a pretty woman can bestow.'

It was impossible not to smile. 'Do tell, Mr Lefroy, which lady has the credit of inspiring such reflections.'

'I cannot tell, I am sworn to secrecy, for if the lady ever found out, her vanity would know no bounds.'

'But, I should not tell a soul, Mr Lefroy. Your secret will be safe with me.'

Tom grinned and stood up. 'Come, Miss Austen, I see her moving to the dance floor ... let us join her, and I will point her out.'

The dances were starting. I caught my mother's eye and she smiled broadly. Her hopes for me were written on every line in her face, and every anxious word. From the very beginning she'd formed my earliest opinions, urged my good behaviour and instructed me in the importance of attracting a wealthy suitor. Well, such subjects I would never be serious about, and I knew I'd not been the willing pupil my mama found in my elder sister with her ease of temper for education in matters of love and money. Not that Cassandra had followed her advice.

What did I care for money? Like my sister, I desired only love. My Tom was not rich, but his future was bright, and my mother had already professed her opinion that a connection with the Lefroys could not be a bad thing. And yet, I knew she wished for something more. She had married for love herself, a brilliant clergyman with mixed prospects, but her own connections with the aristocracy still held their steadfast roots. If she could persuade me to take someone with land and property, I knew she would feel a job well done.

We danced twice, with such looks and feelings as to set every nerve tingling at every quivering touch. Eyes and lips, hungry for the other, fingertips electrifying, hearts beating in tune and in time. His eyes held mine, we were the only people in the room, except we soon found we were not – a resounding burst of applause erupted as Tom escorted me from the floor.

Mrs Bramston came rushing over. 'Oh, such dancing is rarely seen, my dears. What a picture! I have not enjoyed such a spectacle so much since Mr Bramston courted me … oh, ever so many years ago. Now, do not be shy, I must know when you are to announce your engagement. I never saw such a happy couple, so well suited, so handsome and everything good.'

I bit my lip. It was difficult not to smile, and besides, I was so happy that the world could see how much we were in love. I could feel the ring next to my breast, and imagined everyone could see it burning a way through my heart. I could not speak, and looked to Tom for help.

'Mrs Bramston, would you do me the honour of dancing with me?'

I suppose I could not blame him. He'd completely ignored her question and was quick to divert her thoughts into an activity he knew she would not be able to resist. It was then that I noticed Madame standing not two feet away, and it was obvious from her expression that she'd witnessed the conversation. Tom led Mrs Bramston away, and suddenly, I wished to be anywhere else but in the room.

I dashed through the hallway, oblivious to anyone who tried to stop and engage me in conversation. I realised in an awful moment that after tonight I should never see Tom again. He knew this, and however much I tried to fool myself that his response to Mrs Bramston did not hurt my feelings, my disappointment at his reaction gnawed like a blunt knife on a butcher's block, painfully and slowly hacking my heart in two. If he'd hesitated for one moment, smiled, or shared a secret look, I could have forgiven him but his reaction was so guilty and dismissive. I took the stairs two at a time and reached the sanctuary of Madame's room. It was absolutely necessary to compose myself and think clearly. I was so cross for having let my guard down so much. How could I ever have believed that Tom truly loved me? Not that the words were ever spoken, but every word he'd said to me, every look that had passed between us and each love song he'd sung to me had convinced me that he was falling in love with me.

Gradually my breathing settled. I brushed away the tears I felt rising, and made a great study of the painting above the mantelpiece, concentrating on anything else to quieten my mind, though that was not entirely possible. It was a summer landscape, a rural scene in Ireland, a place and country I was sure I'd never visit now. Silly, silly girl, I scolded. Dreams of Ireland, of settling there and running barefoot in the green grass were puffed away like dust along with the visions of the house we'd have there. I had seen it all.

What would Cassy say, I wondered? I knew what she'd do. She, who never let others know how much her feelings were affected, would be resolute in her determination to remain undisturbed by an arrow to the heart. I heard her voice in my head, and I knew I must go back downstairs and face everyone as composed as ever. I'd be polite to Tom but not expect him to talk or dance again.

Standing up, I brushed down my gown, checked my appearance in the looking glass and tugged on my gloves, smoothing every wrinkle until I felt ready to leave the safety of Madame's room. I was disposed to laugh at myself – how could I have imagined that Tom might make me an offer of marriage? No doubt, his family were on the lookout for a wealthy heiress for him, and I was deluding myself to think anything else. Stepping out into the gloomy corridor, I could hear the party noises below me. The sounds of pleasure reached me: Pretty laughter, booming voices, glasses clinking, satin rustling, music playing, feet pattering on wooden boards. It was loud, the gentlemen's raucous voices rising above the strains of violins, the harp and the pianoforte, the ladies' chirruping voices like excitable sparrows. At least I'd be able to slip back into the crowd without being noticed.

Tom stood at the top of the staircase. 'Ah, there you are.'

He'd appeared, as if by a sorcerer's wand, and was at my side in a second. He took my hand and led me along the corridor before opening a door, pulling me through it into the darkness. We were enveloped in black velvet, cocooned in the night with Tom's arms wrapped around us. The room smelled of him – fresh limes, a hint of summer geranium in the cologne he used, aromatic and evocative of all the time we'd spent together. A finger of moonlight probed a slit in the shutters and I glimpsed a carved bed in the silver beam, and a chaise longue set in the corner between the windows with views of the hanging wood beyond. There were no words, only the faintest sounds as his mouth found mine, and lips sought lips with hungry kisses. Tears gathered at the corners of my eyes spilling over my cheeks and down to my throat. I scarcely breathed, as Tom embraced each one, soft lips caressing each damp curve of my cheek, exploring every moist dip and hollow. We fell onto the chaise, and Tom spoke my name with a groan. His kisses were urgent, demanding, ever more passionate. A finger traced the swell of my breasts through fine muslin – I felt his mouth, and his hands on my skin – fondling the line of my hips, clutching at the layers of stiff muslin and pink satin. He was calling my name over and over, as I pulled him to me, opening like a hothouse orchid into his loving arms. Nothing else existed … time was no more. I was away with the moon, riding the stars, and reaching into infinity. No one could separate us, we were joined forever, body and mind.

Ellie came to with a sudden jerk; her eyes wide open. She didn't know where she was, until she realised with some shock that she was in Jess's room. To say that she felt troubled was a bit of an under-statement. Flat out on the chaise longue, breathless and stirred by intense feelings of longing, she felt as if she'd woken from a dream. She'd been dropped back through heaven and space to stark reality, plunged into the present like a returning space probe into a cold ocean of certainty. She was sure it had been a dream – more than that, pure wishful thinking on her part, and she felt quite shocked that she could have imagined such a scenario, if not for herself but for Jane Austen! The trouble was that every second had felt so convincing that she almost wanted to check under the chaise longue to see if Tom were hiding there. The more she thought about it, the more she realised that she must have dreamt it all, and as she lifted her head to sit up, another idea came to her as pain seared across her temples. The drink Greg had given her was surely spiked. He'd intended to drug her for whatever wicked ideas he had of his own, and her splitting headache told her that one glass of champagne could not have made her pass out so easily or given rise to such erotic fantasies. It was little wonder she'd sleepwalked her way to suffer alarming visions even if, truth be told, the experience had not been an unpleasant one. Ellie did not want to admit quite how much she'd enjoyed lying in Tom's arms even if it had all been a product of her imagination. Every cell in her body was alive to the memory of being touched by him, every sensuous moment etched and burned into her flesh as her blood coursed with the memory of the intimacy they'd shared.

There was a storm brewing outside. Thunder rumbled above in the leaden skies, and lightning crackled in the clouds, lighting up the room with a blinding flash. She felt the dried tears on her face, remembering how he'd kissed her, and felt the tender bruises of love on her skin. Rain drummed on the windowsills, drenching the gardens and the people outside. Ellie could hear girls screeching, and the sound of heels tapping on the courtyard below as lovers and friends rushed inside to find a dry space. She lay for a moment, listening to the cascades of water gurgling down the drainpipes, splashing from the dormers above, washing the flagstones on the terrace. Something shifted beneath her dress as she lay back amongst the pillows, and a gold ring suspended on a scarlet ribbon tumbled out from its place next to her heart to fall at her side in plain sight. A dragon crest engraved into its surface confirmed that she'd seen this very same ring before and her heart leapt in response. The scent of limes and geranium hung in her nostrils, as if Tom had just walked out of the room.

## Chapter 26

When Ellie woke the following morning, her thoughts were very muddled as to what had actually taken place the day before. It was all confused, especially about exactly what had happened between her and Tom, though there was no denying that she had physical proof of their spending time together at the lake. She wore the ring round her neck, and played with it on her finger as if it would bring him back to her. How such a thing could have happened, she couldn't work out. Ellie only knew she'd experienced such intense emotions that if it were possible to have wished the ring through time and space, she'd done it.

Last night, she'd managed to make another appearance at the party even though she felt as if she inhabited another world. Avoiding Greg had been easy: he'd disappeared with one of the television crew and she'd guessed they were probably spending their time discussing the finer points of lovemaking in boats. Liberty and Cara had danced the night away, though the former seemed cross all night long. Martha had looked the happiest of them all, as she and Donald had spent the entire night glued to one another. Jess had tried hard to be light-hearted but she'd felt subdued, yet Ellie understood all the reasons why they were both glad when at last the evening had been over and they'd said their goodbyes to everyone.

One thing Ellie had yet to resolve before she started packing for London was to find Nancy and talk to her about the portraits in the cushion. There just hadn't been a right time to discuss it the night before. When Nancy wasn't helping out, she'd been giving it her all on the dance floor. Jess had the hassock in her room. They'd promised to mend it before they left and Ellie knew nothing had yet been done. That would have to be sorted out before they left that afternoon.

When Ellie got downstairs, the house seemed very quiet. By some miracle, all the detritus of the party seemed to have been cleared away, and she guessed Mrs Hill and her ladies from the village had probably accomplished that early in the morning. Her footsteps strayed to the drawing room and she couldn't help thinking of Tom. Where there now stood cabinets of Dresden porcelain, occasional tables scattered with silver frames, and winged chairs of faded damask and pale flowered chintz, she'd danced with Tom on the wooden boards beneath the rose-covered Aubusson rug. Last night's summer ball, its heat and thunderstorms, had been a complete contrast with the winter ball of snow and ice in January 1796. To think of leaving the house where she'd fallen in love was hard, but she knew for her own sanity it was probably the right thing to do, and she reminded herself that her thoughts, feelings and emotions connected with Tom were not entirely her own, however much she wished them to be.

Beyond the green baize door, the kitchen was humming with domestic activity. There were delicious smells of oven-cooked sausages slowly roasting in the Aga for breakfast, a tray laid out with pots of marmalade, honey and lavender jelly for the breakfast table in the morning room, and the scent of Darjeeling tea rising into the warm air from a Spode teapot. Nancy was in command, slicing mushrooms and tomatoes, beating eggs and frying bacon.

'Mrs Hill has just gone to take the dogs for their walk,' she said, 'she won't be long. Breakfast's almost ready.'

'It was you I came to see, actually, Nancy. Can I do anything to help?'

'There's the toast, if you don't mind, Ellie. It's always those last minute jobs when it's all coming together that makes it a fiddle.'

Ellie took the loaf from the bread crock, slicing it thickly. 'I've got something I need to talk to you about ... to do with the reticule.'

Nancy was standing at the stove, scrambling eggs in a large pan. She stirred slowly and thoughtfully. 'If it's them pictures, I know all about those.'

Ellie was taken quite by surprise. She put the knife down and looked over at Nancy who didn't stop concentrating on the methodical stirring of her wooden spoon.

'But, *you* know something about them too, don't you?' Nancy stopped, to look up and scrutinise Ellie's face.

Ellie blushed. She wasn't sure she'd heard correctly. Nancy spooned the yellow egg into a dish, covering it with a lid before turning to face Ellie again. 'I couldn't think where I'd seen you before when I first met you,' she said. 'And it was only after we'd talked the other day, that I realised. It's always been in the family, that reticule. My Granny was most insistent that it came from Jane Austen, and I've always believed that one of the portraits was of her.'

'And the other was of the young man that she loved,' Ellie said. 'His name was Tom.'

'He lived here for a while, didn't he?' asked Nancy. 'He's the young man who won't leave you alone. We've all seen him from time to time, but I must admit, I've never felt him so strongly as the day you arrived, Ellie. I haven't seen the portraits for a while, but it struck me how similar you are to the picture of Jane.'

'Jess and I thought you should know about the portraits because they could be historically very significant. If they are of Jane and Tom, the whole world will want to know about them.'

'And that was precisely what Jane didn't want,' said Nancy,

picking up the tray. 'My Granny's letter states there was a great secret about the portraits, and that Miss Austen had left them in the possession of our ancestor because there were very few people she could trust. She had a bit of a thing about immortality, apparently, and I don't know exactly, but there were verbal instructions about what was to be done with them, and the little bag they came in. The portraits were to be hidden from the world until the time was right.'

'I see. Yes, that makes sense. I'll make sure they're replaced, exactly as they should be, Nancy.'

'Well, there's no need for that. The time is right, Ellie, and I think you were meant to have them.'

'Nancy, I couldn't possibly be the guardian of such precious portraits. I didn't mean to make you think I should have them.'

'But, my ancestors told my Granny that someone would come for them. They didn't say exactly when, but I know the time is right, and I also know the lady named Elizabeth has to be you. Ellie, I'm uncertain where this might lead, and I don't know if this is the beginning or the end for you and Tom, but I do know that I've rarely seen two people so in love.'

'I don't know what you mean, Nancy.'

'On the night of the Ashe ball, I dressed Jane's hair, and I watched her dancing with Tom, albeit from the corridor with the other servants. And, I think I am right in saying that you witnessed it all.'

'*You* were there?' Ellie could hardly get the words out. 'I can hardly believe it.'

Nancy nodded. 'He loves you just as much as you love him.'

'Does he, Nancy? Does he *really*?'

'I can only tell you what I saw, but it's obvious to everyone. It's no wonder they all tease him so much about you.'

'But, that's just the thing, Nancy. It's not really me, is it? I'm a shadow from the present; he's a shade from the past. It's already happened, and I'm merely a channel for someone else's feelings, someone else's life.'

'When you're there, do you have any recollection of where

you've come from?'

'No ... none. I am Jane in mind, body and soul.'

'In that case, we have no need for further discussion. Come on, let's get this breakfast on the table before the eggs go cold.'

Ellie was stunned. She could hardly come to terms with what it all meant, but surely Nancy was quite wrong. It seemed she was trying to say that she and Jane Austen were one and the same person, or that they shared the same soul or something. And that seemed too ridiculous to think about. She picked up the teapot and the plate of bread just as Mrs Hill came bursting through into the kitchen.

'That's very kind of you to help,' she said picking up platefuls of food. 'How are you, Ellie?'

'I'm very well, Mrs Hill, thank you.'

'Well, just you take care – you've some exciting challenges ahead.'

Betty Hill smiled and her blue eyes twinkled, and for a second it struck Ellie how similar she looked to the Austen's housekeeper, Nanny Hilliard, before she reasoned that she was just getting carried away. Ellie could hear Jess laughing in the background at the antics of Mr Darcy and Mr Bingley, bringing her back to the concerns of the present. Besides, she'd better get used to living in the real world, she thought. After today, her ties with the house and Tom would be cut forever, and she would never see him again. That thought made Ellie feel desperately sad. She felt physically possessed with an aching to see him such as she'd never felt before, and the idea of being unable to go back filled her with despair.

Breakfast started as a quiet affair. Only Liberty, Martha and Donald seemed excited at the prospect of going to London, and all three made up for any lack of conversation in the others.

'Martha, we must go shopping for your wedding dress as soon as we get there,' said Liberty. 'I know a shop just off Oxford Street where my cousin went. She had this amazing Cinderella dress, all tulle and net – it was so wide there was hardly room for the groom!

And crystals, you have got to have crystals all over it, especially the bodice, which should be low-cut and plunging for best effect!'

'Thank you, Liberty, but I've got my own ideas about how I want to be dressed. I prefer something simpler – a vintage dress of ivory silk will be perfect, though I doubt I shall get away with that if my mother has anything to do with it. She wants me to have a designer gown, something by one of the big fashion houses, and I can't bear the thought of it – fishtails and ruffles, ugh ... Donald, you don't know how lucky you are; it's so easy for a man.'

Donald, who was thickly buttering a slice of toast, paused for a moment. 'There are still considerations to be made and visits to Locke's to buy my top hat, not to mention being measured for my shirt and morning suit in Jermyn Street.'

'Aren't you going to hire it?' said Liberty. 'What a waste of money. I can think of a million things I'd rather spend my money on than buying a morning suit you'll never wear again.'

'Oh, but I fully expect to wear it on many occasions. There will be Ascot, of course, and presentations at royal garden parties, and the like.'

Liberty nearly spat out the sausage she was chomping. She waved the remainder, which was stuck on her fork, in Donald's direction. 'I'm sorry, but who is going to invite *you* to anything royal? I thought you had to have done something worthwhile for that to happen. My uncle Ted was invited once – he was a lollipop man at the local school – been there at the school gates, boy and man, for fifty years before *he* was invited. He said Prince Charles was really nice, though he didn't actually speak to Uncle Ted, but the man who was next in line. Still, he really enjoyed it, even if there wasn't very much to eat and a lot of standing about, which he said made his bad leg play up like merry hell.'

'In my work as a curate and, inevitably, as a rector, and who is not to say bishop, eventually,' Donald interrupted, 'I hope to prove myself worthy of many an invitation. Besides, I have connections through my godmother who is intimately associated with the royal family.'

That silenced them all.

'My mother's second cousin, twice removed, is Henrietta Dorsey, and also my godmother. She is related to the queen's mother somewhere along the line.'

'Dorsey!' Ellie exclaimed, more shocked than ever. 'Is that the same family as Henry Dorsey?'

'I believe there is a familial association.'

'But, you and Henry didn't even speak to one another at the dig.'

'Well, the Dorsey connection is a very distant one. I do not see my godmother very often.'

'I bet he's never even met her,' Liberty whispered rather loudly to Cara.

'My godmother lives in Scotland most of the time, and as such, we do not see one another often, but she is expected to attend the wedding, of course. There will be many Dorseys attending, including Henry and his sister, Pippa, as a matter of fact.'

'He's coming to your wedding, even though you don't really know him?' said Ellie, incredulous.

'My dear, there are three hundred people attending on my side alone. I couldn't hope to know all of them. Naturally, my mother has invited family members, and he is one of them.'

Ellie noticed Jess was very quiet. With the mention of Henry and Pippa, she was clearly thinking of Charlie. It was not very likely that they'd see him in London but she hoped Charlie would still try and get in touch. She could see Jess's heart was breaking, and despite what Zara had hinted about Charlie and Pippa, Ellie didn't believe a word of it.

After breakfast, the girls went to their separate rooms to pack, and each found their own precious places they particularly wanted to see as a last memory. Ellie walked down to the lake where the willow trees fringing the water dipped their branches like trailing fingers, their leaves falling in cascades like green fountains. She remembered the icy scene where Tom had given her the ring she had hidden round her neck. If only he would magically appear now, she thought, yet knowing that would be impossible. Tom had left Ashe in winter; she would not see him in summer. The sun shimmered on the lake and two swans swam majestically in perfect harmony, mirroring the other in their movements. How she would have loved to stand with Tom and enjoy the scene. Looking up at the boathouse rising from the water with its verandah and windows, unchanged over the years except for fresh paint and the addition of some gothic decoration, she imagined him standing there, waving to her. Tears misted her eyes and spilled over her cheeks. Dreaming of her Mr Darcy would never be enough, but there was absolutely nothing she could do about it.

Saying goodbye to Mrs Hill, Nancy, and the dogs, was one of the most difficult experiences Ellie felt she'd ever endured. Watching them standing on the step as the taxi rolled away brought more tears from all the girls. Even Liberty was dabbing at her eyes, though pretending she'd just got dust from the road in them, and she took a long time either staring fiercely out of the window or asking Cara to see if she could find anything else causing the irritation. Ellie took one last look as the car turned out of the gates before the house was gone forever. Glancing up to the window where she'd first seen Tom, Ellie blinked in disbelief. There he was, his hand to his lips, blowing her a kiss. Craning her neck to see, she lost sight of him as the car manoeuvred into the road, and when she managed to look again, he was gone.

## Chapter 27

The girls travelled by train to London, and lugged their cases onto the underground at Waterloo. It was all rather overwhelming especially in the muggy heat, and they were glad to come out into the sunshine at Green Park Station. Mayfair and Hay's Mews were a relatively short walk away, but they were very happy when, at last, they found the right house. Converted from stables many years ago, the house was compact and could have fitted inside Ashe several times over, but there was a good-sized kitchen, a large sitting room, which doubled up as a dining room and three spacious bedrooms, fitted out with twin beds.

'We've been so spoiled these last few weeks,' said Liberty, 'I wish we could have brought Mrs Hill with us. The thought of cooking and cleaning for ourselves is awful! I'm starving now, and I don't suppose there's a thing in the fridge.'

As it turned out, there was a note left by someone who signed herself Magda. She'd left some provisions: cheese, ham, eggs, milk, butter and bread to be going on with, and when she came in to do the weekly cleaning she would also do their shopping if they wished.

'Thank goodness for that,' said Liberty. 'I daresay she'd cook for us if we asked her.'

'Well, we're not going to – poor woman, she's probably got enough to do,' said Ellie. 'I always felt uncomfortable at the amount of looking after us that Mrs Hill did. It will do you good to learn to cook, Liberty. One day you're going to have to do it.'

'Not if I can bag myself a rich husband like Donald,' Liberty retorted. 'But, he will have to be good-looking too. No offence, Martha, but I couldn't settle just for the money.'

'I *am* in love with him.' Martha shot a look of pure contempt at Liberty.

'I expect knowing he's got aristocratic connections is very helpful where that's concerned,' said Cara, chiming in.

'Oh, please don't be spiteful.' Jess knew that Liberty and Cara needed reining in from time to time. 'I'll do an early supper, and then perhaps we can all go out for a walk. The journey has made us all irritable.'

Jess whipped up some ham and cheese toasties whilst Liberty and Cara laid the table. Martha fetched glasses of water, and Ellie put on some coffee for after they'd eaten.

'Greg Whitely is working in London somewhere,' said Liberty. 'He's got a new telly programme, I think.'

'Well, we're not likely to bump into him, are we?' said Ellie. 'It's not as if we move in the same circles – and a good thing too. I don't think he's the kind of guy I want to hang around with.'

'Just because he likes a good laugh,' said Liberty. 'He's fine; you just have to know how to handle him. Like all men, keep them dangling, and they'll come back for more.'

Ellie noticed Liberty still wore Greg's wristwatch, but she was fairly convinced Greg had tired of her. Anyway, it was pointless to argue with Liberty, she always had the last word.

Someone's phone was bleeping. Ellie saw by Jess's expression it was hers, and that it must be a text. She also knew despite not hearing anything from Charlie that Jess had not stopped hoping he might get in touch.

'Aren't you going to take a look?'

'I don't suppose it's anything important – just someone trying to sell me something.'

Ellie got up and picked up the phone. 'Here you are, I know you're being polite because we're eating, but it might be important.'

Jess couldn't help sighing before checking her phone, but when her eyes widened in surprise, they were all interested to hear what it said. 'It's from Zara. She says Will MacGourtey told her I was coming to London and would I like to meet up.'

Ellie grinned. 'See, I told you everything would be fine. Charlie's just been busy, that's all.'

'Well, she hasn't mentioned Charlie.'

'Just text back and say you'd love to meet up. Who knows, maybe Charlie will be there.'

Jess was animated and excited when she'd finished the exchange of texts that passed between her and Zara who suggested they meet at Fortnum and Mason's for afternoon tea the next day.

Ellie couldn't have been more pleased for her friend. Tomorrow was going to be a busy day for them all. Martha was going to meet Donald's mother for the first time at Peter Jones department store in Sloane Square, and they were going to be looking at the church and making wedding plans. Liberty and Cara were off on a shopping expedition, which left Ellie who was meeting Will and his friend Oliver at the gallery in Cork Street. She was really looking forward to it but felt incredibly nervous. It was impossible to believe that anyone could like her work enough to put it in such a prestigious gallery, and a little part of her still doubted that it was really happening. Thinking of the paintings and the inspiring landscape of Steventon naturally led to thinking about Tom, and the last time they'd been together. She tried to tell herself that she should forget him but it was so hard when the memories were so strong. Determining on going to bed early when they got back from their walk, she tried to put all her anxieties and thoughts of kissing Tom out of her head. Tomorrow was another day.

Ellie was up early the next morning for her ten o'clock appointment with Will and Oliver. She tried on several outfits before she was satisfied that she looked just right. She wore a floaty shirt-dress with contrasting ankle boots and topped it off with a black boater. It was comfortable but modern, and she felt ready for anything. Cork Street was not very far away and Ellie knew she was bound to get there too early, but she hated to run out of time and would rather be pacing up and down outside for ten minutes than arrive breathless and late. Hugging Jess and wishing her luck, she waved goodbye before setting off through the mews.

Early mornings and Londoners did not generally go together. The streets seemed very quiet apart from the noise of the traffic, and such a contrast after being in the countryside. The unmistakable smell of London seeped from its yellow brick walls, of damp clay and soot after rain, of iron black railings in the heat, spilt wine on wooden bars emanating from pub doorways, fried chips and curry, Italian coffee, and the intoxicating scent of Lime tree flowers. Ellie took a route past Berkeley Square, not quite as romantic as she'd imagined it, along Hay Hill, Grafton Street, and New Bond Street, which was filling up with taxis and chauffeur driven luxury cars depositing expensively dressed shoppers. She was starting to feel less confident about what she was wearing, and wondered if she should have worn a more formal dress for her first meeting, then told herself off for being ridiculous. Turning into Cork Street where the majority of buildings were given over to art galleries, she soon found Oliver Fitzwilliam's, a gallery converted from an old Georgian house. Pushing the glass doors on the right of the frontage, she took a deep breath and entered the cool vestibule inside. After the bright light outside, it took a moment for her eyes to adjust to seeing, but she was aware of someone standing at a reception desk. He had his back to her as he rummaged in a drawer, but Ellie saw enough to appreciate broad shoulders, dark hair, and a pair of long lean legs encased in light chinos.

He obviously hadn't heard her come in and so Ellie thought she ought to speak. 'Excuse me, I'm here to see Oliver

Fitzwilliam.'

She jumped what felt like ten feet in the air when he turned round. Ellie could not believe her eyes. Henry Dorsey was standing in front of her grinning from ear to ear.

'Hi Ellie, Oliver's expecting you. If you just go through that door on the left, you'll find him.'

'OMG!' It was out before she could stop it. 'What are *you* doing here?'

'I'm working in the gallery, mostly on reception, as it happens ... helping out.'

Ellie realised she'd probably sounded a little rude. 'I'm so sorry, it's just such a shock to see you.'

'Don't worry, you didn't know I was going to be here, I expect Will forgot to mention it.'

'Have you been working here long? This is such a coincidence.'

'Not really ... Oliver is my uncle. I often help out in the holidays. How are you?'

He was smiling at her, and, for once, Ellie had only charitable thoughts about Henry. He looked genuinely pleased to see her.

She found herself smiling back at him. 'I'm fine, thank you. How are you?'

His eyes, dark brown and freckled with amber, and fringed by the thickest black lashes she'd ever seen on a guy, were twinkling under dark brows. His shirt was pure cotton, with sleeves rolled back showing tanned forearms, and his long fingers were hooked into the pockets at his hips. He stared at her a moment longer before smiling broadly, showing off beautiful white teeth. 'I'm really good, Ellie. Look, it would be lovely to chat afterwards. Are you up for a coffee?'

Henry was being so nice, and caught as she was in such an astonishing situation, she felt she could hardly refuse him. 'That would be great. Thank you, Henry, I'd really like that.'

The phone rang then, and Henry picked up the receiver. He sounded in charge, and was talking very knowledgeably about the work on display in the gallery. Ellie turned to head off to the door Henry had pointed out, and glancing back couldn't help noticing that Henry was still staring at her even though he was in full flow on the phone. It was slightly unnerving, but Ellie managed to put him out of her mind as she knocked on the door and went into the next room.

Will MacGourtey seemed so happy to see her, throwing his arms around her and kissing her on both cheeks. It was wonderful to see such a friendly and familiar face. He swiftly introduced her to Oliver, an older, slightly greyer, and more distinguished-looking version of Henry.

'Ellie, what a pleasure – I've heard so much about you.'

'Oh dear, I hope it wasn't all bad.'

'Gosh, no – all good – wonderful, in fact. Henry has hardly stopped talking about you, isn't that right, Will?'

Ellie relaxed immediately, warming to Oliver's easy attitude. He was like a laid-back version of Henry, and considering he was at least twenty years older, she was surprised she found him quite so attractive. If only Henry wasn't so jumped up and snobby, she thought, he would be just as nice as Oliver and twice as handsome without the scowl he usually wore.

Will nodded. 'I think we can safely say he's your biggest fan ... next to me, of course. Actually, he was really keen that we tell Oliver about your work, though he wouldn't suggest it to you himself. I think he's a bit shy, to tell you the truth. I was sworn to secrecy, but it doesn't really matter. It worked, and you're here!'

Ellie wondered if she'd been dropped into some sort of alternate universe for a moment. She was aware that her mouth had fallen open, and thought she'd better close it for fear of appearing completely dense, rude, or both. The idea that Henry had been part of the scheme to have her work exhibited was too much to take in, and that he not only liked her work, but was also a 'fan' of it, was unbelievable. As the exhibition was discussed, Ellie tried to concentrate on what they were saying, but every now and then her thoughts turned to Henry. She couldn't make head or tail of it. This was a Henry she just didn't recognise. Had he a twin brother he hadn't told her about?

Henry came in ten minutes later. It was impossible to look him in the eye, though she felt his eyes on hers constantly. When at last she was brave enough to return his gaze, he smiled at her in such a way that he made her feel really cherished. He looked as if he was incredibly proud of her, and spoke of her paintings like an expert who'd studied them carefully.

'Now, tell me,' said Oliver, 'how have you been getting along with my nephew? I believe you met in Hampshire on the dig.'

'Yes, we met in Steventon, though I couldn't say we got along, exactly.'

Oliver threw back his head and laughed. 'Don't tell me, Ellie. I suppose he's been rather reluctant to mix, and kept himself to himself. He's always studying. I'm always trying to get him to go out a little more.'

'I don't know about his studying,' said Ellie, staring back at Henry with laughter in her eyes, 'but, he was more than reticent about talking to anyone very much, or dancing. In fact, he told me in not so many words that socialising with the volunteers on the dig wasn't really something he was interested in doing.'

Oliver roared with laughter again. 'No, he never would give himself the trouble of getting to know anyone.'

Henry was laughing now. 'I give up. I shall never understand how some people want to know everything about other people or how in wishing to do so, they find such conversation easy. I hate talking to people I don't know, and there's the end of it.'

'But we all have to do things we don't like, and we should be careful not to hurt other people's feelings by ignoring them or when giving our opinions so forcefully,' said Ellie wondering if she'd said too much.

'Okay, I admit you're right. Maybe I wasn't as friendly as I could have been in Hampshire, but perhaps I had my reasons. Anyway, let's not discuss it further. I mean to make it up to you, if you'll let me, Ellie. Can I take you for lunch?'

Ellie didn't know how to answer, though she supposed she'd asked for it with the way she'd attacked him in front of his uncle. What could she do? Coffee was one thing but lunch was quite another. It would mean having to talk to him at length.

The words were out before she could stop them. 'Yes, that would be lovely.'

Oliver and Will said their goodbyes, saying they'd look forward to seeing her the next day, and the next moment found her walking down the street to the Italian restaurant a few doors down. Henry held open the door for her. She couldn't think of any other guy ever having done that before, and when he placed a protective hand in the small of her back, as they were ushered to a table downstairs, she felt almost sorry when they parted to sit down opposite one another at the table. Ellie was lost for words, for once, though the open kitchen meant they could watch the cooks preparing the food and pass comment on the rotisserie behind them, roasting large legs of lamb, fillets of beef, shoulders of pork and racks of chickens. Henry asked for the à la carte menu, and if anything was guaranteed to put Ellie even less at ease it was the sight of a menu where everything cost more than she'd ever spent on a meal in her entire lifetime.

She scanned the pages trying to find something that didn't look too expensive, but failed miserably. A poached egg with a bit of salad was the price of three of her favourite luxury boxes of seashell chocolates, and that was just the starter.

'I can recommend the lobster to begin with,' Henry said, 'and then the beef is very good ... though, of course, you might want something else, entirely. The Dover sole is always excellent and a little lighter for lunch, if you prefer fish.'

Henry was trying really hard, going through the menu and explaining any dish she was unsure of, and he did it in such a lovely way, Ellie didn't feel stupid at all. When she'd made her choice of the lobster followed by lamb cutlets, she started to relax. He took charge and ordered for them both, and Ellie really appreciated the way he did it, always asking and checking with her first. He had impeccable manners.

'Why didn't you tell me that you had something to do with arranging the exhibition with your uncle?' Ellie asked, tucking into the lobster when it arrived.

Henry put down his fork. 'I had a feeling it wouldn't go down very well. I knew if I asked you myself, you'd probably say no. I'm really sorry we got off to a bad start, Ellie.'

'It's all forgotten. I was probably just as much to blame as you, anyway. I should be apologising too.'

'No, there's no need. I hope we can be friends now.'

'Of course, and I want to thank you, Henry. I am so thrilled that you asked your uncle to take my paintings. It was very generous of you.'

'I can't take all the credit. Will was very keen for your work to be seen in London. You're so talented; Ellie, and I know how hard it is to break into the art world. Besides, I want to be there when you make it big.'

'Well, I wouldn't hold your breath, if I were you.'

'I've no doubt you are going to make a name for yourself. All your friends will be very proud of you.'

Ellie was thoughtful. She really wanted to ask Henry about Charlie, but she knew she'd have to ask very carefully. It was important to her not to spoil the lovely time they were having. In the end, she decided a direct question would be best. 'Talking of friends, how is Charlie?'

'He's well. We've been recording some new songs, and then we've been out gigging at a lot of new clubs. It's hard work, but he's got a record label almost on side. Charlie's very busy with the band. It's an important time for him.'

Ellie couldn't keep quiet. 'What a pity it's so important he's forgotten all his friends. He made Jess think she was someone he considered significant, but he can't even be bothered to send her a text, let alone phone her.'

'I don't know anything about that. He's just got a lot on his plate.'

He looked sincere, and Ellie decided not to press him further. It was hardly Henry's fault if Charlie didn't want to contact Jess. Henry changed the subject almost immediately, which showed just how uncomfortable he felt about it. They were soon discussing painting again, and Ellie couldn't help but be impressed with his knowledge, which wasn't surprising considering he'd been working with his uncle for a few years.

'I like to be independent and earn my own money, and anything I can add to help fund the digs I like to go on is always really helpful.'

'So, archaeology is your true passion?'

'I wouldn't be telling the truth if I didn't say my music was equally important. I consider myself really blessed to have so many interests. I love travelling, and if I can combine all three, I'm in heaven.'

'I would love to travel, and paint pictures of all the places I'd visit. If I sell any of my paintings, that's what I plan to do.'

'Wow, what an exhibition that will be – Ellie's world travels. So, where would you like to go first?'

Before she knew it, three hours had passed by, and they hadn't even had their coffee. It was five o'clock before either of them realised how late it was getting and it was time to say goodbye. Ellie couldn't believe how much she'd enjoyed Henry's company, and all the way home she still asked if she hadn't dreamt the whole episode. She was anxious to see Jess, not only to tell her all about the difference in Henry, but also to see how she'd got on with Zara. When she opened the door, Ellie wasn't expecting to see Jess as she knew she was meeting Zara at four, but when Liberty greeted her at the door saying Jess had come home in floods of tears, she raced upstairs to find out what had happened.

## Chapter 28

Jess was sitting, dry-eyed, in their room. She was reading a book, looking quite her usual self, but for the fact that her eyes were red-rimmed, and her nose was a little swollen. Ellie waited for her to speak.

'Did you have a lovely time? Was it exciting discussing your paintings at the gallery?'

Ellie nodded. It was very obvious that Jess had had an awful time. She decided it would probably be best not to mention the fact that she'd seen Henry, and that she'd been out to lunch with him, let alone tell her that he was actually related to Oliver. That piece of information could wait. 'Oliver is a really nice guy, and it was quite amazing to be discussing my work with him. How about you … do you want to talk?'

'I don't know why I'm so upset. Zara was perfectly friendly, though our conversation was a bit awkward, I must admit. I asked after Charlie, and she told me he was out that afternoon with Pippa. I don't know why I held on to the idea that we would somehow get back together if I was here in London, but … it's just so hard, Ellie. I've never felt for anyone the feelings I have for Charlie, and the thought of him being with someone else is so hard to bear.'

'Look, Zara told you he was with Pippa – it doesn't mean he is *with* her in that sense. Perhaps they were rehearsing or something. We've only just got here. I think you should give him a chance, just in case work has been too overwhelming.'

'But, he hasn't even tried to contact me by phone. He gave Zara no message for me, and I think I'd be pretty daft to think there's any chance of getting together now.'

When Ellie thought about Henry's reaction she began to wonder if she'd been entirely wrong about Charlie. It was hard to see Jess trying to be brave but so obviously heartbroken. There were only three weeks before Martha's wedding, and then she must think of something they could do to take Jess's mind off Charlie. There was a favourite music festival coming up near Bath, and if Ellie could still get tickets that might be the very thing to help.

Ellie spent the next couple of days at the gallery. Henry wasn't there on either occasion, but she was quite pleased not to have any distractions as she collaborated over the design of the exhibition and made her wishes felt. Besides, she didn't really want Jess to know about Henry just yet, and if he was busy elsewhere that suited her fine. She had to admit, when she thought about him, she'd really enjoyed his company. There was still much she'd like to ask him about, regarding Greg Whitely. She was beginning to wonder if Henry's assessment of Greg might have more truth in it, but she'd have to wait until the time was right to ask him. Oliver wanted her to go back in on the following Monday to see how she liked what had been achieved, so she hoped she might see Henry then. Ellie had decided she might ask a little more about Charlie too. For now, she was free to spend the rest of the week, as she liked.

The girls were all eager to go sightseeing. They'd all had days out in London before, but never the luxury of time as they had now. They enjoyed a trip to Buckingham Palace, and watched the changing of the guard, sailed on a boat down the river Thames and saw the crown jewels in the Tower of London. They took in some culture, visiting the National Gallery in Trafalgar Square, and the portrait gallery, gasping at Jane Austen's portrait and her writing desk at the British Library, which had even Liberty staring in awe. The weekend was taken up with pure pleasure, and they all had a wonderful time. Martha hardly mentioned Donald or the wedding, which was a relief to them all, and Liberty didn't moan once, not even when they were in the library. It had to be said she was spending quite a lot of time texting on her phone, but there was nothing new in that, and the fact that she was happy to be with them all and seemed to be enjoying herself, was a plus. Morale was high, and even if Jess looked wistful on occasion, it was clear she really loved their outings.

Ellie went off to the gallery on Monday morning with a happy heart. Jess had received news about her work experience that she was taking up in September as part of her course, and that had seemed to cheer her up. She was already making plans for the lessons she was going to teach, and studying the timetable. Ellie was glad she had a lot to keep her occupied. Liberty was going to visit an old school-friend, she said, so Cara and Martha were going on a shopping trip for ideas on Martha's dress.

Henry was in reception looking very handsome, Ellie thought. He was wearing a dark denim shirt, which made his eyes look blacker, and he smiled when he saw her.

'Ellie, I hope you're really excited, and if you're not, you will be when you see it. Oliver's just popped out, but he said you were to go in and take a look. He seemed to think you might want to do that on your own, but I'm longing to see your reaction.'

'Your uncle is a very sensitive man. Your aunt must be a very lucky woman.'

'Yes, he is a wonderful man. I gave up trying to emulate him years ago.'

Ellie laughed at that, and followed him as he pushed open the door. His enthusiasm was infectious, and she decided that it really was fun to have him share the moment with her. Ellie couldn't wait to see her paintings, and when she walked through the door, she felt completely overwhelmed. Every one was mounted in its own space and lit from above. All through university she'd dreamed of having her own exhibition, something she thought she'd have to wait a very long time for, and now it was a reality. It was all she could do to stop throwing her arms around him.

'Isn't it amazing?' Henry came and stood next to her. He was watching her face, and Ellie could hardly disguise her emotions. Tears misted her eyes, and she hastily brushed them away with her fingers. In the next second she felt an arm steal round her as Henry pulled her into his shoulder. 'Oh, bless you, Ellie ... are you okay?'

Ellie looked up to see Henry looking down at her with genuine empathy in his eyes. She felt him touch her face, and his fingers brushing her cheeks where the tears lay in a wet trail. He was looking at her steadily, and she didn't know where to look.

'Ellie ...' His fingers brushed her jaw-line and tilted her chin towards him. Those dark eyes gazed down at her before he lowered his lips on hers, and she closed her eyes in response. She felt his arms slip around her waist, as he pulled her closer. Henry's lips were soft; he held her head in his hands, as his kisses grew more passionate. She was completely swept away by the feel of him, and his powerful presence. He dwarfed her, held her protectively, and she allowed him to take possession. Her arms went round his neck, her fingers caressing the curls that fell on his collar. How long they stood there, she was uncertain, but when they finally separated, Ellie couldn't think what had happened. It frightened her a little, and she didn't quite know what to do with it.

Before either of them had a chance to say anything, Oliver was through the door. Ellie hardly heard a word he said, and hoped she didn't sound completely unintelligible. When she managed to glance at Henry, he looked exactly as he always did. Had he really kissed her? The situation was so bizarre she almost couldn't believe it had happened. She could hear Oliver and Henry talking, but her mind was elsewhere.

'If it's all right with you, Uncle Ollie, I thought I'd take Ellie along to the summer exhibition at the Royal Academy this afternoon.'

Ellie looked up in surprise but smiled at the suggestion.

'That is, if you're not doing anything else, and you'd like to come,' Henry added, his eyes pleading with her to accept.

'I'd love to visit the Royal Academy,' Ellie said at once. 'I've always wanted to see the summer exhibition.'

It crossed Ellie's mind, as they took the short walk to the Royal Academy, how one never knows what life has in store. If someone had told her a fortnight ago that she'd be visiting galleries in London with Henry, she would never have believed it. The other matter of the kiss, she hardly wanted to think about. She glowed with embarrassment at the very thought, and couldn't account for any reason that she'd been so willing a participant. Missing Tom was a factor she knew, and missing his kisses made her ache with emotion. Perhaps she should have declined the offer of the trip but she knew there was a treat in store. Henry had wanted her to go with him so much; that was clear. If anything untoward happened again, she'd be ready. They'd been swept away by the moment, and she'd put money on the fact that Henry was not really interested in her romantically.

Over the next few days, Ellie started to get to know Henry really well, and she began to wonder how she could ever have misjudged him so much. Every afternoon, when he was supposed to be working Oliver allowed time for a different excursion each day, and Ellie was being really spoiled. He'd taken her for tea at Claridges and breakfast at the Wolseley, there'd been walks in Hyde Park and Kensington Gardens, and they'd enjoyed a tour round Kensington Palace. Henry was kind, considerate, and talkative, so much so, that Ellie soon forgot the Henry of old. She'd been reluctant to talk about him to Jess, but she knew she would have to say something sooner or later. As it was, Jess seemed happy caught up in the planning for her teaching course next year, and was occupied with visits to the school where she was to be doing her teaching practice in September.

Ellie still thought about Tom from time to time with such an ache that she didn't like to dwell on those memories too often, but it was impossible not to let the thoughts intrude. Besides, she had no control over them. Something would trigger them: the scent of a fresh cut lime, the sound of a voice with an Irish lilt or the sight of early Christmas cards set out in Harrod's department store, would bring him clearly into view, and her heart responded with a bitter sweet sadness she'd never experienced before.

On the following Tuesday, Ellie rushed to the gallery with hopes of seeing Henry. She was really enjoying getting to know him, and was relieved that there had been no repetition of any kissing scenes. They'd both been caught up in the moment, she realised, but despite sometimes wishing things could be different, she was glad they were friends, at least. It was more than disappointing when she found he wasn't going to be there. Oliver said he was working with Charlie and that Henry had sent his best wishes, and would catch up with her as soon as he could.

'Henry is helping Charlie's sister to transpose some music,' said Oliver. 'Do you know Zara?'

'Yes ... a little,' Ellie answered. 'Charlie, I know better. He seemed such a lovely person when we were in Hampshire. He and Henry are great friends, aren't they?'

'Yes, they have been very close for a number of years. My nephew likes taking people under his wing, looking out for them, that kind of thing.'

'Yes, I can imagine.'

'And from something that he told me the other day, I have reason to think Henry's been doing a good job of taking care of his friend. Charlie not only needs Henry looking after him, but also he's very much indebted to him ... though it's all guesswork on my part. He could have been talking about someone else.'

'What do you mean?'

'Well, it's something Henry wouldn't want generally known, I'm sure.'

'I wouldn't repeat it, I promise.'

Oliver hesitated. 'Just remember, that I am not absolutely certain that it's about Charlie. He told me that he recently saved a great friend from the clutches of a gold-digger, but without mentioning names or any other circumstances. I only suspected it to be Charlie from believing him the kind of young man to be gullible enough to fall for someone who was only after his money, and from knowing them to have been together the whole of this summer.'

'Did Henry say anything else about this girl?'

'Only that the girl in question was highly unsuitable. He said she was a typical example of someone from a poor background, seeing her chance and throwing herself at Charlie. Henry was really worried for him, as this girl had got her talons into him in just a matter of weeks.'

'And how did he split them up?'

'He didn't talk about how he managed it, said Oliver, smiling. 'He only told me what I've just told you.'

Ellie made no answer, and stared ahead, as if deeply perusing a painting, her heart swelling with indignation. After watching her a little, Oliver asked her why she was so thoughtful.

'I've been thinking about what you've been telling me,' she said. 'I don't really see that it was any of your nephew's business. Why was Henry to be the judge?'

'Do you think Henry was wrong to interfere?'

'I don't see what right Henry had to decide on his friend's preference for one girl over any other, or why, he was to influence his friend in such a personal matter. But,' she continued, 'as we don't have all the facts, it's not fair to completely criticise him. Perhaps, as you say, there wasn't any real relationship there.'

'That's true,' said Oliver, 'though that rather takes away from Henry's victory in the case.'

Though his last remark was made in a jokey way, Ellie could only think of poor Jess. It was obvious to her that Charlie's gold-digger could be no other. Infuriated by what Henry had done, firstly to influence his friend into believing that Jess held no affection for him, and then to have told his uncle and to have used such awful expressions about the sweetest girl in the world, was unforgiveable. How could she have been so blind? Swept away for the moment by his charming and lavish ways, Ellie scolded herself for her own behaviour. She admitted to herself that however lovely Henry had seemed there had been other forces at work, and she felt ashamed. His confidence, a natural result from the power he wielded as a consequence of his moneyed background and education had swept her along, and was as much a part of his attraction as his good looks. Ellie had fallen for it as she was sure many women before her had too. Good-looking men would always be attractive, but those who were handsome and rich, were ultimately irresistible. Except, she'd been brought up rather sharply, and was glad of it. What had she been thinking? The more she thought about what Henry had done, the crosser she got. It was impossible to think of staying at the gallery any longer, and she left as soon as she could. At least, she wouldn't have to go there any longer. The only reason she'd been going so much was at Henry's insistence. Now that the exhibition was up and running, there really wasn't any reason for her to be still turning up every day. Ellie didn't know how she'd speak to Henry ever again, but she was determined to let him know her true feelings. Not one used to writing letters, she felt it was the only course of communication left open to her, and boy, was she going to let him know exactly how she felt.

As she turned the corner onto Grafton Street walking at top speed, she ran headlong into Henry.

'Darling girl,' he shouted, picking her up and twirling her round in his arms, 'where are you going in such a hurry?'

## Chapter 29

'I'm going home,' Ellie said, struggling out of his arms, and brushing him away. 'Don't you dare call me your darling girl. I am not, nor will I ever be!'

'Gosh, Ellie, what's wrong?'

'I know why Charlie hasn't been in touch with Jess. How *could* you, Henry? Because of *you* she has a broken heart!'

'What are you talking about? Listen Ellie, forget all that nonsense, I came to tell you something *really* important. It might be the most incredible moment of both of our lives – and even more momentous for *you* in many ways.'

For a second Ellie wondered if she might have been mistaken about Henry and the part he'd played in splitting Charlie up from Jess.

He took her hands, and kissed them both. 'Ellie, this may not be the right time or place, but I have to tell you something ... I know it's crazy, and it's been really hard coming to terms with what is essentially so flawed and absolutely wrong from every point of view, but in the end, I've just given in to it. There's no other way to say it – I'm hopelessly in love with you. Despite everything that's dubious about starting a relationship with you, I've decided to go along with every damned feeling. Wow, Ellie, I've never felt like this before.'

'What do you mean ... it's been hard, and despite everything that's wrong, you're going along with it?'

'Well, we're so different, aren't we? I've money; you have none. My family are connected in the highest society circles, yours are ... not. Let's face it, my mother is hardly going to be impressed – she's expecting me to marry a lady, at the very least. Look, Ellie, you must know, this is a relationship with a very wretched beginning.'

'Hang on a minute, Henry. Whatever feelings you think you have for me, let me tell you now that if I have ever considered having any for you, and I can assure you that *love* has never been on my mind, this last speech of yours has entirely blown them away. You have to be the most arrogant and conceited person I know. How dare you!'

'I don't understand, Ellie. I've just told you that in spite of everything, I love you – I can't help myself!'

'Exactly, and let me tell you that there is no way on earth you could have told me in a less inviting way. You have the nerve to tell me that you've fallen in love with me although everything about me is wrong. I'm not good enough for you or your mother, but you love me anyway! Did you really think this 'love proclamation' would have me falling into your arms because it has had the very opposite effect. And, besides all that ridiculous stuff you're spouting, even if I was very slightly tempted, for a millisecond, to go out with you, I would not. I know you were behind Charlie's dumping of Jess. How *could* you?'

'I've been kinder to him than I've been to myself.'

Ellie groaned. 'The trouble with you, Henry, is that you think you have the right to control other people's lives – to have influence and power over them. The rich are all the same, manipulating everything from friendships to business with no one except themselves and their own ends in mind. It's disgusting. Just as I thought you weren't quite as bad as your character had been painted. Greg Whitely is another case in point. Your family thought nothing of trampling all over him!'

'You're very interested in him and his welfare,' said Henry, his complexion turning scarlet.

'Anyone who had an ounce of compassion would feel really sorry for him, and the way he's been treated by you.'

'Oh, yes, he's been treated very badly.'

'There, so you do not deny it!'

Henry hung his head, shaking it from side to side. 'And this is all that you think of me? I'm very sorry to have been the cause of such anguish. I completely understand your feelings and am only ashamed of what mine have been. Well, my uncle is expecting me, and I think I've said all I wish to say.'

Ellie was so cross she couldn't speak. She turned on her heel leaving him staring after her, before he decided it was pointless to follow. Everything he said just seemed to make it worse.

The following day, Ellie awoke with a sore throat. Feeling really unwell, she was glad that she had a legitimate excuse, if she needed one, not to go to the gallery. She felt so miserable, but she was determined to hide her emotions from Jess who would want to know why she was feeling upset. It was enough to indulge in a silent cry in the bathroom, but she quickly pulled herself together for fear of Jess seeing her red eyes. She padded downstairs to make a cup of tea, and passing the front door en route noticed a letter just poked under the door with her name inscribed upon it.

Ellie snatched it up, stuffing it into her dressing gown pocket before anyone else could see it. Everyone upstairs was still sleeping so Ellie took a chance by taking it into the sitting room to read.

*Dear Ellie,*

*This is not a love letter; I want to be very clear about that from the start. You asked me about G. W. and so I will tell you, though in the interests of all concerned, I would ask that you destroy this letter after reading.*

*Whatever else you may think, one thing we have to be clear on. Greg Whitely is a complete waste of time and space – there are no words I can write here that I feel would adequately describe the low-life that he is, and I cannot stress that enough. He and my family go back a long way – his father and mine were in business together, as you know. Greg's father made some unwise investments and was bailed out by my ever-forgiving father, but unlike HIS father who made genuine mistakes that could have been the error of anyone in business, his son decided to take greater risks. He put the company in danger – almost entirely ruining the business and leaving us with debts that took several years to recover from. He was sacked, of course, but fortunately for him, he was given a job from a friend in the family, though Greg considered, at the time, that nothing but a partnership was acceptable. He drifted for a while, and became hopelessly lost, as he struggled with his own demons of drug abuse and alcoholism. As if all that wasn't enough, a few years ago, after his father died, he went after my sister with nothing but malice, revenge and her seduction in mind. He'd become a presenter by then and was becoming well known. She was very young, just fifteen, and dazzled by the 'bright lights' and his circle of 'celebrity friends'. He made her believe that he was in love with her – when all he was interested in was destroying her life as a way to get back at the family. He had plans to get her out of the country, but I've no desire to tell you of all his sordid campaign to wreck my sister's very existence. Fortunately, I found her in time to save her, but I hope you can understand why I have never been able to forgive him for his actions.*

*As for your friend, Jess, I admit I did warn Charlie against her. He has all too often been the easy prey of fortune hunters, and has always suffered for his kind and generous nature. We have known one another since we were boys and I've always sought to protect him. Whilst Jess seemed a perfectly pleasant girl, it was very clear that they were from totally different backgrounds, and I saw nothing in her behaviour to suggest that she was in love with him. I told him as much, but whether that has anything to do with*

the way he has behaved since, I can't say. He is quite capable of making up his own mind, and making his own decisions though, of course, he has always been under my influence to an extent and looks up to me quite like a brother.
 I have nothing more to add, and can only wish you well.
 Take care,
 Henry.

 Ellie seethed with indignation on her first reading of the letter with particular reference to the part he'd played in splitting up Jess and Charlie. He'd known exactly what he was doing, as far as she was concerned. Charlie was clearly following Henry's advice, and Ellie was sure that the latter had really driven his point home in order to manipulate him. She meant to destroy the letter there and then, but found herself re-reading parts, especially the beginning, and what Henry had said about his sister. The episode with Greg she thought had a definite ring of truth about it. She knew how charming he could be, and she'd been convinced that Greg had tried to drug her on the evening of the party at Ashe. It was perfectly horrifying to think that he'd tried to seduce Pippa and to realise he'd concocted a hideous plan to destroy her life – it was no wonder Henry was so cold towards him, and reticent about forming new relationships. Although Ellie was finding it hard to forgive Henry for his part in separating Jess from Charlie, she couldn't feel anything but sympathy for the way Greg had behaved towards Henry and his family. She felt ashamed to think she'd been so taken in by Greg, and she couldn't think of either he or Henry without feeling that she had been blind, partial, and prejudiced.
 Ellie decided she would go to the gallery, after all, if only to make her peace with Henry. She dressed quickly, leaving a note for Jess to say she would not be long. Stepping outside, there was a definite hint of autumn in the air. Summer was on the wane, and rain was falling steadily from the skies. Grabbing an umbrella from the stand in the hall she set off into the grey streets, uncertain exactly what she was going to say to Henry when she saw him.

When she reached the gallery, the glass outer doors were shut against the weather, and when she peered inside she couldn't see clearly if Henry were there or not. Taking a deep breath to settle her nerves, she pushed open the door.

It was a complete shock to find nothing of the familiar reception desk inside and when she turned back on herself, the door by which she'd entered was completely altered, too. The door opened, and there was Frank, her brother in another time, with another who surely must be brother Edward, and when she looked again, Tom was there to welcome her in.

## Chapter 30

I stood rather shyly, sandwiched between my brothers in the narrow hallway. Hardly able to look at him, I thought he'd grown taller in the seven months that had crawled slowly by, every day stretching out like an eternity.

'Welcome to London, how do you do, sir?' Tom addressed Edward first, shaking his hand warmly. He passed along the line, giving mine an extra squeeze, reassuring me that he was as thrilled to see me, as I was him.

'My uncle is sorry he is unable to welcome you himself, but he will dine with us later this afternoon.'

'Thank you, Mr Lefroy, that is most kind,' said Edward. 'We are indebted to you and your uncle for opening up your home to us.'

'Friends and neighbours are always welcome, Mr Austen. When my Aunt Lefroy found out you were coming to London she alerted us immediately. It's a pleasure to be of service. We have taken the liberty of procuring some tickets for an evening's entertainment ... I hope you are able to join us at Astley's tonight.'

I felt so excited at the prospect and remembered Tom's words all those months ago, though it was impossible not to feel nervous at the thought of meeting Tom's Uncle Benjamin. The honour of being invited to stay I knew had been engineered by dear Madame. My hope that I might make a good impression weighed heavy on me.

'How delightful,' answered Edward, turning to grin at me. 'I've heard Jane say how much she has wanted to visit Astley's, and we would love to join you.'

'Excellent!' said Tom, 'Now, would you care for some tea?'

Mrs Dawson, the housekeeper, brought in the tea things and the gentlemen chatted about sport and country pursuits, and the races that my brother Henry had not managed to attend after all. I was happy to look around. This room was where Tom spent his evenings with his uncle. It was a very masculine space with dark panelled walls, and robust furniture. Gentlemen's periodicals were stacked on a table in the window; along with a selection of worthy books, not a novel in sight, and the only other decoration were one or two good oil paintings on the walls. I couldn't imagine that Tom would have found it much fun living here. I formed an idea of Uncle Benjamin as a very sober and serious sort of gentleman, and I felt more nervous than ever.

'Mrs Dawson will see you to your rooms, and my manservant John can help with anything you might require. Do not hesitate to ask if we can make your visit more comfortable,' Tom said.

'Thank you, Mr Lefroy,' said Edward, rising to his feet. 'I have a little business to attend to in town that I must see to immediately, if you will excuse me, and Frank, I believe, you also have a commission to make. Please forgive us for our hasty departure, but we look forward to seeing you later on.'

'I will look after the young lady, Mr Austen,' said Mrs Dawson.

My brothers seemed satisfied, and left. We heard the front door shut, and Tom caught my eye and smiled. 'Mrs Dawson, what do you say to a trip out this afternoon? Would you please be chaperone for my friend and I?'

'I would be happy to oblige if your young friend wishes it. In the meantime, please follow me, Miss Austen, and I will show you to your room.'

I looked back at Tom as she swept out before me. He was standing in the window and the light was so bright I could hardly make out his expression, yet I knew his next words were spoken in humour, as he bowed deeply. 'I will eagerly await your return, my lady.'

Up three flights of stairs my small bedroom looked out onto the street. Simply furnished, it contained a narrow bed, a chest of drawers, a looking glass and a chair. When Mrs Dawson left the room, I took out my writing desk. I wanted to send a quick note to my sister.

*Cork Street: Tuesday morn.*

*My Dear Cassandra,*
*Here I am once more in this scene of dissipation and vice, and I begin already to find my morals corrupted. We reached Staines yesterday, I do not know when, without suffering so much from the heat as I had hoped to do. We set off again this morning at seven o'clock, and had a very pleasant drive, as the morning was cloudy and perfectly cool. I came all the way in the chaise from Hertford Bridge.*

*Edward and Frank are both gone out to seek their fortunes; the latter is to return soon and help us seek ours. The former we shall never see again. We are to be at Astley's tonight, which I am glad of.*

*I hope you are all alive after our melancholy parting yesterday, and that you pursued your intended avocation with success. God bless you! I must leave off, for we are going out.*
*Yours very affectionately,*
*J. Austen.*

Tom and Mrs Dawson were waiting in the hall.
'Where should you like to go, Miss Austen?'
'I would like to see the immediate vicinity, Mr Lefroy. I've

always had a fancy to see Mayfair.'

'And, no doubt, en route you will be finding homes for all your characters. Miss Austen is a writer, Mrs Dawson, but it is a huge secret, and must not be talked about.'

'I should hope you know that I would never impart anything you were to tell me, sir. I have no use for idle gossip.'

Tom took us along to nearby Bond Street where I had already decided Mr Willoughby would be lodging in London. At first, Mrs Dawson stayed closely at my side, but after a while, she forged ahead leaving us to dawdle behind. There were booksellers and printsellers, linen-drapers and perfumers, glove-makers and tailors, with their shops displaying their wares in the most fashionable way, and all far above my pocket.

'It's very grand, but my few shillings will not go far here,' I dared to say.

'We'll have a change of plan and go on to Ludgate Hill,' said Tom. 'The shops there are generally cheaper, and if you like, I can show you Lincoln's Inn on the way.'

'I should love to see where you are studying, Mr Lefroy. And Ludgate Hill sounds perfect!'

Tom lowered his voice. 'How long it has been since I had the pleasure of seeing you and talking to you. I believe it must be above seven months. We have not met since January 17th, Miss Austen, when we were dancing together at Ashe.'

'Yes, Mr Lefroy. I believe it is almost seven months, exactly.'

'Thank you for your letters,' whispered Tom quietly, when our companion was out of earshot. 'I've looked forward to each one. You are the greatest comic writer of our age, Miss Austen, as fine a wit as any man.'

'High praise, indeed, Mr Lefroy. But, I must tell you how very diverting I have found your correspondence, and I've been impressed. For a gentleman, you write a long letter.'

'That's schooling by my sisters, Miss Austen. I have been used to write in a feminine style for more years than I care to think about!'

I laughed at that. We were soon passing the gatehouse entrance to Lincoln's Inn on Chancery Lane, the great oak doors open to views of the hall and chapel. How I envied Tom. To be in charge and command of one's life, to study and practice the law – I felt inordinately proud of him at that moment. I knew he would fulfil all of his ambitions and more.

'In another year I will be called to the bar, and I will be making my way in the world, Jane. Time passes slowly, but I believe waiting never killed anyone.'

He looked at me with such sincere looks just then, that I could not doubt his meaning.

Tom leaned across and whispered in my ear. 'Do you still have my ring?'

I nodded, and my hand flew to my breast. 'Of course, I always wear it next to my heart. Do you wish to take it back?'

'Yes, its absence has been noted.'

It was difficult not to show my disappointment but when Tom took my hand and squeezed it for a precious few seconds, my heart soared with pleasure. Thankfully, Mrs Dawson looked neither to right nor left and strode on ahead. As we reached Ludgate Hill I could see St. Paul's in the distance, its huge dome rising above the smoking chimneys that belted black smoke even on this warm summer's day. The shops stretched in front, a theatre of luxury goods selling everything from silks and silver to fans, glass and jewellery. It was outside a shop selling watches and jewellery that we stopped. Tom said his pocket watch should be ready for collection. It had been losing time and his uncle Benjamin was a stickler for punctuality. Mrs Dawson said she needed to visit the linendraper's next door and so we were alone at last, if only for a short while.

'Ah, Mr Lefroy,' said the shopkeeper grinning broadly, 'I have your pocket watch here, and I believe there is some other trifle you picked out ready for inspection.'

A small leather box fetched out from under the counter sat upon the glass. The shopkeeper bowed towards us, before bustling away to disappear from view into a curtained doorway at the back of the shop.

Tom was suddenly serious. I'd never seen him look so grave, and I was tempted to say something to bring back his smile. But, I could see he was gathering his thoughts and was clearly looking for the right words.

'Jane, this is a small token of my affection, and one I hope you will exchange for the ring you wear next to your heart.'

Tom picked up the box from the counter, opening it to reveal the most divine piece of jewellery I ever saw. Fashioned from gold with a large turquoise cabochon, it was exactly the kind of ring I'd have picked out for myself.

'I wanted to make you a present to seal our friendship. I hope you like it. I remember you saying that your preference was for simplicity, and I hope this fits the bill. The gemstone has associations with your birthday month, and I hope you will agree that it's as pretty as its recipient.'

I removed my glove and Tom took up my hand, slipping the ring on my finger, which fitted perfectly.

'Tom, it's the most wonderful gift I have ever received, though I am certain I do not deserve such a treasure. I can hardly find the words to thank you. How clever of you to know exactly what I should love.'

We were quite alone in the shop. Time seemed to stand still though the ticking clocks on the shelves behind the counter marked the seconds and the passing minutes. Tom was looking at my mouth and when I raised my lips to his he kissed me with such tenderness that I could swear the clocks stopped for an infinite moment as time took us out of this world to another realm.

'I dreaded giving you back the ring, but I do so now with a glad heart,' I said at last. 'Thank you, I will always cherish it.' I hooked the ribbon out from under my cloak. Tom's fingers reached around my neck, and in pretence of untying the ribbon he pulled me closer to kiss me again. When he drew away he took up the ring on his finger and kissed it, still joined to me and dangling on its scarlet ribbon.

'Oh, that I could nestle so closely to your heart – it's still warm from your skin, Jane.'

'My heart is your own, Tom, and you will always occupy that place.'

'It is a place I often dream about, I admit. That last time at Ashe ... such cherished memories are not easily forgotten, real or imagined. When I talked of waiting, I meant every word. Will you wait for me, Miss Austen?'

'I will, Mr Lefroy!'

We were almost late back to Cork Street for an early dinner before going on to Astley's Amphitheatre. Fortunately, we'd not been missed and no one was any the wiser. Uncle Benjamin was stern, but civil. I do not think he looked my way or made any comment to me other than a perfunctory nod when we were introduced. I knew how it would be; I'd met the type before. Women were to be endured, ignored and suffered until they were gone from his presence. He inhabited a gentleman's world, and women were considered to be nothing more than a nuisance. He was uncomfortable in their company, and ill at ease in their society. I tried to nod and smile in all the right places and was careful not to give too many of my 'pert opinions' or stare too much at Tom who constantly winked at me, as I was so keen to make a good impression. And just when I thought we might not escape after all, Uncle Benjamin declared he was retiring for the evening and would not be joining us to my great relief. At last, the ordeal was over and we were free!

Tom sat by my side in the box at Astleys, and I experienced the delights of the evening with feelings of rapture. Every time I moved, I felt the cold metal of the ring smooth against my breast, a constant reminder of Tom's caresses and the soft words he'd spoken. We laughed at clowns and conjurors, were amazed at feats of daring bareback riding, and all the while I was aware of his eyes on mine and the new understanding we had.

Four white horses trotted in sideways marching in time to the music of the band. A troupe of young men in skin-tight breeches leaped and jumped from one to the other drawing gasps of approbation from the crowd.

'Do you think you're up to the challenge of a bareback ride, Miss Austen?' Tom whispered, as the sight of the steaming horses diverted my brothers' attention. Thundering round the circus arena, two of the riders stood aloft, performing acrobatics as if it were the most natural thing in the world.

I laughed and whispered back, 'I could do anything if you were willing to catch me.'

'And I should be most happy to oblige, Miss Austen.'

His fingers found mine for a second, and when the inevitable happened and my brother Edward remarked on the warmth of my complexion, I made the excuse that it was the heat of the August night that made me so pink.

My admiration for Tom was as great as it had ever been and his continuing to love me was irresistible. On quitting the box, we found ourselves in such a crowd as to make me uneasy. People pressed on every side and the surging horde pushed and pulled in all directions. I was separated from Tom and my brothers and thought I'd never find them again. It was a stampede, and for a minute, I believed I might be dragged and trampled on by the throng, until a hand found mine pulling me along in the sea of people. Tom's fingers were laced with mine but the multitude still threatened to tear us apart. I felt his fingers slipping from mine, and a giant of a man pushed past me in the opposite direction. I looked about wildly, but couldn't see Tom anywhere. I didn't know what to do. I wasn't sure which way to go at the exit, and I had no idea where our coach was to pick us up. All of a sudden I felt completely alone and quite helpless. But, just as I began to despair, I felt strong arms around me, and the masculine scent of one I loved. Tom picked me up as if I were no more than a dried leaf, and carried me away. I buried my face in his chest, inhaling the very essence of him, and when at last we came to rest in the engulfing darkness, he kept hold of me as we exchanged smiles, and snatched kisses, making every moment matter.

'Meet me later, Jane?'

'I will try, Tom, but I am certain it cannot be safe.'

'Uncle Benjamin's library is tucked away at the back of the house. There are doors, which lead out into the garden. No one will know we are there if we wait until they are all slumbering.'

'Tom, I do not know if …'

He took my hand to his lips. 'Please, Jane, it may be our last chance for a while.'

My brothers were relieved when we found them, thanking Tom for bringing me safely to them. In the carriage on the way back to Cork Street I was grateful for the dark shroud of night, which enveloped us all, hiding my transgressions from the world. Tom's scent emanated from my skin, my hair and my mouth, and I felt sure if I moved, his perfume would betray me.

In the drawing room of his uncle's house, Tom served my brothers with brandy and gave me a glass of Constantia wine. Every time I caught Tom's eye I felt guilty about the plans we'd made, but with each sip of wine, I felt any caution waning. My head was light; I was filled with longing, and could no longer meet Tom's eyes. He was seated directly opposite, and appeared to be entirely engrossed in my sailor brother Frank's tales of the sea. I listened to their voices, and with every passing minute my heart quickened its pace. I was resolved to meet Tom even if my mind told me I was being very foolish. Tom looked so very handsome, and I loved him with every part of my soul.

It was after midnight when lying on my bed, I tuned in to listen to the sounds of the house sleeping. The house creaked, its wooden panelling and staircases settling down after constant usage throughout the day. I thought I heard footsteps at one point, and caught sight of a yellow beam of light under the door, which diminished seconds later. I lay in the dark straining my ears for any little sound. Still dressed in my evening gown I removed my stockings and lay upon the counterpane waiting for time to give me a signal. A cool breeze blew in from the hot night beyond the sash window, lifting the muslin on my gown into puffs of white cloud. Yet, for a moment I was frozen by fear. What if we were discovered? My mind reeled with the possibilities and I wavered. If I stayed here Tom would understand, I was sure. But then, I wanted to see him more than I could admit. Sitting up, I swung my legs round and planted my bare feet on the ground. Feeling the connection with the floor felt safer, and I stood, hardly daring to breathe in case the wooden boards groaned. It was now or never. Creeping down the moonlit stairs, I felt every step must be heard, but the rhythmical sounds of snoring from all quarters assured me that everyone was asleep. I crossed the hall quickly, tiptoeing over bare boards and silken rugs to the room at the far end of the corridor. In the library, the dying embers in the fire and a single candle threw shadows against the walls highlighting the gilt picture frames and the spines of books. The doors to the garden stood open, the night breeze blowing back the curtains like a ship's sail. Hurrying through and down the steps into the dark garden my heart was beating so fast I thought it might suddenly stop altogether.

I couldn't see Tom anywhere. In the walled garden, heat rose from the gravel warmed by a summer sun as the moon threw beams of silver light across the sundial. Beyond, sheltered by trees, lantern light glimmered through the trees.

'Tom, are you there?' I called softly, but there was no answer. I ran along the flag-stoned path, avoiding the gravel terraces where the stones might hurt my toes, and crossed the garden to a wilder corner where a large apple tree, already laden with fruit, bent its branches to the ground. The smell of the garden at night was intoxicating, and I stood on the dew-drenched grass inhaling the sweet smells of fruit and flowers. Even if I'd missed Tom, it felt good to be outside with nature all around me. I was so disappointed not to see him. Twinkling above in the heavens, stars were sprinkled like handfuls of diamonds cast against the cloudless sky. It was breathtaking and I wished Tom could share it with me.

But, I might have known I was not really alone. Warm fingers shielded my eyes, and a voice whispered from behind me.

'Is that you, Tom?' I said, turning to face him. 'I couldn't find you.'

'But I found *you*, my sweet Jane.'

He took me up and lifted me into his strong arms. In a few strides we were at the end of the garden where the doors to the summerhouse beckoned us in to the stillness and tranquillity of the night.

Ellie stumbled against the dustbins, gashing her leg in the process. She couldn't think where she could possibly be for a moment until she realised she must be standing in what was left of the garden in Cork Street. But, it was daylight and her surroundings hardly resembled those she'd left behind with its dustbins, tea crates, plastic plant pots and buckets, set amongst the paving of a modern patio clearly unused for anything but a dumping ground.

'What on earth is going on?'

Ellie heard the familiar voice behind her and turned to see Oliver. She was firmly back in the present, and with little understanding of what had just happened. Was it possible that she was in the same house that Tom Lefroy had lived in all those years ago with his uncle? The garden was probably half the size but the high walls looked pretty similar, and she could see the same steps and double doors leading into the back of the gallery. The flash back to the present left her feeling completely bewildered especially as the two scenes could not have been more contrasting. Not to mention the coincidence of all that was happening, which was quite terrifying and unsettling. But, the images were fading fast, and when she tried to hang on to the elusive memories, they vanished, bursting like iridescent bubbles drifting in a summer sky.

'I'm sorry, Oliver, I'm not feeling too well.'

That was the truth and thankfully, Oliver didn't seem to expect any further explanation. He was his usual charming self, and so kind that Ellie felt she might burst into tears. She was totally confused about everything that was happening. When she was in the past, the experiences were so vivid and her emotions ran so high that she felt it was all beginning to take its toll. Her throat ached, and her head throbbed. It was very warm outside, and to make matters worse, she was feeling feverish and overheated.

'I think you need to go home and put yourself to bed. I'm sorry Henry isn't here if you've come to see him, but he told me he was going to be busy with Charlie for the next week or so. It's a good job we have a flexible working relationship ... I can't keep up with all his concerns.'

Ellie did her best to pull herself together and smiled weakly. 'I will go home. I feel so tired.'

'I'll get you a cab, come in and sit down for a while.'

'No, I'll be fine,' Ellie insisted, making for the door before Oliver could stop her. 'I can walk ... the fresh air will do me good.'

'I'll tell Henry you called,' said Oliver, taking her hand and looking at her with some concern. 'I shall only let you go if you promise me that you'll text me the minute you're home to say you're back safely.'

Ellie left with promises to do just that. Jess fussed around her as soon as she saw the state she was in. She administered tablets, hot lemon and sympathy before urging her friend upstairs. Climbing into bed, Ellie gave into sleep just as soon as her head touched the pillows. She slept fitfully, and when she woke in the early hours she crept out of bed so as not to wake Jess. Finding that Tom's ring was no longer round her neck did not really surprise her – she'd never quite worked out how it had managed to travel through time in the first place. She couldn't be sure that she hadn't just lost it, but remembering that she'd given it back to him in exchange for his gift of a turquoise cabochon made sense of its disappearance. That the beautiful ring he'd given her was no longer in her possession was disappointing though she wondered if anything she was experiencing was quite as it seemed. In the sitting room on the first floor, she watched London wake up to a misty day. Ellie was feeling cold after the fever of the night before. She pulled up her knees beneath her on the sofa and drew her dressing gown around wrapping it closely. Feeling exhausted, she knew tears were threatening to spill down her cheeks. It was all so confusing. When in the past she felt love as she'd never known it, and she didn't know what to do about that. It was an impossible situation being in love with the ghost of a man. And then there was Henry. Henry made her feel so angry, and yet, she hated the fact that he probably thought badly of her and her friends. On the one hand she felt glad she hadn't seen him. In hindsight, she didn't think she had any reason to apologise to him. He was clearly a snob and he'd been the reason her best friend was so unhappy. On the other, she knew she'd seen a side of him that probably most people didn't get to see very often, and she was vain enough to think he liked her. *That* Henry she'd found charming and loveable. Ellie admitted she'd really enjoyed his friendship, and now, that was probably over for good. The annoying thing was that she couldn't really decide whether that was a good or a bad thing. In the end, she gave up trying, and let sleep steal over her once more.

## Chapter 31

The day of Martha and Donald's wedding arrived at last. Rain fell steadily, shrouding the trees in the mews and darkening the interior of rooms with its insistent pattering on roofs and dormers, making Ellie wonder if the sense of doom at the prospect of the day was pre-ordained. She was fully recovered, although it had taken a whole week before she'd felt truly back to being herself.

Martha was staying with her mother near Sloane Square, but despite the fact that these two were often at loggerheads, the former had been able to stay calm. The wedding was at noon, so the girls were up early to get ready. Liberty was in a state of complete overexcitement, and spent too long in the shower using up all the hot water so the others had to make do with the briefest of showers in lukewarm water.

Undaunted as ever, Jess and Ellie emerged looking gorgeous, in pale pink lace and blue silk respectively. Liberty managed to wear something both short and plunging, and Cara chose a maxi dress to show off her curves. Martha's mother had kindly arranged for a taxi to take them to the church and so they emerged with large umbrellas into the rain, which bounced off the cobbles in the mews. In the gloomy church they found their seats next to an urn of white lilies, which set off Cara's hayfever, and then were able to take a look round to see if there were others they might know and recognise. Ellie knew her mother and father would be there but it seemed from a casual glance that they hadn't yet arrived. It wasn't long before Liberty was screeching with delight, and running off into the arms of Greg Whitely who was sitting three rows behind them. Whilst he seemed pleased to see her, Ellie thought he didn't look exactly delighted, and wondered whom he'd been hoping to see. She really thought she ought to say something to Liberty about what she'd learned about Greg, but was finding it hard to think how she'd explain knowing so much without revealing her source and the story of what had happened to Pippa. Deciding it might just be easier to keep an eye on her, Ellie thought it highly unlikely that Greg was really interested in Liberty, and when she glanced behind to check up on her friend, she could see he was already ignoring her as Liberty talked at him, nineteen to the dozen.

Melanie Button approached, resplendent in lilac with an enormous hat and a frilled parasol to match. 'May I join you?' she said, shaking raindrops everywhere from flapping the parasol too briskly, and sitting down without waiting for an answer. 'Isn't a summer wedding marvellous, even if it feels like winter? And, it's especially gratifying, in this case, to know that *Project Darcy* is entirely responsible for this love match.'

Ellie bit her tongue. It was easier to let Melanie think that she had something to do with the event that was unfolding before them than to argue against it, and she felt herself start glazing over as Melanie proceeded to tell them how she'd guessed from the very first time she met Martha and Donald, that they would marry before the year was out. She was brought rather sharply out of her reverie, however, when she heard Melanie exclaim out loud.

'Oh, look! It's Henry Dorsey and that lovely friend of his, Charlie Harden. Now, I wonder why they're sitting on the groom's side? I wouldn't have thought they were especially friendly with Donald. That is a mystery. Now, I seem to remember that you were rather sweet on Charlie, weren't you, Jess? Has cupid's arrow struck? You know what they say? One wedding brings on another and all that!'

Jess was smiling through gritted teeth, as Melanie went on and on without a pause for breath. They could just see the back of Henry and Charlie who were sitting by the side of a girl each. One of them was Charlie's sister, Zara, who was busy removing a piece of lint from Henry's lapel, but Ellie didn't recognise the other, and could only assume it was Pippa. She looked like Henry, but was very petite with dark glossy hair. Melanie then excused herself, saying she simply must say hello to them, and the friends heaved a sigh of relief.

Jess was looking very pale. 'I didn't expect to see Charlie here. Martha didn't say anything about him being invited.'

'No,' answered Ellie, squeezing Jess's hand. Privately, she wondered if Martha had invited him especially but thought it best to keep it quiet, though that didn't seem likely, either. 'Still, there are so many people here, that with luck we might be able to avoid them.'

'You never did like Henry, did you?'

Ellie said nothing, and was almost relieved by the sight of her mother and father bearing down on them at speed. She still felt guilty about not telling Jess about Henry working in the gallery and of the time they'd spent together.

'We shall be sitting on the other side, of course,' said Ellie's mother, kissing her daughter on both cheeks, 'behind Donald, the man you rejected ... *You* look very nice, dear.'

Ellie ignored the first barbed comment and wondered if she'd heard the second correctly. Her mother wasn't one for effusive praise, and for her, that was a huge compliment.

'Of course, it's you who should be wearing bridal satin, but you wouldn't listen to me. However, I'm sure you know best,' said Margaret Bentley, fetching out a cotton handkerchief from her large bag and blowing her nose. 'And, perhaps when you are an old maid scratching around in an artist's garret, you'll think about the efforts your mother made on your behalf to keep you from want and starvation.'

Ellie almost laughed when she caught her father's eye. His eyes were rolling and he'd stuck out his tongue for just a second behind Margaret's head. He winked at Ellie before leading her mother to the other side of the church.

'If ever there were an argument against marriage, that has to be it in living form,' Ellie said after they'd gone, which despite herself, made Jess laugh out loud.

The rain stopped just before the bride made her entrance. During the ceremony, shafts of sunlight blazed through stained glass casting lozenges of coloured light along the aisle, and on Martha's heirloom veil, which trailed over the steps behind her. By the time the newly weds were smiling tentatively in the porch for the first photographs, amidst peals of bells and gusts of confetti, the umbrellas were down and the pavements glittered. The steaming marquee at the hotel was barely dripping by the time the guests were seated, and when the Master of Ceremonies announced Donald and Martha, sunshine and champagne had lightened the mood enough to ensure rapturous applause for the entrance of the bride and groom.

Ellie and Jess were both happy to see that they had been seated with Cara and Liberty, and two cousins of Martha's of a similar age. It would not have surprised Ellie to find that Martha had placed Henry and Charlie etc. on their table, but was glad to realise that she must have given it some thought as they were seated on the other side of the room.

'I know we can't really see them,' said Jess, ' but I dread bumping into him. How could Martha have invited Charlie and not told me?'

'Perhaps she didn't realise how awkward that would be,' answered Ellie. 'You know what she's like, she probably hasn't even given it a thought.'

'Yes, and I can't help feeling sorry for her. Martha's mother hasn't stopped criticising her for a moment.'

At the end of the room by the top table, Martha and Donald

were poised by the wedding cake for the photographer. Mrs Knightley fussed about her daughter straightening her veil, and rearranging the train on her dress.

'Hold Donald's arm as if you mean it, Martha,' she scolded, 'and lift up your bouquet so we can see it. Stop slouching, and show off a little. You have an audience, dear!'

Martha tried very hard to follow all the instructions, and what with Donald barking in her other ear about making sure his mother came in on the next photograph to stand between them, they were doing an excellent job of making the bride more anxious than ever.

'I could have predicted such a scene,' said Ellie, picking her moment when Martha's cousins were engaged in conversation with Cara, 'but I feel sorry for her, too. I sincerely hope she won't live to regret this day.'

Jess could hardly eat anything of the wedding breakfast. Though she tried very hard not to look, she couldn't help her eyes swivelling across occasionally even if it was only to see the back of Charlie's head. He and Pippa were talking, their heads very close together. Feeling wretched, Jess struggled to talk to the others and when the speeches started, she resolved upon keeping her gaze very firmly fixed on Martha and Donald. Although a distant sight, seeing Charlie's golden head and the way his hair curled on the back of his collar aroused such emotions inside that she knew it would be impossible to remain self-possessed if she spent any more time looking his way. There was a moment when she felt she was being observed, but the turn of his head when she moved her own convinced her she'd been mistaken.

The wedding went off as well as could be expected. With the speeches over, toasts were proposed and the consumption of champagne increased which had the resultant effect of laughter, some genuine hilarity, and some forced. Everyone agreed the chef was worth his weight in gold, and the rumour spread that the buffet lunch had, indeed, cost a queen's ransom. Bridesmaids flirted, fathers sighed, mothers cried, aunts gossiped, cousins chatted, friends smiled, and uncles tripped up on the marquee ropes after too many glasses of wine. As the sun sank, guests strolled out on the velvet lawns to admire the gardens still drenched with rain.

Ellie and the others followed likewise, picking their way over the grass, kitten heels sinking into the green sward.

'Oh, my feet are soaking wet,' said Liberty shrieking too loudly and drawing attention to their small circle. 'Come on, Cara, let's go and find some young men. Talk about jammy, they don't know just what a treat's in store ... could be their lucky night.'

'Liberty, do be careful,' urged Jess. 'Please look after her, Cara.'

Liberty was already looking glassy-eyed. She scowled at them all. 'I don't need anyone telling me what to do, I'm old enough to look after myself.'

Jess and Ellie exchanged glances. Liberty's behaviour was becoming an increasing problem. She'd always been a handful, but she seemed to have completely abandoned any sense of self-control.

'I'll admit,' said Jess, 'I can't wait to go home. I just don't know if I'm feeling strong enough to cope with any more of Liberty's nonsense and I'm so frightened of seeing Charlie and not knowing what to say or do.'

'I'm sure Cara will keep Liberty by her side. I think you've done all you can. As for Charlie ... Donald and Martha are going away this afternoon, but there is the evening party to get through. I'm totally with you – I don't want to hang around here any longer than necessary, either.'

'Shall we go home once they've left? The thought of watching Charlie and his girl dancing all night is not an appealing one.'

Ellie agreed, thinking that she wasn't in any mood to watch Henry taking pains to glare at her or avoid her. Fortunately, their paths hadn't crossed. With luck on their side they might still be able to steer clear of the Dorseys and the Hardens. There was the music festival to look forward to next week and she hoped some time away with Jess might help them both.

Martha's mother was rounding up the guests. 'The bride and

groom are leaving, everyone. Do come and see them off. There's going to be a wedding arch of clergymen with Donald's old friends from theological college to see them off to their honeymoon!'

Ellie smirked. 'I can't wait to see it. Do you think they'll be wielding prayer books instead of the usual swords for such ceremonies?'

The crowd surged from the gardens and the marquee, out into the forecourt of the hotel. Martha and Donald appeared in their holiday clothes looking far more relaxed than they had done all day. Donald's friends made an arch over their heads, which made Ellie think that they might burst into a chorus of the old nursery rhyme, *Oranges and Lemons*, and before they had a chance to do more than wave goodbye, the couple were whisked away by a sleek chauffeur driven car. Guests strolled languidly, finding chairs in the hotel reception or lounging by the bar before the next activities started. The girls agreed that they would say their goodbyes even if it meant telling a small white lie about Jess feeling tired.

'I'm really sorry, but I just don't think I can avoid saying goodbye to my mother,' said Ellie. I'll never hear the end of it if we just slip away.'

It didn't take long to find her. She was in the hotel lounge with a party of people, all braying at one another in very loud voices. One particular woman, expensively dressed in a pink and grey Chanel suit, was holding forth. She flapped her hands dramatically; displaying gold bracelets and French manicured nails.

'Donald is distantly related to the Dorsey family on his mother's side, and it's very clear to see he has inherited every feature from that branch. There is little resemblance to the true Dorsey lineage where the genes are very strong. My father always used to say you could spot a Dorsey from fifty paces, don't you know. Tall, dark and handsome, the women as well as the men!'

At that, the lady fixed her black eyes upon her audience and smiled, waiting for the sycophantic laugh and murmurs of approval that she expected.

Margaret Bentley was waiting for her moment. 'He's been an

excellent curate, and it's been our pleasure to take him under our wing.'

Ellie groaned inwardly. She and Jess were waiting for their chance on the periphery of the circle to speak and be gone. No one had noticed they were there, and Ellie hoped it wouldn't be too long before they could say farewell. It suddenly occurred to her that the lady must be Donald's godmother and remembering the connection with Henry, for a second it crossed her mind that it was a little like looking at Henry in drag. Henrietta Dorsey was tall and large with raven black hair swept back into a bun under a pale grey hat.

'Oh, *you* must be Margaret Bentley!'

Ellie's mother beamed at the recognition, and for a moment, Ellie thought her mother might curtsey in response. 'I *am*, Lady Dorsey, and my daughter is a friend of your godson's.'

It was too late to tiptoe away though Ellie could have died on the spot.

'That was *your* daughter, was it? The one that turned him down flat. His offer of marriage wasn't good enough for her, I believe. Your daughter sounds a very headstrong young woman.'

Margaret Bentley was turning scarlet. She'd flushed from her neck where ivory pearls disappeared into a powdered cleavage and a crumpled linen dress. Her cheeks matched the crimson of her hat and her jowls wobbled with indignation.

Ellie was just retreating, pulling Jess away with her when she was spotted. Margaret Bentley pointed at her daughter who now stood perfectly still and faced them all. The group of six ladies were all looking at her very curiously.

'I tried to tell her, your ladyship, but she wouldn't listen.'

Ellie knew she would have to speak up for herself. 'But, I am sure you would agree, Lady Dorsey, that Donald has found the perfect partner in Martha. They are well suited, and I believe she will make him very happy.'

Henrietta Dorsey looked Ellie up and down. 'Modern girls do not suffer from shyness or from the fear of speaking out of turn, it seems. In my day, we spoke when we were spoken to and were seen and not heard!'

'Women's liberation has been a wonderful thing, and I think we have your generation to thank for that. We dare to dream beyond the confines of the house and home. Modern girls are very lucky, I agree. We can choose our own lives, our careers and even the men we fall in love with. We have a voice, at last, and are now being heard.'

Lady Dorsey was at a loss for words. Ellie waited for her reply rather nervously, but she was not going to be put down by another Dorsey. She'd had quite enough of them.

'Do not think I am ignorant about you, Miss Bentley. But, your 'voice' and your career would probably have never got off the ground if you'd been unaware of the advantages of having the right connections. Your relationship with Henry has stood you in good stead, and if you are sensible will continue to help you realise the career you desire.'

Ellie was fuming. She was about to reply that they could take her paintings down straight away if that's what they thought, when out of the corner of her eye, she saw Henry, Zara, Charlie and Pippa approaching. One look at Jess was enough to tell her that they should go, but there was an awkward moment where no one seemed to know what to do. Their old friends were standing there in the next second. Henry's expression looked as if he was highly amused, and Ellie hated him for it. However, his sister was smiling as she stepped up to both girls and shook their hands warmly.

'Hi, you must be Ellie and Jess,' said Pippa. 'I saw you earlier and I've been longing to say hello. Charlie hasn't stopped talking about you both.'

Ellie couldn't look at Henry, but she saw Jess turn white as a sheet. Charlie was looking at Jess, and he looked as if he might speak, but before he had a chance, Jess muttered an excuse to be gone and with Ellie hurrying after her friend, followed her out of the building.

## Chapter 32

Jess was even more subdued during the following week, and Ellie began to think that the festival alone was not going to be enough to cheer her up. They were going to Somerset for the festival, which was set in the grounds of a beautiful stately home five miles outside Bath. Ellie hit upon the idea of taking her friend to Bath, itself, for a few days, and she'd managed to find some reasonably priced rooms above a restaurant in Milsom Street, which was just about as central as you could get. Cara and Liberty were going to be joining them later, and meeting them at the festival, so they were to be on their own for a few days, just the two of them. Jess actually looked quite excited when Ellie told her of the surprise she'd arranged, and when they caught the train from Paddington, Jess was totally absorbed in a new book of Jane Austen's life.

'I knew Jane lived in Bath for a while,' said Jess, as they struggled with their backpacks from the train, 'but I hadn't quite appreciated how much she'd visited here before that. Ellie, it will be so interesting finding all the places where she lived and stayed. I've just got to 1797, and the book I'm reading says that she stayed with her aunt and uncle Leigh-Perrot on the Paragon that year in the winter months of November and December.'

'We need a map, that's for sure,' answered Ellie. 'In the guidebook I have, it says there are lots of walks. Bath can be a bit hilly, I understand, but it will be good for us!'

Jess laughed. 'Jane Austen liked a walk, and I will enjoy finding all the places she mentions in her books. *Pride and Prejudice* is my favourite, but *Northanger Abbey* and *Persuasion* actually have scenes of Bath in them. I can't wait to see the Pump Rooms and the Assembly Rooms, not to mention Milsom Street where we're staying. It's the main shopping street and Jane mentions Molland's, the coffee house where there's a most romantic scene in *Persuasion*.'

Ellie was in a contemplative mood. They were out of the station and Bath looked shrouded in cloud and mist coming down from the distant hills. Rain was falling in large droplets, gathering pace, catching the girls unawares as they struggled to find umbrellas.

'Do you want to talk, Ellie? I haven't liked to ask but I know something else must have happened when we were in London. I feel dreadfully selfish being so upset about Charlie when I know you've your own troubles.'

Ellie nodded. 'I saw Tom in London, believe it or not. It was such a coincidence, though I must admit, I have wondered if there's something more at work here. There seem to be a lot of things happening by chance. Anyway, by some twist of fate, Tom Lefroy's uncle lived in Oliver's gallery, in the very same house.'

'In the book I'm reading, there is a mention of the fact that Jane and Tom may have met in London. One of her letters was sent to her sister from Cork Street.'

Pausing for a minute, to adjust her bag across her body, Ellie picked up her case again. 'I know. I had the experience of writing it and of being there for a while.'

'In Cork Street? Then you must also have been to Astley's. I remember reading that and thinking how wonderful that must have been.'

'I was at Astley's, and it was an incredible experience, which followed an amazing day. Tom took me shopping earlier on Ludgate Hill. Jess, he bought me a ring ... he bought Jane a ring, I should say. It was such a special day. I don't know, but it felt like a kind of promise to one another.'

'Like a secret engagement?'

Ellie could not help smiling. 'Sort of, but I don't know that Tom could really promise anything. Jane and Tom were so young. They neither of them had any money. I've resisted finding out what happened, and in a way I don't want to know. I feel if I did, the magic that takes me back would stop. And how could I go back, if I knew the worst?'

'But, you still want to find out what happened. I can understand that.'

Ellie hesitated. 'I do, even if I've a sense of foreboding that I can't describe. Part of me wishes it were over, and yet, the thought of seeing him lights up my very soul with such love that if I could only spend another five minutes with him, even if it was to tell me it was all over, I would do it. And that sounds ridiculous, I know. Tom isn't in love with *me*.'

'I am very concerned for you, Ellie, and yet I know that your feelings are real and true. I don't quite know what else to say except that coming to Bath might grant that wish you desire.'

They'd reached the bottom of Milsom Street and as they climbed higher passing shops on either side, the feeling that Ellie had been there before increased with every step. When they reached the top and found the doorway of the building where they were staying, Ellie was experiencing such strange sensations that she had to stop and catch her breath.

'What is it, Ellie?'

'I just have this incredible sense of déjà vu. This street and those buildings opposite are most familiar.'

Jess looked across the main road where cars were clogging up George Street. There were cafés and restaurants with chairs and tables spilling out onto the pavement, propped under umbrellas so as not to get too wet.

'Come on, let's get inside. What you need is a hot drink and a rest.'

'But, we need to go exploring. I'll be fine in just a moment, believe me.'

They had to collect the key from the restaurant premises, which owned the flats above. Up a flight of stairs they found their rooms on the first floor. In the tiny sitting room, there were double aspect windows with views onto both Milsom Street and George Street, and although it was quite a noisy location, they were glad to be in the heart of town. They sat at the little table in the window watching the comings and goings below. It was a wonderful spot for people watching. Jess seemed thoughtful, and when she spoke at last it was clear that she had to speak her mind.

'I'm sorry, Ellie, but there is something I feel I have to tell you. I couldn't bear for you to have another experience or go back in time and be unprepared.'

'If you think it best,' said Ellie, looking at her friend anxiously, 'I trust you implicitly.'

'The thing is, Ellie, there is a lot that we don't know about what happened to Jane Austen in her life, particularly at the time in which you're travelling. I'm not sure what time, year or month you'll jump into next, but I have a feeling it could well be 1797, as we are here in Bath, and we know Jane, Cassandra and her mother spent most of November and December in the city.'

'What would they have been doing there?'

We know they stayed with family, and I think Mrs Austen might have felt it would be a trip to provide a much needed change of scene.'

'Whatever do you mean?'

'Cassandra lost her fiancé that year.'

Ellie's eyes instantly filled with tears. 'You mean Cassy's Tom? Are you saying that Tom Fowle got lost at sea or something?'

'There are no letters left from her for that year, but we know that Tom died of yellow fever in San Domingo in February of 1797, but the Austens were not to find out until April according to my book. James and his new wife Mary broke the news to Cassandra.'

'Oh, my dear Cassy – how could she bear it?'

'I imagine she bore it as well as she could. Certainly, her heart must have been broken but Jane wrote that her sister coped with her loss as stoically as she always conducted every aspect of her life. It seems she was devoted to the memory of Tom Fowle for the rest of her days and she never considered marriage again.'

'So when they came here, Cassy would still have been grieving deeply for him. And I suspect Jane had probably not seen much if anything of Tom. He was studying in London and most likely went home to Ireland when he had time off. They were writing to one another – Tom's cousin George acted as go-between when he could.'

'Let's start by buying a bigger map, and perhaps we could find a copy of a historical one. In *Northanger Abbey*, the Tilneys lodge in a house on Milsom Street. I've often wondered if Henry Tilney wasn't a little like Tom Lefroy, for all his Mr Darcy ways.'

'I'm going to need a copy of that book too,' said Ellie. 'I've almost finished *Pride and Prejudice*, and I've no doubt in my mind that Mr Darcy was inspired by Tom. Jane was writing the happy endings she wanted for herself and Cassy.'

A trip to the nearest bookshop found everything they needed. There were so many places the girls wanted to see that they almost couldn't decide which to see first. But, after reading the first few chapters of *Northanger Abbey* out loud, Jess and Ellie were both agreed that they'd like to walk down to Pulteney Street where the heroine Catherine Morland stayed with the Allens, and then Jess suggested they take a look at the Pump Rooms along the way. By the time they'd accomplished all that, both girls felt they were getting their bearings, and over supper in the restaurant below their rooms, they planned the route they'd follow the next morning. The Paragon where Jane had stayed with her aunt was a short walk away; then they could cut through Hay Hill, cross the Landsdown Road and find their way to the Assembly Rooms.

'I'd also like to investigate the building over the road,' said Ellie, 'the ones I felt drawn to yesterday. On the map it's called Edgar Buildings.'

'Perhaps you're drawn because it's a wine bar and restaurant,' joked Jess. 'Seriously, I've heard the name before, and I'm fairly certain it's a location that Jane Austen used in *Northanger Abbey*. Let's have a look.'

Ellie passed the book over to Jess who flicked through the chapters, scanning the pages for any information.

'That's it! I knew I was right. 'Edgar's Buildings', as Jane called it, is where the Thorpe family lodged. Isabella Thorpe makes a play for Catherine's brother in *Northanger Abbey*, and John Thorpe tries to trick Catherine into marrying him. They were not the best of Jane's characters.'

'Excellent! I'd like to see it, and we can have lunch there after we've been to the Assembly Rooms.'

The next morning the girls were up early and set off for the Paragon, which was a short walk round the corner. It proved to be rather disappointing on first view as it was a very busy road with cars and lorries thundering along the street, and it took a certain imagination to envisage an earlier scene with carriages and horses. But for both Jess and Ellie, to imagine Jane coming out of the door of number one was a pleasure and delight. Jess had her photo taken at a discreet distance in case one of the owners of the flats decided to walk out, but having had a good look at the ancient steps leading down to Walcot Street, down which they were sure Jane would have lightly skipped, it was time to discover all that awaited them at the Assembly Rooms where Jane had danced all those years ago. To stand in the historic rooms with the delights of the octagon room, tea room and ballroom with their glittering chandeliers, such as neither of them had seen before, was a feast for the eyes, and by the time they'd walked back again passing the temptations of a few shops they couldn't resist, they were starting to feel hungry.

Walking into the restaurant on Edgar Buildings filled Ellie

with such a sense of anticipation that she was surprised that nothing extraordinary happened as they passed through the door. A waitress who greeted them showed them to the upper floor, but as they climbed the ornate staircase higher and higher, Ellie sensed her surroundings were shifting. Although she was feeling strange and light-headed, she convinced herself that she could control the situation. The waitress's back and her long blonde hair which swayed from side to side as she walked were almost hypnotic, and as Ellie felt and saw her surroundings subtly changing, she knew there was absolutely nothing she could do to remain in the present.

## Chapter 33

'My dear friends, how delightful to see you here!'

Madame Lefroy rose to greet us with all her usual warmth. As at home in Steventon, the room was full of friends. We were introduced to a Mr and Mrs Runham with their two pretty daughters from Farnham in Surrey, their friend Mrs Brown and a Miss Tomlinson who hailed from Berkshire, a set of the pleasantest people. My mother shook hands warmly, and my aunt and uncle followed suit, though perhaps with not quite the same enthusiasm. My aunt was an unsociable, snobbish woman, and her effusions merited on a scale depending on her own idea of hierarchy. Morning calls were usually swiftly executed, and I knew we would not be stopping long if she had any say so in the matter.

'What a splendid situation,' said my mother. 'To step outside and have everything on your doorstep, I always find is the wonder of Bath.'

'It is, indeed,' Madame answered, whilst her husband insisted we take our seats. 'There are so many delightful shops and Marshall's circulating library just across the road has made us very happy, has it not, dear?'

Reverend Lefroy nodded. 'I find myself drawn to the library

almost every day – to a good fire upstairs and a choice of forty newspapers. And one never knows whom one might see; there are dukes and viscounts at every turn.'

'We are to have a subscription to Mr Hazard's library on Cheap Street,' I said. 'It's very convenient for the Pump Rooms and will be a reason for having a stroll out every day. Cassy and I are going along in just a little while.'

Cassy smiled at all the faces who looked on her with pity in their eyes. My sister would probably never be as cheerful as she'd once been, but she was making a supreme effort to be as light-hearted as she could.

Madame Lefroy quickly diverted the conversation and the attention on my sister. 'We have tickets for the theatre tonight. I do hope you will be able to join us. Miss Tomlinson says she saw the play performed in London and it is most diverting.'

'My husband has already secured a box for this evening's play,' answered my aunt in a superior tone before Miss Tomlinson managed to open her mouth.

'So, we shall be able to meet later – how delightful!' exclaimed Madame, as if she could not think of anything more splendid than spending an evening with my disagreeable aunt.

'And tomorrow morning, there is to be a public breakfast in Sydney Gardens. I do hope you will be there, Madame,' I begged.

'I have heard the breakfasts are very good,' exclaimed Miss Runham. 'They have Bath buns with a sugar piece as large as a crown!'

'Which is an excellent reason not to miss such an occasion,' answered Madame. 'And, my dear husband enjoys an outside repast above all others.'

'Whereas I cannot find anything to recommend sitting outdoors in the damp and cold and being forced to talk to people of every sort,' said Aunt Leigh-Perrot. 'I much prefer to stay inside, and so I shall.'

We left not long after that leaving the happy company in much discussion on the merits of eating outdoors. Cassy and I managed to leave my mother and our aunt and uncle at the earliest opportunity, and made our way down into the town. Choosing two books apiece from Hazard's took an age, and afterwards we drifted back along Walcot Street where some of the cheaper shops were to be found. I wanted a new ribbon for my hair and I persuaded Cassy to buy one too, even though she resisted. The white silk was very pretty and looked a picture against her chestnut hair.

'It's not as if I shall have occasion to wear it.'

'But, you've been wearing black ribbons long enough,' I said. 'Tom would not wish you to mourn him for the rest of your life. I understand, dear sister, that his memory is very precious to you, but I think he would wish you to truly live again. Indeed, if you cannot do it for yourself, then you *must* do it for him. His life was cruelly snatched away, and he would urge you to do all that he is not able.'

'I know you are right, Jane, but sometimes it is so hard. The thought of dancing with anyone else or wearing ribbons with the thought of attracting another is too difficult for me to contemplate.'

'I know, Cassy, but wearing a fresh ribbon in your hair to the theatre is a much easier prospect, and I think it is time. More than eight months have passed since we lost darling Tom. It is a little step, and one I think you can take.'

'And I will take it, on one condition. You, too, must find it within your heart to put the past to one side. I hate to see you waiting for Mr Lefroy to keep his promises to you.'

'He promised me nothing, Cassy.'

'But, he asked you to wait, Jane, and you have been kept waiting with no guarantees of anything, least of all marriage. I do not say these words to be cruel, but I cannot bear to see you unhappy any more than you can me.'

'I know you are right … it is some time since I even received a letter from him. And the last was nothing more than a treatise on astronomy of which he is particularly fond. There was no affection in it. I am glad he is in London and that there is no possibility of seeing him here.'

I took her arm in mine. At least we had each other, and that would always be the case.

Tom or no Tom, I dressed myself with care for the evening's entertainment and in the murky looking glass, I was quite pleased with my appearance, yet thankful for the small miracle that half-light and candles can perform. I loved the theatre and though there were no actors in Bath of any great note about to be treading the boards, I looked forward to an entertainment that took us away from the confines and the noise of my aunt's house on the Paragon, an apt name for the street in which such a formidable lady lived. I'd always felt that my aunt disliked me for my 'pert opinions', as she called them, but on discovering that my mother and Cassy had been given a room at the back of the house with delicious views of the river and the hills and woods beyond, it came as no surprise to find I'd been given one at the front. The dirt from the street left a layer of dust on my white muslin gowns and the unceasing sounds of carriage wheels and pattens on the pavements clinked and rumbled past all day and night. At home we shared a room, but our aunt always separated us whenever she could. I was certain she knew how much we discussed her when together, but her attempts to quieten us were in vain. We were in and out of each other's rooms as often as we possibly could and we talked late into the night before finding our own beds to fall asleep.

Arriving at the theatre, I was suddenly overtaken by a childish excitement. Cassy looked beautiful at my side and no one would guess the secrets of her soul by looking at her with new ribbons threaded through her tresses, which fell in curls from the top of her head, and were stirred into movement from the quiet airing of her fan. In the soft candlelight, her pretty eyes shone, and her gown of white sparkled with tiny spangles. My mother sat slightly behind us in the box with my aunt and uncle, and so we felt very much on display. I knew my sister was attracting more than a few admiring glances from the audience below who stared and quizzed at every new face on view.

When the Lefroys arrived in the box opposite, they were in a large party. The ladies sought their chairs at the front whilst the gentlemen hung back. Madame and Lucy sat on the left, and three ladies sat to the right of them. I couldn't clearly see who sat behind them apart from Reverend Lefroy, and two gentlemen who I'd never seen before. And then the door of the box opened and I saw the silhouette of a gentleman outlined in the light from the passage. I felt myself start, and put my hand up to my mouth. My first thought was that I must be mistaken, but then I quickly realised it could be no other than the object of all my dreams and hopes. His yellow hair shone under the candelabra as he bent to kiss his aunt on her cheek, and my heart turned over. Cassy hadn't missed my exclamation, and put out her hand to steady and comfort me as she followed my gaze. There was a movement below in the orchestra pit, and the musicians started playing. Red velvet curtains were swept aside and the attention of the audience was on the play at last.

Tom straightened, and it was then that our eyes met. As if held by the ribbon that bound my hair, our eyes locked for an instant before Tom's dropped to the floor. He made a curt bow and took his seat. Thankfully, my mother's eyesight was such that she could not make out who was there or what was going on and the play started before she could ask.

The stage could no longer excite genuine merriment or no longer keep my whole attention. Every other look I directed towards the opposite box; and, for the space of two entire scenes I watched Tom without being able to catch his eye. Not once did he look my way. At length, however, he did look at me, but there was no smile, no continued observance attended it; and his eyes were immediately returned to the stage. I was agitatedly miserable; I could almost have run round to the box in which he sat and forced him to look at me. I'd witnessed his coldness before, but never like this. There was no warmth in his looks, and I felt he was entirely lost to me. Any hopes that he might come to see me in the interval were false ones, and when my mother suggested we go to their box, I resisted. Cassy was happy to stay by my side and we sat in silence, words being an unnecessary supplement. It was such a shock to see him. Madame had made no suggestion of his coming to Bath, but the thought that he might have come to see me vanished as quickly as it started. And by the end of the evening, I was certain he would be as aloof as I'd ever known him.

## Chapter 34

'Madame says her nephew arrived earlier than expected,' said my mother, buttering toast at breakfast next morning. 'I should have thought you, Jane, would have been only too happy to shake hands with him. If I remember, you always liked Mr Lefroy. Indeed, I did wonder if he might not make you an offer at one stage, though his aunt tells me he is destined for great things in Ireland, and I daresay, he will look for a bride in his native country.'

'I am sure we will have opportunity enough to meet,' I said. 'I did not wish to crowd him on his first evening. He had quite enough people to contend with.'

'And I was thankful that Jane sat with me,' said Cassy, taking my hand beneath the table to reassure me. 'I was feeling rather fatigued and Jane insisted on staying. She always lifts my spirits.'

'Well, the rain has put paid to the public breakfast,' said my aunt, ignoring the rest of us, 'for which I am grateful.'

For once I was obliged to my aunt for changing the subject. I'd had quite enough during a sleepless night to think about Tom's reaction. Why on earth had he come to Bath if he were to behave so disagreeably? Had he changed his mind about how he felt for me? My feelings were the same as they'd ever been. Over a year had passed since I'd seen him in London, but I still loved Tom with every feeling of my mind, every pore of my body. That would not change, but I was not insensible to the feelings of others, and in that one evening, Tom had made very plain that his were so completely altered. I'd cried, silently sobbing into my pillow, but then thought myself pathetic. Cassy, who'd been so brave, that we might not suffer her sorrow, had unselfishly put aside her feelings. I could do the same. In any case, I would not let Tom see any alteration in me. Indeed, I was quite prepared to make it easy for him and for myself, and resolved there and then to avoid any connection, however impossible in a place like Bath.

We were very fortunate that for the next few days the weather kept us from walking out very much, and although being shut up with my aunt was the last activity I would have wished for, it gave me time to ready my mind to the alteration in my friend. I must admit, there were occasions when a knock at the front door would have me rushing to the window, but he never came, and after a while I gave up expecting him.

When at last Cassy and I escaped to visit Hazard's library to change our books, I'd almost forgotten that Tom existed. Books were my delight, and so absorbing that finding myself in a new world more than made up for the one I occupied. Besides, I'd put away my own writing. I'd suffered a dreadful disappointment where that was concerned, but I couldn't think about that now. Cassy found books a great distraction too, and so we combed the shelves looking for any volume we had not yet taken up.

To my great delight, I'd just found a copy of Ann Radcliffe's first volume of *The Italian* when I heard a familiar voice. It belonged to Lucy Lefroy, who was gaily chattering to someone, clearly female, in very loud whispers. They were on the other side of the bookcase, and I glanced across at Cassy who put her finger to her lips. I grinned. Lucy was a talkative girl, and as we were enjoying our solitude, our eyes and minds agreed it would be best if we stayed quite where we were and continued our search for books in silence. If we were lucky they would probably pass by in a moment and we'd avoid seeing them altogether.

'Your cousin is extraordinarily handsome,' said Lucy's friend.

'He is, indeed, Miss Grantley, and gaining hearts in every corner.'

'I can well believe that,' replied Miss Grantley. 'He is so very flirtatious, is he not?'

'No more than any other young man, I don't suppose,' answered Lucy, rather defensively.

'And Mr Lefroy is to be a lawyer, I hear.'

'Yes, and he means to practise one day, I believe. He will be called to the bar in Ireland ... at least, that is what my mother says.'

'Does he mean to take a wife? Is he courting?'

'I believe he is in love.' Lucy lowered her voice to a whisper. 'But, it is a secret engagement, and I should be in such trouble if he were to find out that I'd told you, Isabella.'

'Lucy, I would not tell a soul. You know I am discretion, itself.'

My heart was hammering. Surely Lucy knew nothing of the arrangement Tom and I had. Not that it was exactly a secret engagement, but I did not know what to think. Perhaps George had told her of our exchange of letters. Could Tom have told Lucy about me, perhaps?

I felt Cassy's hand on mine, and then she was gesturing that we should go, but I was determined to stay.

'Her name is Mary, and she is the sister of his great friend Tom Paul. He spends every spare moment he can with Tom's family in Silverspring, County Wexford. But, Isabella, I must have your promise to keep my secret. I should know such trouble if my aunt were to find out.'

My heart was pounding so loudly, I was sure Lucy would hear me. I could not move, and felt the colour drain from my face as I gripped the shelf. She must be wrong, I thought, but my heart told me I was not deceived in the truth. Besides, the more I thought about the past, certain memories and snippets of information came surfacing to the top of my mind. These friends he'd known for a long time – I'd heard Tom talk about them. Was it the case that Tom had been in love with Mary for longer than he'd even known me? Had they some kind of understanding all the while that had existed long before he met me? So many conflicting images and emotions rushed upon me in a flash of time. But, I could not envisage my sweet Tom as a villain, however hard I tried. Whatever the case, I could not think the worst of him, even if I felt he was as lost to me as Cassy's Tom was to her.

We left after that, as soon as Lucy and her friend moved away. It was almost as if she'd come to tell me herself, to let me know that I was wasting my time holding onto the hope that one day Tom and I might be together.

A week passed where by fortune or luck we saw nothing of the Lefroys. I was reluctant to go the Pump Rooms and Assembly Rooms, but they were not in attendance, and we heard via one of my aunt's maids who heard it from one of the Lefroys' manservants that Reverend Lefroy had caught a cold after bathing. That certainly put paid to Madame's attendance also, but I was surprised not to see Lucy and Tom who could quite easily have joined any of their friends. I didn't see Tom anywhere, at any of the public places, and began to think he must have gone out of town.

On the following Monday, we were attending a ball at the Upper Rooms. I'd persuaded Cassy out of wearing any mourning now, and though she'd been timid and not wanted to dance, at least I felt she was making strides forward. Aunt Leigh-Perrot decided to stay at home to nurse my uncle who seemed to have caught the same cold that was infecting almost everyone in Bath. I felt stronger; I'd recovered my spirits well enough, and looked forward to the ball. Dancing was guaranteed to lift my mood further, and if I could only persuade Cassy to follow my behaviour I would feel happy. My mother insisted on a chair to take her up the hill, but my aunt's manservant Frank accompanied my sister and me. The evening was mild for November and the humidity in the air only served to tighten our curls. A procession of lantern light wound its way to the Assembly Rooms, throwing yellow lances or darkling shadows against the Bath stone walls.

We met my mother at the top, and made our way through the crush of people at the entrance. New arrivals had brought new faces – eager girls looking for a husband, reluctant young men keen for the card room. The crowd increased as we went along, and my mother complained loudly as a couple of rough young men stumbled into her causing her cap to dislodge. They apologised after a thorough dressing down, and we moved on through the surging throng.

'It's a wonder we're not stripped naked!' exclaimed my mother who loved to exaggerate at every opportunity. 'I've never felt quite so tumbled about. Now, let us find a chair, though I doubt we shall get the bottom tier, but I do so dislike to be sitting at the top. It makes one feel so vertiginous.'

By some small miracle we found three seats just vacated by three gentlemen who looked as if they'd lurched into the ballroom by mistake, and we sat down. It was an excellent spot opposite the door, where we could watch everybody who entered or left the room. Before we'd been there five minutes, two brothers, whom we'd met through my aunt at the last ball, asked us for the first two dances. Cassy agreed to dance; as she knew I would be unable to if she snubbed them. Rather too tall and thin, our partners did not hold the promise of great dancers, but I was glad to have one at all. There didn't seem to be anyone else we knew. I scanned the room, and although I told myself I was not looking for Tom, I knew in my heart I was disappointed not to see him.

The two Mr Haggerston's presented themselves with a formal bow and an outstretched hand. I was dancing with the younger, and he blushed when I put my hand in his.

'I have never seen the rooms so full, Miss Austen,' he began in the usual way as the dancing started.

'No, indeed, Mr Haggerston, it is always a wonder to me that when there are so many people arrived in Bath, there should be such a multitude at the balls.'

He looked at me for a second, as if to query my answer, but I kept my face as straight as it would allow. I wondered on what absurd topic we'd discuss next. The tedium of conversation always spoiled the dancing, to my mind.

'And, how do you like Bath?'

I was floored by such inventive questioning – having never heard such an enquiry before except at least a hundred times in the previous week.

'I like it very well.'

I looked across at Cassandra to see how well she liked her partner, but I knew better than to go by the expression on her face. She always looked like an angel and behaved as one.

I was about to sigh after the next question and pretend not to hear what he was saying when I was aware that I was being observed. I connected with a pair of piercing eyes, and saw not much else for a moment as they burned their way through my soul like spears of flame. I could not look again, but became more animated than my partner was ready for. Every comment he made had me smiling or laughing. I skipped and turned, and I made a display of myself showing my prettiest and most tantalising self. Not for nothing had my cousin Eliza schooled me in the arts of seduction, and poor Mr Haggerston was unaware that my coquettish long looks or flashing smiles were not for his benefit. No, they were for the young man who stood at the side of the ballroom, and I knew he couldn't take his eyes off me.

When Tom came to ask me to dance, I must admit, I had not expected it. I had meant to refuse him, but it was an impossible situation, and I was determined he should not see me indifferent to him. He took my hand, but the moment he did, I was a lost cause.

'It was a surprise to see you in Bath, Miss Austen.'

'The surprise was on both sides, Mr Lefroy. Your aunt did not mention that you were coming.'

'I only decided to come at the last minute. Lucy's letter urging me to come had its influence, I must admit.'

'But, perhaps if you'd had intelligence of everyone who was

visiting, you may have decided against it.'

'Nothing could make me happier than to find old friends here.'

My heart skipped a little, but to find oneself described as an old friend like some day-old leftovers that have been dipped into again and again, only to be discarded at the last, soon quieted my spirits.

'I heard Dublin is the place to visit at this time of year,' I said gazing into his grey eyes. 'Or do you prefer Limerick or County Wexford when you're not visiting Bath?'

I saw him flinch so slightly that anyone else but me would not have noticed. And now I knew, beyond a shadow of a doubt, that what I'd heard Lucy whispering was true. Tom coloured furiously, and I dropped my gaze to the floor. When the music stopped, I curtseyed prettily, thanked him and gave him the benefit of my widest smile. I did not wait for him to escort me back to my chair. I felt so ill with pent-up emotions that it was a battle to compose myself, but I won over my feelings and returned to my mother and my sister as if nothing untoward had happened.

I did not see Tom for a few days. The Lefroys were busy with other friends, and Lucy was practising her riding for a performance at the school in Julian Road. Cassy and I avoided the Pump Rooms, and for a few days after the assembly, Cassy seemed reluctant to go out at all. She struggled with her feelings, she told me, and felt it was wrong to enjoy herself when her Tom lay forgotten in his watery grave. It was unlike her to be melancholy, and although I tried to reassure her, she would not be tempted out. I decided a walk would be the very thing, and I might find something with which to treat my sister at the shops. Walking into the town, I could find nothing in the way of fruit or flowers to cheer up her bonnet, and all the lace seemed far too expensive for my pocket. Inspiration struck at last and I found myself in Molland's, the confectioner's, where large groups of ladies and gentlemen were partaking of hot beverages. Inside, the air steamed with the smell of chocolate and coffee, warm cake and cold, fragrant ices. Displays of iced cakes fashioned like temples with vases overflowing with sugar flowers moulded into roses and pansies in pinks and lilac graced a central table where everyone could stop and admire them. A box of marchpane might be the very thing and just suit my pocket, I thought, wandering to the display cabinet where sweetmeats were arranged on glass dishes, lit by oil lamps, making tiers of candied fruits sparkle in the light. I chose a selection of strawberries, plums, cherries and pears, which made a pretty picture in a box all tied up with a glossy green ribbon.

'I always suspected you to have a sweet tooth,' said a voice in my ear.

I had no time to compose myself. I turned to see Tom smiling at me.

'I cannot deny that, Mr Lefroy, though these marchpane treats will not be giving me the toothache.'

Tom laughed at that, and I relaxed enough to smile back at him. Though I felt hurt inside, I did not want him to be my enemy. If he did not love me, there was little I could do about it, and I could not give him the satisfaction of letting him see how the transference of his affections was making me feel.

'How are you, Miss Austen?'

'I am very well, Mr Lefroy.'

'And, tell me, what news of your book, *First Impressions*? Is it yet completed? The little you were so kind to tell me about was fascinating to such an extent that I long to see it in print. There was something about the hero you described that seemed most familiar.'

As usual, I was not entirely certain if he was teasing me, but I decided to tell the truth. 'Sadly, you will be waiting an eternity for that momentous occasion. My father very recently sent it to Mr Cadell in London and it was declined by return of post.'

His expression changed and when he told me of his heartfelt sorrow, I believed him. His eyes and looks were so sincere; I could no longer look at him, and there followed a moment of awkward silence.

'Would you do me the honour of walking with me, Miss Austen? If you are bound for home, I should love to accompany you.'

'I do not know where I am bound, Mr Lefroy, but some company would be very pleasant.'

He offered his arm and I was happy to be directed. He was my friend, after all, and I could only wish him happiness. Instead of proceeding up the hill as directed, he lead me round the corner to Quiet Street, aptly named after the bustle of Milsom Street, and though we were silent and did not speak immediately, as soon as we came out of Wood Street and started the ascent into Gay Street, I knew he was troubled and wishing to speak.

'I am certain you suspect me of wrongdoing, and it is a crime which, sadly, I cannot deny. I have behaved very ill towards you, Jane.'

'Please, Tom, do not explain. I have no wish to hear that which you desire to tell me. Besides, I am guilty of a transgression also. I overheard and listened to a conversation that was not meant for my ears. I do not want you to feel tormented – the plain fact is that I heard Lucy telling a friend that you were secretly engaged to be married.'

'If I could have written to you on such a matter, I would have. I have made such a mess of everything.'

'No, Tom; you cannot have all the blame. We both knew in our hearts we were a hopeless case. We live in different worlds, on different sides of the Irish Sea, and are both in want of money.'

'I have been such a fool, and I will never forgive myself, much less expect you to forgive me for my conduct. Will you hear me out, Miss Austen?'

I nodded, though the formality in his voice prepared me to hear a speech I knew I would not enjoy.

Tom gazed steadily into my eyes. 'I met Mary five years ago. She is the sister of my dearest friend, and I spent several visits with their family where I was always made to feel welcome, and very much at home. We spent long summers together … I was young, and thought myself in love. We came to an early understanding between us, but Mary's parents, and even her brother had no idea. Then, when I came to England that December of 1795, and I met you, everything was turned on its head. I knew you were someone special; that I'd found a love beyond compare with anything I'd formerly known. I was stupid enough to think, that because fate had bespoken me to another, there could be no danger in my being with you; and that the consciousness of my engagement was to keep my heart as safe and sacred as my honour. I felt myself falling in love with you, but I told myself it was only friendship; and until I began to make comparisons between yourself and Mary, I did not know how far I was got. After that, I suppose, I was wrong in seeking you out as much as I did, and the arguments with which I reconciled myself to the expediency of it were no better. I convinced myself that the danger was my own; and that I was doing no injury to anybody but myself.'

'It may have been wrong, but considering everything ... as foolish as our connection may have been on both sides, and as foolish as it is now proved in every way, it was not at the time an unnatural, or an inexcusable piece of folly.'

'Jane, I beg you will let me finish, even though I know you will hate me forever.'

'Tom, I do not think I wish to hear much more. But, I could never hate you – you must know that in your heart.'

'Oh, how I wish I could be saying words that would make you happy, make you love me. Jane, I have been foolish, vain and reprehensible, but I meant every word when I asked you to wait for me. It was very wrong of me, I know, yet I was sure I'd find some way of making everything work out. I was determined to find a gentle way of letting Mary down, but I am a coward and delayed telling her the truth.'

We turned onto the Gravel Walk, and when Tom put his hand over mine, I did nothing to stop him.

'Whatever I professed on our first meeting at the assembly, I came to Bath to explain everything to you. My aunt told me you were here, and I knew it could not be put off any longer. I cannot ask your forgiveness, but I hope you will think of me with pity. The truth is I am promised in marriage and though my Aunt Lefroy does not yet know of my engagement, Mary's family do.'

'Whatever happened?'

Tom looked down at our hands, fingers linked together. 'Mary divulged her secret. She told me she could no longer keep it from her mama, and once that was known, my position was untenable. I had no choice but to make it an official engagement.'

I felt the tears prick behind my eyelids. 'You are very honourable, Tom, and that is what counts.'

The trees towering above us began to drip through the branches from the mist and rainclouds above. A few birds hopped upon the gravel and pecked amongst the litter of copper leaves beneath the trees. The murky sky was grey, fading to dirty ochre and against it, the branches of the great oaks still wore a few ragged leaves, their branches moving erratically, tossed in the wind. And then the rain started, pelting down on the chimneys and roofs of the houses I could just see along the back of Gay Street and the Circus, falling steadily against the dark trees and whispering through the scanty leaves. Tom pulled me underneath the largest, and opened his umbrella. He looked angry, and I knew his struggle for words came from anger – anger at himself and the situation we were in.

'I have loved none but you from the very first encounter, and I believe I will always love you, dearest Jane. Unjust I may have been and foolish beyond hope, but never inconstant in my heart. If there was any way we could be together ... you must know that ...'

Standing so intimately, we'd never been further apart. But, when he lowered his head, and I saw his eyes penetrate mine, I wanted him to kiss me, though I knew it was to be our last. I was careful to capture the memory, instilling it in my mind, as his lips tenderly kissed mine goodbye. Forever associated with the scent of pine needles and the sound of rain drumming against taut cloth, such recollections of Tom I locked away in my heart.

## Chapter 35

Popping in and out of time always had the most devastating effect on Ellie, but there were no words for this last trip back. The pain and heartache were almost too much to bear, but she kept Cassy in her mind knowing how much she had had to suffer. All she could pray was that time would spare her, and that they could leave Bath as soon as possible. It was hard telling Jess about everything, but Ellie knew she would be able to lay the ghost to rest now that she'd experienced all that had happened. However Jane and Tom had spent the rest of their stay in Bath, they'd known it was the last time they would be together, and she was sure that they'd managed to reach an understanding which Ellie was convinced no modern couple would ever fully comprehend. She didn't think it was possible that they'd ever stopped loving one another, even if they'd made room for others in their lives. And, as much as the pain would eventually subside, Jane had re-lived it over and over again through her work. Ellie didn't need to read the novels to realise that, and knew that although she would relish every word, she would have to put time and distance between her and the books for a while.

The girls only stayed another day during which Ellie spent most of it in tears, feeling very sorry for herself. In a moment of madness, she walked along to where the riding house had once been on Julian Road. Most of it had been pulled down in 1973, she later read, to make way for some hideous architecture from that era, and though part of her wished she could be snatched back in time, she knew that Jane could only have been miserable there. Jess told her that Jane had written a later letter in 1805 where she'd referred to the event in terms of her feelings, recalling the years and months that had passed. Had she and Tom sat together as they watched Lucy cantering round on her pony, knowing that such precious moments were to be their last? Had they imagined their futures apart, and yet still loving one another with a passion that would keep burning? And, when at last Jane and Cassandra had returned to Hampshire for Christmas, Ellie could not imagine what a sober affair that must have been. Now, she needed all her resolve to put the past behind her, and move on with her own life. It wouldn't be easy, but she also had her best friend Jess to think about and looking after her happiness was paramount.

Ellie and Jess managed to hire a tent before they left Bath and found a bus to take them the six miles out of the city to the pretty village of Colerne. It was a short walk from the church to the vast driveway of Doncombe Park, and then a long walk before they joined the queue of festival-goers laden down with tents and backpacks. They could see the house, which gave the estate its name, in the distance. It was a large, stone building situated on rising ground, and backed by a ridge of high woods and hills. A stream with a bridge crossing over it in golden stone made a picture perfect addition.

'Oh look, it's just like Pemberley in *Pride and Prejudice*,' said Jess. 'Isn't it beautiful?'

Ellie gazed at the vast house. 'Do you think anyone actually lives there?'

'I've no idea, though there are still some families who live in these great houses.'

'Well, I'm glad I don't live there. Can you imagine how much it must cost to heat and light, not to mention all the cleaning? Give me a cosy cottage anytime. In fact, the gatehouse is definitely more my style.'

Jess laughed. 'I don't know ... I think the kind of people who live in houses like these have people to look after them.'

'I suppose so, though it seems a bit feudal, if you ask me.'

They were soon through the gates and were given wristbands and directions to the camping area. Putting up the tents proved to be tricky: there seemed to be more tent-holes than poles, and more than once the structure fell down.

'So long as it's up before nightfall, we should be all right,' said Jess, laughing at Ellie who was scratching her head.

'I've never had a problem before, but this tent we've hired hasn't any instructions, and I don't know this make at all. Let's have one more go. Perhaps if we take out all the tent-poles and start again ...'

It was a bit embarrassing. They were surrounded by neighbours, sitting around perfectly taut structures, as they ate their lunch cooked on what looked like portable Aga ovens. Ellie and Jess hadn't even a kettle between them, but were already seeing the funny side of the situation. They'd just managed to get the whole thing up again when Ellie nearly jumped out of her spotted wellies.

She was clinging onto a tent-pole as Jess secured a corner with a tent peg, when out of the corner of her eye she spotted two people she really didn't want to see.

'Jess, duck down!' she shouted, but of course, Jess was already on her knees trying to secure the tent, so when Ellie let go to jump down, the whole thing collapsed again right on top of them.

'Keep still and quiet, and we may get away with it,' hissed Ellie.

'I'm sorry, but I haven't a clue what you're talking about,' Jess replied impatiently. 'I'm sure that was right – you just have to hold it steady for me.'

'Can we help?'

Neither of the girls moved for a moment. But then, they didn't have to. Peering underneath the forest-green fabric at the pair of them were two faces they recognised.

'Do you need a hand?' said Henry Dorsey, barely able to hide his amusement at their plight.

Charlie Harden stood next to him, and to cover his obvious embarrassment set about helping to remove the fabric whilst proffering a hand towards Jess, which she took.

'We're doing all right, thanks,' said Ellie, who was feeling really cross that Henry should have appeared out of nowhere like that. He obviously thought they couldn't put up the tent and that made her crosser still.

'Let us help – it's been so long since we saw you,' said Charlie. 'We could put it up really quickly with everyone helping, and then perhaps we could take you for a drink … or a bite to eat.'

Jess didn't speak, but she was glowing pink, and Ellie noticed neither she nor Charlie seemed to want to stop holding hands. She looked at Henry to see his reaction, but he was nodding and saying what a brilliant idea that would be. Ellie was so pleased to see that Charlie looked as besotted as ever by her friend that she instantly agreed. After all, she needn't talk to Henry if she didn't want to, she decided.

The tent was up in what seemed like ten minutes, and so they all set off for the main arena where they knew they'd find food and a drink. Jess moved round to Ellie's side, and Charlie and Henry followed on behind.

'It's such a surprise to see you here,' said Ellie, at last. 'I thought you were all gigging in London.'

'We were,' said Charlie, 'but I've got this new management team and they fixed us up here at the last minute.'

'Are you playing?' Jess could hardly keep the excitement out of her voice.

'Yes, we're on tomorrow evening … not on the main stage, but in the Big Top. Still, we're really pleased with that.'

'Congratulations, Charlie,' said Jess. 'I know how much you've wanted something like this to happen.'

'Thank you, Jess. I hope you'll come and watch.'

'I'd like that ... I wouldn't miss it for the world.'

'Are Zara and Pippa here?' asked Ellie. Charlie might be behaving in a really friendly way towards Jess, but she wanted to gauge his reaction at the mention of Henry's sister.

'Yes, they're both practising madly. Pippa's boyfriend is on the management team so he's got them hard at it,' said Charlie, smiling into Jess's eyes.

Jess really blushed pink when she heard that. Ellie could see how pleased she was, and when they started talking, she felt she should give them some space. To find out that they'd been quite wrong about Pippa was fantastic news, but Ellie reminded herself that Jess had been persuaded that Charlie liked Pippa by Zara. Thank goodness she wasn't around. Ellie wasn't quite sure she'd be able to talk to her.

They'd reached a festival favourite, the Bumble Bee Inn, a canvas tent serving drinks and snacks, swathed in silks and satins and twinkling with fairy lights inside. Henry and Charlie went to the bar, and the girls sat down at a wooden log table.

'Now that we've met one another, I feel absolutely fine,' said Jess. 'He's as pleasant as ever, and now we can just concentrate on being good friends.'

'Yes, I'm sure you'll be really 'good friends',' said Ellie, smirking.

'What do you mean? Ellie, you cannot doubt me. I'm in no danger of falling in love with him again.'

'Oh, I think you're in great danger of *him* falling even more in love with you than he was before. And, you must admit, you are just a tiny bit pleased to see him.'

Jess scolded her, but Ellie could see she wasn't really upset by her words.

As the evening progressed, Jess and Charlie relaxed. Ellie almost felt envious. Henry made conversation, but Ellie felt there was still a feeling of coolness between them. She wondered what he thought about the fact that Jess and Charlie were getting on so well. Surely he didn't now approve. But, she couldn't possibly talk to him about it.

'Are you camping anywhere near?' she asked.

'No, not exactly.'

Ellie had a vision of Henry and Charlie 'glamping', a kind of posh camping for rich people, and then realised he might perhaps be in one of the luxury teepees on the hill that cost a couple of thousand pounds a throw.

'We're staying in the house.'

'Wow, I didn't realise musicians had such wonderful benefits.'

'They don't as a rule … it's my aunt's house.'

'Your aunt's house?'

'You met her at Donald's wedding.'

'Ah, yes I did, though I thought Donald said she lived in Scotland.'

'Not all the time.'

Ellie didn't think Henry had witnessed what was going on between her and his aunt, but she couldn't be completely sure. She was keen for the conversation to move on.

'Cara and Liberty should be here a little later,' said Ellie. She watched Henry's face for any sign of disapproval but he asked after them straight away.

'I think they're fine, but I haven't really heard anything from them since we came to Bath. I've tried phoning them both, but it's not unusual if they don't pick up. They're either really busy or they've run out of battery. I know they'll just come breezing along later without a care in the world.'

'Good job they've always got you and Jess to look out for them.'

Ellie smiled and took a sip of her drink. 'Well, some people need a little more looking after. I don't like to say very much, but they've both had rough times, and in my experience that usually means they need a little more attention than most.'

'They're very lucky to have your friendship. Most people just wouldn't put up with their behaviour. Aren't you worried that their reputations might rub off on you?'

'Are you kidding me?'

'Most people would assume that because they're a couple of airheads who drink too much, and flirt with every guy in sight, that their friends are exactly the same. By associating with them, you put yourself in danger of getting a name for yourselves.'

'I wouldn't care about anyone's opinion if they thought like that. They'd be people I am not interested in knowing. Are you really serious? Who thinks like that?'

A muscle twitched in Henry's cheek. 'I do, actually.'

Ellie looked into Henry's eyes and could see he was in earnest. She wanted to slap his face and walk off, but she was determined not to spoil things for Jess as she could see how well she and Charlie were getting on.

'Well, I am sorry that is your opinion,' Ellie replied in a measured tone, 'but everyone should be judged on his or her individual merit. That's the way I perceive other people, and I certainly wouldn't lump a whole lot of people together just because they were friends, and then dismiss all of them because a few might not be to my liking. It's like disliking different countries or races of people because of a minority that don't conform to your beliefs. I never heard anything so ridiculous. We will have to agree to disagree on this one, Henry.'

Henry stood up. 'I'm going back to the house, Charlie. It's lovely to see you, Ellie and Jess, but I need to go and wash for dinner. My aunt is expecting us.'

'I'll be there in just a minute,' Charlie answered, but Ellie could see how reluctant he was to leave Jess's side. She watched Henry stride away thinking his arrogance only seemed to get worse, and just as he'd initially appeared to be so charming.

Charlie arranged to meet Jess later on, which pleased Ellie though she wasn't sure she would enjoy Henry's company very much. She thought about what he'd said, and though, in her heart, she knew he might have a small point, she was still very upset with him. It was true that both of her friends were a bit of a handful, but they were still her friends, and Ellie knew they only needed to grow up a little. They were just trying to have a bit of fun, even if it meant that at times they could both be very trying!

## Chapter 36

By nine o'clock that evening, there was still no sign of Cara and Liberty and both Ellie and Jess were feeling a little worried. Finally, about ten minutes before Charlie was due to come and find Jess to take her for a drink, Ellie's phone rang.

'Thank goodness, Cara, we've been worried about you. Are you nearly here?'

'No,' said a voice, barely recognisable as Cara's on the other end of the phone. She was clearly sobbing. 'It's Liberty. I don't know how to tell you, Ellie.'

'For goodness' sake, what is it?'

'She's disappeared. I've hardly seen her lately. She's been going round with Greg Whitely and his friends ... partying and clubbing every night until the early hours. Ellie, I only went to Greg's once, but half of his so-called friends were on cocaine ... I'm so worried about her.'

'What are you saying? Has she been taking drugs?'

'I don't know, though she's been behaving really oddly.'

'Why didn't you tell me before now? Cara, we have to find her.'

'Will MacGourtey is here. He's helping me and he wants to

speak to you.'

There was silence for a moment and then she heard Will speak in his soft tones with a burr of an accent she'd never been able to make out. She felt more reassured now she could hear his voice. 'Hi Will, how are you? I'm sorry you've been inconvenienced like this.'

'Ellie, it's no trouble. I only wish I'd done something sooner. I suspected something was going on, and I know all about Greg Whitely. Look, try not to worry. I've been on to Henry and Charlie, and they're on their way.'

'Oh, no – they've got a gig tomorrow. Of course, I'm really anxious about Liberty, but this really is the limit!'

'Don't worry. Charlie says some things are more important, and he's right.'

'But, we should be there for her – not you. Liberty is not your responsibility.'

'Ellie, believe me, I don't want to expose you to any danger. I'm sure she'll be fine, but I think you and Jess should stay where you are. Promise me?'

'I do promise, Will, but I feel so useless. Isn't there anything I can do?'

'Just stay by the phone; Liberty may try and contact you herself. Listen, you take care. I'll be in touch as soon as I can.'

Under any other circumstances, Ellie would have been really pleased to talk to Will. She hadn't seen him for ages, and she could just imagine him coming to the rescue. He was such a lovely guy and so dependable. Maybe he'd do for Cara if she'd just be a little more sensible. At least Cara wasn't on her own, and with Henry and Charlie leaping into action so quickly, she was sure it wouldn't be long before they managed to track down Liberty.

Jess burst into tears when she heard. 'I should have known something like this would happen. But, I'm sure between them, Charlie, Will and Henry will find her.'

'I am worried about her too, Jess, but it's about time she did something to change. She simply doesn't care how her actions impact on other people or more particularly, on her friends.'

'It could all be a false alarm. Cara may be worrying for nothing.'

'But, it's so unfair on our friends who have had to travel two hours to London to look for someone who probably doesn't want to be found. They'll get no thanks for their trouble, and now they're going to miss their gig. Charlie's worked so hard for this.'

'Yes, but he wouldn't have behaved any other way. He's such a lovely person. Ellie, he's apologised for not being in touch for so long, and asked me to forgive him. He didn't go into any details, but I know he's been working really hard.'

Ellie kept her thoughts to herself. Her only comfort was that she was sure Henry must have said something to Charlie for him to come and look for her. Had he finally realised just how egotistical, and self-important he really was, and had decided to change? The fact that Charlie needed his permission to go out with Jess made Ellie very cross, but if Henry had seen the error of his ways, she was part way to forgiving him. Perhaps Henry wasn't so bad. After all, he had gone to look for Liberty with the others. Whatever scrape Liberty had managed to find herself in now, Ellie hoped it wouldn't be long before they were all together again. She couldn't help worrying about all the implications of what had been said, but she was optimistic by nature, and refused to think the worst.

By the following morning, Jess and Ellie were no longer sure what to think. Each had received a text from Charlie and Will respectively, saying that although they hadn't tracked Liberty down yet, they had good reason to think they'd find her before the end of the day with the new information they'd received. There was nothing the girls could do which was frustrating, and with the festival in full swing, they felt even more miserable and useless. Everyone around them was having a good time. Music played wherever they went, and being surrounded by laughter and fun only made them feel sadder than ever. They didn't feel like seeing any of the bands, and wandered along looking at all the stalls selling crafts and hats, Indian parasols and incense.

Everywhere they went, people cried out to tempt them to look at jewellery, clothes and a thousand different kinds of accessory, or to listen to poetry and songs specially performed for them. Jess bought a garland of silk flowers and looked even more like a midsummer fairy in her long dress, which was the colour of pistachio ice cream. Ellie chose a top hat that she said reminded her of Tom. It had a jaunty feather tucked into the silk band and she could only think how much he would have loved it, which made her feel sadder than ever. Everything had been thought of for the fun of the festival crowd. There was a barber's tent where several men were either having their hair cut or were enjoying a wet shave as the crowd gawped on. The tent with 'massage chairs', and even the Reiki healing tempted Jess, though she didn't stop to try them. Ellie shied away from anything like that and, as they passed the fortune-telling tent, she pretended not to notice the voice calling out to them.

'Pretty ladies, let me tell you what your future holds.'

A rather dishevelled looking man in a long black leather coat beckoned to them. He looked more than a little unkempt with his hair tumbling down his back in matted dreadlocks tied into place by a grubby handkerchief over which he wore what Ellie could only describe as a highwayman's hat. He wore sunglasses, and a scarf wound and muffled round his throat, which fell to the ground in long tails like his grey beard. Ellie didn't think she'd ever had a less inviting offer.

However, Jess seemed intrigued. 'I know it's silly, but I think I'd like to see what he says.'

'Will you be safe?' Ellie whispered. 'I know you shouldn't really judge people by appearances, but I'm not sure I'd go in there on my own.'

The flap of the fortune-telling tent was open, and they caught a glimpse of someone else sitting at a table, dressed in long flowing robes wearing a beautiful Venetian mask with long plumes of feathers.

'There's a lady in there with a crystal ball,' said Jess. 'I'm sure they wouldn't be here if it wasn't all above board. Look, if I'm not out in five minutes, you can alert the authorities.'

Ellie watched her friend disappear inside and when she emerged ten minutes later, she was beaming.

'Don't tell me, you're going on a long journey,' Ellie pronounced. 'You'll meet someone tall, dark and handsome, get married within the year and have half a dozen children.'

'Not quite, but he was incredible. He said I had already met the man of my dreams, which you must admit is true. And then he said that my lover's name began with the letter C, and that we were going to be very happy together.'

'I am slightly impressed, but he could have just guessed Charlie's initial.'

'I don't know what to think, Ellie. All I can say is that I hope he was right. He said we would marry and settle in Hampshire.'

'Well, I expect he guessed that from his preliminary probing questions.'

'He didn't ask me anything at all. He went into a sort of trance and it all came out.'

'Did he say anything else?'

Not much, except to say that you would be going on a journey over the water, somewhere green and emerald, and that it would be sooner than you think.'

Ellie laughed out loud. 'Now, I've heard everything. And, that's not very likely is it? The furthest I'm going is back to London to stay with my mum and dad whilst I consider what my plans are next. Well, they have got a green front door, though I'm not sure I would describe it as emerald.'

'I'm sure it's a lot of nonsense.'

'Maybe not where you're concerned,' Ellie replied taking Jess's hand and giving it a squeeze. 'I believe you and Charlie will have the happy ending you both desire.'

Waiting to hear any news from Cara and the guys was agonising, and though they trudged round trying to find anything to distract them, both girls became increasingly worried as the day moved on. Not having a battery charger or any source of electricity was a problem as both of their phones were running low. Finally, at 6.30 a text came through from Charlie.

'He says they're in the Big Top in ten minutes performing on stage! He can't explain now, but apparently though Liberty is still not found, Will has it on good authority that he knows exactly where she is and that she's safe. Charlie says we're not to worry and he'll explain later.'

'I trust Will implicitly,' said Ellie. 'I'm sure he has it all figured out, but I do wish Liberty would contact us. Though contacting me isn't going to do much good – my battery is flat.'

'So long as she's safe and that she will be found, that's all the news I want to hear,' answered Jess. 'Come on, we've got ten minutes to get to the other side of the site. I am so excited to see Charlie play.'

Walking uphill through the quagmire was hard work in wellington boots, and wreathing through the hundreds of people who surged in all directions proved to be almost impossible. Ellie caught Jess's hand as they tramped through the mud past all the paraphernalia of festival décor – giant animals and larger than life flowers, flaming torches and a myriad of soap bubbles that floated over their heads, adding a touch of fairy tale magic.

The Big Top was full to bursting and the girls squeezed their way to the front just as Charlie and Henry came on with the band. The audience gave them an enthusiastic welcome and then the set began. Charlie blew Jess a kiss as soon as he spotted her, and Ellie watched her face light up. The first song brought spontaneous applause and loud cheers from the crowd. Charlie and Henry looked almost overwhelmed by the reception they were getting, but wasted no time in getting on with the next song. Once or twice Henry caught Ellie's eye and smiled. He did look at home up there on the stage, and Ellie could see the effect he was having on the groups of girls who'd pushed their way to the front of the barriers. Every time he looked their way a cheer went up. It was quite surreal, Ellie thought.

About mid-way through the set, Charlie put down his guitar and pulled the microphone from its stand.

'Thank you, everyone, for coming to see us – we're so excited to see how many of you are here. I just wanted to take a minute to say something. This year is turning out to be a spectacular one for many reasons, not least, because I've just signed with a major record label and I couldn't be happier.'

The tent erupted, and when the applause died down Charlie paused for a moment, the audience holding their breath waiting to hear what he was to say next. 'So, it's time to slow it down ... just a little now. This next song is very special – it's a new composition. I wrote it for the girl I'm deeply in love with, and I know I'm probably going to really embarrass her when I say that, but it's true. She's brought love and happiness into my life like I've never known before, and Jess, I hope you'll forgive me when I say that I'm hoping you're going to want to spend the rest of your life with me because I can't imagine my life without you, and I'm not taking no for an answer.'

The whole crowd turned, oohing and aahing, to look at Jess who covered her face with her hands before blowing a kiss up to the stage. Charlie blew one back, picked up his guitar and started to sing.

'That's the most romantic proposal I've ever seen,' whispered Ellie into Jess's hair.

'I can't believe it,' said Jess, hugging her friend. 'He feels the same as I do!'

'Of course he does, you noodle,' said Ellie with a laugh. 'Just promise me that you won't put me in pink if I'm going to be your chief bridesmaid ... I'd much prefer blue.'

'Oh, Ellie, I think I might just burst with happiness. If only you could feel the same my day would be just perfect.'

'Jess, I'm so thrilled for you, but please don't worry about me. Besides, I don't think I could ever be as happy as you. Only if I had your lovely nature and your goodness could I ever hope to approach anything like your happiness. No, I'll be fine, and you never know, perhaps with good luck I'll discover that Donald has a brother!'

The rest of the gig went down a storm and at the end Jess and Ellie went round by the side of the stage to greet the band. Charlie swept Jess up into his arms and kissed her, hugging her as if she might just disappear if he let go.

Ellie was filled with happiness and turned to Henry who was just coming off the stage. 'Thank you so much – I don't know what you said to Charlie, but I'm sure you had a hand in it.'

'I didn't really say too much, and besides what you think, he has his own mind. But, I must admit, I thought about what you said. I know how much you love Jess, and I can see why you and Charlie adore her. I'm sorry, Ellie.'

'Don't worry about it. All's well that ends well, as they say. It is so lovely to see them together. I've never seen two people so in love.'

'No, it's a rare and beautiful sight. So often it can be completely one-sided, but here, it's a genuine meeting of hearts and minds.'

'Oh, Henry, you surprise me. I didn't know you were so romantic.'

'Well, I have my moments.'

Ellie didn't quite know what to say next and decided to change the subject completely. 'We've been so worried about Liberty. What did you manage to find out?'

'We were right about her being caught up with Greg Whitely and his crowd, but from what we've gathered she may not have fallen into the abyss of complete destruction, thankfully. Will managed to track down some of the film crew who'd seen her last, and they seemed to think that apart from being totally besotted with Greg, she was only getting tipsy on alcopops.'

'Yes, that sounds exactly like Liberty. So, do you have any idea of her whereabouts?'

'They were last seen in Brighton at a club on the seafront.'

'She's always been so thoughtless. How she could just go off like that without telling anyone is beyond me. Surely she must have an idea how worried we must be. And, whatever the intelligence, I won't feel comfortable until I see her myself.'

'We've got other plans, don't worry.'

Henry took Ellie's hand and squeezed it. 'Come on, the night is young. How about a ride on the big wheel? You can see as far as Bath from the top.'

Suddenly, Ellie felt really deflated. However reassuring Henry tried to be and however silly Liberty could be, she couldn't bear to think of her in trouble. And when Henry squeezed her hand, she couldn't squeeze his back. 'I'm sorry, Henry, I just don't feel like it. I'm going to have an early night.'

'Could I tempt you to come for dinner? My aunt loves company. I'm sure Jess is going to dine too.'

'No, thank you ... I'm sorry, I suddenly feel really worn out by everything. Could you just tell Jess I've gone back to the tent. Tell her I'm fine, I'm just really tired.'

Henry didn't argue. He let go of her hand and Ellie walked as quickly as she could through the Big Top, and out into the darkening night. Crowds of people surged past her on every side, but she'd never felt so lonely in her life before as she did at that moment. Everyone else seemed so happy, arm in arm with friends or lovers. There wasn't a single face she recognised, though for a second she thought she saw Will. He was in the distance. Broad shoulders, blonde hair glinting with streaks of pale auburn in the torchlight, and a head height above most people, she almost ran to keep up with him. And then he disappeared, and she realised it couldn't possibly have been Will. If he was really there he'd have found them all by now, and he was still trying to find out where Liberty was hiding and why. Thinking about her friend made her feel helpless, but there was more than that. She didn't fully understand why she felt so low. Henry made her cross; perhaps that was one reason. She was glad he'd done the right thing by Jess, but she couldn't help thinking that the invitation to dinner he'd given her had been out of a desire to please his aunt, not her. It was not like Ellie to feel so miserable, and certainly not when she felt so happy for Jess. But, there was something else nagging at the back of her mind. She couldn't help thinking about Tom though she tried to put him out of her mind. Those last moments they'd shared were a memory seared into her soul. To feel love like that she felt would ever be an unattainable goal, and she could never settle for second best. But, she reproached herself for her foolishness. The feelings and emotions she'd experienced were not her own, she told herself. Maybe she wasn't even capable of feeling such love for another human being.

After a good night's sleep the world seemed a happier place next morning. Jess was back safely and radiating pure happiness even in her sleep. Ellie felt it was impossible to feel miserable when there was such joy emanating from every cell in her friend's body. It was infectious, and as she struggled to get dressed in the tiny space, she was determined to greet the day with a brighter spirit.

'I said we'd meet Charlie for breakfast,' said Jess, rubbing her eyes and propping herself up on one elbow. 'He says there's a stall selling bacon and egg rolls that are to die for, and I'm starving.'

'I thought people in love lost their appetite,' said Ellie, observing Jess who looked back with a huge smile on her face.

'I am in love ... we are in love, and it's almost impossible to believe how things have worked out. I just wish everyone was so happy.'

'You deserve happiness like no one else I know.'

'You do too, Ellie. Henry kept talking about you at dinner last night. I'm really starting to warm to him. He likes you a lot, you know.'

Ellie ignored her. 'Come on, I'm starving, too. Bacon and egg sounds fantastic, and we've still got a ten minute walk to find it!'

After the loud music and laughter of the night before, most festival revellers seemed subdued and as they glimpsed the long and quiet queue who waited for their early morning tea and breakfast, delicious smells of cooked sausage, bacon, eggs and mushrooms drifted across the misty fields stirring people into action. Charlie and Henry were waiting for them. Jess looked as shy as she had on the very first occasion she'd met Charlie, but Ellie noticed it wasn't long before he caught hold of her hand and whispered something into her hair.

'We missed you last night, Ellie.'

'Thank you, Charlie. I just felt so tired all of a sudden, but I'm wide awake today and back to feeling my old self.'

'That's good,' said Henry, 'you'll need your strength. Will has been in touch. He's meeting us in a minute with some news.'

'Did he say it was good news?' asked Jess. 'Has he found her?'

'Yes, she's safe,' said Charlie. 'Will is going to tell you all about it.'

Ellie lost her appetite after that but the combination of egg, bacon and wholemeal roll was so delicious that she soon found it again, and when she spotted Will in the distance, ten minutes later, she felt prepared for whatever he was to say. She watched his progress as he walked slowly towards them. Blue jeans, with a woollen sweater and grey denim jacket to guard against the early morning chill, she saw him rake a hand through his fair hair which was swept back from his forehead save for a curl or two that refused to be tamed and danced on his tanned face. He was tall and broad, his face unremarkable except for his extraordinarily light and clear grey eyes. Ellie met his glance, and felt embarrassed that he'd caught her staring.

'You're not to worry,' Will said, 'Liberty is here and she's fine. But, she's a bit concerned that you're going to be really cross with her, and she's very reluctant to meet you.'

'Well, I am really mad at her, I can't pretend,' said Ellie who was so relieved to see Will. 'But, it's not so far away from anything else she's put us through, and I'm just so relieved that she's been found.'

'Henry is a wonderful sleuth,' said Will. 'Anyway, Liberty

says she can't face Jess just at the moment but she wants to talk to you, Ellie. Will you come with me?'

'You will go, won't you?' urged Jess.

'Of course I'll go, and I promise, I will not shout, as much as I'd like to give her a piece of my mind.'

Ellie followed Will as they set off towards the fields where the craft and clothing stalls were ranged along their boundary.

'It's lovely to see you, Ellie,' said Will, stopping in his tracks. 'How are you? It seems an age since we last met.'

'I'm fine, Will, and I'm all the better for seeing you. I'm so sorry you had to get mixed up in all of this.'

'It's nothing, really, and I knew how worried you'd be until she was found.'

'But, I know what she's like. It's a miracle that she's co-operated.'

'I don't think she means to be so thoughtless – she got caught up in certain events, and in her own way she wanted to surprise you.'

'She did that all right. So, where is she?'

'Just a minute. If you stay right there, I promise she'll be here in a moment.'

They were just walking past the fortune-telling tent. The man who'd read Jess's palm appeared from within its depths and grabbed Will, hugging him and slapping him on the back.

Will was just the kind of person to embrace everyone, but even Ellie was surprised that he seemed to know the fortune-teller quite well. But then the man turned, and when she saw him remove his sunglasses to smile at her, the mystery was solved.

## Chapter 37

Ellie couldn't find the words to speak she was so livid. Greg Whitely was standing less than a couple of metres away from her. He still looked swarthy and unshaven, though it was obvious now that the beard and dreadlocks he sported were very good false ones. She wanted to run and hit him, but Will came over just then, and when he spoke to her so softly and in such measured tones making everything sound so utterly reasonable, she reined in her emotions and just bit her bottom lip instead.

'They'll tell you themselves, but they're really sorry. Liberty didn't think for one minute about how worried you'd be because she was here, and all they could think was that it would be a huge joke if they saw you.'

'And what about Cara?'

'She only knew about them going to Brighton for a few days; she really didn't know they were going to pull this stunt. Apparently, Greg always used to work the festivals when he hadn't much in the way of acting or presenting to do. He thought Liberty would enjoy it.'

'Liberty was bound to want to join him. She's been acting a part ever since I first met her, but did she not realise that you can't just disappear into thin air without people imagining that you've been kidnapped or murdered?'

'No. She realises now that she was very thoughtless and she wants to apologise.'

'I blame *him*. He's the one that led her astray, and he's old enough to know better.'

Liberty appeared at the doorway of the tent. Although still dressed in long flowing robes, she no longer wore the feathered mask that Ellie and Jess had seen her wearing on the day that Greg had told Jess's fortune. And when she sauntered over Ellie witnessed little remorse. Liberty was as apologetic as Ellie knew she would be, which was hardly sufficient.

'Ellie, I am truly sorry, but Greg and I thought it would be such a laugh! We knew you were coming to the festival and though we didn't really expect you to be interested, I thought Jess might like her palm read. And, you must admit, you were both taken in. I wish you could have seen Jess's face when Greg told her about being settled and in love with someone from Hampshire. Luckily, she couldn't see my face, I was shaking so much with laughter that I had to pretend I was sneezing.'

'It's a really shabby way to treat your friends, Liberty. I don't mind for me, but Jess doesn't deserve to be duped like this.'

'We haven't duped anyone ... anyway, it's obvious she's going to marry Charlie. Just like me and Greg.'

'You're getting married?'

'Well, I'm going to stop at Greg's for a while, and then we'll see. I've turned out most of his loser friends and he needs me to keep him off the drink and drugs. He's going to find me a job at the television studios when we get back.'

'So, you're not planning on fortune-telling full time?'

Liberty laughed raucously. 'No way! We just thought it would be a bit of a laugh as Greg has done it before. He's got his own camper van just over there. We neither of us like camping and it's really cosy in the van, just room for two in a bunk.'

'Spare me the details, please. Liberty, will you just think for once in your life. I don't think you should be with Greg – he's a really bad influence.'

'I know he is, Ellie, but I also know I can change him.'

'Don't you think every girl thinks she can change a man who hasn't her best interests at heart?'

'Ellie, you must stop worrying. Greg needs me to keep him in check – he's already admitted that. Besides, I can't help the fact that I've fallen in love with him.'

Suddenly, Ellie felt she had no more to say. It was clear that Liberty believed every word, even if she was deluding herself. 'I can't stop you from making your own choices, but please think carefully before you end up living a life of regret. And you must make it up to Jess who's been so worried about you. Just promise me, Liberty, you'll apologise properly to her as soon as you can.'

Ellie couldn't bring herself to speak to Greg and when he started to say something, she ignored him, and said her goodbyes to Liberty as politely as she could. Everything Henry had ever said about him was true, she realised, and there wasn't a thing she could do to help Liberty. She was obviously in deep with Greg and didn't care what anyone else thought. Ellie would never change her and there was absolutely no point in trying to any more.

Walking back to the others, Ellie was quiet. She was thinking what an awful imposition it had been on Will and the other guys who'd spent so much wasted time trying to find a girl who simply hadn't cared about how much trouble they'd been put to.

'I'm so embarrassed, Will,' she said at last. 'I don't know what we'd have done without you looking for my friend, and yet, you can see, she doesn't care one bit about the inconvenience, not to mention the heartache that she's caused.'

'It's nothing, Ellie. I was in the right place at the right time, that's all.'

'But, you've spent hours and days of your life looking for her when she couldn't care less about the danger she was exposing herself to. That was so unselfish of you.'

'I did want to find her, but I must admit, it wasn't really just for Liberty that I spent all that time searching for her.'

When Will suddenly stopped in his tracks, Ellie stopped too. She could see he had something on his mind and that he wasn't quite sure how to say it. He was searching the ground with his eyes and when he looked up, she knew he was going to say something important.

'I knew how worried you were. I did it for *you*, Ellie.'

Will towered over her. He was standing against the light, almost blotting out the rising sun, and she couldn't quite see his expression, but his grey eyes, which were flecked with blue, gazed at her intently.

'You did it for *me*?'

Will nodded his head slowly. 'Listen, I know this might sound a little weird, but I have to know something, Ellie.'

'Anything ... ask away, Will.

His gaze was steady as he took a step nearer. 'Are you in love with Henry?'

There wasn't a minute's hesitation. 'No, I'm not.'

She surprised herself when the words came out, but she knew what she was saying was true. She was growing to like Henry, but no, she knew she would never be in love with him. Not only was the chemistry quite wrong, but also their worlds were too different. Besides, he needed someone who would knock some of that arrogance right out of him or failing that, be with someone like Zara who positively relished it. Ellie knew if there'd been any attempt at a relationship she'd have probably ended up hating him before she could love him, if that was even possible.

Will smiled, though Ellie could see that he was trying to stop himself.

'I probably shouldn't say this, but I decided if I found Liberty, there would be no holds barred.'

Something about the scent of him was like a pure shot of nostalgia, which coupled with his nearness, aroused a physical response to surprise her. The fragrance of fresh limes prompted a stirring deep within, mixed with such bittersweet emotion to produce equal measures of exquisite pain and pleasure. Ellie held out her hand to him and he took it, wreathing his own long fingers between hers. 'What is it, Will – tell me?'

He could hardly find the words for now he was so close to Ellie, her beauty overwhelmed him. She was wearing a vintage dress of grey satin with splashes of red poppies here and there. Cut on the cross, it clung to her curves and swept over her tiny hips flaring out into a skirt that stopped short of the wellington boots, which somehow seemed to finish off her look to perfection. Her hair, caught up by a scarlet ribbon, showed off her long white neck and the slope of her creamy shoulders. Taking a deep breath, he began. 'I am in love with you, Ellie. I have been since the first time I met you and saw you sketching at Steventon with your hair blowing back in a summer breeze and your forehead wrinkled in concentration.'

His hand dwarfed hers, his large fingers holding her tiny ones protectively. Ellie couldn't stop staring at them. 'I had no idea, Will.'

'I couldn't stop thinking about you, but I thought you were with Greg or Donald, and then when Henry started showing an interest in your paintings, I naturally thought it would be a matter of time before you'd be together.'

Ellie saw immediately how it had been all along. At every stage, Will had been looking out for her, being appreciative of everything she did and said, and even looking after her friends. He'd encouraged her work, and she knew it was Will who'd made sure her paintings were exhibited.

'But, it was you who really believed in me, wasn't it, Will? You made me feel good about everything I did.'

'Listen, Ellie, please forgive me for speaking my mind. I don't know if you think you could ever return the love I feel for you, and maybe it's selfish of me even to ask, but I had to tell you how I felt.'

Will was looking at their entwined fingers as if he beheld some precious treasure. Ellie put up her hand to his face. 'No one has ever said anything so beautiful to me before.'

'I feel as if I've known you all my life,' he said. 'The very first time we talked at Steventon, it was like déjà vu … Oh, you'll think me stupid if I say anymore.'

'No, I won't,' said Ellie, drawn to the eyes that stared so steadily into her own.

'I do know you, intimately, as you do me … and I think you must remember.'

'What do you mean, Will?'

It was his eyes she noticed then. They were the colour of the sea on a wintry day and as restless as the waves crashing to the shore. The grey jacket he wore intensified the shade – one minute they were as lavender as sea thrift, the next as pale as pebbles in sand. The grey eyes that pierced hers looked across the centuries, and settled in their rightful place. 'We've been in love before, I'm sure.'

The connection between them was one that felt so familiar, she knew that time had brought them together again. He was not Tom and she certainly wasn't Jane, but the emotions felt the same and the feeling of souls having found one another over time and distance was so strong that she understood every word Will was saying. True love was never lost, and what had been in the past was as much a part of them as it would be forever. He slipped his free arm around her slender waist and pulling her closely to him, he bent his head before tenderly placing his lips on hers. There was no hesitation. Ellie kissed him back as if she had been waiting to do so all her life. Time took her back to another place and another person, and when she finally drew back to look into his eyes, so full of love for her, she knew their souls had found one another once more.

'I don't think I recognised it before now,' she said, 'but I do believe you are right.'

'Do you really feel it too, Ellie?'

'I do.'

'I feel as if I've been waiting my whole life to find you again.'

'Will, I'm so glad you found me.'

'Would you stay with me if I asked you to, Ellie?'

She could not tell if he was teasing her. His grey-blue eyes reflected the hues of the sky, and she glimpsed amusement twinkling in their depths.

'That is a question I cannot answer ... as you have not yet asked it.'

Will laughed and raised her hand to his lips. He kept his eyes on hers, and Ellie felt herself sinking into those limpid pools. She watched him kiss her fingers. 'Give me the ribbon from your hair,' he said.

Ellie reached up to untie the scarlet ribbon, and he slipped off a gold ring from his little finger, which he threaded onto the piece of silk before he lowered it over her head. 'It's a talisman, to keep you safe, and a token of my love.'

A smile played upon his lips. His fingers tied the ribbon round her neck, and she felt them brush her ears, as he held her head in his hands, tangling his fingers in her hair to kiss her lips again.

The ring, enamelled in royal blue with white crosses and flowers engraved upon its surface, was the most beautiful Ellie thought she'd ever seen, and told him so.

'It's the family crest of the Darcys and MacGourteys,' Will explained. 'The blue is symbolic for their high status, the white stands for purity and honesty.'

'Why the Darcys?' asked Ellie. 'You surely must be joking!'

'We're all related to one another in Ireland,' he said, laughing. 'That's where I'm from ... I've a family home on the outskirts of Limerick. It's not quite Pemberley, but it's a big old house, which dates back to ancient times. You see, I'm distantly related by marriage to the very first Mr Darcy.'

'Now, you have to be pulling my leg.'

'Seriously, the name Magourtey is a derivative of the name Darcy, as unlikely as that seems. It means 'son of the dark one', so you can see how closely I'm related.'

Ellie laughed at that as she looked at his blonde head. 'Jess will be thrilled that she knows you. She's always wanted to meet a real-life Mr Darcy.'

'And, what will she say when she learns that Mr Darcy is in love with you?'

'Oh, I don't think she'll mind. After all, she has her very own Mr Bingley.'

'Will you stay with me, Ellie?'

'If you're asking, Will.'

'I am, with all my heart.'

'Then I shall say yes, with all that my own heart has to offer.'

'It means a journey to Ireland, and it's a draughty old house in winter, but I think you'll love the countryside where I grew up. You'll be coming as the leaves are turning and the days are growing shorter, but there's the promise of an Indian summer with days of misty mornings and golden afternoons. You'll never see the like of wildflowers as there are in Ireland, planted by the pixies they say.'

'And are the buttercups as large as saucers?'

'How d'you know that?'

'I think you told me once before.'

'Aye, and we'll walk barefoot together across the dew-drenched fields of emerald green.'

*The End*

# About Jane Odiwe

Jane Odiwe is the author of five Austen-inspired novels, *Project Darcy, Searching for Captain Wentworth, Mr Darcy's Secret, Willoughby's Return,* and *Lydia Bennet's Story*, as well as a contributor of a commissioned short story for the anthology, *Jane Austen Made Me Do It*, edited by Laurel Ann Nattress.

Recent television appearances include a Masterchef Special, celebrating 200 years of *Sense and Sensibility*, and an interview for the 200 year anniversary of *Pride and Prejudice* on BBC Breakfast.

Jane is a member of the Jane Austen Society; she holds an arts degree, and initially started her working life teaching Art and History. With her husband, children, and two cats, Jane divides her time between North London, and Bath, England. When she's not writing, she enjoys painting and trying to capture the spirit of Jane Austen's world. Her illustrations have been published in a picture book, *Effusions of Fancy*, and are featured in a biographical film of Jane Austen's life in Sony's DVD edition of *The Jane Austen Book Club*.

Website: http://austeneffusions.com
Blog: http://janeaustensequels.blogspot.co.uk
Austen Authors: http://austenauthors.net
White Soup Press: http://whitesouppress.com
Facebook:http//facebook.com/JaneOdiwe
Twitter:@JaneOdiwe

# OTHER BOOKS BY JANE ODIWE

## Searching for Captain Wentworth

Sophie's story travels 200 years and back again to unite this modern heroine with her own Captain Wentworth. Blending fact and fiction together, the tale of Jane Austen's own quest for happiness weaves alongside, creating a believable world of new possibilities for the inspiration behind *Persuasion*.

## Mr Darcy's Secret

After capturing the heart of the most eligible bachelor in England, Elizabeth Bennet believes her happiness is complete-until the day she unearths a stash of anonymous, passionate love letters that may be Darcy's, and she realizes just how little she knows about the guarded, mysterious man she married ... Mr Darcy's Secret is a story about love and misunderstandings; of overcoming doubt and trusting to the real feelings of the heart - Elizabeth and the powerful, compelling figure of Mr Darcy take centre stage in this romantic tale set in Regency Derbyshire and the Lakes, alongside the beloved characters from *Pride and Prejudice*.

## Willoughby's Return

In Jane Austen's *Sense and Sensibility*, when Marianne Dashwood marries Colonel Brandon, she puts her heartbreak over dashing scoundrel John Willoughby in the past. Three years later, Willoughby's return throws Marianne into a tizzy of painful memories and exquisite feelings of uncertainty. Willoughby is as charming, as roguish, and as much in love with her as ever. And the timing couldn't be worse—with Colonel Brandon away and Willoughby determined to win her back, will Marianne find the strength to save her marriage, or will the temptation of a previous love be too powerful to resist?

### Lydia Bennet's Story

In Lydia Bennet's Story we are taken back to Jane Austen's most beloved novel, *Pride and Prejudice*, to a Regency world seen through Lydia's eyes where pleasure and marriage are the only pursuits. But the road to matrimony is fraught with difficulties and even when she is convinced that she has met the man of her dreams, complications arise. When Lydia is reunited with the Bennets, Bingleys, and Darcys for a grand ball at Netherfield Park, the shocking truth about her husband may just cause the greatest scandal of all ...

## REVIEWS

### Searching for Captain Wentworth

Searching for Captain Wentworth will send you on a magical journey through time, and your heart, that you will not soon forget -Austenprose

– *Mr Darcy's Secret*

### Mr Darcy's Secret

Jane Odiwe comes to it steeped in Austen, in all her renditions; Odiwe's sentences often glint with reflections of the great Jane ...

–*Historical Novel Society*

### Willoughby's Return

"Odiwe's elegantly stylish writing is seasoned with just the right dash of tart humor, and her latest literary endeavor is certain to delight both Austen devotees and Regency romance readers."

– *Booklist*

### Lydia Bennet's Story

Odiwe pays nice homage to Austen's stylings and endears the reader to the formerly secondary character, spoiled and impulsive Lydia Bennet ... devotees will enjoy

– *Publisher's Weekly*

Milton Keynes UK
Ingram Content Group UK Ltd.
UKHW040736301024
2459UKWH00026B/108

9 780954 572235